THEY WERE DEF[...]

ROSE MACAULAY was born on 11 August 1881 at Rugby, where her father was an assistant master. Although she read history at Oxford she was primarily interested in writing and her first novel, *Abbots Verney*, was published when she was twenty-five. During the First World War she worked in the War Office, but she was already well on her way to a successful literary career, and the post-war decades saw the publication of such celebrated novels as *Potterism* (1920), *Crewe Train* (1926) and *They Were Defeated* (1932). Repeated disasters during the Second World War interrupted this success: her home was destroyed by a bomb, she was bereaved more than once and she suffered serious ill-health. However in the 1950s she overcame her misfortunes. Her novel *The Towers of Trebizond* won her the James Tait Black Memorial Prize in 1956, and in 1958, shortly before her death, she was created a Dame of the British Empire.

SUSAN HOWATCH was born in Surrey in 1940, and after an uneventful childhood spent writing she attended London University where she obtained a degree in law. Abandoning a legal career in order to pursue her writing ambitions she emigrated to America in 1964 and shortly afterwards published a mystery novel, *The Dark Shore*. However it was not until 1971 that her long novel *Penmarric* became the first of four international bestsellers. In 1975 she left America, and after spending four years in the Irish Republic she returned to live in England. She and her husband have one daughter, Antonia, who was born in 1970.

ROSE MACAULAY

They Were Defeated

Introduced by

SUSAN HOWATCH

Oxford Melbourne Toronto

OXFORD UNIVERSITY PRESS

1981

Oxford University Press, Walton Street, Oxford OX2 6DP
London Glasgow New York Toronto
Delhi Bombay Calcutta Madras Karachi
Kuala Lumpur Singapore Hong Kong Tokyo
Nairobi Dar es Salaam Cape Town
Melbourne Wellington
and associate companies in
Beirut Berlin Ibadan Mexico City

First published 1932 by Collins
First published with a new Introduction as an Oxford University Press paperback 1981

British Library Cataloguing in Publication Data
Macaulay, Rose
They were defeated.—(Oxford paperbacks)
1. Title
823'.912[F] PR6025.A/
ISBN 0-19-281316-1

Printed in Great Britain by
Richard Clay (The Chaucer Press) Ltd.
Bungay, Suffolk

CONTENTS

To my Uncle

WILLIAM HERRICK MACAULAY

this story of Cambridge

and of one of our distant relatives

NOTE

I HAVE done my best to make no person in this novel use in conversation any words, phrases, or idioms that were not demonstrably used at the time in which they lived; though I am aware, for all the constant and stalwart aid of the Oxford Dictionary, and the wealth of literature, letters and journals of the period that we possess for our guidance, that any such attempt must be extremely inadequate; or, at least, that mine is so. I must apologise both for its inadequacies, and to those (if any) who may think that I have used too many words which now sound somewhat peculiar in our ears; ghosts of words, " old and obsolete, and such as would never be revived " (as Sir Thomas Browne said of heresies), " but by such extravagant and irregular heads as mine." If they should vex any reader, I should be sorry, but would assure him that I have rejected so many more of these ghosts than I have admitted, that I am surprised (and hope others will be grateful) at my own moderation. As it is, they are not so frequent after all, and can, like other *revenants*, be ignored.

As it seems to be the habit to furnish such information, I would add that only a very few of the people in this book are imaginary.

INTRODUCTION

by Susan Howatch

WHEN Dame Rose Macaulay, witty and erudite to the last, died in 1958 at the age of seventy-seven, she left behind a collection of novels, letters and miscellaneous writings which had dazzled literary London for decades. Moreover she was still dazzling her readers when she died, for at an age when most writers are either dead or in their dotage she produced the international bestseller *The Towers of Trebizond*, a work acclaimed by many as one of the two finest novels she had ever written.

The other novel was this book, *They Were Defeated.*

The most interesting feature of these two books, published twenty-four years apart, is their diversity, but diversity was the keynote of Rose Macaulay's long literary career. A graduate of Somerville College, Oxford, she eventually made her home in London, and long before the end of the First World War she had made a name for herself as a novelist. However it was not until the nineteen twenties that she found widespread popularity when she published a series of novels satirising post-war life. Following hard upon the heels of Lloyd George's exhortations about the way the world should be ("What is our task? To make Britain a fit country for heroes to live in!") came Rose Macaulay's entertaining but cold-eyed appraisal of the world as it really was. In the novel *Potterism* her target was vulgarity, the burgeoning world of shoddy standards as represented by the popular press, and in *Crewe Train* the world of publishing was scrutinised with the same merciless humour. Hypocrisy, snobbery, pretentiousness, the cheap, the cynical and the profane—all were winkled out of the social woodwork with a skill and wit which captivated both critics and public alike. Then, at a point when lesser writers might have been content to continue in the same safe profitable style, the satires stopped. The twenties ended, the mood changed, and the other Rose Macaulay, graver, deeper but infinitely more profound, began to emerge on paper.

In *They Were Defeated*, published in 1932, she revealed herself to be more concerned with themes of eternal interest than with the current mores she had explored in the satires, and although she continued to write fiction throughout the nineteen thirties she also turned to essays, criticism and biography. For some years following the outbreak of the Second World War she wrote no novels, but 1950 saw the publication of *The World My Wilderness*, a sombre and often unconvincing treatment of the theme of moral disintegration. The aftermath of decayed civilizations continued to fascinate her. Retreating once more into non-fiction she produced her long learned work *Pleasure of Ruins*, but after this the call of the novel proved too strong to resist, and in 1956 *The Towers of Trebizond* crowned her career by combining the wit of the satires with the moral and intellectual depth of her other masterpiece, *They Were Defeated.*

No understanding of this triumphant literary synthesis is possible without examining the part religion played in Rose Macaulay's life. As her great friend and correspondent, the Reverend John Hamilton Cowper Johnson of the Cowley Fathers, once wrote to her biographer, Constance Babington Smith: "You know her real mind, and about the extreme seriousness and centrality of her religion . . ." Religion was indeed at the centre of her personality, and permeated steadily although often stealthily into the very heart of her books. Both her father's family, the Macaulays, and her mother's family, the Conybeares, had been actively connected with the Church of England for some generations, and as both families also had a strong tradition of scholarship, religion was approached from an intellectual as well as an emotional point of view. With her older sister Margaret and the four younger children, Jean, Aulay, Will and Eleanor, Rose Macaulay grew up in an atmosphere in which stimulating debates on clerical issues were frequent, and in later life she always welcomed with zest the chance to discuss the finer points of some intricate moral problem. For the Macaulays religion was no gloomy skeleton to be dragged out of the closet once a week on Sunday. It was a continuing source of the liveliest intellectual entertainment and spiritual satisfaction.

It is against this background that one of the most crucial events in Rose Macaulay's life must be measured. During the First World War when she was in her thirties, she fell in love with a married man and for many years she lived apart from the Church which had always been such an integral part of her existence.

The playwright Athol Fugard said recently that we cannot grow without pain, and this paradox of the human condition in which spiritual growth can only be achieved through suffering is illustrated by Rose Macaulay's life. In the words of C. V. Wedgwood, Rose Macaulay became absorbed in "the conflict between human and divine love", and out of her personal experiences of this painful conflict came the deepening of her personal vision which led to her triumphs as a writer.

Ever aware of the striving of the soul towards God, yet fully recognising the power of the craving of one human being for another, she was drawn to explore the tragedy which occurs when these two great yearnings of the human spirit are irreconcilable. In *The Towers of Trebizond* the narrator Laurie is in the grip of this tragedy, and over twenty years before Laurie was born in the author's mind, Julian Conybeare, the heroine of *They Were Defeated*, is presented with a conflict which is equally intractable: she longs for the world of the intellect, but finds it cannot coexist with her longing for John Cleveland, a man of sophistication, glamour and irresistible sexual charm. Thus the power of the senses is pitted against the hunger of the intellect; the need for another being is brutally set in opposition to a spiritual quest which is less tangible but no less vital to survival. This is an ancient conflict, and one which is so universal that its consequences are of interest even to those who do not belong to any branch of the Christian Church.

Rose Macaulay came back to her Church in the end. The man she loved died, and after a long correspondence with her distant cousin, Father Johnson of the Cowley Fathers in America, she was reunited with the world in which she was intellectually and spiritually so much at home. In this end there was indeed a new beginning, and after the success of *The Towers of Trebizond* she had just begun a new novel, *Venice Besieged*, when she died of a coronary thrombosis at the very height of her literary powers.

After her death it was possible to see her work as a whole, and beyond the satires, which now seem dated, and the writings on travel and literature, which appeal to a more specialised public, her novel *They Were Defeated* stands out as unique. This is not merely because it was her one historical novel and her own personal favourite. It is because while she was exploring the history, literature and religion of her beloved seventeenth century, she was creating characters so multi-dimensional that they refuse to become dated; she was writing of people with whom the modern reader can still identify.

However, despite this it must be said at once that of all Rose Macaulay's novels, this is the one that provides the most challenge to the modern reader. One of Rose Macaulay's virtues as a novelist is that she is supremely readable. She made nonsense of the popular notion that readability and literary merit are incompatible, yet *They Were Defeated*, its dialogue constructed in the idiom of the 1640s, may send the reader temporarily into shock. Persistence is required, but this is worthwhile for the shock soon passes, the strangeness becomes familiar and the reader receives a more vivid picture of seventeenth-century England than would otherwise have been possible. Meanwhile, interspersed with the dialogue, the prose is Rose Macaulay at her ironic, economical best, and this merging of the language of one century with the language of another achieves not only a *tour de force* of literary skill but a triumph over "the rags of time" which separate us from those people who lived so long ago.

Rose Macaulay was particularly fascinated by the years which led up to the Civil War, not only because of the religious issues which were involved, but because she was captivated by the intellectual climate and literary excellence of the times. Widely read in seventeenth-century literature she found the poets of the day so familiar to her that it was inevitable that many of them became characters in *They Were Defeated*. Much of the action of the book takes place in Cambridge, then experiencing one of the brightest epochs in its history, and here Milton, Cowley, Cleveland, More and other illustrious figures meet to discuss and read their work. To the heroine Julian Conybeare, Cambridge represents the magic City of the Mind, symbolic of man's intellectual achievement and all that is most inspiring in the human spirit as it strains to rise above an ignorant, cruel world. Julian is enrapt by Cambridge, and wastes no time regretting her father's decision to leave their home in the Devon village of Dean Prior.

The opening scenes in Dean Prior are remarkable for their realism. The countryside of Devon is shown in all its pastoral beauty, but this is no glimpse back into the fantasy of Merrie England. The people are ignorant and bigoted, cruelty is accepted as a fact of life and religion is streaked with paganism. When Julian's father, a man who despises superstition, tries to help an old woman damned as a witch, local animosity is so strong that he finds it safer to retreat to Cambridge with his daughter, and on their journey from Devon they are accompanied by the parson Robert Herrick, himself a poet, who has been teaching Julian Latin and Greek. For Dr Conybeare, detesting the stupidity of uneducated women, has long since reached the eccentric decision that his daughter should be a scholar.

Conybeare and his friend Herrick form an interesting contrast to each other. Both are kind, humane, intelligent men but Herrick, in his position as parson, is an accepted member of society while Dr Conybeare, the atheist, is always in danger of becoming an outcast. Men like Dr Conybeare who place truth above conformity are always people whom society finds difficult to tolerate, and Julian's unusual education has pushed her equally far from the mainstream of seventeenth-century life. However on her arrival in Cambridge she does not at first realise how unorthodox she is. She is too absorbed in her reunion with her student brother Kit, and too enthralled with the stimulating atmosphere generated by the University. It is not until she falls disastrously in love with Kit's tutor John Cleveland that she comes face to face with conflicts which she had never before realised could exist.

Julian is fifteen years old. Although a talented scholar she has seen nothing of the world, and when her father becomes diverted by Kit's troubles, Julian is unprotected from the danger which Cleveland represents. Yet Cleveland, although cast as the villain of the piece, emerges as a much more interesting character than the convention of the wicked seducer usually allows. Cleveland is not just an idle rake. He is a poet fluent in Latin, a conscientious tutor who cares for the welfare of his students, a man of consequence at the University and a loyalist who stands fast for the king's cause later during the Civil War. Kind to Dr Conybeare and also to Herrick (whom the younger poets regard as *passé*) he is genuinely charmed by Julian. Although we blame Cleveland for seducing her, we almost blame Dr Conybeare more for his failure to ensure that she remains properly chaperoned, and this success in making Cleveland a sympathetic character is all the more remarkable when it becomes clear that he is concerned only with sexual gratification. Julian's mind means nothing to him. He cares only that she is pretty and can provide him with a delectable new conquest.

Modern opinion could justifiably label Cleveland a male chauvinist, but ultimately this late-twentieth-century tag fails as fully as the Victorian cliché "the wicked seducer" to catch Cleveland in all his complexity. Above all else he is a poet, and it is through poetry that Julian finally touches his heart. Seeing at last into her mind, he mourns genuinely not only for what he has lost but for what he in his bigotry has never cared to know. It is Cleveland's tragedy that he has the sensitivity to recognise the enormity of his mistake, and in his tragedy he becomes not a stereotyped anti-hero but a living breathing being with all his virtues and vices inextricably mingled in the complicated web of his personality.

And Julian? Julian is one of the most appealing of the unconventional heroines to whom Rose Macaulay gave names which can belong either to men or to women. More intelligent than Denham in *Crewe Train*, quieter and more feminine than Stanley and Rome in *Told by an Idiot*, more serious-minded than Laurie in *The Towers of Trebizond*, Julian underlines more clearly than the others the point behind the asexual name: that women can be the intellectual equal of men, and that the differences between the sexes are not as vast as social conditioning throughout the centuries would have us all believe. Julian's dilemma is the dilemma so frequently encountered by clever women. She wonders how she can remain true to herself while she seeks happiness with a man who finds it necessary to regard women as an inferior species. It often seems that the woman who is equal has to become a woman who is second-rate if she is not to be denied the happiness she wants from life, but the acceptance of a second-rate role means the suppression of the true self. The result is that although the joys of love can be bought by role-playing, the price paid is nothing less than the mutilation of the personality.

Yet Julian's dilemma is not confined to women for she represents all those people, male and female, who are too original in character to conform to the standards which society classifies as normal. Society sees any threat to its stability as abnormal; insecurity leads to bigotry and bigotry leads to witch-hunts as the deviants are hunted out and destroyed. The tragedy of Julian is mirrored not only in the witch-hunt at the beginning of the book but in the gradual disintegration of England into civil war as the Puritans gain the upperhand with the fall of Strafford.

Julian's society decreed that only men were fit to become scholars. It is her brother Kit who attends the University, and Cleveland only gives her private lessons in order to have a better opportunity to seduce her. Mocking Julian's love of learning and scorning her ambition to be a poet, he makes no secret of his belief that Julian's sole ambition in life should be to please him in love. This attitude certainly reveals the bigoted, insecure side of John Cleveland, but more importantly it reveals the bigoted, insecure society which produced him. For Cleveland is not a social outcast. He is a typical product of his times, and it is left to Dr Conybeare, the intellectual outlaw moving inexorably towards exile, to see his daughter not as a mindless cypher but as an individual as uniquely gifted as the man who treats her with contempt in the name of love.

Accustomed to her father's humanity Julian finds the encounters with her lover emotionally bruising, but so deeply is she drawn to Cleveland that she feels she has no choice but to accept him as he is and to be as he wishes her to be. Suppressing her true self in order to gain his love she thus unconsciously connives with Cleveland to bring about the tragedy which forms the climax of the novel.

This climax will have a special significance to the reader living in the late twentieth century when random violence is rife and the threat of senseless death is constantly present in even a stable society. Violence explodes between Cleveland and Julian's elder brother Frank, and in their fight we see not merely the confrontation between Anglican and Puritan, but the glimpse of the war which achieves no victory but only the destruction of innocence and beauty and the psychological maiming of those who survive.

Cambridge, Julian's City of the Mind, was ravaged by the Civil War, its treasures smashed, its intellectual glory dissipated. All the characters in the novel share this terrible defeat, yet this was neither the end of Cambridge's history nor the end of Rose Macaulay's novel. The book ends with Robert Herrick, representing not only all the poets but all that is best in the Anglican tradition. He has been dispossessed of his living but he has survived to fight another day, and in shattered Cambridge learning is being kept alive by those few who remain to pass the tradition to the next generation. It is a historical fact that the living of Dean Prior was restored to Herrick after the Restoration, while Cambridge rose again from the ruins to become the world-famous city of learning which exists today.

The title of the book is *They Were Defeated*, but despite this the book's message is that such a defeat is ultimately unacceptable to the human spirit. Buffeted and bludgeoned by the brutality of an imperfect world, the human spirit continues not only to strive for the unattainable perfection which God represents but to build those cities of the mind which signify all that is noblest in man's achievements. Rose Macaulay's work is a tribute to this indestructability of the human spirit, and because of this, *They Were Defeated* is not a novel merely for today and yesterday but for all time.

PART I

BUCOLICK

I sing of *Brooks*, of *Blossoms*, *Birds*, and *Bowers*:
Of *April*, *May*, of *June*, and *July*-Flowers.
I sing of *May-Poles*, *Hock-carts*, *Wassails*, *Wakes*,
Of *Bride-grooms*, *Brides*, and of their *Bridall-cakes* . . .

ROBERT HERRICK
The Argument of his Book

More discontents I never had
Since I was born, than here;
Where I have been, and still am sad,
In this dull *Devon-shire*.

ROBERT HERRICK
Discontents in Devon

I

THINGS WERE going none too well this morning, the vicar felt. The church was full enough; the villagers and the squirearchy were ranged in their seats, and the Miggle family, who were "Church Catholics," sat at the back, dark and solemn, their black Spanish eyes goggling, like everyone else's, at the fruit, corn, pumpkins, barley-sheaves and vegetable marrows. That was the trouble: the harvest decorations. They were new in Dean Prior; the vicar had himself conceived the notion of bringing the rejoicings of harvest home and the hock-cart into the church itself, and carrying on the good old pagan custom of decking the altars of Ceres with the fruits of the earth. His congregation had fully entered into the idea, and had spent a happy Saturday piling the window recesses, chancel steps, and pulpit with ripe pumpkins, melons, apples, pears, plums and enormous loaves, erecting wheatsheaves on the altar, twining barley and hops about the pillars, and standing great jugs of Michaelmas flowers in every corner. The vicar had sent fruit from his orchard, and sunflowers and Michaelmas daisies from the parsonage garden, and had himself directed Prudence, his housekeeper, in the arrangement of them. He had been delighted with the look of the church yesterday, when the decorators had gone home to make ready for the hock-cart festivities and the great harvest supper at Dean Court. Theocritus, thought he, would have thought it very apt; Virgil, too, would have found it not unworthy of the occasion. To bring the fruits of the earth into the temples of the gods, to pile them before the altar, to hymn God's praises among his gifts, this was certainly a good custom, even if Christendom had never used it, even if it would not please those sour-faced, meddling visitors of the Archbishop's, those beagles who objected to the passage of carts across the churchyard, and to the parson's pointing at members of his congregation when he preached about their faults and insisted on the communion table being moved up against the east wall and railed off. Meddling prelatical fools; the vicar, himself a man of the cheerful middle English way, hating Puritanism, heartily damning all extremes of piety, classed the Metropolitan Visitors with the Puritans and the Papists, as finicking, kill-joy nuisances, to whom a spell in the village stocks would do no harm. Unlike some of his brother parsons around, who had got themselves into trouble by amending the prayer-book and using impertinent extempore prayers, he was no Puritan. He liked order and seemliness, and had enforced it on that first Communion Sunday after the table had been moved and railed in. Himself, he cared not one way or another for such details, and had been irritated alike by meddling authority and by his recalcitrant flock, who shied at the unaccustomed and unpopular use. He had stood in the chancel at communion time and commanded them sharply, as they sat sullenly in their seats, to "Come up to the rail as I telled ye, plague take 'ee, for ye'll get nought sitting there." He had broken them in to it, all but a few old ones, who still wouldn't budge, for the new mode minded them, said they, of the days of the old stone altar that had been moved away fifty years back and replaced by the good new table, and they weren't going back to them days at their time of life.

But—to return—the morning service was somehow going ill. The people, confound them, weren't attending. When the vicar climbed into the pulpit, and stood, a burly, Roman-headed figure, among the corn and barley-sheaves and apples (too many apples were ranged round the pulpit's edge; he moved some of them away to make room for his elbows) the plaguey congregation tittered. As for the young Yardes, sitting with their grandparents in the Court pew immediately beneath the pulpit, they were obviously overcome with ill-suppressed mirth. Those graceless young imps, Giles and Meg, were nudging and giggling without shame. But their friend, the doctor's daughter, little Julian Conybeare, sat with them as usual, serious as a judge, her pale, pointed face, almost overweighted by its high forehead and enormous grey eyes, turned up thoughtfully, awaiting the vicar's words. Julian Conybeare was his pupil, and an apt little maid; she was turned fifteen, and had for the last three years come down the hill thrice a week from Deancombe to the vicarage to read Latin and English with him, for her father, himself something of a student, and reputed to be that almost unheard of monstrosity, an atheist, was set on giving his daughter learning. She sat between her friends, Giles and Meg Yarde. Giles, a handsome lad of seventeen, was at Cambridge, and should have been back there long since but for an attack of measles. As for Meg, that long, copper-headed limb, she did nothing at sixteen but run wild, and wouldn't either open a book or the door of the still-room. It had been different when their great-uncle, Sir Edward Giles, had been alive; he had kept order in his household, a stern, kind, good gentleman, now kneeling in painted stone effigy with his wife, both of them ruffed and prayerful, in a niche in the church wall, with their rhymed epitaph, composed by the vicar, beneath them. Behind the Court pew sat the vicar's widowed sister-in-law, Mrs. Elizabeth Herrick, plump and good-natured, with their guest, Sir John Suckling, but lately back from brightly though somewhat ineffectively leading a troop of horse to assist His Majesty in the little matter of the Scots and their service-book. He was a slightly-built young man, with a very merry quizzical expression, and lolled back in his seat, staring lazily round the church between yawns, for the country noises had kept him awake last night. The vicar had desired that this gentleman should receive a favourable impression of the service and congregation, of his own esteemed position among his rustic flock, and of his powerful gifts of preaching. He often derided and lampooned his bucolic parish, but had no mind that his occasional guests should carry back to the London wits stories of poor Robin piping in the wilds of Devonshire to a flock which would not so much as listen. Still, there was no getting round the fact that the flock only too often did *not* listen, witless churls and louts that they were; nor that this harvest-feast Sunday was, apparently, one of the occasions when their inadvertence was conspicuous.

The vicar, growing displeased, rolled out his discourse ever more loud and emphatic. "Robin grows heated," thought his placid sister-in-law. "In another minute he'll be calling 'em names." And so, to be sure, he was. He called the Lord God, who had sent them all this fine corn, all these melons, apples and pumpkins, whose providence had dropped fatness on their soil throughout the year, to witness that they were hard of heart, blind of eye, alive only in belly and in malice . . . "Aye, you, Prig, snoring there in your corner, come to snore in the church because your own hovel stinks. And Mrs. Batt, staring round about ye as if ye'd never seen good food before and was all agog to get your teeth into it. And you black Miggles at the back there, pox take ye for the papistical outlandish hypocrites y'are, sitting in church to save a fining, and slinking home to tell your Spanish beads safe and quiet. And all you children giggling there, ye little michers, asking for a whipping and never getting it, what d'ye say God and his blessed angels think of ye, as they look down from heaven on your dirty little grinning faces? A plague on y'all, sitting thankless among God's gifts, goggling at his fruits and his corn like pigs in a melon-plot . . ."

At this the children fell to laughing in earnest, for all that Mrs. Prudence Baldwin, the vicar's housekeeper, turned and frowned at them. As to that, many of the adults laughed as well, and the vicar, growing, as his sister-in-law had remarked, heated, caught up the manuscript containing notes of his sermon (from which, however, he had considerably diverged during the last few minutes) and flung it with violence at his congregation in general. A moment's pause followed, and then there sounded from immediately beneath the pulpit a little squeal, another, and a third. The vicar, starting, craned his head over and peered down between luxuriant vegetation at the floor, and saw, tethered by its collar to a sturdy apple-branch that stood against the pulpit's base, a small plump sucking-pig, munching enthusiastically, and with shrill and sudden cries of joy, at the mixed produce within reach. Quiet enough this happy occupation had kept it until now, though the vicar had, as he stood in the pulpit, observed rustlings and munchings; but now either the excitement of seeing its pastor and master (for it was, indeed, a parsonage piglet) fling self-restraint to the winds and his discourse at his flock, or else the intolerable delight of getting its snout into a ripe melon, had snapped its manners and its dignity, and it squealed aloud.

The vicar, an unaccountable clergyman, and none too easily shocked, took it calmly. Possibly a consciousness of how sharply the Archbishop's Paul Prys would have condemned pigs in church sweetened his temper; possibly he was softened by the discovery of the reason for the inattention and the mirth of his flock; or perhaps the little porcine offering appealed to his classical fancy. After all, animal, as well as vegetable, fruits of the earth had always been offered in thanksgiving both by pagans and Jews. Anyhow, for whatever reason, his eagerly and hopefully attentive parishioners (for in Dean Prior in the year 1640, as in other parishes in other years, people did enjoy a good scene in church) saw their vicar's countenance relax into something near a smile, and instead of a picturesque string of oaths flung at their heads, all they got was a much less comprehensible and satisfactory " Et minor ex humili victima porcus hara. But we'll be kinder to the creature than were the priests of Juno." He then commanded Will Pratt, the lad who worked in the parsonage garden and orchard, to " Carry back that animal to its dam, and see ye make haste to 't "; which Will accordingly did, but made no extreme haste in the business of untying the little porker, disengaging it from its meal, and bearing it, shrill in complaint, from the church, followed by Prudence Baldwin, who did not mean to have Will loosed alone about the parsonage premises.

The last squeals dying away as the disappointed little creature was borne out of the churchyard and across to the parsonage, the congregation settled down, their joke at an end. Indeed, they speedily looked sober enough, for it was Brief Sunday, and their vicar proceeded, since the thread of his discourse was now irrevocably broken, to command them to give their bountiful and liberal contributions to the redeeming of captives in Algiers, taken prisoner by the Moors. The plate was firmly carried round for this object by Mr. Pringle, the churchwarden, and Dean Prior produced its pence, reluctant indeed, but perhaps less so than they had been on recent Brief Sundays, when their charity had been sought for Protestant ministers in the Palatinate, and for the rebuilding of the church of Widecombe-in-the-Moor, struck by lightning such a long while since that the Widecombe folk must surely by now be used to doing without a church. But as to the unhappy prisoners in Algiers, they were certainly in a piteous plight, though Dean Prior saw no adequate reason why they should ever have put themselves in the way of capture, causing all this expense in Devonshire.

But young Julian Conybeare did not think of this. At the mention of the Algiers prisoners, her wide grey eyes filled with tears, which hung beading her thick black lashes till she winked them away, and she dipped into her pocket for the largest coin she could find. Dreadful, dreadful it was to think of the sufferings of those poor gallant men in the cruel hands of black infidels.

Sir John Suckling, just behind her, caught a glimpse of the diamond tears glistening on the lashes of the pale, pretty child, and approved her mightily. A pretty little maid; an extraordinary pretty, tender little maid, thought he. Robin must make her known to him, and also the long, copper-headed wench next her, who looked a gay young spark with a good spirit. The pale little maid seemed shyer and more solemn; she was perhaps over young to afford much entertainment. She did not seem more than thirteen.

"For young thou art as blossoms
That blooms upon the tree,"

Sir John hummed beneath his breath. She might better suit his cousin Charles, who liked them but just out of making dirt pies. Still, he would like to tease the child, pretty little sucker. Sir John whispered a question to Mrs. Elizabeth as they knelt for the prayers. "Why, the Yardes, to be sure," she replied, in her round, comfortable voice that scorned concealment. "From the Court, ye know. And t'other little wench is the doctor's."

At that, Meg Yarde turned her copper head about, stared at the strange fine gallant with frank inquisitiveness, and, turning back, whispered to her friend, "That will be Sir John Sucklin, July." But grave Julian was intent on her prayers and answered not. Julian, the atheist doctor's daughter, knew how to behave in church, if her young friends did not. She brought to church worship the same earnest attention which she gave to her lesson books; you could not distract her from either, once she had settled down to them. "So solemn as a judge," thought Sir John. "A proper solemn little Daniel. What young spark will tickle it up, I wonder? I'd as lief wear his shoes as some. All the same, I like 'em best when they save a man the trouble of doing the whole of the going himself. That wears a man out. I swear little Daniel would tire a man, looking at him like a puritan at a conventicle, when he spoke to her. I'd liefer try the red-headed giglet, for all she stares at a strange gentleman like an impudent urchin out of school and never a blush, and for all she's got freckles on her dear little nose. Amen," he remarked, loudly and cheerfully, at the end of Robin's last collect. Poor old Robin, he thought, was a good fellow, and wonderful witty company, and a confounded ingenious and pleasant poet, though he did think too much of his own verse and not enough of other men's (but then that was a way of all poets). But he didn't seem much of a hand at minding these few sheep of his in the wilderness. He let 'em get out of hand. And pigs in church—Lord, that was a pretty state of things; it was almost blasphemy. What would the bishops say? They were getting very stern in these days about seemly church observance, and would never stand for pigs in church, even if they stood for pumpkins. If Nat Brent and his merry men had chanced to pay a visit to Dean Prior this Sunday, they would have had a pretty report to carry back to the Archbishop.

But Robin's choristers sang very pretty; no one could deny him that. He had trained them well, thought Sir John, himself a musician. They were singing some harvest hymn, or was it a metrical version of a harvest psalm, as the congregation went out. And the vicar, his eye commandingly on them, was beating time with his hand. No one could call the vicar of Dean Prior a zealot or a mystic; he was no George Herbert, or Dr. Donne, or John Hales, and not given over much either to religious controversy, to pious painful preaching, or to prayer, or even to conspicuously godly living: but he did see to it that his church music was good, or as good as barbarous rusticity could manage. You could not, his friend knew (himself feeling some interest in such topics, and having lately written an excellent discourse on Socinianism), rouse him readily to debate on the Arminians or the Latitudinarians, or John Cosin's book of devotions, on the rights and wrongs of bowing to the altar, or the merits of Sir John's own reasoning as to Socinianism; but he would discuss music as eagerly as he would discuss Latin and English poetry, the old days at the Apollo Tavern, the quality of sack or the shape of a woman.

2

The vicar, crossing the churchyard from the vestry, caught hold of a tow-headed urchin by the arm.

"Where's thy father, boy? Where's Ned Cuffe? He surely warn't in church?"

The child conveyed, in the peculiar idiom natural to him, that his father, owing to rheumatism, had this morning remained in bed.

"Keeps his bed, does he? Feels his rheumaticks, does he? Strange, how those rheumaticks of his ever seize him on Brief Sundays. He seemed well enough last night at the supper; I'll warrant he ate well enough, too. Ate too well, perhaps, did he? See here, Dick, tell thy dad from me that the warden will be waiting on him shortly to collect his brief-money, and he must see he has it ready, rheumaticks or no. Don't forget, now."

He released his parishioner's arm, gave him a shove, and walked up to the group who stood talking at the lych gate—his sister-in-law, Sir John Suckling, the party from Dean Court, and Julian Conybeare. "Harky, Jack; how's this for an epigram?

'Cuffe stops at home from church and keeps his bed
Those Sundays only when as briefs are read.
This makes Cuffe sick . . .'

A pox on't, thou canst finish it, I'm not in the humour for verse-making this morning. Good-morning, Squire; good-morning, Mrs. Yarde. Well, my young friends, I saw 'ee tittering beneath me all service time. If Mr. Brent had paid us one of his visits, he'd have had ye up before the Bishops for indecent conduct in God's house. And now, pray, can anyone of ye cast a light on how my sucking-pig found himself in church? If 't was that young knave Will Pratt, he shall get the stick for 't."

"'Twarn't Will, Mr. Herrick," Meg Yarde said, in her deep loud voice like a breaking boy's. "'Twas Giles and me. July kept plaguing us with a Latin piece that she'd read with you, about bringing he-goats to the altar for a sacrifice to the gods for the crops, and we ha'n't gotten a he-goat, so we thought as a he-pig would serve, and we caught one of your little porkers this morning, as it ran loose in your orchard, and tied it up beneath the pulpit among the fruit. 'Twas a marvellous good little piggy and munched away like an angel, till you threw the sermon. Lud, Mr. Herrick, you should have seen how sweetly pretty it looked, among the pumpkins and earth-apples. July thought as you'd be pleased, di'n't you, Jule?"

"I di'n't know," replied Julian, a literal girl.

"Was ever such a vulgar, impudent hoyting wench?" Meg's grandmother, Mrs. Christian Yarde, a downright Elizabethan lady of sixty, inquired of Heaven. "A pig in church, forsooth! Marry come up! Even those nasty Brownists 'd know better. Pray, what d'ye think Sir John Sucklin here will say to such pranks? I'll be bound he a'n't used to young ladies and gentlemen behaving so in London. If I'd ha' done so when I was a maid, I'd ha' got the rod, indeed I should. But there, I was wed before I was thy age, and a mother before I was turned seventeen. I was indeed, Sir John."

"Had you said fifteen, madam, I would have believed you still more readily."

"Zooks, sir, none of your court flattery here. But I could a' been wedded to a fine young gentleman at twelve, that I could, only my parents woun't hear on't. Look, husband—where's he gone?—Why, husband! I thought you was at hand. We must ask Parson and Mrs. Herrick to bring Sir John to sup to-morrow, must we not?"

Mr. George Yarde, who had been examining the hinges of the churchyard gate, turned round, politely; a slow, solidly built, kind-faced elderly gentleman, in sensible country clothes that contrasted with the Londoner's gay fripperies. "Surely, surely. You must come and tell us the news from London. Things are going but badly, I fear."

"Now, squire," his wife protested, "no politics of a Sunday. You know as I can't endure politics of a Sunday."

"Quite right, ma'am," Sir John agreed. "His Majesty bids us pray and play on the Lord's Day, but never to talk politics. Is't not so, Robin?"

"A sad topic enough presently, any day of the seven,"

gloomily said the parson. "The Archbishop might well have ordered it of a Friday, with the rest of the fasting he's so fond on. God's wounds, ye'd think the country and parliament was run mad, flouting and denying and insulting His Majesty the way they do."

"To be sure ye would," his sister-in-law tranquilly and absentmindedly agreed. She was sitting on the churchyard wall, beside Mrs. Yarde, finding the gentle Michaelmas sunshine very agreeable and soothing, and wondering how Prue was getting on with the dinner.

"None the less," said the squire, who, though loyal, did not care about paying taxes, and was of a cautious, constitutional turn of mind, "none the less, His Majesty's advisers urge him a thought too far. No good'll come of all these levies. Don't you agree as to that, Sir John? Why, dammit, sir, our estates won't stand it. Furse of Morsehead was saying so only yesterday, and you know, parson, what a king's man he is. 'Tis rousing a great amount of unpleasant feeling round here, and that's a fact. And there's none too much loyalty in these parts, anyhow; th'are a lamentable discontented lot, eh, Parson? It don't do to push us too far. Her Majesty Queen Elizabeth ne'er did that. But these new Scottish kings hadn't her sense."

"Well," Sir John courteously deprecated the politics that Mrs. Yarde could not endure of a Sunday. "I'll give you my views on the matter, an ye want 'em, to-morrow at dinner, Mr. Yarde, since your good lady's ordained this a day of abstinence from such gossip." He turned to the two girls, agreeably conscious that they were observing him with interest, and, he hoped and believed, admiration.

"What of the young ladies? Art interested in affairs of state, Mrs. Meg?"

"Not I, sir," she bluntly returned. "I think politics is lamentable tedious. But then I've no intellects. Neither ha'n't Giles. Julian here is the learned one; she knows about politics and books and all, don't thou, July?"

"No," replied the girl of few words.

"All the same," thought Sir John, "a pox on't if she don't think she do! Lord, but I'd like to teach the little great-eyed elf something that an't politics, nor books neither."

"Julian's spack and diligent enough," the vicar put in, patting her shoulder, "and her Latin goes on tolerable well. But no maid of her years is a doctor of learning and wisdom, and don't thou be setting my pupil up with thy nonsense, Meg. Better if thou'd try and learn something thyself, imp, before it grows too late and th'art a know-naught wife."

"Aye, marry, Parson, 'twould indeed be better," Meg's grandmother agreed. "Why the girl won't so much as embroider her own handkerchers, or learn to make piecrust, or play on the harp. It's horses, horses, all day, or else dogs or falcons, or running wild about the moor. She's a sad madcap, Sir John. Why her little step-sister, Bishop Potter of Carlisle his girl, already knows more than she about household matters. But her older sister, that married Mr. Northly, she's very different. She knows what's proper in a lady, and can embroider and play the harpsichord, and sing and make preserves like a bird. Isn't our Lettice a proper accomplished young lady, Parson? I know you think the world of her. He made some marvellous pretty verses on her wedding, did he not, Mrs. Elizabeth? She has 'em framed, the vain chit. No one will ever write verses to *you*, miss, unless you behave prettier, you may be sure."

"To disprove that, ma'am," Sir John said, "I shall compose some to Mistress Meg this very afternoon, while Mr. Herrick polishes up his epigrams on his misbehaving parishioners. What d'ye say, Robin? Shall we sit and versify together, you on your friend Master Cuffe, or who ever he is, and I on Mrs. Meg's gold locks? Should I please you so, Mrs. Meg?"

"I don't care. I don't read verses. You may write 'em if you please. But my hair's not gold, it's red. My sister Lettice is the one for that kind of thing. You should know her, as my grandmother says."

A forward, unabashed kind of a hussey, certainly. They were an odd pair of chits, the one outspoken and blunt like a lad, the other with a wide grave stare, like an observing baby's, and not a blush anywhere between the two of them. Indeed, the boy, young Giles, seemed the shy one, for he hung in the background, switching the grass with a stick and saying nothing. Perhaps he was bored by so much talk, or perhaps abashed in the company of a strange, fine gentleman. "Well, come, we mustn't loiter longer, squire," Mrs. Yarde said. "Good-day t'ye, Mrs. Herrick; good-day, Parson; good-day, Sir John. We shall be very happy to see y'all to-morrow to supper."

With suitable compliments they parted. The Court was up by Lower Dean, a mile from the church, and the Yardes' coach was waiting in the road to convey Mrs. Yarde there. The squire went on foot, having to see some of his tenants on the way, and the three young people struck up a steep lane, to see Julian back to Deancombe.

3

"Lord, how old people do talk!" Giles exclaimed on a yawn. "I thought they'd never a'done."

"I don't suppose they *have* done," Julian said pessimistically. "They'll talk all day, I think. Mr. Herrick always does, and now he has that friend of his with him, they'll be at it all the night too!"

"What dost think of that gent?" Meg asked. "I think he's a *flirt*, with his curls and his eyes and his verses."

"'Tis said he gambled a fortune away at cards and bowls," said Giles, half admiring him for it, "and got it back by selling his cribbage cards over the country. He invented cribbage, you know. And he's just back from the Scottish wars. But they say he didn't do much there. I read a lampoon on't at Cambridge. They say he got a hundred horse and dressed them all up in scarlet coats and white breeches, but never got to blows with the Scots."

"Sir John got him an ambling nag,
To Scotland for to ride-a,
With a hundred horse more, all his own, he swore,
To guard him on every side-a.
No errant knight ever went to fight
With half so gay a bravado;
Had ye seen his look you'd have sworn on a book
He'd have conquered a whole armado."

Julian quoted.

"That's it. That's the lampoon I read," Giles said.

"Aye. Mr. Herrick has it in a collection of verses newly

published, called *Wit's Recreation.* It goes on how Sir John wouldn't face the enemy but ran away. Sir John Mennis wrote it. But Mr. Herrick says 'twas somewhat spiteful and unjust of him, and from envy, he being a poet too, and there's no cause to think as Sir John Sucklin ran away swifter than the others of the king's troops. They *all* ran, the vicar says. The Scots are such rude barbarous wild men, they'd strike amaze into ye just to see 'em."

"Then Sucklin was a fool to go out against 'em. No one forced him. He's no soldier really, even though he did serve in the foreign wars; he's just a poet."

That was enough for the Yarde brother and sister; they flicked Sir John on to the horizon, where gesticulated in harmless folly poets, playwrights, lawyers, parsons, and all such sedentary beings.

They were scrambling up the deep lane by Moreshead Brook, the smell of bonfires drifting to their noses, the golden Michaelmas noon day lying on the reaped fields, a light, cool wind on their cheeks.

"Yoicks away!" cried Giles, as they started a hare from the ditch. "Look, she's lepping away to Widow Prowse's cottage. Yoicks, puss, yoicks!"

They scrambled out on to the field above the brook, and there stood one of the black-eyed Miggles, crossing himself rapidly as he watched the hare bounding across the field towards a tiny tumble-down hovel at the far corner by Deancombe copse. He was a tall lad of fourteen, black, graceful and handsome; the Miggles were of Spanish blood, and this boy's grandfather, old Hoon Miggle, as they called him, had settled in Dean, a good-looking young fugitive strayed up from the coast after the wreck of the Armada fifty years back. He had shortly taken to wife a daughter of a farmer of the old religion, who had befriended him, and had propagated a large Anglo-Spanish family. The third generation still looked more Spanish than English, and, though they came to church, were still partly Catholic in tradition and habits, as Mr. Herrick had seemed to indicate at morning service.

"What's the matter, Peter?" Meg asked, as the boy still crossed himself and muttered.

He looked at her with sullen black eyes.

"'Tis the witch's hare, mistress. I saw un crouched in the ditch; then her jumped up and ran to the cottage there. 'Tis old witch herself, belike."

"Nonsense, Peter Miggle," Julian told him severely. "You know my father said you weren't to talk so foolish about old Mother Prowse."

Peter Miggle looked sulky, frightened and unconvinced. *He* knew old Mother Prowse was a witch; every one knew it; and that she'd wished the smallpox on his little sister, who'd died of it. And that she had a hare for familiar, and could take its shape when she chose, and that her master, the devil, could take it too, and did. It was no manner of use Mistress Julian standing there and repeating the nonsense doctor talked. Doctor couldn't cure the smallpox, whereas Widow Prowse could kill you with it, which just showed. She ought to burn, so his father said; and so said many of the people about. When next the witchfinders came round, it wouldn't be the fault of Dean, nor of Deancombe, nor of Addislade neither, if they didn't get old witch.

They left him there in the field, stubborn representative of country knowledge, knowing what he knew.

They were come now to Deancombe; a cluster of steep-eaved thatched cottages, deep in rosy-fruited orchards, huddled beneath the steep bank of a bracken-gold, furze-gold, brambled hill. Just ahead of them, where Addislade Water crossed the lane, stood the small grey stone house where Dr. Conybeare had lived for three years with the only daughter left him, the youngest of his family; a queer, learned kind of a leech, who had once held clerk's orders at Cambridge, renounced them and taken to medicine, and who seldom, if ever, was to be seen in church, though, owing to the vicar's friendship, he had been able to avoid fining. He was known for a violent temper, which he was apt to let loose when he met, among his patients, with the obstinate application of prescriptions other than his own. And, since Dean and its neighbourhood had always been rich in prescriptions of all kinds, for all diseases, he spent much of his professional life in anger. He was believed, and doubtless rightly, to have occasioned many deaths by his removal from the sick of what he called old wives' nonsense, and the substitution of his own remedies. It has always, of course, been, and was then as now, an open and hotly debated question whether the sick would die in any case, or whether this consummation is hastened by the physicians in attendance. The vicar inclined to the latter opinion; still, he liked Michael Conybeare, one of his few country neighbours with whom he could exchange views on classical literature and on the foolish superstitions of the countryside, and when he was laid up he would have the doctor in, and endure his remedies for the sake of his caustic and acrid conversation. Even when this took an anti-clerical turn, as it not seldom did, the vicar made no objection. Religion, thought he, could look after itself well enough, and was more than a match for a sarcastic, disgruntled leech.

" 'Tis all very well, Jule," said Meg, as the three young persons climbed down into the lane through a gap in the hedge, " 'tis all very well for your father to call it nonsense, the way folk talk of old Mother Prowse, and I know as you think she a'n't a witch; but she is a witch, and everybody knows it. She wished the murrain on Farmer Mudge's cattle, and the smallpox on the Miggles, and sent her cat to smother

Mrs. Jolly's baby in its cradle when Mrs. Jolly was out at the wake fair; and all kinds of wicked doings. She *is* a witch; for when they took her to the river, and dropped her into Hound's Pool, with her toes crossed, she swam and never sank."

"So'd you swim, if you was dropped into a river. So'd anybody who could. That don't prove aught," said Julian crossly. "And Mother Prowse a'n't a witch, for my father says there a'n't any witches, and it's all cruel, superstitious, ignorant nonsense."

"How can your father know?" Giles asked. "There's always been witches in all lands. How could they stop of a sudden, just now?"

"My father don't think there ever was witches," said Julian, a little doubtfully mentioning this very curious opinion, conscious that it was one of the paternal oddities, which occasionally made her shy, like the doctor's habit of abstaining from his parish church.

Giles Yarde looked at her with compassion. Fortunately his grandfather did not trouble him with any such odd and ignorant thoughts.

"But they come in history. History's full of 'em. Why, they come in the Bible—the Witch of Endor. Parson could tell thee that, Jule."

"I know that. But my father don't believe on 'em all the same." Julian did not like to say, "My father don't believe all the Bible;" she concealed this monstrous and wicked and most perilous oddity so far as she was able. She knew it was perilous; she would sometimes wake at nights in a sweat of terror, dreaming that the Archbishop's men had come after her father for non-attendance at church, and were dragging him befoie some dreadful court; and, once get Dr. Conybeare answering questions before a court, he would, his child knew, say anything, utter the wildest heresies, getting ever wilder and wilder as he was opposed. And then—why then, he might be flung into jail for life; he might lose his ears; Julian wasn't sure they mightn't burn him, as they burned the poor old witches. Abroad, in the countries where the inquisition was, they did still burn heretics. There was no inquisition in England now, but there was a Court of High Commission, and blasphemy laws, and church attendance laws, and Julian felt that, once her father's tongue got wagging, he might easily be entangled among them.

Her two friends now gave her a pitying look and said no more; for, after all, it wasn't poor Jule's fault if her father chose to be so perverse and blind to well-attested facts. No witches! You might as well start declaring that there were no beggars, and that the men and women arrested as such were unjustly whipped. Facts were facts, after all. As to old Moll Prowse, she had been actually seen, talking in the most suspicious manner to her cat, whispering commands into its ears, bidding it, doubtless, go and smother the babies of such parents as had offended its mistress.

"Never you mind, July," Giles slipped his arm through his friend's as they went up to her father's house. "Never you trouble your head about old Moll. She's be cared for all right by her master."

Julian was on the point of retorting that the same master had not cared very adequately for his other servants; but she didn't want to talk about witches in her father's presence, it would only cause a violent scene, that would startle the Yardes and embarrass herself. So she deferred her reply for future use (no Conybeare ever abandoned an argument) as the doctor came out of his door to greet them. He was a small, wiry man, pale like Julian, dark-haired too like her, and with her large grey eyes and high, broad brow; he had even her pointed chin and small, firm mouth, though above that he carried a big, arched militant nose, while hers was small and straight. There was more of acrimony and irony in the father's face, and less of dreams. Dr. Conybeare's was a fighting face; his daughter's was a student's or a poet's.

"Good day t'ye, young people. Back from your harvest praying? I'll warrant parson was delighted with his church full of vegetables."

They told him about the pig, which pleased him. "Aye, that's the style. There's never aught to be had from on high except ye slay some creature for it. 'Twas ever so. Parson ought to have held piggy over the altar and cut his throat, and caught the blood in a goblet, and offered it up."

"No, sir, why? Poor piggy!" Mistress Meg was a literal young woman, not given to discerning ironies.

"Poor piggy, ye say, do ye? Yet ye'd eat up poor piggy blithely enough if he came to table on a trencher, with sage in his mouth. And what about the poor foxes and hares ye chase, and the stags too? Ye don't say poor Reynard and poor stag, I'll be bound."

"Why no; that's sport. Sport's very well, and pleases the horses and the hounds and the men and women and all. Even the fox enjoys the run, 'tis said."

"'Tis said! That *'tis said*, miss, is the villain of the piece, the arch-fiend that has ever deceived human kind. *'Tis said* sends innocents to the gallows, poor old women to the flames, keeps men's minds in swaddles and scholars groping beneath blankets of darkness, contents people to endure that their fellows should suffer torture and poverty and death, because *'tis said* as they deserve it, or as there's no help for't, or some other plaguey infernal trash. I don't let July quote Mr. 'Tis Said at me, do I, Jule? Except only she means, ''tis said round about, and what can we do to stop the lie?' There's only one medicine for Mr. 'Tis Said—a fist in his mouth, to send his teeth rattling down his throat, the dirty brock.

So, Meg, don't thou be 'tis saiding me, for it heats my blood."

"I won't, sir. Nevertheless, don't any one ever say a true thing? And if they should, are we quite forbid to mention it?"

"None of your impudence, miss. They that mock their physicians have cause to be sorry when next they fall sick."

"When the artless doctor sees
No one hope, but of his fees,
And his skill is on the lees,
Sweet Spirit, comfort me!

"When his potion and his pill
Has, or none, or little skill,
Meet for nothing but to kill,
Sweet Spirit, comfort me!"

The cheerful young lady quoted the only lines she appreciated from her vicar's Litany to the Holy Spirit, which he had composed last winter after a fit of fever and circulated among his parishioners.

"A plague on the lot of ye," the doctor returned. "Parson making a figure of fun of his leech, and teaching his flock to do the same, and July here bringing you young limbs back with her to mock a God-fearing physician in his own house. If it's dinner ye want, imps, ye'll get none here, for there a'n't none, only a rabbit pasty for July and me and our old woman. So ye'd best be getting back home, an y'are hungry."

"W'are going," Giles said. "Good-bye, sir. I go back to Cambridge to-morrow, you know."

"Time, too," said Dr. Conybeare. "You look quite well enough for your books."

"Oh, I'm never that, sir, plague take 'em. Still, I like

Cambridge; 'tis well enough. Good-bye, sir. You'll walk as far as the cross with us, Jule?"

"Don't thou be long, July," her father bade. "That pasty waits, so does my stomach." He watched the three start up the steep lane that climbed up beyond the village to join the road that ran alongside the end of Dean Wood towards Lower Dean and the Court. "Limber monkeys," he muttered, with affectionate scorn. "Not a notion in both those red heads o' theirs together. Still, th'are good children, an' I'm glad July has 'em for friends. My little wise-head sticks too close to her books, and I forget she's only a little maid, and get talking away to her about the world and its troubles, as if she was a grown man, she's so much sense and ingeniousness in her questionings and sayings. It's she should be away learning with her brother, instead of young Giles. Still, I couldn't spare her—my last nestle-chick, and the best. And to think her mother, poor soul, lacked the intellects ye could shake in a walnut-shell, so that from the time I took her to the hour God did, she never once got a notion into her head beyond how to make elder wine and mix preserves and see the serving-wenches di'n't eat and drink 'em up behind her back. Lord, Lord, there was a poor fool! Well, she was happy enough. Wits don't always bring joy in this Bedlam world of ours."

4

Giles, at the cross-road by the wood, into which Meg had run after a badger, was saying, "You'll write letters to me, July?"

"Aye, Giles." Julian believed that she wrote good letters.

"And you'll not stuff 'em with Latin verse and trash y'have been reading? Remember now, I don't want to hear of books, but of what y'have done and seen. You must divert me, July. Women should divert men while men work."

"You don't work, silly. Aye, I'll write. But you must write to me too."

"Faith, I will. But not so often, July, for you know I hate writing, and love to get letters."

"Kit writes. He writes me news of Cambridge, and of all the poets and wits and scholars and learned men there; and the masques, when they have 'em, and all. But he don't write often."

"Oh, I think that's all tedious stuff. And I know no poets well. My friends don't write poetry, only Latin verses when they must, and they get others to write those for 'em when they can."

"Well, there's Mr. Cleveland of St. John's, Kit's tutor. He writes marvellous ingenious verses."

"Aye, and I like Cleveland well enough; he's a pleasant droll. If all poets was like him. . . ."

"And there's Mr. Richard Crashaw of Peterhouse, and Mr. Abraham Cowley of your own College. Mr. Cowley's a wonderful good poet."

"So they say, and so he thinks. I don't quaint with him much. Why do you make so much pudder about Cowley? Y'are for ever pestering me about him."

"I a'n't."

"Y'are."

"I say I a'n't. But y'are such a stupid lad, you never can tell me what I ask you, as Kit does. So does Mr. Herrick. He tells me all about the poets that he knows, and their poetry. I dare say Sir John Sucklin can too."

"Let him; pox on him for a chicken-liver that ran away from the Scots. When I go for a soldier, I shan't run from the enemy anyhow."

"Indeed," said Julian distantly. "They that brag loudest run fastest, 'tis said."

"*'Tis said!* There you go; the doctor said he never let you say that. Oh, pox take it, July, let's not brangle and squabble my last day at home. Kiss me and be friends, sweet-heart."

Giles was the sweeter tempered of the two, but Julian could always be won from ill-humour by a generous word. "I'm sorry, Giles," she said. "And I know thou'd never run in battle, and thou doesn't brag. And I'll surely write. But I wish I could go to Cambridge too with Kit and you, and read all the books there, and see the colleges and the learned men. I know, if I could, I could write something myself."

"Why, July, y'are always writing. Y'have filled books full of manuscript. You never lin."

"Aye, I know. But I would like to write something famous; a masque that should be performed before the King; or to have my poetry printed in a book for men to read. Kit told me Mr. Cowley's *Pyramus and Thisbe* was printed when he was a schoolboy, and he wrote it when he was but ten years old. And here am I, turned fifteen, and nothing done yet."

"Well, Mr. Herrick's poems, that he thinks so much on, ha'n't been published in a book yet, and he'll be turned fifty soon. I can't see, July, that y'are so much behind."

"Poor Mr. Herrick! I would he had gotten his poems published when he went up to London for all those months last spring. He came back quite sad. But now he says he will write a great number more, before he prints 'em, and 'twill be a book will live for ever. I should like to write a book would live for ever. I would I had your chances, Giles. Particularly as you don't use 'em."

"I do use 'em, only not to write books. I'd rather see cock-fighting anyday. Lord, all this pudder about books! A'n't there enough books in the world already, then? You won't find me wasting my time over books, nor Meg neither. All the same, July, I like you best. Aye, faith I do, I love you better than Meg or any one. Y'are so *pretty*, July; your face is like white violets." At this, they both coloured a little, because it was not the way they normally talked to one another, and both of them found it embarrassing.

Meg swung up whistling from the steep wood. "I cou'n't track him. I shall bring Dash to-morrow and seek him out. Come, Giles, we're late, we must get home. Good-bye, Jule. See you to-morrow. My grandmother means to ask you and your father to sup, along with the vicar and Sir John Sucklin. Mind and you come. Have you done with saying July good-bye, Giles? I left you long enough for't."

"Don't be stupid," Giles replied, and reddened again through his freckles. "Good-bye, then, July."

"Good-bye, Giles. Give Kit my love." Abruptly and casually they kissed and parted. The Yardes ran down the lane towards Dean.

5

Julian strolled back to Deancombe. She was very fond of the Yardes, but she thought she liked best to be alone; they chattered so much that she couldn't see the country properly as they walked together.

She saw it now, as she stood at the top of the lane that dipped steeply down from Dean Wood to Deancombe village. The smoke of bonfires drifted sweetly on the light, cool air; behind her stretched the long dark gorge of the wood, climbing densely up Dean Bourne to the wild moors; unyellowed yet, it climbed, a tangled dark-green forest of oak, birch, holly, beech and fir, on either side of the brawling river far below. Julian loved to climb up all the river's wild length, from Dean village to where the long steep ravine opened out on to the purple moors at the ford where the old Abbot's Way started across Lambs Down towards Buckland Abbey in the far south. But now she turned to where Deancombe lay huddled away in rosy orchards beneath steep copses golden with furze, and beyond it to the south the blue landskip swelled and dipped. The day, the landskip, and the world, were so beautiful that they burned Julian's heart in her breast. A sober little prig she might be, but she sang aloud and ran down the lane as swiftly as the merry Yardes themselves, alive and exultant not with their hoyden spirits, but with the starry, supermundane frenzy of the poet, that will turn its pleasure later into song. For Julian wrote poetry with the zeal and resolution of any reveller at the lyric feasts made at the Sun, the Dog, the Triple Tun, or even at the Apollo Tavern, of which her pastor, Mr. Herrick, had so often told her tales.

She would be a poet; she knew she would be a famous poet when she was older. She was emulous of Mr. Abraham Cowley, with his list of famous poems and plays already behind him and *Poetical Blossoms* published when he was but twelve. Giles was right that she harped on him, for she was not only admiring but jealous. Poets *were* jealous; that was obvious to any one who met any of them, or even heard tell or read of them. Even Mr. Herrick. . . . So Julian felt that for her to be jealous of Mr. Cowley was quite in order. Questionless, Sir John Suckling would have some malicious tales to tell the vicar of his fellow-bards, and particularly of that Sir John Mennis who had written the spiteful skit on his Scottish expedition. Julian, wise already in her chosen profession, was not to suffer shock or disillusion from the manners of literary persons.

6

"Prue, Prue," called Mrs. Elizabeth Herrick, bustling to the kitchen, "more canary for the gentlemen. The gentlemen have drunk up all the canary sack."

Prudence Baldwin looked as if she disapproved this action on the part of the gentlemen.

"The master has taken to the sack again," she coldly remarked, "He drinks a plenty sack since he's gotten home from Lunnon."

"Aye, 'tis pity," Mrs. Elizabeth agreed. "'Tis pity he wou'n't drink cider instead. But there, gentlemen know best what they like to drink. So you must draw them the canary, Prue, for they grow impatient."

Grimly Prue drew a great earthen jugful from the hogshead in the buttery, bore it into the parlour, and set it with a discouraging thud on the oak table. Here were goings on: her master, who had given up wine with a fine flourish last winter, on the doctor's advice, and even written a poem called *Farewell to Sack*, had trapsed up to London in the spring for three months, got into bad ways, no doubt (indeed, there had been pretty tales going about) and returned to his parish as fond of sack as ever; and the carrier seldom now came from Totnes without something to drink for the Vicarage—canary, or sherry, or Jamaica rum, or new Florence wine. And here was one of his plague fine gentlemen friends from London to encourage him in it. As to Mrs. Elizabeth, much use *she* was with the vicar; Prudence thought it a pity that her master should have given a home to his widowed sister-in-law. That was another ill result of his London visit. You didn't want ladies about a house; even if they were as placid, kindly, and uninterfering as Mrs. Elizabeth, you couldn't away with that fatal fact of nature that had made them ladies and not gentlemen, and therefore such that you didn't want 'em about a house.

Mrs. Elizabeth had settled herself now with her embroidery in the ingle-nook, beside the bright apple-log fire, the oil lamp at her side, for it was past eight o'clock, they had finished supper, and the curtains were drawn against the misty October evening.

The vicar and his guest still lounged at the table, with mugs and pipes. "Drink about, Jack," said Mr. Herrick, filling his friend's mug. "The evening's young yet. O thou the drink of gods and angels! Wine, that scatter'st spirit and lust, whose purest shine . . ."

"Yes, well," said Sir John, stemming his host's flow of poetry, "what was I saying? Aye, about parliament. We've come to a time, Robin, when all His Majesty's friends should rally round him, and try and serve him as best they can. So

I have accepted Bramber: aye, I shall sit for Bramber when parliament meets, as they say it will in November, if only to provide the king with gold to buy those damned greedy Scots out of England. The more of loyal men get into that plaguey assembly the better, now. Lord knows in what a mood they'll meet, after the way the last one was dissolved all in a hurry. Pox take me if they won't have too great heads on 'em to be brought down without much ado. I tell thee, Robin, w'are on a mine's edge. Look now, I have wrote a letter to Harry Jermyn, that I will shortly send, and told him straightly that all wise men look to the King now to do something extraordinary to compose these differences. All men's eyes are on him, said I; for majesty in an eclipse, like the sun, draws eyes that wou'n't look t'ards it when it shined out, said I."

"That's good," said Mr. Herrick, as his friend paused for approval. "Aye, that's a good figure. Drink about, Jack." Sir John drank about.

"And neither must he delay to act, I wrote to Jermyn. Look, said I, the King must act forthwith. He must haste and make the best of a bad market. He must make a union with his people. There are two things in which the people expect to be satisfied, religion and justice. And the King must more than satisfy 'em; he must do something of his own, give 'em things they expect not, and so cure all jealousy. Else, said I, 'tisn't safe to imagine what may follow. For the people, you know and I know, Robin, is naturally not valiant, and not much cavalier; the rabble is cowards, and mayn't consider 'emselves safe even with royalty fettered; they may want to do away with royalty, all-thing. That's what I told Jermyn. And, said I, the Queen must join in the good work; she should dismiss those papist counsellors of hers; she should meet the people in that. And the King should let my Lord Strafford go, and the Archbishop too, for the service of suspected servants does a king no good. Mind you, Robin, I respect those ministers; I respect Strafford, and I look to the Archbishop for the keeping of the Church's order against all the damned vagabond zealots and predicants; still their service will only harm the King now. What think you, Robin, of that letter?"

"Faith, Jack, so fine a letter as never I heard. It should save the realm. Toast it, man. Here's to His Majesty's health and wealth, so long as he'll leave us ours!"

"Oh, and I forgot: I said to Jermyn, too, that the people of England have ever played like wantons with their sovereigns; they pull and tug against 'em, but when the princes ha' let go, they put the rope into their hands again that they may play on, as we saw in Queen Elizabeth."

"And as you may see in Tracy here." The vicar pulled his spaniel's ears. "He ever does that with a rope or stick. Aye, the people is as senseless as dumb beasts. I'll warrant they be so in Dean Prior. Hark 'ee, Betsy, how will Master Cuffe like this?" He tossed his sister-in-law a half sheet of paper on which he had been scribbling while his friend talked. "Read it out, Betsy. Let me hear how it goes now."

Mrs. Elizabeth held the paper to the light of the lamp, and read it through to herself first, familiarity with many of her brother-in-law's epigrams on his parishioners having taught her caution. Jests were all very well, but some of Robin's jests were not seemly, even to her unsqueamish tolerance. However, this on Cuffe was harmless enough, and she read it out, in her placid, drowsy, good-natured voice:

"*Cuffe* comes to Church much; but he keeps his bed
Those Sundayes onely when as briefs are read.
This makes *Cuffe* dull; and troubles him the most
Because he cannot sleep i' th' Church free-cost."

"Well, will that do, think ye? Will that please Master Cuffe?"

"Very droll," said Sir John, somewhat bored, and reflecting that small country parishes were not beneficial to poetic wit. Old Robin should be above concerning himself in verse with the petty misdemeanours of villagers. Mrs. Elizabeth looked relieved that it was no worse. Really, some of Robin's epigrams! She hoped that Prudence had not heard them all, but no doubt Prudence and the whole village had, and it could scarcely make for good feeling in the parish.

"You know, Robin," she said mildly, "that I never do like your poetry about the village people so well as your other verses. The parish don't like it, being called names in verse, and the verses being said about. No one don't like that, do they, Sir John?"

The vicar burst into a laugh.

"Ay, marry, do they, Sir John? Sir John's a man should know that, in truth. What of Mennis his lampoon, Sucklin? Didst like it? I'll warrant thou didst. No errant knight ever went to fight with half so gay a bravado! How goes the rest? Betsy, sister, I hadn't guessed thou hadst such malice in thee."

"Why, la you, brother, you know very well I ha'n't thought o' that. You know that, Sir John, I am sure." Hospitable Mrs. Elizabeth was flustered. But their guest seemed unconcerned.

"Pray, ma'am, don't mention it. 'Tis a most tedious silly squib; I had thought better of Jack Mennis his wit than to have made a lampoon so mean and poor. But 'tis odd how flat men's wits become when envy sours 'em. If ever you see me wanting to lampoon a man I envy, Robin, bid me give over, if you love me, and I'll do the same by you. D'ye recollect Dick Brome's malicious hit at my *Aglaura* in folio, with its goodly wide margins, that made it look so fine? Like a child in the great bed at Ware, he said it was. Pox take him for a jealous cat. And he only Ben's serving man, when all's said. How we poets do love one another ! I tell thee, Robin, I am sometimes sick to death of literary men, with their spites and rancours and follies, and think I shall get me to politics; but then, thinks I, politics is only another game played by the same poor human kind, and questionless they hate one another there, too, when they get scuffling for place and power. It's a sorry spiteful world, Mrs. Elizabeth, once you get beyond the green fields and hedges of the country, where I am sure all is peace and amiability, hey, Robin?"

Mrs. Elizabeth shook her head as she put away her embroidery.

"Alas, Sir John, even in the country there's sometimes spite. Why, you'd never believe the feuds there is in Dean, the malice and brawling, and the wicked lies some tell of others. Robin preaches at 'em from the pulpit about it, but, Lord, each looks at t'other and thinks the discourse is meant for 's neighbour, not f'r 'imself. I swear I could die laughing to see 'em."

"The way o' the world," Mr. Herrick said. "Dean Prior's the same as the rest o' the world there; though, shrew me, it's a cursed ill-speaking, ungrateful, churlish village, devil take me if it a'n't. A'n't it, sister?"

"What, brother?" Mrs. Elizabeth, looking for her needle, was not paying much heed to the gentlemen's talk.

"I say, a'n't Dean Prior a damned spiteful, ill-speaking, ungrateful village?"

"Aye, to be sure it is, Robin. Wonderful ungrateful indeed. But there, I always say, the poor a'n't grateful, do what you will for 'em. Good-night, Sir John. Good-night, brother. I always seem to get drowsy, Sunday evenings, and shall to bed. Pray, Sir John, don't let him sit up all night talking. I know what he is when he has old friends with him."

Sir John gave her her candle and held open the door. How pretty-mannered a gentleman he was, Mrs. Elizabeth thought. She was glad Robin had his company; Robin enjoyed company; he sometimes got moody with her alone, and missed his London friends. And it was more seemly for him to have gentlemen friends in the vicarage than ladies; Robin with ladies was wont to get a little gay, for a clergyman, and Prue might get thinking things, indeed, even saying them. Mrs. Elizabeth was a little afraid of Prue.

Sir John sat down again, saying, "Art for a game of cribbage? I have a pack in my pouch here."

"Aye, we'll play suddenly. Drink about, man, drink about. But I've not your skill or practice at the game, as you know, and shan't play high. Or look, damme if I don't play my benefice against your seat in parliament. Though, as to that, you can have the benefice with all my heart, an you win it, but I've little mind, even could I, to be a parliament man, though I like well enough to stay in Westminster. Ah, Jack, I would I was back there. It was like the old days, the months I spent in Little Aumry last winter and spring. I like Devonshire well enough in summer, and 't is a pretty sight to see the spring flowers and the may, and the maids going a-maying with the dew on the fields and on their hair; in sunshine and song-time I'm content enough, and indeed I've wrote my best verses here, I do believe. But when the lanes are knee-deep in dirt, and the fields in mire, and there's cold white mist on the moor and a frog in my throat, and the weather's so dirty a man can't ride out and see his friends, why then Dean Prior's no place for Robin. My beloved Westminster was so like Paradise when I got there, intending to stay a month, that I stayed on till May. I lodged in Nick Wilkes his house; he had his sister's two daughters living there—d'you mind 'em—old John Parsons, the organist's, wenches, Dorothy and Thomasin. 'Swounds, Jack, but Thomasin has grown a proper pretty maid. She was brought to bed of a bastard while I was there, and plague take it if one of Mr. Dell's jackals didn't come prowling around, trying to make out 'twas my get. I heard as he had wrote up about it to Dell, and that Dell reported it to the Archbishop, and I mayn't have heard the last on't yet, the church courts is so hot in these days on the track of poor parsons."

"And was it your get, the bastard?"

"As I live, no. I've had sins enough in my day, God forgive me, but Thomasin Parsons's bastard a'n't one of 'em. Marry, Jack, this world without wenches would be a sad dull place, but more free from care!"

"It don't bear thinking on, Robin. I'll die a bachelor, I trust, but never live long without love."

"Ah, Jack, but you're not a parson. God knows, I do often try and live without it, I swear I do, but he knows, too, that 'tis a hard task, and mortal nature can't always reach perfection. All the same, Jack, God forbid any one should judge my life by my wanton verses. I'll have Ovid write my epitaph for me—

> Crede mihi, mores distant a carmine nostri.
> Vita verecunda est, Musa jocosa mihi.

But I've wrote some nobler numbers of late, with more of religion in 'em. Did I tell ye, Jack, I thought of printing my poems—I've over five hundred on 'em—when I was in London; Andrew Crooke had 'em in hand, and put in for a licence and all. But my friend Weekes—you know John Weekes, now parson of Sherwell, near to Barnstaple—counselled me to delay a while, for he liked very well the grave, religious poems I showed him, and thought I should write more of those, and so give my book a graver, more pious, parsonical air. Further, all said it was a bad market for poetry just at this time, with all this trouble and unrest about, and the critics all hot on politics, so I stayed Crooke, and took the poems back again to complete. After all, where's the haste? I can wait. Immortality's a long word; and, having stayed near fifty years for glory, I can stay another year or two. Not longer, though. I can stay as patiently as any man, but the years haste on, and I'm not young no more. I think my book will bring me glory, when it comes, eh, Jack? I don't doubt that, do you?"

"Why, you never know. It's extraordinary pretty verse, to be sure, but you never do know in what humour critics and readers be."

"I look past the moment; I wait on all time for my bays."

"Why, then you know still less, for you don't even know what the fashions in verse will be. Look at Ben, hissed off the stage in the end of his days, and for a mighty good play too. None can tell they'll wear the bays in this unaccountable life, till they win heaven and the angel's crown. And even that turns on the toss of a coin, or so we must believe if w'are to be good Arminians and not to side with the predestinating rogues. Well, I care little for poetic fame myself, and had as lief have a win at bowls."

The vicar looked coldly at him. "So ye say, Jack. So ye say, I remember, in your *Session of the Poets*."

"Aye, marry, did I? Aye, marry, I think I did. 'Tis true enough. I have ever been a careless knave about the bubble reputation."

"So careless, Jack, that when you went to seek it i' the cannon's mouth, you burst it and left it on the field."

"How's that, sir? Wa'n't I a soldier of Gustavus nigh on a year, and was there any man ever called me coward? I don't hold it friendly in you to take up the silly, tedious foolery of that malignant oaf Mennis to taunt me with what never was. As my host, as, thought I, my friend, and as a divine, I hold it damned uncivil in you."

"I grant, Jack, I grant. Crave your pardon. Drink, man, and wash it out, as I do. But you nettled me, with your talk of caring nothing for fame. 'Tis a thing we say of ourselves; a thing we like to credit ourselves with, that carelessness of fame. But never yet I heard of a poet had it."

The vicar still spoke disagreeably, because remembering his friend's *Session of the Poets* had recalled a rankling grievance to his mind. He did not hesitate to mention it, after three years' vexation.

"'Swounds, Jack, 'twas a strange thing that, among all the poets and wits you mentioned in that drollery of yours, you said no word of Robin Herrick, that was used to be called the music of a feast when you was still being birched at school. Ben and Selden, Tom Carew and Will Davenant, Porter, Waller, Falkland, the Bartlet brothers, Toby Matthews, Jack Suckling as grand as ye please, not caring a fig for fame, and a whole rabble more, but no Herrick. Am I a less poet than Tom Carew, then? Am I become nothing since I left the London taverns for Devonshire?"

"I'm sorry, Robin. I suppose that, not meeting you about the town I didn't turn my mind on you when I wrote. Come, man, 'twas but a squib thrown off in a hurry, a piece of the nonsense that men write about their circle of gossips. 'Twasn't a serious assize of fame, and I swear I never thought any man would feel wounded to be out on't."

"Wounded? Not I, Jack. I don't give a fig for any such stuff. The loss is to the verse, not to me. It was just that I marvelled how it came about. As I marvelled, far more, how it came that I, one of Ben's own tribe and his foremost disciple, wasn't asked to write a verse to his memory in

Jonsonus Virbius, in which half the little poetasters in the land wrote their little elegies, while I, that knew and loved him as his son—Aye, forsooth, but I do know why: there was malice in 't."

"Aye, surely," Suckling amiably agreed.

"But I care not," said the vicar. "I don't write for glory, no more than you. Here, I'll give you a toast, Jack. To ourselves, the only poets in London or in Devonshire as don't give a fart for glory. Drink deep, man; 'twill take a deep draught to wash down that lie."

"I swear, Robin, I believe I care more for my repute as a theologian. Didst read my *Account of Religion by Reason*, that I wrote at Bath?"

"No," said Mr. Herrick, who did not care about religious treatises.

"Why the devil not? I sent it you, since it dealt with religion, and religion's a parson's subject, thought I. John Weekes of Barnstaple praised it enough, and Hales of Eton spoke extraordinary well on't. Indeed, though I should scorn to boast, 'twas a devilish ingenious piece of work, and would have done credit to a divine. Art not interested in Socinianism and the like, Robin?"

"Not I. I'm a religious man enough, I hope, and try and serve God both with my prayers and my life, so far as a sinful man may, though I'm not one of your pious painful strivers that make a great ado and pudder to win heaven. But as to your Socinianism, what is't to me? I hope I can believe in the mystery of the Trinity without such close enquiry into Nature, Substance, Essence, Hypostasis, Suppositum and Persona, as they plagued me with when I took up Orders. I ne'er think on 'em now."

"Tell me this, at least. What d'ye think of the state of church matters to-day? The ignorant populace say the Court'll go Papist before it's done, and Canterbury and his pet clergy with it. It's already growing to be the shortest way to royal favour, for the Queen's influence greatens daily. But the populace err concerning the Archbishop, who hates Popery as much as he fonds the Arminians. You know the jest—"What do the Arminians hold?" Answer: "All the best bishoprics and deaneries." But the vulgar who confound Arminianism with Popery are much wrong. Howbeit, the country don't like all this interference with its old use. 'Tis angering both the gentry and the rabble, and siding 'em together against the new clergy, with their bowings, their duckings, their doppings, their square caps and long coats, and their railed tables in the east, and forbidding business and conversation even in Paul's itself. For my part, I like decency and order, but I swear I think Canterbury's party goes too far."

"Well," said the vicar, "damme if I care aught for any on't. But I'm in a plaguey awkward predicament, since the Bishops quarrel with one way of doing things, and the squires and people quarrel with t'other. What I say is, let the table stand east, west, north or south, behind no rails or behind a whole forest of 'em, so long as it's God's table the people must e'en come to it, like it or no, aye, and the squires too. Zounds, sir, it's not for them to dictate where God's altar shall stand. It shall stand where I place it, and I have been ordered to place it against the east wall, so there it stands, and there the people shall come to 't. And if I choose to swing incense for a feast, as God's chosen people did, and as the very pagans did to their gods, who is the Squire of Dean Court to say no?"

"He don't like it, then? Nay, I'll swear he don't. Was there ever a Church of England squire to like censing and ceremony, since the Church first renounced 'em? 'Tis alienating the squires from the Court and Church party, and that's pity."

"Not," added the vicar, "that I go along with Canterbury. He's in the right, say I, to punish the conventiclers and Brownists, the damned canting predestinating knaves. But he's in the wrong to go so easy with the Papists. Some of 'em need the pillory as well as the Puritans. Those Miggles, now. . . . And I'm sick and weary of those pestilential Church Visitors of his, with their 'Cease this,' and 'Do t'other,' and 'No carts through the churchyard,' e'en at hay-cutting, and 'No meat in Lent,' and, God help us, no pointing at our own flock from the pulpit, to show the man or woman we preach of. And this Mr. Dell's man, with his impudent lying tales of myself getting a bastard on little Mrs. Thomasin. They o'erstep their bounds, these inquisitioning beagles. God knows, as well as any man I stand for the clergy leading chaste lives, but inquisition does no good. We hear of clergy losing their benefices now for a stumble. Is that God's mercy? It can come to no good, such harrying as that. Give every man his chance, I say."

"Y'are right, Robin." Sir John knew that it would not be fruitful to proceed more deeply into the topic of the state of the Church, or to touch on Socinianism, Calvinism, Arminianism, the Cambridge Platonists, or the like, as was often his fancy when he talked with the clergy, for he fancied himself as a theologian. Mr. Herrick cared for none of these things; he was a rather peculiar clergyman, and something of a misopatrist, in a good-humoured, indifferent way, for, instead of St. Thomas, St. Augustine, St. Ambrose, and the other Church Fathers and Doctors, he read Anacreon, Horace, Virgil, Ovid Catullus, and Martial. So Sir John reserved his Church conversation for a more worthy companion, such as Dr. Hales, or Lord Falkland and said, instead, "Does that pretty little pupil of yours come and construe with you to-morrow morning?"

"Aye, Julian comes. W'are reading the Georgics together.

Hence that notion those young limbs got of catching a pig for the church."

"There's a pretty trim little maid, Robin. What eyes, what a brow, what a skin like milk! And what a cool, quaint, distant air the rogue carries! There's a manner, a *je ne sais quoi*, about that little lady, that would fit her well for the court, with a trifle of instruction added. I could give her that myself; an you please, Robin, I'll teach her something of court ways to-morrow, instead of your Georgics. Faith, I should like the task."

"I swear you would, Jack. And I swear I'm hanged if you shall do't. She's my charge; her father the doctor entrusts her to me to get learning, not to be exposed to any seducing young spark from London."

"Nay, Robin, you know I'm a safe man with a maid."

"I know no man less so, Jack. My little Julian is like a white snow-blossom, before rude hands have touched it; she's the most innocent pretty young virgin in the world, and she's to learn Latin, not philandering. Her father swears that, since she's as good intellects as either of his two sons—nay, better—she shall have as good learning, and since she can't get it at school or university, like her brothers, he's put her to me for't. He had, says he, a plaguey silly woman for a wife, one of those fools of women, who trapse gaping through life and know so little of letters that they can scarce tell a Bible from a ballad book. So, long before God relieved him of her, he swore as he'd never have another silly woman to live with him, and that his daughters, at least, shouldn't grow up fools. None the less, says he, one of 'em did so, her mother being too strong in her, and the Lord not having seen his way to giving her intellects. So he married her off quick to a schoolmaster, hoping he might put some sense into the brats they'd get, since she hadn't any to give 'em herself. But he swore as his youngest should get learning; he schooled her himself when she was a little maid; he's too busy to give her the hours she needs now she's grown a great wench, so he sent her first to a schoolmaster near by, but, Lord, she got beyond him, and when they came to live here, he prayed me to read with her and better her in her Latin and Greek and English. And, on my life, I never had a pupil who did me such credit. She takes to learning as a kitten sups milk. Her Latin verses wouldn't disgrace a bachelor of arts, and there's no puzzling her in construing, or satiating her at reading. She'd read all the English plays and poetry in my library an I let her."

"Does she read mine?" Sir John carelessly inquired. Mr. Herrick a little grudgingly admitted it.

"Aye, she'll read anything."

"What—*Aglaura* and *The Goblins*, as well as the poems? Perhaps she's done better by my work than you have, and read even my *Discourse on Religion*?"

"She prefers it to your love-poems. I warn you, Jack, she don't relish all your verses."

"Not?"

"No. She thinks you don't manage the conceited, metaphysical style well, and that, when you try and Clevelandise, not only Cleveland but young Cowley leave you a mile behind. Oh, she knows her mind, little Julian. And some of your verses she finds too jocund and unseemly."

"Aye, does she? And what of some of yours, pray, reverend poet?"

"Oh, I ha'n't let her read 'em all. There's some, God forgive me, as she'd not like. But she's pleased to like my country verses, and my fairy pieces, and many another."

"And what does Mrs. Innocence say to your Julias, Celias, Corinnas, Perillas, and the rest of 'em?"

"Why, nothing. She knows a man's life must have had

women in it. And she knows, too, as the most of 'em are but fancies, jewels to adorn a verse with. She's not a prude, the child, and she's read romances and plays. But she don't like unseemly jesting, such as thou and I both have on our heads, Jack. But she quarrels with you for more than that; she can scarce forgive your taking to yourself Donne's line about the lover's ghost. The dean's a god to her; so is Ben. She wept for his death as much as I did myself."

"Did she so? Will Shakespeare's the only god I'd set up for young things to worship."

"He can reign on one altar, but my Ben's must be the higher one."

"Aye, I mind you ever said so. But you're wrong, Robin. I could make your pupil a heretic there, an I had her for a day. Shakespeare's the one immortal, to my mind."

"If a man should believe your verses, he'd think Will Davenant to be the immortal, Jack."

"My beloved Will! Aye, marry, Will Davenant's a mighty fine poet; nevertheless, he's also my friend, and the laureate, and you must grant me a little licence on both those counts. We can't judge no man fair but the dead. Why, when I'm dead, Robin, you'll even judge me fair—except that, to be sure, y'are older and will be first underground. So then I'll judge *you* fair, and perhaps give you that crown of bays you don't covet. Well, now, what of that game of cribbage before we sleep? Come, I'll stake you a keg of canary against an hour of little Mrs. Julian to myself to-morrow morning. How's that, reverend master tutor?"

"As you will, fool. But, an you win, you must swear me on your honour to respect the child, and play her no saucy tricks."

"On my life, I swear it. D'you think I'd do or say aught to sully that little dew-bud? 'Pon my honour, Robin, you should know Jack Sucklin better by now. I'll read poetry with her; I'll make her love my verses by the melting voice I'll read 'em in. I'll tell her of my new play, *The Discontented Colonel*, that you won't listen to. I'll make those eyes of hers stretch bigger with tales of the poets and wits, of the court and foreign lands."

"Of Scotland, belike. Well, tell her what you please, and I'll to my orchard meantime and see to the planting of my new bergamots and standard apple-trees. That lad of mine never trenches deep enough without I have an eye on him. Deal on, Jack."

7

"Hoc pinguem et placitam Paci nutritor olivam," read the vicar.

"In this manner nourish thou," said Julian, "the plump olive, and pleasing to Peace. The olive, plump and pleasing to Peace."

"Continue, child."

"Poma quoque," read the pupil, in her clear, soft treble voice,

> "ut primum truncos sensere valentis,
> et viris habuere suas, ad sidera raptim
> vi propria nituntur opisque haud indiga nostrae.

Apples, also, so soon as they feel their trunks. . . ." A shadow fell across the page. Looking round for its cause, the diligent pupil's grave grey eyes met a merry pair that watched her through the open lattice window. The late-lying gentleman had at last arisen, and was standing in the garden, leaning his elbows on the casement sill, his brown hair moved lightly by the breeze.

"Good-morrow, pretty maid. Art as deep in thy olives and apples as a fruit-wench at Covent Garden. But why read of 'em, when they wait outside in the orchard for thy picking?"

"Out on you, Jack; and don't waste our time. And when sprang olives in a Devonshire orchard, pray? Continue, child. Apples, also . . ."

"Climb hastily towards the stars . . . so soon as they feel . . ."

"Stay the lesson, Robin. I am come, like Mephistopheles, for my bargain. Go dig thy apples and olives about, and dung 'em well, so as they may bear fruit, for you know the garden lad don't do't to thy liking. Young Mistress, will you cease climbing hastily towards the stars, and let me take your tutor's place a while? I have some poetry I would wish to read with you—not Latin, but English. They tell me you've wrote some pretty verses yourself; I would hear them, an you please."

A very amiable, handsome, ingenious gentleman, Julian perceived him by this to be. She looked inquiry at Mr. Herrick, who said, "Why then, I suppose you must have your way. We'll follow the apple-tree to-morrow instead, child. Come in, then, Mephisto, and remember what I told you. Look ye, Jule, this poet is fain to make you better acquaint with his own verse. Can you bear with him an hour? He's a tedious proud man, and will weary you, belike. As you know, he's a plagiarist, a thief of better men's words, and mars 'em in the thieving."

Julian blushed, for she had said this herself, and it now sounded rude.

"But, sir," she protested, "I like a great part of your verse very much. Indeed, I think some of it is marvellous pretty. Mr. Herrick knows I do."

"Mr. Herrick's envious, little mistress. And as to plagiarism, isn't a large deal of his own poetry from his Latin masters, and much of it through Ben Jonson, his English one? Look now." Picking up the thick manuscript volume from a shelf, he turned the pages.

"Hark at this:

"To read my book the virgin shy
May blush while Brutus standeth by,
But when he's gone, read through what's writ,
And never stain a cheek for it—

Straight from Martial, as I live. Is't not, Robin? Here's another, on when he would have his verses read—Martial again, with a dash of Catullus. And here's Anacreon translated, and never a word of gratitude. And here he copies Ben, who got it himself from the Lord knows which heathen. Ovid, Virgil, Theocritus, Horace, Catullus, Martial, Propertius—why there's scarce a line of the man's own!"

"'Tis near all his own," Julian spoke now coldly. "All the most beautiful verses. The Latin and Greek poets warn't never in Devonshire, so how could they have written about our maying, and daffodils, and primroses? 'Twas all olives and figs and gourds and myrtles and vines with them, though to be sure they had harvest home like us."

"Thank 'ee, July child, but don't trouble your head to protest against Sir John's nonsense. 'Tis all his envy and malice. I forgive thee, Jack. Quod nimium lives nostris et ubique libellis detrahis, ignosco. And as to the getting of my verses, you may find it defended in some lines I wrote down t'other day—

" What off-spring other men have got,
The how, where, when, I question not.
These are the Children I have left;
Adopted some; none got by theft.
But all are toucht (like lawfull plate)
And no Verse illigetimate.

Look 'ee now, I shall leave you to't, and go mind my trees."

8

The baronet and the young lady were left alone, facing one another across the oak table. She still regarded him something distantly, for speaking slightingly of Mr. Herrick and his verse. For her part, she regarded much of her vicar's poetry as straight from Paradise; it had that lovely, direct cadence and colour that seemed to drop into one's soul like dew, to grow like flowers, to run like brooks. If it was sad, it brought tears, if gay, laughter; it had a clear grace and candour that scarce any other poet had. Certainly not Sir John Suckling, though much of him was pretty and pleasing. But who was he, to slight Mr. Herrick? Julian had heard of the envy of poets, and sure enough, here it was.

" Come, my dear," Sir John gently rallied her, " ha'n't you a smile for your new tutor? Why so solemn and stiff? You're not displeased?"

" Yes," she replied gravely, " I admire how you can speak so of Mr. Herrick's verses, which are so marvellous beautiful, and you his friend and his guest."

" Why, if it teases you, child, I ask your pale little ladyship's pardon. I meant nought; I only jested. Robin's welcome to use all the Latin poets of antiquity to adorn his verse, for aught I care. He has good authority for't."

"Aye, and so he has. But a great number are all-thing of his own devising, and those the most beautiful."

"I grant, I grant. Lord, I esteem Robin's verses as well as any man do. Nevertheless, he's too rustic, mark you; too much out of the mode. Conceits and quiddities is all the mode to-day. Dr. Donne set the fashion, and we all run after it."

"I know that." The young lady was diverted from her resentment by her eagerness to talk and hear of poetry. "There's Mr. Cleveland—his is wonderful conceited verse."

"Aye, he chases the fashion faster than any of us. Young Cowley too."

"Oh, Mr. Cowley," Julian kindled pink; it was, thought Sir John, as if a white pansy blushed. "You know him, sir?"

"Aye, surely, a little." Sir John was off-hand concerning Master Cowley, remembering the vicar's reference to him. "He's but a lad at Cambridge, and 'tis early yet to say what he'll do. He's the faults of youth on him still."

"But, sir, already he's done a pretty many noble plays and verses. Why, he was but ten when he wrote *Pyramus and Thisbe*, and at twelve he wrote *Constantia and Philetus*, and while yet at Westminster he——"

"Lord, child, don't recount me young Abram Cowley's life. I know already that the young cock has crowed more than there was any call to in such a hurry. Give him time; he may grow out on't."

She regarded him rather gravely. More jealousy, she supposed. "I wish," she said, "as I was him. I am turned fifteen, and never have printed a line. And soon it may be too late."

"How too late, pretty madam?"

"Why, I might die," she explained, with the negligent

pessimism suitable to her years. "There's a vast deal of the smallpox round about, in Exeter and the towns, and I might take 'em and die."

"Lord forbid you should! Let all Exeter, and all Dean Prior, perish on't first."

"Or I might get married." She still meditated on the various assaults of fate, unheeding his prayer.

"Aye, so you might, on my life. That's a happier and a likelier chance."

"And married ladies have an uncomfortable deal to do, without writing verses and plays. But indeed I don't intend to marry, but to stop with my father, and learn of Mr. Herrick and write."

> "And after to lead apes in hell,
> As maidens doomed be;
> That fairer are than blossoms
> That blooms upon the tree,"

Sir John trolled. "Not for all the writing in the world, I think. . . . You've written much already, perhaps?"

She coloured pink. "Some few things."

"Wilt show 'em me?"

"I han't 'em here, sir."

"Nay, but let me wait on you and your good father in your house, and show 'em me at leisure there. For indeed I'd enjoy to see 'em."

"Truly, sir?" Like other authors, she was always ready to believe this. "Mr. Herrick's seen 'em," she added. "He tells me how to mend 'em."

"And do you mend 'em as he says?"

"Not always."

"I thought not. No one mends his own verse to order; 'tis not in human nature. It delights me, Mrs. Julian, that you don't lack human nature after all. Look now; if you read me your verses, I'll read you my new play. Is that a bargain?"

"Yes, sir, if you choose."

"And look, keep it to yourself. Take no notice on't to Mr. Herrick or Mrs. Elizabeth or any other soul. Regard it as *sub sigillo*, and 'twixt us two. For I'm a modest man, and don't care to have my plans noised abroad, more particularly when they concern literature. I'll warrant you feel the same, and that we shall well fadge."

Julian was solemnly watching him.

"What now, sweet chuck? A penny f' your thoughts."

"I was wondering," she replied, "how you and my father will fadge."

"Well, well. Well, I know. I have determined it shall be well. Why, is your father not easy? Will he mislike me?"

"I don't know. My father a'n't easy to guess at."

"Oh, I shall make myself so agreeable, he'll think me the pleasantest cheerful gentleman as ever waited on him. Oh, you need be in no case about that, my dear."

"I am not," said Julian. "I don't care."

"Little baggage, you seek all the time to disconcert me, with your *don't knows* and *don't cares*. Look, child, you'll like me, whether your father takes a fancy to me or not?"

"Oh, yes," she politely answered.

"Oh, yes; oh, yes! What kind of a cool, prim, fishy answer is that? Look 'ee, my dear, say, On my life, Sir John, that will I. Say, Dear Sir John, sweet Sir John, as I live I like 'ee extraordinary well already. Come, say it, little bud! Or I swear I won't read not one of your verses, but will instead read out to you my *Account of Religion by Reason*, from end to end."

"I need not listen," she replied. "And, if you read it also to my father, 'twill be very cordial to him, for he has already an answer prepared to't, and longs to give it you."

"I sha'n't read it t' your father, little cat; I shall read it to you. Come, say it, or—Pox take it," he muttered, for the door opened and into the parlour fluted feminine voices and rustled feminine skirts—Mrs. Elizabeth and a pretty gay young creature, over-dressed and merry-eyed, and behind her a pale, elegant and languid young gentleman.

"Why, July, good-morning t'ye," cried the young lady. "At your studies, as ever, but, I protest, with a new tutor! Make us known, pray, dear Mrs. Elizabeth."

"Surely, my dear. 'Tis our guest, Sir John Sucklin. Sir John, let me make you known to Mrs. Lettice Northly, and Mr. Henry Northly too. Mrs. Northly is the eldest granddaughter of Mr. Yarde of Dean Court, and the sister of the red-haired boy and girl as you met at church."

"Your servant, ma'am. Your servant, sir." As he bowed, Sir John observed that Mrs. Lettice was remarkably pretty, and looked amusing. He did not anticipate that books would play any part in his acquaintance with *her*.

"Your servant, Sir John Sucklin. I heard as you was to church yesterday, and encountered my good grandparents and my bad sister and brother in the churchyard. Mr. Northly and I warn't in church, for, Lord, the vicar'd dressed it up so with vegetables and fruits as it stank like a fruiterer's, and we can't abide a stink. Can we, husband?"

"Never in the world, my love," Mr. Northly yawned his agreement.

"And it seems as there was a pig too, to make matters worse. A pig and apples and punkins in church! I am sure, Sir John, you think Dean Prior a sad vulgar village; and you'd never see the like in London. I admire as dear Mr. Herrick thought it fitting to make such a show and to-do on the Lord's Day! Still, I am sure it delighted the vulgars. Lord, they'll run after anything."

"Indeed, ma'am, I found nought amiss in the church but one thing, and that an empty pew."

"La you, Sir John, y'are the politest gentleman that ever I met, if you sat lamenting my room afore ever you knew as I lived. But I'll swear you had a pretty plenty to stare at, with piggy and the punkins and all the country wenches, and never wanted anything. But look now, let's talk sense. I want to know of the new fashions. Is it true that lace collars is to be worn deeper this autumn? They say the Queen doth so. And I shall be mortified to death if, when we go up to London, I find I have gotten the wrong clothes, and am all out o' the fashions."

"More likely, ma'am, as you'll set 'em."

"Oh, God forgive you, Sir John, pray don't give me your nonsensical replies to such grave questions. Make him tell me, Henry."

"Indeed, sir, till you do so we shall get no peace. And, while y'are at it, you might inform me if our hair's to be worn the fraction of an inch longer. They say the King doth so, and if I find myself in London with my hair cut wrong, why, I too may die of shame, and that would be a sad pitiful case for our young children, both parents to have died of ill-dressing."

"Well then, to tell you the truth, Mrs. Northly, I've never observed. You take me for a man of fashionable tastes, with his eyes ever on his neighbour's apparel. Instead of which, I'm but a poor scribbler in peace, and a soldier of the King in war, and diligent card-player, bowler and gambler as well, and, on my life, I swear my time's too full to be observing the fashions. I dress as I can; I hope to pass in a crowd, and that's all my ambition. But as to ladies' collars—well, I'll inquire of my lady friends, an you please, and you shall be informed to the last fraction of an inch."

"Gentlemen's hair too, sir; I pray you won't forget gentlemen's hair."

"I promise you shall know on't, sir."

"We're dying for London, a'n't we, Henry? Lord, how weary I get of Denshire and its dirt and barbarous dull souls. Mr. Herrick and I are of a mind as to that, a'n't we, Mrs. Elizabeth? Don't the vicar grow weary of Denshire and hanker for his dear London?"

"What d'ye say, my dear? Why, yes, my brother enjoys London, to be sure. But his duty's here, a'n't it, and he's ever set on his duty and to serve his flock. And look how happy he is, minding his garden and his orchard, planting his vegetables and digging 'em up, and shouting at that stupid lad. Lord bless me, yes, Robin dotes on the country. But look ye, my dear, about that maid Sukey who minds your children; you should know as Prudence tells me she's five months forward, and in no case to care for innocent children. You must send her off, and I can tell you of a good honest maid to take her place."

"Pray, Mrs. Elizabeth, don't let's talk of maids and their bastards. To be sure Sukey's five months gone, but I never take no notice on't till the seventh month. She must go then, but, Lord, let's have such peace as we may till then. She washes and mends my ruffles well, and keeps the children from crying, and goes quiet about her work, and I'll not make a pudder about what don't concern me. I am sure as the vicar would counsel Christian charity. Wou'n't you, dear Mr. Herrick?"

The vicar, earthy and mopping his brow, strode in.

"Charity? Aye, always, my dear, save to that garden lad o' mine."

He kissed her on both cheeks so heartily that she gave a little cry of dismay.

"Parson, parson, mind my complexions! Put on newly

this morning, to delight you, and to air my new pot of paint. They say the Queen do go in more than ever for paint; does she so, Sir John?"

"'Twould be disloyal of me, madam, to peer so curiously into my sovereign's cheek as to distinguish the true rose from the false."

"Nay, but they say she has no roses these days, but is all gone sallow and dark, and looks but ill without her paint."

"Well, well, poor lady, she grows no younger," Mrs. Elizabeth kindly said. "And she has to do credit to the King."

"Aye, forsooth, and to keep him fond, too. They say he hangs on her least word now, like a love-sick swain. So, you see, paint is some use, vicar."

"None to you, my pretty. There, Jack, I got that said before you, for all your courtier's habit. To paint cheeks like yours, and like little July's here, is to profane nature's finest handiwork. Go wash it off in dew, pretty child, for I swear we'd all like thee better without it. Wou'n't we, Jack?"

"My good husband would not. My good husband likes to see a little paint on a female cheek; it persuades him that the female has took some pains to please him, and that he likes. Don't you, husband?"

"Well enough. Why shouldn't the creatures be at pains to please us? Pox on't, we do more than that to please them. We maintain 'em, and support 'em, and gratify their whims, and I'm hanged if they don't ought to be at pains to please us. A painted face mayn't be fair to look on, but, 'swounds, it indicates a good godly desire to delight us; ergo, I am delighted, with the intention, if not with the achievement. Are you with me, Sir John?"

"Nonsense," Mr. Herrick interrupted. "Why, according to that reasoning, you'd be delighted if the creatures should paint their noses red, thinking to please you."

"And so I trust I should," Mr. Northly replied. "Like the Lord, I look on the heart and not on the outer skin. As a learned and discreet minister of God's word, you should do the same, sir."

"Why, who am I to usurp God's function? As mortal man, I don't pretend to look so deep."

"Why," exclaimed Mrs. Elizabeth, "don't I hear the carrier?"

The grinding rumble of cart wheels up the lane outside the vicarage garden seemed strong evidence that she did, and she and the vicar, joined by Prudence Baldwin from the kitchen regions, hurried out to see what he had brought them from Totnes.

"Lord help us, the Totnes carrier," young Mrs. Northly commented, for she ordered from Exeter. "I'd as lief order stuffs for my gowns from Buckfastleigh or Brent, wou'n't you, July?"

"I think I do so," Julian simply replied, not being able for the moment to recollect where she ordered anything from. "Aye, 'tis from Higgins at Buckfastleigh."

"Whom I heartily congratulate," Sir John quickly put in, turning his flattering eyes from Mrs. Lettice, that pretty piece of malice and mirth and furbelows, to the pale, grave child in her plain, ill-made gown of blue woollen. In truth, the young lady had had Mr. Higgins's stuff made up by a somewhat inexpert Deancombe cottager, since she herself disliked sewing, and could afford no better sempstress. She did not know how ill-made it was, nor greatly care; but she rightly believed those who told her (including her glass) that the colour went well with her eyes and skin, for few young ladies are so deeply sunk in their books as not to heed such matters as that.

Mrs. Elizabeth came bustling back, a list in her hand. "Eight ells of the best Holland for sheets, four breadths of green figured silk, patterns of damask, an ell white cambric for a stock, the clock back from the menders, ten pounds best raisins, a barrel of fat oysters, a dozen fresh herring, quarter of loaf sugar, hogshead of canary, six pints white wine. . . . Robin, Bodger han't sent the sugar. That's the third time in five weeks as Bodger has disappointed us, and I am sure we must go elsewhere. Where d'you get your sugar from, my dear?"

"Oh, Churton's, of Exeter. You should send to Exeter, dear Mrs. Elizabeth, not to Totnes. I am sure we never buy from Totnes."

"Your uncle, Sir Edward Giles, ever did so," the vicar said, rather irritated by the young lady's airs.

"Aye, so he did, to be sure. But then he had kept house there, being its Burgess, and knew 'em all, and didn't like to disappoint 'em. I assure you we think the Totnes shops are the saddest poor things. Look 'ee, Sir John, have you drunk *tea* in London much?"

"Now and then, ma'am. I've been given it by travellers home from the east. 'Tis queer, bitter stuff, better for Chinamen than for Englishmen, to my mind. 'Twill never be liked here. I'd liefer drink Guiana coffee, as begins to be drunk among the nice and forward sparks at Oxford and Cambridge."

"Lord, sir, that'a nasty muddy stuff. An't coffee extraordinary nasty muddy stuff, beau?"

"Extraordinary nasty, my life."

"But tea, Sir John, is lighter to a nice palate. It has a thin delicate flavour, though bitter. Henry had a pack on't sent him from his brother in the East India Company, and we drink a little now and then as a rarity, though indeed 'tis nasty too. But lest the Lord should cause it to be the mode, we drink it, don't we, Henry?"

"You'd do better to drink coffee too, madam, lest the

Lord should please to make *that* the mode, and you would be found wanting."

"Lud, Sir John, y'are always in the right. We must get some coffee suddenly. As to tea, Mrs. Elizabeth, you and the vicar will drink some this very evening after supper, for my grandparents too was sent a packet."

"What do I want with a drop of hot water and dried leaves, hussey? Ale, wine and sack are good enough for a country parson, and the squire always gives me plenty of those. Come now, minx, will you see how my garden grows, and pluck a posy?"

"Indeed, I won't, sir, for it's past time I was gotten home to feed that tedious greedy son of mine. Come, my life. Adieu, ma'am, adieu, parson, adieu, Sir John. We shall all meet again presently at my grandad's."

She fluttered out, a bright, ridiculous posy on the breeze, the scent of her drifting lightly after her as she tripped, her languid spouse behind her. Mr. Herrick and Sir John Suckling saw them out at the gate in the garden wall.

"There steps so pretty a little giglet flirt as never I saw," Sir John commented. "Godsnigs, Robin, she's wasted on Dean Prior. She should be in town."

"So thinks she, Jack, so thinks she. But you must leave us a few bright country flowers in our wilderness. Mrs. Lettice has ever been a merry pet lamb of my flock. She's above the deserts of that fantastical, dandified fellow I married her to."

"Oh, she'll lead him a dance; I'll warrant her she'll lead him a dance. If she don't make Actaeon of him before she's done, I'm a bishop."

"In that case, she's bound for't. Well, you ogled her as if you thought to join the dance with her yourself."

"'Sdiggers, and so I would if she'd let me. The pretty wanton!"

"Well, so long as you don't turn the head of my little Jule, you can flirt your fill with Mrs. Lettice. Jule's a maid apart, dedicated to the moon and the stars; she's a little Pallas, with the bird of wisdom on her shoulder, and no man's meat for the nonce. Marry, her day will come, but 'twon't be an unhallowed spark such as you as'll enjoy her, but some grave, discreet, learned young man, with his head in the clouds and his soul already in heaven. She's too good for such coarse worldlings as thee, Jack."

> "Hast thou seen the down in the air,
> When wanton blasts have tost it?"

Sir John trolled,

> "Or the ship on the sea,
> When ruder winds have crost it?"

"Another of your profane thieveries," remarked the vicar. "Now that verse of Ben's might have been wrote for Julian herself."

"Aye, I grant. But a burlesque's honest theft, whereas yours, Robin—What of your night-piece to Julia, I ask? And, to speak of Mrs. Julia, hast seen or heard any news of her of late years?"

The vicar oddly flinched, before he said, carelessly, "Not I. She belongs to my wild unhallowed past. Canst picture her in Denshire lanes? 'Slife, I'm glad she left me in the lurch, and I care nought for her now. If I still write verses to her lashes, her lips and her legs, 'tis from old habit. . . . Nay, nay ——" He stopped short where he stood, and violently struck at a marigold with his stick. "Nay, nay, why should I lie? I know not if I love Julia or hate her, but 'sbread, she's always in my dreams. I know and have adored many lovely ladies and wenches, country and town but when I shut my eyes to reflect on 'em, 'tis my lost, merry Julia, pox take her, swims like a full-sailed ship into my soul, all roses and cream, roguery, and merry black eyes. Ah, there was a woman, Jack. She loved me a little, too; I swear my Julia loved me a little, though she left me. . . . But enough of such foolish talk; my little pupil seems deep in her books, even though both her masters have deserted her."

They entered the parlour, where at the oak table sat Julian, diligently reading her Virgil.

"Shut thy book, Jule; school is over for to-day. I have to go see old Miggle at Deancombe, who thinks his last hour to have come, for the hundredth time this year, though your father says he may live to see a dozen more harvest-homes, despite all his ministrations and potions. So I'll walk up to Deancombe with 'ee, and wait on your father on my way. Look, Jack, an you desire to see a pretty walk, a pretty hamlet among apple-orchards, and a most ingenious learned profane physician, you can walk with us."

It seemed that Sir John did desire it, and they started off together up the hill, the young lady between the two gentlemen. Gaily Sir John sang snatches of a country jig:

"O mine own sweet heart,
And when wilt thou be true:
Or when will the time come,
That I shall marry you?
That I may give you kisses,
One, two or three,
More sweeter than the honey,
That comes from the bee.

"For now me thinks thou seemest
More lovely unto me;
And fresher than the Blossoms,
That blooms upon the tree."

9

They found Dr. Conybeare in his shirt-sleeves digging fiercely in his vegetable garden. Hailed by the vicar, he plunged his spade into the earth and came forward, wiping his forehead with his handkerchief.

" 'Morning, parson. I hear fine tales of your doings in church yesterday, y'old heathen, with your corn-sheaves and your punkins and your pigs. A'n't you 'shamed to lead your flock along such pagan paths? No, y'are not, I know it. What would busy Mr. Laud say to you and all your disorderly doings? He belongs, sir," he turned to Suckling, " to ancient Rome, not to our modern England, as doubtless y'are aware."

" Oh, Sir John Sucklin knows all my sins, doctor, but still bears with me for friendship's sake. But as for the Romans, they were wiser than we, for all they had no knowledge of the true God, for they war'n't infested and plagued with all these crop-eared sectarians, Brownists, Amsterdamians, Papists, Presbyterians, precisians, and the rest of the damned zealot crew, who set 'emselves up to pray in their own places instead of in God's house that's appointed for 'em."

" There were, to be sure, the Christians," the doctor maliciously remarked. " Though I grant they made little pother till Rome was in her decline; and that the authorities made brisk work of the most part on 'em. What we need in England's a few arenas full of hungry lions. That'd soon settle the sectaries, eh, Parson? "

" And not," added Mr. Herrick kindly, " as I've the least objection to sectaries, if they'd but keep quiet and not mention it. I'm no inquisitor, to inquire into the thoughts of their hearts."

"Nemo cogitur credere invitus, as Theodoric said to the Jews," Suckling put in.

"Just so, just so, Jack. No inquisition into men's beliefs, but a decent orderly practice. For instance, doctor, I'd not throw you to the lions, only on those occasions when you get talking too free and fly out at godly and Christian worship. For the rest, you can go your way for me—dig your vegetables, kill your patients, quarrel with me about Latin texts, and I'll not have you molested for the blaspheming unbeliever y'are. But, look now, I'm on my way to visit old Miggle. How does he do?"

"Reasonable well, the old rascal. He should have his health pretty well, if he'd but take my treatment and leave plastering himself over with the nasty concoctions they get from old Betsy Jollie, who sets herself up for a wise woman and claims to cure by her spells and verses the evil that poor old Widow Prowse has wished on folk."

"You've a local witch, then?" Sir John asked; and Julian saw her father's face set into its fierce, damn-the-world look.

"Aye, forsooth, have we, poor soul. I never pass her hovel but I fear to see a rabble gathered about it flinging stones or laying firewood to burn her out. We're a barbarous people, we human kind, and still sunk to the eyes in the dirty black bogs of our ignorance. Witch, forsooth! How d'ye regard that superstition, sir?"

"Favourably, favourably. I'm a highly superstitious man. There's God and there's the devil (Lord forgive ye, sir, if you doubt it) and there's persons in league with both on 'em, busy to work their will, as has been proved all down history and is still proved to-day. No man in his senses—pardon me, sir—can well doubt of that."

"Dr. Conybeare's scarce in his sense," said the vicar. "Irreligious men are all mad. Witches! Why, man, an you should take a walk on the moor on a black night, I'm told ye'd see whole covens on 'em flying around on their broomsticks. I don't never walk on the moor myself, night or day, for it's a horrid dismal country, and I've no wish to be pixie-led or to drown in bogs, so I won't say as I've seen the old hags, but there's scarce one of my flock won't swear to 't."

"Oh, your flock'll swear anything, I'll warrant. Since when d'ye take *them* as evidence, I'd like to know, the poor simpletons? And you a man of education and learning. You should think shame on yourself, parson."

"Y'are in the wrong, sir," said Sir John. "You have well-nigh all the scholars and learned men against you, even in your own profession. There's Dr. Thomas Browne, who's near the best-read physician in the country and the closest inquirer and exposer of the errors of the vulgar; he's just on completing a marvellous witty and ingenious discourse on his credo, and he don't throw doubt on witches; I'm told he swallows 'em, broom, cat and all."

"Oh, yes, I know Browne." Dr. Conybeare waved Browne out of his way. "A very ingenious, learned, witty fellow, but with maggots in's head, and overmuch of religion. Nay, sir, you can't daunt me with Thomas Browne, or any other medico."

"No, faith," said Mr. Herrick, "since y'aren't to be daunted by the whole testimony of Christendom, by the word of God in his old and new testament, and by every Father of the Church and holy and learned writer of all ages, not to tell of the pagans."

"I am not," said Dr. Conybeare. "Neither by the Emperors Constantine and Charlemagne, the Angelic Doctor, the Malleus Maleficarum, Pope Innocent VIII., his late majesty

King James, nor all the witch-finders and magistrates of England and inquisitors of the continent. I don't give a fig for the lot on 'em."

"My poor friend, ye'd deny all magic? All working with evil spirits for harm? What d'ye make of history, not only that of Christendom, but of the ancients? Ye'd have spared Lamia the sorceress, belike? Ye'd have taken Medea to bed?"

"Not I. She was a nasty termagant creature, and 'oon't be a safe bedfellow. But away with your ancient fables; we live in the seventeenth century, little heed as you ever take on't, parson. I subscribe to none of your old credulous philosophies, unless that of Epicurus, which did deny sorcery. All the same, it was left to Christendom to hunt out and torture poor old women on so fantastical a charge. That came in with your tailed and hoofed devil, and 'twon't go out till he do, I fancy. Meanwhile, they shan't get old Prowse unless across my body, as I've often said to Jule, ha'n't I, child?"

"Very often, father."

"So you can tell that to the Miggles, parson, with my blessing, and be damned to 'em. By the way, why should you concern yourself with the old papist? That priest of his own persuasion who creeps over from Buckfastleigh, dressed as a Puritan, and calls himself Mr. Harrison, comes to see him every little while, to shrive him and drag him from the jaws of the hell he deserves for attending the heretic church all these years to save his pocket. He's no care of yours, my friend."

"I'm his priest and pastor, doctor, while he lives in my parish, just as I'm yours; and he's had the grace to sit under me, which is more than you've often done. In any case, he likes a word with me, now and again, about this world, if not the next, and he thinks it discreet to keep in with me. Old Miggle and I've always fadged tolerable well; he tells me tales of his youth in Spain that I enjoy to hear, though they grow stranger as he grows older; and I give him the blessing of his foster-mother my Church, and he crosses himself and mutters prayers to set a vacat on mine that they mayn't harm him, and so we part friends. Look now, I must wait on him immediately; it grows late, and they'll be at their dinner. Jack, wilt walk up with me to Lower Addislade and see this old señor?"

"No, I'll wait for you here, if Dr. Conybeare will give me leave, while he digs his vegetables. I've no taste for sick-beds, and I'd liefer talk with the physician about life than with his patient about death."

The vicar gave his friend a suspicious glance, but, after all, it was the affair of the doctor to look after his child, and he left them all to it, striding away up the deep lane between the heavy-fruited orchards.

10

The clear golden October sun illumined the charming landskip to an exquisite radiance; all was gay, tranquil, lovely, English, like the Henry Lawes airs that Mr. Herrick sang, to his own words, as he walked. At such times as he was discontented with his remote country life, irritated by his slow, tiresome, ungrateful flock, and oppressed by his own lonely obscurity while his friends realised social and literary ambitions in the lively world of London, days so lovely and benign as this would turn the lanes, hedges and hills of his parish into a fairyland, and himself into its enchanted poet. Then he would forget his long exile from a more congenial life, and grow intoxicated with beauty, and content, like

Horace on his Sabine farm, to pace his fields far from the turmoils of towns. Then his soul and mind and heart would soar triumphantly together in song, his thoughts would run in lovely rhythms and whimsical conceits, like jewels tumbling forth from a suddenly opened casket. The irritated clergyman would devoutly worship his God, make poetry of his loves, his friends, and his dreams, and sing of brooks, of blossoms, birds and bowers, of April, May, of June and July-flowers, of May-poles, hock-carts, wassails, wakes of bridegrooms, brides, and of their bridal cakes. He became again the young Herrick of the taverns, the music of a feast. In this mood his parishioners thought him agreeable but peculiar. Rather an ado, they thought, to make about common, though jolly, events such as the hock-cart, the may-pole, and the church wakes. He would be a stranger and a cockney among them to the last; but, when he was happy, a lovable and amusing pastor, full of strange, merry, witty talk to be only half understood, and of verses of which they were, as a parish, proud. Parson Dolbeare, over to Buckfastleigh, Parson Bumfield to Rattery, sporting old Parson Beanes to Brent, they were good enough parsons in their more humdrum way, but they did not make and read out verses like Mr. Herrick. And when the verses were about individual parishioners, all but the victims enjoyed them. Mr. Herrick was surely a fine kind of show parson to have, even if he often flew into rages, and was often absent. And no parson more effectively upheld cakes and ales, and may-poles and fairs, against the cursed, kill-joy precisians whom he detested. He would get tipsy with the best, and his idea of decorating the church for harvest was fine, and he never made a sour mouth at folks' pleasures, as some parsons did; he understood life and the warm blood of men, and was not for ever ramming heaven and hell and the Bible down their throats. The children, whom he would cuff or kiss according to their conduct and his mood, liked him for his jests and the diverting rhymes and tales he made for them, and the apples and cakes he would give them. The pretty girls liked him for his merry, facetious, applauding way with them, though sometimes his jests, cheek-pinchings, and teasings would make them shy and their lads surly. The older folk differed about him, according to the way he treated them; some regarded him sourly enough; others loved him for his practical generosity, and his good tales and jests; but whether you liked or hated him, you could not help feeling him a pride to the parish, something of a raree-show among parsons. He was a kindly and warm-hearted man, too, though impatient; he would sometimes prevail on the magistrate and constable to lessen a sentence, shorten a term of the stocks or spare a vagrant a whipping; indeed, he would at times fall into a passion on hearing that some beggar, and more particularly if it should chance to be a woman, was to be whipped at the post. He had, on one memorable occasion, seized the whip from the parish constable and struck him with it, and made so much ado that the sentence, to the disappointment of the village, was not proceeded with. That had been when Sir Edward Giles was magistrate, and a quarrel had ensued. Sir Edward had been a just, firm man, and had known and administered the law, unhampered by the hot moods and impulses that seized the temperamental vicar. The vicar had dark and dreadful lairs in his soul where ugliness and cruelty lusted and ravened; he hated them, but they haunted him, itched him, sometimes obsessed him, taking hold of his verse, twisting it into ugliness that matched the ugliness of those who disgusted him, jarring the loveliness of blossoms, song and love into fragments. Angrily into the face of an alarmed parishioner he would fling the charge that she stank, that her teeth were black, her breath poison, and then he would go home and write a spiteful verse about it, reinforcing (had the parish known it) his own malignant inventiveness with that of Martial and other coarse Roman gentlemen, who had, perhaps, felt less than he but had said even more.

His complaint about the Miggle family was that they had always, when he encountered them, just eaten onions. As to the farm-house, wherein three generations of the family lived patriarchally, it smelt strongly, to be sure, but then so did most people's houses; one was used to that; it was one of the crosses of a vicar's lot. The atmosphere in Lower Addislade, a thick aroma of wood-smoke, children, adults, goats, pigs, poultry, and the respective food of each, washed and unwashed clothes, and worse, lapped warmly about Mr. Herrick as he entered.

II

The living-room was full of Miggles. Old Mrs. Miggle, Hoon's wife, and her eldest son, James, a stout black Anglo-Spaniard of close on fifty, smoked their pipes on either side the hearth, while James's wife, a plump and rosy Devonshire lady, stirred a pot over it, and various members of their large progeny sprawled about the room among the animals.

" Good-morrow t'y'all. Good-morrow, mother," said the vicar. " And how's Mr. Miggle this day? "

It seemed that every Miggle in the room shook a lugubrious head. " 'Ee's uncommon sick, parson," the younger Mrs. Miggle cheerily replied. " 'Ee lieth so quiet as a corpse. Doctor talks a might get well if a drunk the physic a gies mun. Doctor pulls off Mother Jollie's dirt plasters and plucks out hedgehog's spines from's hair, and saith we'm not to give mun broth of mouse's tails, but feed mun cow's milk, which do worrit us terrible, for old witch Prowse hath wished evil on the cows and they'm not safe to drink by."

"Old witch hath by-gaged mun," her mother-in-law quavered. "A's tedious sick, parson, and the dowl's fighting for's poor soul. Priest's up there with mun, praying, but 'ee's mortal tedious sick."

Her son coughed to drown her voice when she said "priest," and looked dark uneasiness at the parson.

"Her be half a vule, poor soul," he explained. "Thou must excuse mun, parson."

"'Tis no matter, my friend. Ye need be in no case about that." Mr. Herrick, except when his personal antipathies were roused, was a tolerant, live-and-let-live man, and made no ado about clergy of rival denominations, so long as they went quietly about their business, as Mr. Harrison did. He never, like Parson Beanes to Brent, set out to run them to earth with a tally-ho and a yoicks. His chief complaint of them, as of the local Puritans, was that they were too straitly pious and made over much painful ado for heaven, which might, surely, be given the credit of being more easily stormed by men of good-will than the sectarians thought.

The family looked relieved, though James and his wife and children were in their hearts still offended by the parson's reference to them at Sunday morning service. After all, if they obeyed the law and came to church, what affair was it of any man what religion they might privately observe?

"But we'm got old witch's mammet," the old lady told him. "Chillun, show parson old witch stuck with pins."

Black-browed Peter and his younger sister, crouched on a settle in a corner of the dark room, were amusing themselves by driving pins into a wax doll dressed up in a black cloak and mob cap.

"Mother Jollie got it this moon off White Witch over to

Ashburton," their mother explained. "White Witch said to stick mun full o' pins and then set mun against fire till her's nighly run away, and as wax melts, sick man gets well. It ha'n't cured mun yet, though we'm melted witch down and built mun up again three time, I reckon. But third time's lucky time."

"Why, my dear soul," said Mr. Herrick, who was interested in charms, "I admire as you don't know better witch charms than that old wax doll."

"We'm lifted the toad for mun," the little girl piped. "We sent mun flying proper, and Peter cut's legs off first."

"That's no part o' the charm." The vicar spoke sharply; physical cruelty always angered him. "Ye'll get no good o' tormenting God's creatures, Peter Miggle. Di'n't ever you hear as for every hurt ye do 'em, the devil'll do same to ye in hell? Aye, 'slife, he'll cut the legs off ye and send ye flying. Look now, Mrs. Miggle, I'll write ye some charms in verse as'll undo witcheries if witcheries there be. With them and with the holy crust beneath his pillow, Mr. Miggle should defy all the old witches in Denshire. But, 'slife, my dear souls," he added, recollecting himself, "what can a poor old witch do against Almighty God and his loving power? No, forsooth, a little true prayer is worth all the charms of the world. All the same, I'll say Mr. Miggle some charms, on my life I will. If they do him no good, they'll not harm him. Is not that Mr. Harrison on the stairs now? Bring him in, boy. I'll speak with him before I go up."

Peter glanced inquiry at his father, who nodded. Since parson didn't object to the priest's presence, there was no reason why they should not meet. Peter opened the oak door on to the passage and admitted Mr. Harrison.

A pale, prim, grave-faced young man, dressed darkly and plainly like a Puritan, with white bands and broad hat, the young priest made a queer contrast to the middle-aged parson, with his great head of grizzled black curls, his full jowl, arrogant Roman nose and florid, careless manner. Mr. Harrison bored Mr. Herrick rather, for he somewhat lacked both wit and learning, and was of little use with a table, a bottle, a may-pole, a lady, or a book other than a breviary. Instead, he had zeal, courage, kindness, virtue, personal modesty, and religion in plenty; and these, of course, should have been enough. Mr. Herrick respected the young fellow, despite his false theological opinions, but his company was of little cheer to a parson who was, like Thomas Chaloner, Esq., "as far from a Puritan as the east from the west; of the natural religion, and one who loved to enjoy the pleasures of this life." Nevertheless, to put the young man and his flock at ease, the vicar greeted Mr. Harrison cordially enough.

"Good-day t'ye, sir. And how's our sick friend? Shall I wait on him, or hath he seen enough of our cloth for one day, d'ye think?"

"Indeed, Mr. Herrick, he is far from well to-day. I left him nigh sleeping, and I think he should not be disturbed further, though I know 'twould be cordial to him to see you at another occasion."

"Well, man, if ye've tired him out I won't plague him, but will begone home to my dinner, and time too. D'ye walk my way, sir?"

"I am bound for Buckfastleigh, sir, so we may start together, if I'll not trouble you."

The fellow was too plaguey humble, thought Mr. Herrick; came of representing an unlawful false church, mayhap. Though, as to that, papists were safe enough and pampered enough now the Queen ruled the roost at court. Even when a priest was informed against, the odds were he'd not suffer ought, for he probably had a grace signed by the Secretary of State.

"By your leave, sir," added Mr. Harrison, "I'll speak a few words with our good friends here and o'ertake you on the road."

"As you will. Ye'll mark I'm a good-natured man, Mr. Harrison; 'tis few parsons enough would allow a priest of your persuasion to go poaching on his preserves as I do. *Your* church wou'n't do the like, sir, were it in the saddle. And there's many of my brethren would say I'm i' the wrong, and so, like enough, I am. But, by Bacchus, I'll leave your Spanish friends and you to make your souls together; I'll bear no responsibility for any o' ye. Good-day, my friends. And look 'ee, boy; there's to be no tormenting of old Mother Prowse or stoning of her cat and chickens, as I've heard tell of too much of late. She may be a witch or she mayn't, but if she is, the less she's meddled with the better for all, and if she a'n't, 'tis unjust and unkind. Leave her to God and her master Satan, and keep civil tongues in your heads." With that the vicar swung out of the house, his pipe between his teeth and his hat on his head.

"'Slife, it's good to breathe the air again and see the pretty day," he muttered, as he strolled down the deep lane. "If that puking fellow's long at his prayers and farewells, I shan't stay for him."

But Mr. Harrison's light, quick steps were soon heard behind, and the two clergymen walked on together.

"May I offer you tobacco, sir?"

"Thankye, no, Mr. Herrick. I don't smoke."

"Ye should, man. It's extraordinary good for the temper and humour. Tobacco and ale; they keep a man fit for's duty, as I ever tell the precisians when they look sourly on God's innocent gifts to man. Lord, what a set o' canting rogues! What's England done that she should be plagued with 'em?" Mr. Harrison looked as if he knew quite well what England had done, but he was too polite and discreet to mention it. The vicar nevertheless read it in the young man's serious face, and was irritated.

"Aye, sir, aye; I know what y'are thinking. Y'are thinking England broke from the true church, and the Lord sent her a plague of zealots, precisians and Puritans to punish her, as he sent Pharaoh frogs. But y'are in error, young sir, for some o' the worst precisians are of your persuasion, and England's been plagued with 'em for the past thousand years. What of Dunstan and his sour-faced monks and his gaping hell waiting to swallow men up, and his army of little devils to torment 'em on earth? I'll tell ye, lad, the mistake men have made is to conceit God ever in a rage. Lord knows he's cause enough for't, but I do dare to think he pities us his poor babes, and lays on stripes with mercy, and don't grudge us pleasures; faith, I'll swear he enjoys to see us laugh and sing; I'll believe he don't desire us to be ever in a melancholy fit, or ever making ado for to save our souls. Ha'n't he given us his gifts to merry us—flowers and wine and oil and meat and corn, aye, and love and laughing too? When we taste 'em to excess, be sure he'll chide us, but does he mean us to flee 'em wholly? Our religion teaches us to bear afflictions with patience when they fall on us, but not to force 'em on ourselves. God knows as we're frail enough, and can scarce stand out against life as it is, and have little need making it harder yet. What d'ye say, Mr. Harrison?"

"I am sure you are right, Mr. Herrick, when you speak for yourself. God, through his holy church, bids us be moderate in all things, and that is a hard saying. There be those can't be moderate short of abstinence, and those must fast much and subdue the flesh. You and I, sir, must needs guide discreetly the souls in our charge, each according to its needs and the church's ordinances, and what serves one will scarce meet another's case."

"Aye, like enough. But hark'ee, young man, here's a word in your ear. The less ye go about the countryside speaking of 'souls in your charge' the wiser ye'll be. Why, devil take it, man, the law of England don't allow ye souls in your charge. 'Sdeath, man, y'are a Papist, and any man, woman, or child around could inform against you to-morrow. Hast forgot that?"

"Nay, sir, I surely ha'n't," young Mr. Harrison gravely replied. "Our lives and liberties are carried in our hands, and in those of God and his blessed Mother and the angels."

"Y'are confident, sir," the vicar testily told him, "by reason the Papists are in favour at Court and with the Archbishop. But don't strain your liberty too far, for it might break. Whatever the Court may think of 'ee, the people and the country don't want 'ee back. And, mark, I've no prejudice myself, though I think much of your church's teaching as false as you think mine. I'd as lief every man was let alone with his conscience, so long as he don't make disturbance for others. But, damn it, man, you mustn't get a head on you and become flown with pride and confidence, or you may rue it. . . . Lord, what an extreme fine day! Dost want thy dinner, man?"

"I don't take notice of such things, Mr. Herrick."

"Marry, don't ye? That'll be the reason as ye look so pale and thin. Well, I do, and I'm going home now to mine. Will you come and have a bite and a sup with us?"

"I thank you much, sir, but I must make haste to Buckfastleigh. I shall eat something there, with a friend."

"Do so; mind you do so. Always mind your belly as well as your soul, and see they work harmonious together or one'll break the bridle and run away with t'other. Good-day t'ye, Mr. Harrison. I stop at the doctor's and call for my friend Sucklin. God b'w'y'."

"God b'w'y', Mr. Herrick."

Mr. Harrison's thin, sombre young figure hurried away down the lane that led along the wood to Warm Bridge. Mr. Herrick walked on alone, in some relief. A sad, dull, spiritless fellow was Mr. Harrison. Though, as to spirit, he would doubtless face the gibbet and hangman's knife if need be, without a murmur, as did the other zealots and fanatics, Papist and Puritan. "Lord save us from zealotry," said the vicar, and crossed himself, giving thanks for Ecclesia Anglicana. Stopping outside the doctor's garden, he shouted, "Jack, art coming, man?" The poet appeared at the cottage door, wiping his mouth with a napkin. "Go you on, Robin. I dine with the doctor."

"The devil you do. Who bade you?"

"Why, the doctor, of course. We talk of life, philosophy, and letters together."

Dr. Conybeare's shabby figure and pale, sardonic face appeared at the door. "Come, join us, parson. I can't promise you much, but there's still a bite of something left."

"No, thankye, doctor. I am hungry, and shall go eat my own dinner. Jack, come down at your own pleasure, or when Dr. Conybeare is sick of you, but bear in mind that we go to sup at the Court this evening at six."

"Oh, I'll not be long." He returned into the house.

The vicar stepped inside the garden, and whispered to the doctor, "A word to the wise—that's a marvellous amorous inconstant gallant; let him not play his games with Jule, for I can tell he's ravished by the child's face. Mark 'em well, an you love her."

"'Sdeath, parson, Jule's as cool a little virgin as ever I knew, and the least like to have her head turned by any London spark. She thinks of nought but books and poetry, never of human men."

"Lord, man, there's no such maid ever stepped; no more

than was ever a scholar who cou'n't be carried away by a fair face. Look to her, sir, if you love her."

"Aye, I'll look to my daughter, parson. But your thoughts, if I may make bold to say it, sir, run o'er much on love and the like. It was myself Sir John Sucklin desired to speak with, on matters of interest to us both, not to a maid of Jule's age."

"Jule's age, my friend, is the age that most pleases gentlemen such as Jack Sucklin. 'Swounds, my friend, d'ye fancy Jack would prefer her to be thirty? Or forty, belike? Lord, the folly of a learned man when he's also a father! Let me tell 'ee, doctor, if ye conceit as 'tis by reason of *your* bright eyes and wise tongue as Sucklin is even now eating your pasty, ye conceit awry, and God forgive and help ye. There; I'll say no more, but be off to my parsonage and my dinner. Do we meet this evening at the Court?"

"Aye, they've bid Jule and me. Good-bye till then, friend parson."

12

Drinking and smoking round the great oak table in the armoured hall of Dean Court, the full-fed gentlemen spoke of politics and trouble, of the Scots army lying sinister and threatening in the north, calling for bribe-money, of His Majesty driven willy-nilly to summon parliament to pay it them.

"Aye, the writs will shortly be sent out," Sir John Suckling told them. "The King sees no hope but that, for neither Spain nor the Pope nor the city will lend. He must call parliament."

"It is over time," Mr. Yarde shook a grave, disapproving head. "All these taxes levied on no authority—the country grows restive under them. What d'ye say, Sir Ralph?"

Sir Ralph Furze, the High Constable from Moreshead, who had his face in his tankard at the moment, lifted it up to remark, "A pox on all taxes, say I," and returned it to where it belonged.

"And that's honest sense," said Dr. Conybeare.

"No man," began Mr. Yarde, with his elderly sententiousness, "is readier to pay rightful taxes than the Englishman. . . ."

"He a'n't ready, sir," Suckling interrupted. "No man's ever ready to pay away to his country good money as might be buying him what he desires. But he has to pay, and he'll pay with not too ill a grace, if he thinks 'tis lawful and can't be helped. But when it's a matter of new levies and tolls, demanded on royal warrant only, and seemingly no end to't, as now, the Englishman's not so obliging. In fact, he gets most damnable insolent. For look'ee, squire, there's no generosity in the rabble. They won't strain a point for their king. And I'm damned if they don't sniff a taint of Arminianism, aye, and Popery even, in the levies, so reasonless are the vulgar."

"A pox on Popery," absently but heartily commented the High Constable, momentarily setting down his tankard again.

"Amen to that," the squire endorsed. "In truth, the country's i' the right to be uneasy on that head, and to suspect a Popish plot, with Her Majesty and others so active in the cause, and with fresh news of conversions at court each day. Zounds, sir, 'tis past a jest."

"Aye, zooks, sir, so 'tis," said the Constable. "Devilish past a jest."

"'Tis but a fashion." Suckling carelessly soothed the

country gentlemen. " 'Tis silly enough, and they but do it, for the most, out of coxcombry, thinking it the mode, and to keep well with the Queen. The King's a sound Church of England man, and so's the Archbishop, and they don't like it, but they can't no way keep Her Majesty in order."

"Why, Sir John," young Mrs. Northly broke in from the background, where she was helping her grandmother to make tea, "if Popery's the mode, I must look into't before we go to town. I vow I'll get that solemn Mr. Harrison to wait on me and instruct me in't. What do you say, vicar?"

"I say that I'll instruct you myself, child, in all the religions you inquire of, from that of Jupiter to that of the Pope. You won't need Mr. Harrison."

"Oh, but I've a mind to talk with Mr. Harrison; he looks wonderful pale and interesting. Don't Mr. Harrison look pale and interesting, Henry? Shan't he instruct us in Popery?"

"By all means, if you please, my love. But I'll not pay your church fines."

"Alack, those fines; I had forgot 'em. 'Tis pity, for 'twould be wonderful entertaining to be a papist."

" 'Pon my soul, child, you want whipping," her grandmother tartly told her. "Don't let me hear any such wicked talk under my roof. Pray, what d'ye think we had the blessed Reformation for?"

"I can't think, ma'am. Aye, I mind; 'twas because King Henry wanted to rid himself of one of his queens. But now as he's done it, and now as we've gotten the monks' lands too, and built all our beautiful homes on 'em, why now I think we can be papists again if we like."

"Enough, Lettice." Mr. Yarde gravely stopped her. "Y'are a forward, thoughtless girl, and know not what you speak. If you remembered, as I do, as a boy, hearing tales of the barbarities of the Spanish Inquisition to our honest sailors——"

"Honest pirates!" Dr. Conybeare snorted.

"Aye, and the tales too," went on the squire, "of such as my father, who'd seen Protestants burnt alive for the faith at Smithfield under Queen Mary——"

"And Papists disembowelled under Queen Elizabeth," muttered the doctor.

"——Ye'd not play with such grave themes," the squire finished.

"To be sure you wou'n't, you silly trifling minx. Come, cease your prating and serve the tea in the cups. Mrs. Elizabeth, I want your judgment on this tea."

"Aye, surely, Mrs. Yarde. Why, I declare, I was all but asleep. You must forgive me; I supped so well."

"Speaking of popery," Suckling said, "they've apprehended Tobie Matthew for a papal spy t'other day. Didst hear that, Robin?"

"No, poor Tobie. What'll come to him?"

"Exile, at worst. Aye, and I think 'twill be exile, for by now they're heartily sick of his plottings and conferrings with Barbarini and the legate and the Queen. They call him a paid spy, of course, but old Don Tobiah a'n't that; I swear he never took a penny for his work. I shall miss old Tobie; a wonderful good gossip and tattler, and the most devilish fine company in the world is Tobie, though a trifle spoilt by his piety. Lady Carlisle and Her Majesty may get him out on't, but I doubt it. He's gone too far."

"We have no need of these Italianate Englishmen in our country," Mr. Yarde observed.

"No, dammit, they're un-English," said Sir Ralph. "Dammy soul, I'm damned if we want any Italian spies. I say, an Englishman should behave English, for it's that as has made England what she is, and thank God for't." He glared across at Dr. Conybeare, whom he suspected of some lack of patriotism, and the doctor was roused to say, " Sir, you blaspheme, in thanking your God for what England is. I wou'n't thank a heathen deity for that, myself."

" Come, gentlemen, drink about," their host tactfully intervened, and quenched his friend Furze's reply in ale.

" But you'll drink some tea with us, gentlemen." Mrs. Yarde had finished her preparations of this strange beverage.

" I'll be hanged first," said Sir Ralph, who was busy elsehow. " I'm drinking ale, madam."

" Aye, surely will I, ma'am," said Suckling. " So will Robin, I'll swear."

" Nay, Mrs. Yarde, not I. I'm grown too old to sample new drinks. I conceit 'tis something of a lady's drink, too."

" And the better for't, Robin, the better for't. Since when wert against ladies and their drinks, like a woman-hating celibate? Here, we'll drink a happy issue to old Tobie, and may he slip out of his enemies' snare. Spy or no, he's a better man than his canting, prating foes, pox take 'em."

" And pox take the Pope. Aye, marry, the devil fly away with him," Sir Ralph earnestly added. " And with all interfering, prying bishops too, as send round to spy on us and on what we do in our own churches, aye, and in our own fields too, dammit." The Constable had in the summer been fined for employing labourers to cut his hay on Sundays, and was an embittered man.

" Aye, the clergy wax too powerful," Mr. Yarde agreed. " If you won't take it ill that I say so, Mr. Herrick."

" Say what you please, sir. No man can accuse *me* of being too powerful, I take it. Zounds, I've no power at all over all you wooden-headed people."

" The clergy," said Mr. Yarde, with courtesy, " are very well in their place. But, 'sblood, the Archbishop would lift 'em out on't and set 'em o'er the laity, and that's out of nature and reason and all English tradition. Why, sir, is my parson to tell me when to kneel and to bow in church, and to keep from beef and mutton on a Friday, and to walk up the church and receive my communion behind rails like a prisoner? Drink up, Mr. Herrick, and answer me that."

"Aye, sir, drink up, and answer us that," Sir Ralph echoed.

Mr. Herrick drank up, and answered them roundly. "Aye, sirs, by all means. The parson's the ruler in his own church, and the congregation must do as he bids 'em. If he says to 'em, come up the church, damme, and kneel at the rails, come up and kneel at the rails they shall." He thumped home his resolution on the table.

"There was a parson indicted at the Plymouth assizes, sir, for refusing communion to's flock in their seats," Sir Ralph told him.

"Aye, I know it. And there's been mobs as has torn up the rails and made bonfires of 'em. There's many an unruly insolent thing done by the rabble."

"Parsons can't rule the country, sir. They warn't born for that, nor ordained for't neither. As to that Jack-in-office, little Mr. Laud, he'll be lucky, if *he* an't made a bonfire of one day. Who the pox is he, to say we mun't talk o' the price o' corn i' the church, and the rest o't?"

"Aye, and the village women complain," said Mrs. Yarde, "as they have now to wear white veils for churchings, for all the world as if they was doing penance for sin. And they mayn't bring their mending to church with 'em neither, and it do put 'em back with it, and why we listen better with idle hands, the Lord knows, for I don't."

"La, grandmother, 'tis more seemly, a'n't it, Mr. Herrick?"

"It surely seems so to me, but who am I to judge? I'm only a poor parson."

"You must forgive our heat, Mr. Herrick," Mr. Yarde said, seeing that his vicar was becoming rather sarcastic and irritated. "And as to seemliness and decency in church, I'm of your opinion, and see no cause why women should not sit in the Lord's house without other occupation than prayer, like Mary in the story. No; 'tis this meddling with secular matters by the Church that is oversetting England. For the power in the country must rest with the country gentlemen, or all is lost."

"And the City thinks it must rest with the City, and the Parliament with themselves, and the Archbishop with the Church and the High Commission, and the King with the throne. So wags the world, and it's pull devil, pull baker, and let the strongest win, amen," said the doctor.

"But as to the High Commission Court, I read as it was mobbed t'other day for its findings in the case of some miserable conventicler. I doubt it's nearing its end, with feeling running so high as it is."

"The Archbishop would be wise to go softly," said Suckling. "And His Majesty'd be wise to keep him in hand. Mark you, I wish no ill to Canterbury. He's a narrow, over-zealous, indiscreet man, and he pushes things too far, but he's doing the Church good, and keeping its worship seemly, and preserving us from the sectarians. But for Laud and his fellows, the Church would be in some danger from the pre-destinating city on the lake, and we don't none of us here want that."

"The Church of England, Sir John," Mr. Yarde said, looking dignified, "has been preserved by God in her chosen path for many years, and will doubtless continue to be so. She needs neither Geneva, Rome, nor Canterbury to guide her."

"But only her country gentlemen, hey, sir? Well, well, I grant it you. You must fight that out with Robin here."

"Nay, Jack, I'll do no more fighting this evening. Look now, as your parson I propose a truce to argument and politics, and that Mrs. Lettice gives us a tune on the lute. I have here a song or two of mine that Harry Lawes set for me when I was in London in the spring. Shall we try 'em? Here's a prayer to the virgins to make much of time, that Lawes has given a pretty air to."

"That would be very agreeable, Robin," his sister murmured drowsily over her tea.

"To be sure it would, parson," Mrs. Yarde agreed. "Meg, child, where art thou? Bestir thyself and fetch the lute for thy sister. Thou'rt too idle to learn to play it, but at least canst bring it."

Meg unfolded her long length from the corner where she had been sitting with Julian, her little sister Joan, and the dogs, trimming arrows, and went to unhook the lute from where it hung on the wall. She was rather dejected to-day, and missed Giles, and was a little bored by all this tedious talk. As they had agreed yesterday, old people did certainly converse to excess.

The vicar produced a page of music, and gave it to Mrs. Northly to read as she tuned her strings. She was quick and skilled, and picked out the melody without trouble, with a light, precise, pretty touch. She played it through, then Mr. Herrick sang, in his full, rich, merry baritone, his appeal to the Virgins to make much of Time. Suckling, watching from his seat the pretty young woman so sweetly plucking the strings, envied his friend his present position and his fine voice; yes, and his genius; he had to grant old Robin that. Who else, since Will Shakespeare and his contemporaries had sung their songs, and Ben had died, wrote such melody as this? What were the trifles of the court crowd, what were the conceits of young Abraham Cowley, of John Cleveland, poor Tom Carew, Denham, even Davenant, when Robin

Herrick in his country glebe was bidding the young virgins gather rosebuds while they may?

> " The glorious Lamp of Heaven, the Sun,"

trolled the vicar,

> " The higher he's a-getting,
> The sooner will his Race be run,
> And nearer he's to setting. . . ."

Did old Robin know how fine a poet he was? Of course he knew; all poets knew that of themselves, even were there none to tell them. And here he was surrounded by rustic admirers.

Suckling's glance, half ironic, half touched, strayed round the dark, candle-lit old hall. Round the supper table sat the country gentlemen, their tankards before them; Mr. Yarde, elderly, grave and attentive, moving his gouty foot stiffly to the tune, smoking a long pipe, and thinking how prettily his granddaughter played; Sir Ralph Furze, flushed and drowsy, drinking himself still stupider than God had made him, but beating the measure with his tankard; Mr. Henry Northly, pale and languid, sipping tea, twisting his curls round his long fingers and looking tolerantly on his wife; the truculent little physician, his aggressive chin on his hand, his dark blue eyes for once dreaming and remote behind the clouds of tobacco smoke which he was emitting. These were England, thought Sir John; the stuff on which King, Church and State must, in the last resort, rely for their maintenance. These, and the noisy country fellows making merry over the harvest ale without. And the women: old Mrs. Yarde, upright and sharp-eyed, nodding approval to her granddaughter's playing and the vicar's singing, tasting and sniffing at her tea with some disapproval, for, in truth, she found it poor stuff; Mrs. Elizabeth Herrick, plump and drowsy, the other side of the hearth, smiling kindly at them all, and pleased to hear her brother so gay and loud; the pretty creature at the lute—(Gad, she'd let me sport with her, thought Sir John; I vow she'd let me, and she's so pretty a piece of mischief as never I saw) and the three young virgins in the corner among the dogs, long Meg trimming arrows, her little round-faced sister playing with a puppy, and Julian, her hands clasped about her knees, her great eyes dewy like wet violets as she listened.

The vicar sang now of young Leander drowned—

> " When as Leander young was drown'd,
> No heart by love received a wound——"

and the child's eyes almost brimmed.

For her now, thought Sir John, life's all books and songs and dreams; no man has woke her yet. Robin's right; she's a flower too young for plucking, for all she's turned fifteen years. I shall do better to divert myself with Mrs. Lettice while I stay here than to waste good wooing on one so inapt. A pox on't, pretty maids shou'n't be brought up bookworms; there's a plenty of ugly ones for that. These great eyes of hers—and, Lord help me, her little mouth and chin, and the half of a dimple in the white curve of her cheek—but what's the use of 'em, if she won't look at me but to stare and consider what manner of extraordinary peculiar creature I may be? I swear I'll have more amusement with the pretty lute-player, and none to run after me and call me off, neither, as the parson and doctor'd do if I was to tease their chick. " Aye, Robin," he said aloud, " those was right good songs, and well sung. Your words go well with Lawes his airs; they have the right spirit and lightness. You should give him some for his next air-book."

" I have so. But I would fain print my verses all together before they appear scattered about the song-books."

"In truth, Robin, they've no need of music, for they make their own. Aye, y'are a prettier poet than us all, when it comes to that light country stuff of flowers and meads. None living does it half so well, and not so many o' the dead neither. W'are too taken up with conceits and quips and philosophisings these days, and have forgot the face o' the earth."

"Aye, Jack, d'ye say so?" The vicar's black eyes kindled in his flushed face. "D'ye say that, indeed? D'ye think as my verse will please the wits and the court? I've feared at times as 'tis too simple, pastoral and Roman for these dull untunable days—and that the court don't want bucolicks, and that I shall be mad to send my country muse, poor maid, to seek contempt in the city, where no man wants to hear of blossoms, birds and may-poles. Yet I'll adventure her there, I swear I will, for, zounds, I know she's a good pretty maid and will win me fame, eh, Jack?"

"As to that, who can tell?" Sir John always felt somewhat cold when his brother poets spoke of fame. He felt that it was not fame of which they should be thinking. "Fame's a fickle chancey jade, as waits on us at her own will, and it's useless to seek her. And though to my mind, which dotes on Will Shakespeare and a fashion of song that's past, your verses are devilish good stuff, there's no denying as they a'n't much to the present mode. Howsoe'er, Robin, they'll merit fame, if they don't win it, and that should satisfy a Roman philosopher."

"There, brother," said Mrs. Elizabeth. "Ha'n't I always said your verses was pretty? And now you see as I'm right, for Sir John says the same. Thankye, ma'am, I'll take another drop, for I think it extreme pleasant stuff, and good for the stomach. Robin, you should sample Mrs. Yarde's tea, for it's excessive good drink, and wholesome for the belly."

"Have you any more songs, Mr. Herrick?" asked Mrs.

Northly, who liked to play, and knew that she did not look amiss in doing so.

"Nay, 'tis some one else his turn." The vicar subsided into his chair and lit his pipe. "I'm old and out of date, as Jack here says. But I don't care. As he says too, I'm a philosopher, and content enough.

> "Cur non sub alta vel platano vel hac
> Pinu iacentes sic temere et rosa
> Canos odorati capillos,
> Dum licet, Assyrioque nardo
> Potamus uncti? Dissipat Euhius
> Curas edaces.

But I've yet to learn that tea dissipates care, so I'll not trouble you for your potations, ladies. My belly thrives well enough on sack. . . . Thankye, sir, I will. . . . Now Jack, give us one of your songs, man, and show us how 'tis done at court."

"Nay, I'll sing one of Ben's, as you said this morning I profaned by burlesquing. Have you the music of 'See the Chariot at hand here of Love,' Mrs. Northly? It goes to a rare pretty air." He hummed it.

"To be sure, it's among our music here—or have I it at home? Nay, here it is. I know the air well, so don't require to try it over."

Sir John stood behind her and sang, in a light, pleasing tenor. He was seen to divide his gallantry between the matron and the maids, for his eyes rested on Mrs. Northly through the first stanza and most of the second, and when he sang—

> "Do but look on her hair, it is bright
> As Love's star when it riseth,"

he flung a smiling glance at copper-curled Meg, but through the last stanza, which he sang with softened voice, his eyes gazed at Julian.

"Have you seen but a bright lily grow.
Before rude hands have touch'd it?
Have you mark'd but the fall of the snow
Before the soil hath smutch'd it?
Have you felt the wool of beaver,
Or swan's down ever?
Or have smelt o' the bud o' the brier
Or the nard in the fire?
Or have tasted the bag of the bee?
O so white, O so soft, O so sweet is she!"

The words died softly away on the shadowed air, and still the singer looked at the white-gowned young lady in the corner. His accompanist, glancing brightly up, thinking to meet tender eyes, perceived their direction, and rose with a titter.

"Upon my soul, very moving, Sir John. Extreme moving and melting and pretty indeed. But I am sure I'm tired of playing. Perhaps July there would like to take her turn."

"Jule can't play," said Meg casually.

Mrs. Northly's slender brows gracefully elevated themselves. "Can't play? Why, I thought as every young lady played the lute, di'n't you, Sir John?"

"No, you di'n't think it," her sister bluntly contradicted, "for you know as I don't. You're only peacocking, as usual."

"Lord, child, y'are excessive uncivil. What'll Sir John think of us country barbarians? Sir John, you must excuse my hoyting sister. She and her friends are sadly country-bred; they never pay visits abroad, or get the chance to learn civil manners."

"Madam, you decry yourself and your friends without reason. I know not where your sister could learn better manners than those I have met here; or indeed, than her own."

"Aye, to be sure, Lettice," her grandmother chid. "I

admire as you'd speak so. To be sure, Meg speaks oft with little civility enough, but it a'n't for lack of precept and ensample, for you know very well as often we have the house full of guests from London and else, aye, and from foreign parts too. Aye, and Edward's friends from the inns of court (Edward's our eldest grandson, Sir John; a went travelling in Spain and Italy last year), and Mr. Herrick and his ingenious notable friends as come to wait on him; where'll you meet such company in London, I'd ask you, Mrs. Pert?"

"Peace, peace, wife; let the girl be. And you, child, talk not so foolish. Women, Sir John, are great chatterers; they like it better their tongues should lap the air than lap good liquor. But look ye, I want more news o' the town and of this parliament that's to meet. What will be its first measures, think you?"

"Lord knows, sir. Pay off the damned meddlesome Scots, I trust, and raise money to pay our own army, for if they a'n't paid suddenly, there's no answering for 'em; they grow extreme sullen and unruly. But how we'll raise the money, that's another matter."

Mr. Yarde shook his head, as he always did at the mention of raising money.

"But parliament," added Sir John, "won't be in over much haste to pay the Scots, for their leaders like the Scots army very well where it is, and think it a good discipline for His Majesty to have it there."

"I hope," said Mr. Northly, "that they'll proceed suddenly to inquire into those devilish monopolies. Virginia tobacco is a most devilish ruinous price."

"Aye, I warrant they will. Be sure they'll inquire into every device as His Majesty has set up to replenish his purse. And then they'll have at my Lord Strafford, and inquire into the Irish army plot, and at the Archbishop and the High Commission Court, and take the part of every snivelling stubborn minister against enforced ceremonial; and then they'll begin on the Popish plot, and the Queen's Papist favourites, and make out that Laud is playing cherry-pit with the Pope for the coercing of England. Aye, they have it all planned out, the impudent censorious fellows. I hope His Majesty'll act wisely by 'em; he walks on a precipice, did he know it, for the people are devilish sullen in all parts o' the land."

"They be so here," Mr. Herrick gloomily agreed. "Devilish churlish crafty knaves, with no gallantry and no loyalty to Church or King."

"'Tis only to be expected, so far from London," Mrs. Elizabeth tolerantly excused them. "People is very crafty and censorious so far out of town, a'n't they, brother?"

"Madam, the most censorious people in England at this time are the City of London," Sir John told her. "The most censorious and malicious and insolent to the King."

"You say insolent, sir," Mr. Yarde, in his cautious elderly voice remonstrated, "but they surely have some show of reason on their side. God knows, I mean no disloyalty to the King, but in these monopolies, taxes, shipmonies, and making us raise and clothe troops at our expense, and the like, and all without a shadow of constitution behind it, he has outstepped his sovereign rights, aye, 'sblood, he hath, and there's no question on't."

The vicar set down his mug with a thump. "'Sbread, squire, the King can't outstep's rights. He may be unwise in pressing 'em, but, 'sbread, a can't exceed his rights as God gave him with his crown. To say he can is to blaspheme."

"These be novel notions, parson," the squire said. "The King his divine rights is a plaguey perilous novel notion, and 'twarn't so put forward by Her late Majesty and her ministers." Her late Majesty was to Mr. Yarde, and would always be, Queen Elizabeth, in whose glorious and freebooting latter years his patriotic youth had been lived. He had never got quite used to these upstart Stuarts from Scotland, with their strange, tedious follies, strange lack of charm and tact, their preposterous claims, their new-fangled Arminianism, their exalting of the power of those usually low-born and always interfering persons, bishops, their perpetual shortness of money, and their coquetting with Spain, the ancient foe. Definitely, Mr. George Yarde's loyal Tudor mind was mistrustful of the Stuart family.

"Whoever picks my purse," said Mr. Henry Northly, moderately and simply voicing the general view, "exceeds his rights, whether divine or earthly. A'n't I right, my life?"

"In what, husband? I di'n't hear you, for I warn't listening, but I am sure I'll support you against the world in whatever mighty truth 'twas you spoke; for that's a wife's first duty, they tell me."

"Mrs. Northly is better employed than to hark to our prating," Sir John said. "Shall we play some game, ladies? Shall I show you my new cribbage, or will you try primero or mumchance? Come, I'm sure y'are an apt carder, Mrs. Northly. You have the hands for't, and the quick eyes and quicker wits."

Mrs. Northly began to forgive him for his own misdirected eyes during his song, and was framing a careless consent when there was a knocking at the door and a serving man entered.

"A strange gentleman from Plymouth to see Sir Ralph Furze. I've left mun in t'porch. He says 'tis mortal particular business."

"'Sblood," observed the High Constable, annoyed. "It's a fine matter if I am to be followed about to my friends' houses on business. Say I'm busy and he must wait on me at Moreshead to-morrow. Aye, and ask his business, for belike he's from the Stannary Court; or to inspect the weights and scales, a pox on these inspectors that descend on us without notice. Or is he mayhap from the tinners, the devil fly away with 'em for pests. Did I tell ye, Mr. Yarde, of the tinners' latest impudent demand?"

By this time the servant was back, and resolved these uncertainties by remarking, "Says as he's the witch-finder to Plymouth."

"Why, begod, I'd forgot." Sir Ralph wiped his mouth and sat up. "Aye, I heard as there was a witch-finder there, and I sent him a message by the carrier to come and try his skill here, as it seems from all accounts as we've a witch in our midst. You mind as I mentioned it t'ye, Mr. Yarde."

"Yes, yes, so you did, Sir Ralph. Well, I mislike these methods, but we must by all means root out sorcery from this neighbourhood if it exists, and we can but try Mr. Witch-finder. They speak they have gotten good results from these men elsewhere."

"But Lord, what a nasty-looking fellow," Mr. Henry Northly murmured, for the visitor had followed the servant into the hall, and stood behind him, hat in hand, bowing to the company He was not, indeed, personally attractive. He was fat and pale and pimpled, and clad like a Puritan, and his bright, ardent, fanatical stare might well strike terror into the hearts of any witches on whom it should turn. The poor old ladies would scarce have a chance with him, thought the vicar, who, while not approving witches, thought they should have a sporting chance. He disliked the look of this fellow, who had a zealous, greedy, tedious air about him.

"Gentlemen, your servant," said the visitor, bowing again and scraping his foot. "Do I address Sir Ralph Furze, the High Constable?"

"Aye, sir, I am he. I suppose they sent you here from Moreshead; but by God, they shou'n't a done so, for I can't talk with 'ee to-night. I must ask 'ee to wait on me to my house to-morrow, at ten of the morning. Where d'ye lie to-night?"

"At the Half Moon Inn, sir. I had thought to hear from you to-night of the affair in hand, that I might get to work betimes to-morrow. I am no time-waster, sir, for time costs money, and Peter Wilkin was ne'er one to waste one nor t'other. Once gi'en a few facts, I can sniff around for witchery alone, but I must know where to look. But mayhap the good villagers will tell me so much."

"I dare swear they will," said the vicar.

Dr. Conybeare sprang to his feet, overturning a bottle and glass and his chair. A red colour suffused his face, and his eyes glared angrily blue.

"'Sdeath, gentlemen, will ye permit this? On my life, if ye turn this fellow loose to try his devil's tricks on poor old village dames, I'll not answer for myself as he gets through with it with a whole skin. Damme, sirs, have ye neither pity nor sense, neither hearts nor yet heads, that ye put such gulleries on folks? Parson, I appeal to you, by the God ye believe on, not to suffer this hellish cruel business to proceed."

The vicar shrugged his great shoulders.

"Indeed, I like it little enough. What d' ye say, squire?"

Mr. Yarde was fingering his pointed beard, perplexed and grave, as if he too liked it little enough.

"I am of a mind with you, and with the doctor, in that I have small liking for such means. But I have less for sorcery and such devil's work, which I truly fear do walk abroad in our country to-day, and which I would by all means uproot from this neighbourhood if it be here, as many tell."

"Why yes, damme, sir, can't have witches about. No, nor warlocks neither. No, by God, can't allow that," Sir Ralph firmly said.

"Witches be damned, sir," returned the doctor. "Aye, and all who've spread their idiot tales of 'em. Pox take the fools: there *is* no witches, I say, but in the silly gaping minds o' their conceiters."

"Come, sir," the high, scandalised voice of Mr. Peter Wilkin broke in, "y'are agen all reason, religion and history there. Why, His late Majesty King James himself writ a treatise on 'em."

"Aye, truly he did so," Mr. Yarde agreed. "He bringed a more fiercer heat to't than e'er did Her Majesty Queen Bess, who was ne'er much froward agen 'em, for all her ministers passed new acts and statutes on 'em. Thou shalt not suffer a witch to live, Dr. Conybeare."

"Yes, sir, I *shall* suffer a witch to live, if by a witch ye mean some poor old doting defenceless fool of a woman. Yes, sir, we all here know who is thus suspicioned, and I say to this—this gentleman here, that if he lay a hand on her, or on any woman of this neighbourhood, I'll have him cudgelled and ducked beneath Bourne Bridge. Do I make myself clear, sir?"

Mr Wilkin glanced somewhat nervously from the doctor to Sir Ralph and Mr. Yarde. He began to wish that he had not taken on this job. They had not warned him that there was a madman in Dean Prior; yes, a very Bedlam, he seemed, with his clenched fist beating on the table, and his voice rising in an angry shout.

"Well, for Godsake," young Mrs. Northly, delighted with the scene, murmured in her husband's ear. "What a praemunire! I don't like witches, the nasty things, but I hope the doctor'll get the better o' that horrid foggy fat fellow there, I am sure I do."

"We must leave the matter for to-night, doctor," the squire was saying. "Nothing will be done, in any event, before to-morrow. Mr. Wilkin, we will bid you good-night. My servant shall conduct you to the steward's room for some refreshment before you go."

"God-a-mercy, sir; I shall be very content at that, for I have had a long and busy day. Aye, I smelt out a brace of witch at Plymouth early this morning, and had 'em trussed up in chairs to wait my return. They'll have time to reflect on their misdeeds, I warrant, afore I get back to 'em. Well, ladies and gentlemen, I'll bid ye good-night. I shall wait on you to-morrow at ten of the clock, sir."

"Aye, do so."

Mr. Wilkin retired backwards, keeping a wary eye on the doctor, who, being mad, might suddenly rush on him.

"Look 'ee, doctor," said Sir Ralph, when he was gone, "you must be reasonable, man. All we desire is to see justice done, and to protect the poor folk, their children, beasts and crops, from ill. If this old 'ooman bean't a witch, why 'twill be proved so, and she'll be cleared afore her neighbours, and we'll see no harm comes to her. And if she be a witch, then she should die, and none can doubt that."

"Aye, and how is't to be proved? By trussing her up in a chair and watching if flies and gnats come in to her; by sticking her with pins to see if she bleed; by throwing her into water to see if she swim; by torturing confessions out o' her till she tell ye her cat's an imp o' Satan and she herself his bride. By God, I know how 'tis done, and 'twon't be done in Dean while I'm here. I've a mind to go round to the Half Moon to-night with a couple o' stout fellows and carry that mammet off and drop him in a bog on the moor."

"I'll help ye, doctor," Mr. Herrick promised. "As nasty a canting sly rogue as never I saw. 'Slife, a looks for all the world like one o' those Puritan ministers outed their churches for recalcitrancy."

"A very ugly foggy coystrell fellow, on my life," Sir John Suckling observed. "Still, Robin, you had best not let him in his work. The poor devil's got to earn his bread, like the rest on us."

"Y'have heard me," Dr. Conybeare said, fallen cold and calm now, and addressing his host and the Constable. I've said what I mean and hold by. Neither that fellow nor another shall touch old Prowse while I'm here to let it. Julian, child, thou and I must go home."

Julian, looking pale and unhappy, rose from among Meg and little Joan and the dogs and said good-bye to her host and hostess.

"You may rest assured, doctor," the squire said, "that no injustice will be done to this poor old woman. You may put that out o' your mind all-thing."

"Meaning, squire, as it's no affair o' mine and I am not to meddle? As to that, I have said my say, and there's an end on't. Your servant, gentlemen. Your servant, ma'am, and I thank ye kindly for my supper. Good-night, ladies. Good-night, parson; I may call on ye for help yet. Come, child."

"There goes a wild, proud, windy-headed man, for sure," the squire commented. "'Twas great pity he chanced to be here when Mr. Wilkin called, for we shall have a brangling with him over this matter. He'll see no reason when these hot fits are on him."

"A mighty uncivil rixy man," his wife tartly added. "Marry come up, who's he to set himself up agen you and the Constable of the Hundred and all religion, custom, authority and sense? Just a country leech, and the son of a country schoolmaster, and a spoilt parson withal, as ran his ministry. Depend on't, a di'n't lose his religion and his orders for nought. Well-nigh an atheist, I call him—saving your presence, parson."

"Oh, as to that, I know he'd call himself an atheist. None the less, he's mistook, for never an atheist lived with such honesty and charity. Indeed, an atheist be a sort of monster, that's hard to credit, and Conybeare's no monster, but an extreme honest, right-meaning man, rixy and mistook though he be. He'll tush at sorcery in the face of all reason and evidence, part out o' tachy perversity, and part from the kindness of his heart, as would deny the devil's own existence to's face. But I'm with him as to this old dame Prowse, for I believe she's no witch."

"Whether she be or no," said Suckling, "if that witch-finding gentleman get on her, it's all the world to a China orange as she's proved so, and in that case she'll have short shrift enough. Why not pack off the old dame bag and baggage by the carrier's cart to a new part o' the country, where she may start afresh, none knowing her?"

"Aye, Jack, you speak sense there. Aye, Jupiter Ammon, that's the way to do."

"No, damme, sir," Sir Ralph shouted. "Either the woman's a witch, and in league wi' the dowl, and should die, or she bean't, and shall stay where she is, unmolested."

Suckling shrugged his shoulders.

"Y'are hopeful, sir. I'd wager you what's left of my estate—but I must warn you it a'n't much, owing to that cursed cribbage and those damned bowls—to a tankard of ale, as she won't stay unmolested for long, now the hunt's up, be she as little of a witch as you or I. There be a few of witches, and a great many of old women, and if half the old dames as is conceited to be witches was truly so, this country, and indeed all Europe, would be in a sad bewitched plight. I think better of God's providence then to credit him with permitting his world to be ruled thus by the devil, though I'll allow he gives the devil a mighty long rope. But I trench there on thy field, Robin."

"Y'are welcome to't, Jack. God's ways is above my interpreting, and you or any man may do your best at 'em. But I dare swear 't a'n't his will as we should let old Mother Prowse burn for a witch."

"Zart, sir," Sir Ralph cried, "d'ye set yourself up to tell God's will to me? What a plague, sir, this is what comes o' making nestlecocks o' the church and the parsons, as these damned bishops now practise. Varjuice, sir"—(Sir John Suckling observed that the Constable's oaths were very country, for, indeed, he but seldom left his home)—"I 'on't be telled my duty, no, nor God's will neither, by a parson. Dowl take 'ee, Mr. Parson, my fathers owned Moreshead and was gentlemen of substance in the land when as yours was snivelling tradesmen and prentices. Aye, by cock, let you not stand up and huff me wi' your talk o' God and his will, you as have no holding in the country."

Mr. Herrick was on his feet, angry and red.

"'Sbread, sir, you think fit to insult my church, my calling, and my fathers. Let me tell you, Mr. High Constable, as my fathers was people of substance and credit in Leicestershire, and as for city trade, 'tis a circumstance might befall any family, and if to be a skilled master goldsmith, as was my father, and my uncle, Sir William, is scandalous and low, 'tis a scandal as many might envy. No holding in the country, say you? I tell ye, as parson of a parish, I have as much right to my glebe and tithe as you to your land and your fortified manor house. Aye, even if John Selden were right when he said tithes weren't *jure divino*, but we know th' Archbishop made him take that back. And as for my calling, 'tis from God, unworthy though I be, and 'tis my duty as his priest to declare his will; aye, and I'll declare it to the end, though I mayn't greatly perform it. Not all the Constables and squires in this damned dull Denshire shall let me in that duty."

"Why, for Godsake!" his flustered sister-in-law exclaimed. "Robin, thou'rt all-to hot and out o' humour, I declare. He don't mean it, ma'am," she explained to Mrs. Yarde. "He grows heated sometimes o' nights, and after he's mellow."

"Marry come up," was all Mrs. Yarde found to say, divided between her duty as hostess and her natural sympathies with the right and respectable side.

"Come, gentlemen," the squire intervened. "This is unseemly in you both. Sir Ralph, you went too far, and I think you would do well to crave pardon of Mr. Herrick for your hot words. We should differ as gentlemen, not with huffing incivility."

Sir Ralph snorted. "Gar, I meant no offence, Mr. Parson. But, a pox, an ye cry up witches and seek to exonerate 'em, you do strangely forget your Christianity."

"I cry not up witches, sir. Cock's body, d'ye take me for a Sadducee or an atheist? D'ye charge me with denying the devil and his armies on earth? Ha'n't I read Scripture, the Endor witch, the Gadarine swine, Simon Magus and the rest? Ha'n't I read the Greeks and the Romans, and a'n't they full of magicians and sorceries? Don't Apuleius tell me of men turned into beasts; don't Horace speak o' witches and their wickedness? A'n't there murderous and lustful wizardry all down history? Though, mind you, I don't go along with Walter Mapes, who has Satan change Ceres, Pan, Bacchus and the fauns and dryads into demons. That was a poor credulous conceit, as was only apt for those dark papistical times. And I'll still believe 'tis Almighty God minds our crops and cattle, and sends the rain, the shine and the blight at his pleasure, and that the devil has not that power. Howbeit, there is demons and devils walking the earth sure enough. Satan's like a king outed his country, as is for ever prowling about seeking to make him links with such vassals as'll ope their gates to him, and any creature with an evil will may do't and let him in. And as to the old hags, why, many on 'em has owned to't themselves, and who'd confess to such vile unholy intercourse if they ha'n't it? 'Tis agen nature. So, Mr. Constable, I don't cry up witches, nor witchcraft neither, but only speak for a poor silly crazed old creature as ha'n't the power to harm a soul if she will to."

"We've heard else, Mr. Herrick," old Mrs. Yarde said. "There's been shocking sorry tales and scandals for long, and growing worse of late. The village folk is sure as Mother Prowse hath overlooked old Miggle and is wishing him to's death, and hath blighted James Miggle's cattle beside, and soured their milk, and caused five children of late to sicken with the smallpox, and sent Margery Mudge's daughter into fits and delivered her of a monstrous child, and a hundred ills else. I swear I am weary of hearing on 'em."

"I won't listen to 'em," Mrs. Northly declared. "The horrid vulgars, if you but wish 'em good-day they'll begin and tell you the shockingest uncomfortable tales, and never lin till you move away. Denshire's an extraordinary scandalous place, Sir John."

"So's London, madam," returned the baronet. "The truth is that the Lord's planted us in an extraordinary scandalous world, fuller of tales, troubles, lies, wickedness and witches than are eggs of meat. What of it? I'll not complain, for it contents me well enough in the main, aye, witches and all, mistress. Come, Robin, forget witches and witch-hunters in another song. But first I'll give you a toast—here's to witches, so long as they be young and fair, and to witch-hunters so long as they be gallant and gay. Drink that with me, Mrs. Lettice."

"Lock, Sir John, witches never is young and fair."

"A'n't they? A'n't they indeed?" He held her with his eyes until she faintly blushed.

Meg whispered to her small sister, "Lettice is happy now. Don't she look a fool," and made the child giggle, drawing her grandmother's attention.

"Why, shrew me, child, to bed with thee. Thou'rt late

already. No, leave the pup; no, thou mayn't have it to bed. Get off with thee, poppet, this minute."

Joan made a general curtsey to the company and went. Rather bored, on the whole, by the evening, Meg wished the guests would depart. They all seemed to have witch-mania, she thought.

But, if they had, they soon forgot it in music and drink and games.

13

It was half-past ten before Mr. Herrick, his guest, and his sister (who had been nodding for an hour) left the Court.

"Well, Jack," said the vicar, as they took the path across the misty moonlit fields, "there's a country evening for thee. And it seemed much to thy taste, if I could judge."

"Aye, I grant. Give him wine, women, cards and song, and Jack Sucklin's content enough. I tell thee, Robin, I like thy bucolics very well. And a witch thrown in too; what more could a man get at the play itself?"

"They shan't get poor old Moll," Mr. Herrick began muttering. "'Sbread, they shan't get her," and Sir John, bored long since by poor old Moll, yawned and changed the subject.

"Plague take thee, Robin, let's talk of young women, not of old."

"Aye, well, talk on, Jack. But mind as Eliza's with us."

"Indeed, I'd say no word to offend Mrs. Elizabeth. My tongue's pure as the fall o' the snow before the soil hath smutched it. I would but praise Mrs. Lettice's lovely cheek and merry ways. There's a sweet pretty merry rogue for you, Jack Sucklin."

"Not for Jack Sucklin. For Henry Northly. None of your pranks among my flock, Jack."

"As to that, we'll see. But since when have you grown a puritan, Robin?"

"A'n't I my people's pastor and God's minister, bawdy fellow?"

"To be sure y'are, brother," his sister-in-law approvingly agreed, pleased to see him remembering it. "Aye, Sir John," she added, "Robin's an extreme good pastor, though he may on occasion talk wild and write loose."

I wonder, Suckling speculated idly to himself, if Robin's as very a wencher as his verses would show him. Aye, is Robin a wencher at all, since his Julia left him? And if he be not, why does it so run in his mind and from his pen? Poor Robin; Julia hit him hard, the handsome quean, and I opine it's run to lewd and envious fancies in him, so as he conceits himself surrounded ever by fair maids and madams—but I'm damned if I see many on 'em in Dean Prior! Where are his lovely Corinnas, Sapphos, Lesbias, Antheas and the rest? All in's head—or in Catullus, Horace and Martial? Or has he had 'em all in his arms? Pox take it, I daren't ask him, for it's his own secret business, and if a man may hold any secret fast, 'tis surely that. But Lord, he's a mighty singular parson, and ever was, as his brethren of the cloth complain . . . I wonder has he seen Madam Julia of late years, as I have, and, if so, if she still seems fair to him. She's grown as bouncing a coarse quean as never I saw. Robin was well quitted of her.

"Well," he said, "this country life is odd; here are we on the way to bed, just when a gentleman's night should be beginning."

"'Twill seem odder in the morning, Jack, when you hear

Will pulling the bell for matins at six, just when a gentleman should be going to his rest."

"D'ye tell me so? You go to church at that hour? Does the Christian religion ask so much of poor human nature, to be astir and praying when all should be at their slumbers but those plaguey birds and cows? Faith, Robin, the Almighty never meant me for Holy Orders, that's certain."

"'Tis very certain, Jack," Mr. Herrick agreed, "for all your treatises on theology. As to that, who shall say as he meant me? But here I am, and here I must bide in my wilderness, and do the best I can wi't. There's worse lot than to be a parson in Devonshire when the sun shines and the spring flowers blow, or the corn's gotten in and the orchards are heavy with golden fruit like the trees of the Hesperides. There's times when as I feel in myself the content of Virgil's old Corycian hind—

> regum aequabat opes animis, seraque revertens
> nocte domum dapibus mensas onerabat inemptis,
> primus vere rosam atque autumno carpere poma,

and times I don't. But God bears with me, and pardons me my rebellions and my wanton moods—or so I trust, so I trust. Aye, and so I'll ever believe, for a'n't he the King of all mercy, and don't he know as w'are but the frail dust he made us on? So I get me to his house, Jack, and I cry him mercy for my sins, and give him God-a-mercy for his kindness, and hope to win to heaven after all."

"And shall Prue bring you your caudle when she wakes you, brother, or will you have it when you return?" Mrs. Elizabeth inquired.

"When she wakes me, in course. D'ye think, Eliza, as I'll tempt the gout by going out on a dewy autumn morning through the wet grass to the cold church without a sup or drop in me? God don't ask that of me, and I'll not do't."

14

Dr. Conybeare and his child walked from Dean Court through the dark village, in the soft misty twilight of the yet unrisen moon. In the lanes between the thatched cottages, with their little twinkling eyes that shone out beneath deep eaves, a few people stood, talking, laughing and courting. The river ran gurgling in its rocky bed through the meadows, singing and whispering, thought Julian, as if naiads chuckled there beneath their breaths, as perchance, thought she, they did. For Julian's country training, her classical instruction, and her natural good sense combined to assure her that naiads, dryads, nymphs, pixies, fairies, fauns, satyrs, and all the other creatures of the countryside, abounded now as ever. She knew better than to believe that

> Since of late Elizabeth,
> And later James came in,
> They never danced on any heath;
> As when the time had been,

for she had seen and heard them time and again.

But to-night she heard little either of fairies or of the river's voice, for her father's impatient anger, gushing like a geyser out of Dean Court, rushed on through the quiet night in a torrent of hot words.

" 'Sdeath, the damned addle-pated fools shan't have their way. They'd do the poor old creature to death, would they, with their nasty credulities and conceits? Are we no better still than a pack o' savages, then? 'Pon my soul no, I think w'are worse. Nay, we *are* a pack o' savages, and that's all there is to 't. And this is the seventeenth century; this is the year of grace (save the mark!) 1640. And here we are, living in so-called civility, and acting as our forefathers acted three hundred, five hundred, nay, a thousand years back. Aye, worse than a thousand years back in this matter, for 'twarn't till long after that as Europe ran all-thing witch-mad, like a pack o' dogs on a blood-trail, throwing old women into fire by the hundred. God-a-mercy, England's never been so fierce on witches as her neighbours abroad, though bad enough; 'twas Scotland catched the infection so strong i' the last century—there's a damned wild superstitious people for ye, curse their red heads—and that infernal silly gabbling fool of a king of theirs brought the fever South with him and fanned it up, with his demonologies and his cowardly Highland dreads and cruel French hates—Lord, how I mislike these Stuarts!—and now every murderous fool as hunts a poor old woman down can plead royal support and Christian approval to boot. For look, the Church has ever led these hell-hounds on the trail; let 'em but cry heresy, anti-Christ, and the devil, and any folly'll be credited. What did they to the Waldenses who were used to meet for worship o' nights? Charged 'em with sorcery, racked 'em till they owned to communing with the devil, then fined the men of substance among 'em and threw the poor old dames into the fire. And when they desired to be quit of the Templars, king and pope must cry 'Sorcery,' and 'witches' Sabbath,' that they might wipe 'em off the earth and take their goods. The English and French between 'em burned Joan for a witch, as was but a poor crazed deluded maid; and then came that cursed Bull of Innocent's, and Europe turned to a bonfire and a torture-chamber, and men took to witch-finding for a paying trade, like water-divining or killing rats. And now here's one of 'em come here on his devil's work. But, by God, a shan't do't. A shall burn me first."

" Oh father, how shall we save her? "

The lovely night, lit already by the rising moon, that sent its soft glow across the misty fields, had turned to blood and fire and terror—a monstrous devil's bonfire, in which old women shrieked.

" Oh father, we must save her. But how? "

The doctor darkly brooded.

They crossed Warm Bridge, beneath which Dean Burn glittered now in a thousand golden facets, and turned up the lane that climbed the hill in the long shadow of the wood.

" Aye, how? She must not be catched; she must not be took for trial, or 'twill be the end of her. She's three parts addled already, and rough usage will finish the work, and she'll confess to anything."

" If y'are present when as she's tried, father, you and Mr. Yarde could see she warn't hectored and hurt, but treated fair . . ."

" Fair? Whoever heard on a fair questioning of suspicioned witches? Was old Moll treated fair before, when they flung her into Hound's Pool? The manner for the questioning of witches is laid down in the Malleus Maleficarum. They'd put her infernal questions, and stick pins in her to find the devil's spot, and make her screech out that she was the devil's slave and bride, and her cat her familiar, and that she'd wished the plague on her neighbours and the blight on their beasts, and ate up babies in secret. Then they'd have her, and 'twould be the hangman's rope were she lucky, the fire if she warn't. No, she must ne'er get into the hands o' that nasty whey-faced fellow and that blustering fool Furze. We must take her out her cottage and hide her for a while, till I can get her away from these parts. But where? There's not a farm-house 'ud take her in. Skerraton, Addislade, Reddicleve, Nurston—no, not one. Every man and woman around here, gentle and simple, clerk and lay, is soaked in this credulous conceit. The parson would shelter her, but with those two prating women in the house, 'twould get abroad, and the Constable and the squire'd demand that he give her up, and, were he well mellowed, he'd do't, and all would be up. No, we must hide the old body ourselves, and this very hour."

"Oh, yes," Julian eagerly breathed. "'Tis a lucky chance as Tib's away till Friday. We can shut Moll in her chamber, and none will discover her—if we can but make her keep quiet. Shall we go and fetch her now, father?"

"Aye, forthwith. There's little time to lose."

The doctor drew his daughter's arm within his as they climbed the deep, shadowed lane.

"Thou'rt a good maid, July, and hast a head on thy shoulders. I thank God I can trust thee in plights and troubles . . . Thou dostn't believe on witchery or any such nonsense, in thy heart, child?"

His child's wide eyes roamed over a haunted moonlit country, where, behind every tree and bush, fairies and spirits lay leaguer; followed the long black line of Dean Wood, up and up to the hidden moors, which would be lying mist-wreathed and last beneath the moon, alive with mocking pixies, pale with straying ghosts.

"I don't know, father," she murmured. "But I don't believe as old Moll's a witch."

"Thou dostn't?" he mocked her. "Godamercy for that, at least. Ne'ertheless, thou dost believe on witches, thou little addle-pate. Well, well, why should I expect in thee more sense than I find in any others, young or old, just by reason thou'rt my daughter, and ingenious at thy books? Natheless, child, thou shouldn't credit such nonsense, after all my teaching. I suppose parson misleads thee, and tells thee of pixies, imps, spirits, and all the rest o' the rout."

"I've no need to hark to parson, father. There *is* pixies and fairies. Everybody knows it, and has seen and heard 'em in the meadows and woods, and on the moor. I've heard 'em tee-heeing often, and seen 'em flitting around corners as I come nigh, or lurking in the vuzz. And the pixies colt folks astray on the moor, and tumble 'em into bog-holes. But the kind good people help us, they say. And, whether they be good or bad, th'are all around and about, father, for I've heard 'em."

"Heard 'em, hast thou? Credulent, superstitious, silly wench that thou art. Thou and thy tee-heeing pixies. I tell thee, thou hasn't heard 'em, for there be none to hear."

"But father, there's all the old tales; the Greek and Roman tales, and our own . . ."

"Aye, I grant, there's tales enow, if tales prove aught. Well, believe on fairies and white magic if thou must, though 'tis silly, but ne'er believe on black magic and sorcery."

"Oh, I don't wish to, father, but how can I not? I must believe on the devil, and that he tries to work his will on earth through men."

The doctor shrugged his shoulders.

"If thou must, then I can't let thee from it, 'tis plain. But see here; how did belief on sorcery grow up, think you? From human nature, only. From men's fear and folly, that peopled the dreadful earth they lived in with spirits and powers as could help or harm 'em. Ergo, they must have witches and wizards and wise men to mediate for 'em, so that business began early. Then in came the Christian's devil, with all his nasty hosts, and the Church took o'er the whole army of spirits and made saints or demons of 'em, and took the magicians with 'em, and some they called good magicians, or priests of God, and some bad ones, or slaves of the devil. And all as seemed evil to 'em they put to the score of the devil and his servants; aye, and in all good faith, since they conceited Satan and his merry men to be anti-Christ and rivals to God. And look ye, so double and divided is man's nature that he is foul but yet hates his own foulness, and so, needing a scapegoat for't, he loads it on to this devil and his servants, and delights to imagine in 'em all the filthiness as lurks in his own heart, and when he hunts down and harms some poor old creature who, he's persuaded, is devil-ridden, he fulfils a many needs in himself; he defends himself and his from the harm and the evil eye he fears; he joins in a hunt, and that's ever sweet to our bloodthirsty human kind; he feels a righteous fellow, in league with piety and virtue for to punish sin; and he wreaks vengeance on the wickedness he knows on in himself and his dreams. Add to all this the love of the general for a raree show, or of any sport, and the teaching of Church and State the world over, and human credulence and the love of strange portents, and you'll not marvel that scarce one has e'er owned to doubting witchcraft, not even the unhappy creatures themselves. Why, they have often cried 'emselves up for witches without the aid of the torture; they've believed it. An ingenious physician would be able to tell 'em better, and that they was crazed, epileptic, or had St. Vitus his dance, or had worked 'emselves into a frenzy and needed blooding or a purge. But the poor silly bodies are ne'er treated for sickness, only tried for sorcery. And then there's this: men have hated women in all ages—and mind, I'll not say as men ha'n't been in part right, for women are often mighty angering and plague a man's life out—and so they've piled the world's wickedness on 'em, from Adam on; and women being more fantastical, conceited, romantical, and easy crazed, they accept a charge of sorcery more easy than do men, and that's why there's ever been more women witches than men. Who ever, since Erasmus, has writ in doubt of witches? Those few as have questioned their diabolical powers, and apprehended in the business much error and superstition, have still half opined the old ladies should die from their evil will, and none all-to denies demonology. There's a few doubt it in secret, or in familiar talk, but they'll not confess it openly, since 'tis publicly affirmed by every divine and layman of weight in all lands. Even our Mr. Hobbes keeps an open door behind him. If our most learned men are either cowards or else slaves to their time, what's to do? There's small hope, Jule, for the world, or for the life of man upon it. The best hope's in the philosophers, and they're chained and fettered . . ."

"Yes, father." Julian agreed, having heard him say so before. "Look, here's the path across the field to Moll's cottage. We climb through the gap in the hedge."

"Soft, then. We must not be marked. Not as any one's like to be abroad in the fields by the witch's cottage at this hour . . . There's no light in the windows; she's asleep, belike. Knock soft on the door, not to fright her. She's been so rabbled and mobbed of late as to moider her wits. 'Twere best to call her, so she'll know who 'tis. Moll, Moll! Mrs. Prowse!"

"Moll! Don't be feared. 'Tis but the doctor and his daughter. Will you let us in?"

There was a shuffling within, and the latch lifted. The low door opened a crack, letting a slant of moonlight into the dark interior. The old lady stood there, shrivelled and bent, with scared, malicious, peering eyes.

"Moll, you must let us in. We would speak with you."

Mrs. Prowse made the peculiar sounds that served her Devonshire and anile tongue for sentences. They understood her in Dean, which was all that concerned her. So when she said "Gar, vor vy, cham abed," the doctor replied, "Aye, but you must make haste to rise. Y'are in danger."

"Lock, chell warndy," observed Mrs. Prowse. "Tha muxy trash do rabble ma and roily upon ma fra cockleert till dimmet. But by night mun's skeered o' pigsnies i' the vuzzy-park and o' being by-gaged of old Moll, and tha don't come vort. Aye a vengeance, hey go, a'll by-gage mun."

Her visitors had pushed through the door and closed it. They stood in the low little room, close and dark, lit only by the dying ashes on the hearth and by the moonlight that slanted through the tiny window in the thick wall.

"Art dressed?" the doctor asked. "Aye, thou art. Then wrap thy cloak about 'ee and come with us. Y'aren't safe here. They'll come to fetch 'ee in the morning for a witch. You must come and bide with us, and not discover yourself to a soul."

"Come vet ma vor witch, what a vengeance? Hey go, varjuice, chall be zlopt i' the burn again and buddled to death, chall be prinked and punged and glammed and vulched and drashed and brent, hey go, hey go, a vengeance."

"Come, Moll, don't waste time talking. Thou'lt not be fetched if thou come with us. I promise ye no harm shall come to thee. But make haste."

Julian was raking out the embers. Their last glow sparkled on green eyes shining from the corner. Mrs. Prowse was understood to say that Puss must accompany her, and also Nan her goat and Pork her pig.

"Can't be," said the doctor. "Their presence would discover you forthwith. We'll turn 'em loose in the meadow. There, puss, out with 'ee, begone."

"Plague rat tha muxy volk vor tha roilying. Gar, cham a-troubled wi' the bone-shave, doctor. Chall be all-to dugged i' the wet vuzzy-park."

"Thou'lt be worse dugged i' the burn, Moll, gin they catch thee. I'll give thee physic for the bone-shave suddenly. Art ready?"

The old lady was gathering up her various possessions and handing them to Julian to carry for her, truly remarking that she was not very likely to see them again if she left them there.

"Dowl fly away wi' tha kee," she added, in pious hope that some ill might befall her neighbour's cattle.

At last, having slung a shawl about her neck filled with miscellaneous objects, turned her back and with great privacy dropped some coins down her stockings, remarking, "Ma hozen's rumpled," collected some cheese and part of a manchet from a cupboard and given them to Julian, placed in a conspicuous position on the table another loaf, too stale to take, and stuck a needle into it, saying, "Gar, hope tha pink mun vinely," Mrs. Prowse was ready to leave her home.

"Soft now," Dr. Conybeare said. "We had best go mumchance, and keep close along the hedge in the trees' shadow."

They did so, creeping down the steep, wet field in the dark of the moon, among munching cattle.

"Please God and the pigs," Mrs. Prowse muttered, "they kee'll sicken and rat. Hey go, hey go, sicken and rat. Ees fay."

"Pray don't talk," the doctor sharply requested. Julian thought it certainly was a pity that Mrs. Prowse expressed herself as she too often did with regard to the animals and persons of her neighbours. There was no doubt but that she had had provocation; still, Julian did occasionally think that, even if not a witch, she behaved rather like one.

They were now in the doctor's orchard, where the heavy apple boughs drooped laden, like the boughs of those tropical trees on which a score of rosy, plumed birds sleep balled like apples. The silvered trees, the long, dew-wet grass, stood still and enchanted in shadow and in pale light; no wind breathed, no pixies tee-heed; only the hoarse, asthmatic panting of the aged refugee and the slurring of dark footsteps in heavy orchard grass broke the quiet.

They dropped down into the garden, and stood before the dark, shut little house. Dr. Conybeare let out a sharp breath of relief, as he unlocked his solid oak door.

"Godamercy, here we are without mischance. Take her up to Tib's room, Jule, and I'll mix a cordial for her. There, mother, you'll be safe enough here, please God and the pigs, as you say."

"Vield war wet," said Mrs. Prowse, sadly.

"Oh don't be grumbling, 'ooman. Be off to bed, and be thankful 'twas the field and not the burn as wet ye."

"Gar, dowl splet mun," said their guest, and, clutching her bundle tightly to her, she creaked after Julian up the worm-eaten stairs.

Ten minutes later, while the doctor sat lighting his pipe and sipping a glass of the hot rum he had brewed for his visitor's rheumatics and his own, there came a beating on his door.

"Who knocks?" he cautiously and somewhat testily enquired. Really, the sick . . .

"Es Peter Miggle," he was answered. "Granfer's mortal sick. Vauther suspicions as a'll die vorewey, and please be so good to come suddenly."

"Zart, a plague on't," the doctor muttered, as he gulped down his drink and drew on his wet shoes again.

Going to the foot of the stairs, "Jule," he softly called, "I'm called out to old Miggle. I shall lock the house and take the key. Go you to bed. I might be long."

Hearing him, the old lady now huddled in blankets in Tib's bed observed, "Hey go, hey go. Dowl's come vor Miggle, dowl ull vet mun vore cockleert, hey go. Gar."

"Oh hush," Julian whispered. "There's a Miggle boy at the door; he'll hear you."

Mrs. Prowse disappeared beneath the blankets, so that, even if heard, she might not be seen.

The doctor went out into the moonlit orchard country and up the deep, miry lane to Addislade.

Juan Miguel died before cocklight, muttering faintly and

hoarsely in Spanish, with his doctor one side of him and his priest on the other, and his descendants keening in the background. No doubt, no doubt at all, but that he had been by-gaged.

" 'Sbones," growled his swarthy son, " her'll smart for't, the horry old hag. Aye, a vengeance her shall."

" Shall her indeed," Dr. Conybeare said within himself. "We'll see about that, my friend."

15

The quarry had fled. Round the deserted lair the huntsmen rabbled and mobbed. Mr. Wilkin the witch-finder, accompanied by two stout constables and armed with the authority of magistrate, sheriff and High Constable, had waited on Mrs. Prowse at eleven of the morning, and found already assembled a crowd of neighbours, desirous, it seemed, of avenging the decease of Mr. Miggle, and other local mishaps. They greeted Mr. Wilkin with approval, but informed him that he would have to seek elsewhere, for the watch was abroad. They showed him how they had broken the door and the window and tousled the cottage and its contents, flinging the latter pell-mell out into the field, and how Malkin the cat, the witch's familiar imp, crouched on the thatch and spat at them and none dared touch him for fear of bewitchment, for he might well turn into the devil in their very hands. The same with the goat, who browsed and bleated in the meadow near by.

" As to that," said the witch-finder, " I shall suddenly prove these creatures, whether they be natural or of Satan," and bade one of the constables bring him hither the goat.

The young man, after some demur, gingerly approached the animal, and, taking it by the horn, led it back.

" 'Tis very well," Mr. Wilkin said. " Truss the beast to a tree, and I will later deal with it before the Lord. Now bring the cat."

No one moved to do this.

" Be so good to bring yonder cat from the roof," the witch-finder said again to his assistants. Then, " What, are you feared? 'Tis but those yet in their sins as Satan's imps can harm. The Lord's elect shall touch any deadly thing and it shall not destroy them. Is none of the elect here? Are ye all yet in guilt, and shivering lest the devil should claim his own?"

Some of the Miggle family and a few others of conservative habit were observed to cross themselves, which annoyed Mr. Wilkin.

" Leave those vain, popish and superstitious signs," he adjured them, " for what will they avail you when Satan's on your heels? Nought can save you, my friends, but faith and a pure heart before the Lord, and little enough you seem to have of *them*. Come, doth no man or woman of this assembly walk with God so as he fears not Satan?"

" Go vet puss thaself, gin thou'rt so bold," said the assembly, hoping to see him scratched or worse, for they did not care about this fat precisian from Plymouth, who turned up his eyes and insulted them in his mincing voice.

" We will leave puss for a while," Mr. Wilkin said at that, " since our first task must be to discover his mistress. Where, think you, friends, will she be? Somewhere down in Dean village, belike, with friends?"

" Old witch ha'n't no friends. There's none hereabouts 'ud let her within the door—none but parson and doctor. Belike the dowl's vetched her i' the night and vlown away wi' her or dropped her i' the bog. Aye, very like he'm dropped mun in Dockwell Hole."

"Not very like," Mr. Wilkin disagreed. "I have had great experience of the ways of witches, and that but rarely occurs. She may, truly, have wandered on the moors for herself, and have been entrapped in bog; nevertheless, 'twould be more like her master would deliver her, as I am telled he did from the water when she was cast therein."

"Aye, her swam, th' old chum; her 'oodn't sink for nought. Aye, he saved her for burning, the dowl did."

"Even the devil," Mr. Wilkin assented, "must work the Lord's appointed will in the end. And now, my friends, if you will guide me to this old dame's likely haunts, we will lay hands on her."

The day passed, and their search was still vain. Mrs. Prowse had not been seen walking abroad the night before, nor that morning; she had not been heard of down in Dean, nor in Deancombe, nor anywhere in the neighbouring lanes and coppices. She did indeed seem to have been spirited away, and there were those who had heard galloping horses in the air at midnight and after, and a strange wild screeching as of souls in torment, or devils in triumph, at the very hour when Hoon Miggle had died.

"Her's rid off t'hell with old Hoon," was commonly believed, and there were members of Hoon's family who suspicioned that this might indeed be the case, though his widow averred that, since he had died in grace, Mrs. Prowse's efforts to secure him as fellow-traveller to her own destination must certainly have failed, and that her screech had been one of frustrated rage.

Meanwhile, the old lady's neighbours stopped her earth by first smashing all they could of her cottage and then setting fire to the thatch, thus giving their defrauded desires some solace. "If witch don't burn, witch's home do," they remarked. At this occupation they were discovered by the squire and the vicar, who walked up from Dean together to see that the search was lawfully and properly conducted, neither putting much faith in the wisdom of their hot-headed friend the High Constable. The squire exercised his magistrate's jurisdiction by arresting several ringleaders, including some Miggles, for malicious damage and arson, pending a trial next day at Dean Court.

"I admire Dr. Conybeare an't in the thick on't, laying about with a cudgel to defend the old dame's property," Mr. Yarde observed. "We waited on him to inquire if he knows aught of the old body, but he said he was too mightily occupied to be running about after old dames, and shut his door in our faces. D'ye think he knows aught on't?"

"Not he," said Mr. Herrick."

Presently he crossed the fields to the doctor's house, his spaniel at his heels. Arrived at it, he leant on the old garden wall and so stayed for a minute or two. He saw his pupil's face peeping at him from the parlour window, and presently the doctor himself stood in the doorway.

"Good den, parson. I can't ask you in now, for I'm extreme busy with a drop of blood, proving a notion I've gotten concerning it. I'll walk with you so far as the coppice, if you go that way." He came out, laying a finger on his lips. "Pray not a word," he whispered, "of yonder hoyting mob and their doings. I don't want that Jule shall hear on't; 'twould vex and fright her. The devil fly off with the lot of 'em for the spiteful ramping rabble they be. Come, let's walk a moment, so we can speak."

He led the vicar away down the lane, to where they could see, across two fields, the fire leaping from the burning cottage.

"Lord," he muttered, "the cursed nitwit devils. Aye, th'are burning the poor old body's house because they'd like to burn herself but can't lay hands on her . . . Don't it fear you, parson, to think o' that poor weak moidered creature, if she was to fall into the hands o' such a pack?"

"Aye, does it. For they be gotten so reckless as there's no holding 'em, and if they should find Mrs. Witch now they might well make quick work o' her first and have her proved for a witch after, for all we and the squire could do. God send as the creature's safe hid somewheres."

"God send it indeed; if you think 'tis within his providence. I'd almost say my prayers again if I thought as he'd listen to 'em and save poor old Moll."

"Where is she, Michael Conybeare? Or, no, don't tell me, for I'd best be able to tell the squire and Furze as I don't know."

"Aye, surely say 'em so. I've said 'em the same. Do they believe me? I don't know and don't care, but 'tis all they'll get from me. I'm biding home to-day and leaving my sick to mind 'emselves, lest these beagles should come and trouble July with their questionings."

"And how's it to end, my friend?"

The doctor shrugged his shoulders. "The people'll presently quieten down and it'll pass from their silly minds. Moll can't ever return here, but she can settle down in another part o' the county, with a pig and a goat and a hen, and scrat her poor livelihood somehow."

"And be soon suspicioned for a witch again, I'll warrant. I wou'n't say it to Sir Ralph and the witch-finder, doctor, but she's the most damnable like a witch of any old creature as ever I saw. Talks like one, too, I'm cursed if she don't. There's times as I half conceit her one myself. All the same, I don't want her harried to death by the rabble, or t'have this pursy fellow from Plymouth sticking pins into her. Even if she be a witch, leave her to God and her master, say I."

Dr. Conybeare impatiently snorted.

" No use to talk on't, since we don't agree. However, we both want her saved, and can aid her in that. But look, I must back to my business and my house and child. Do you go and reason with your flock over there, and endeavour to instil some sense and virtue into 'em if you can."

" Even their God, doctor, can't do that, much less their parson. This is the first raree-show they've had since the June mumming when the little hunchback was tossed up in a blanket and broke his leg coming down. Look, they've gotten hold of a mammet; 'tis that doll as the Miggles were sticking pins into for old Moll. Th'are building a bonfire in the field to fling it on. Come, Tracy, we'll go see. Lord forgive us all, what a nasty sort of evil children we be! There's old Bunce grinning at the show with his two snaggle teeth, and his dirty-faced wife, that fights him all day and all night, holding on to his arm in love. How a good hate binds us together, for sure! Those two old stinking creatures'll sleep in amity to-night, likely, muttering curses through their rotten teeth as they snore."

Thus pleasantly musing, the vicar approached his busy and eager flock. He too liked a raree-show well enough when he got one, and out of a rabble dancing round a bonfire in a meadow could make poetry as well as of a troop of maids gathering cowslips. He began in his mind to fashion a verse apt to the occasion—a hymn to vulcan, to receive the witch's image, and not spue it forth.

" Thou fiery Godhead, take this waxy *Doll*,
Since sure 'tis all thou'lt get of poor old *Moll*—
Devour her, drown her in thy raging sea,
Till her wax witchship's melted quite away.
Then, if th'art hungry still, gape wide thy maw;
We'll fling thee Zelots, all uncooked and raw.

Wilt spue 'em forth? Thou serv'st not witches so.
Witches thou'lt take; but them that burn 'em, no.

I should follow Mr. Hobbes his example, and carry an ink horn in my cane. Well, Jack, is our rustic revelry to your gust?"

"Very rustical, Robin. Very merry and rustical indeed. How does't compare with a Bacchic orgy, think you?"

"Ill, I fear; very damnably ill. Still, we do our best. See how they grin and leap and wave their arms at the mammet as it burns. They'd do the same at old Moll, were't she that burnt."

"Lord forbid they get her. I've no liking for such plays as that. Has the medico spirited her away, as we surmised? He's a marvellous ingenious resourceful fellow, your Dr. Conybeare; I'll back him for a gold purse against your country mob. What's he done with the old dame?"

"Gently, man, gently. You and I know nought of the matter. Ask him, and he'll tell you there's no such matter. With the authority of the magistrate, the Constable, and the law against us, it's well to know nought. Conybeare may cock his nose at 'em if he will, but, as vicar of the parish, I can't be party to't—except *sub sigillo*."

"Well, whisper it *sub sigillo* in my ear, Robin—has the doctor got her hid away in his house? Nay, don't tell me; I'll go see for myself. Yes, *sub sigillo* I'll wait on the good physician and his fair daughter, and, if I hear sounds as of a witch witching, I'll take no notice on't; it shall be *sub sigillo* with me, hid in my breast."

"You can spare your pains, Jack; they'll not admit you. They keep as close as broody hens to-day. As to the witch, they must have smothered her under a dozen blankets to stint her from creeking out loud about her troubles and her neighbours' wickedness. Look, Jack, d'ye see that sour-faced fellow there? Aye, him with the long hair."

"A gentleman's hair and a zealot's face and garb—aye, by cock, and a zealot's crop ears, too, which his hair don't hide, though he'd like it should. What of him?"

"Only that there's a fellow got his deserts of the Archbishop. What must he do, a year back, but start protesting and complaining of the incense and ceremonies used in Rattery church, where the parson's a mighty solemn, ceremonious fellow. Laud heard news of this Mr. Peason's complaining and sent for him to come and relate his grievance. So Mr. Peason hied him up to London, as pleased as can be to get a hearing, but it seems the Archbishop di'n't like the sound of his whining voice so well as he liked it himself, for a had his long ears off in a trice and sent him packing. Little Canterbury's something over fond o' the shears and do dearly love, so they tell, to see the blood flow and make a Puritan to screech; but for my part I cou'n't be sorry for Peason, the man's as plaguey a canting knave as e'er I saw, and makes himself a pest to all the parsons around; aye, and to the laity too, whining of sin and grace and perdition, and turning a man's peccadillos into crimes. I swear, if Laud hadn't cropped the fellow, some one here'd suddenly have done him that justice—perhaps our hot-headed High Constable himself, for Peason's gotten in his road more than once, and he's a damned choleric impatient man."

"And if the Constable had spared the gentleman's ears, perchance the parson himself might have seen to 'em, for he's not such a patient man, neither. Well, if that was the worst folly Canterbury had committed, he wou'n't have gotten himself and the king into the devilish nasty plight he hath. Lord, it's a pretty praemunire. How the people hate him! You should hear 'em mutter and curse when he passes through the city, devilish churlish uncivil dogs that they be. They mayn't like the Peasons, but I'm poxed if they don't hate the Arminians and the prelates considerable worse. But they and Laud would fadge in one thing—they do both dearly like to see a witch burn. If His little Grace was to appear here in this minute, he'd lead the village in the hunt for this old lady, and win their hearts by his zeal. There the learned and the great vulgar meet . . . Look, here's your High Constable leading a mighty cavalcade, all hot on the chase."

A group of riders were trotting down the lane, local squires, clergy, and a medley of farmers on cobs, labourers on cart-horses, and boys bareback on moor-ponies, "They've been searching the near parts of the moor," said Mr. Herrick. "'Tis as good as a fox-hunt. There goes my brother Beanes of Brent."

A jolly clergyman on a great bay mare trotted by them, and waved his whip in greeting. "Ye should have been with us, Herrick. Right up to Ford we went, and all about Lambs Down and Wallingford and along Abbot's Way. We thought we'd got the scent of her once, but rot me if 'twarn't an old bitch fox arter all. But yoicks, we'll run her down yet, wherever she's gone t'earth. Sir Ralph has a notion as that ill-spoken leech o' yours knows summat, and he's got out a warrant to search his house. But I'm varjuiced if I wou'n't sooner gallop her down in the open, for the old fox she be, than dig her out of a hole. Yoicks, then, Jenny lass; over ye go!"

With these words he caused his mare to leap over a hedge and canter across the next field, endeavouring to persuade her, by oaths and gestures, that she followed a fox.

"Lord, a wonderful barbarous merry parson," said Sir John.

"Aye, friend Beanes is a merry soul. And why not? I mind hearing Mr. George Herbert once say as such hunting, swearing, drinking, gaming country parsons was a curse on the

Protestant Church and should be outed from their office. But Mr. Herbert was too much of the saint and the recluse for the common man to live by. We parsons are flesh and blood, and can't be for ever at our prayers or our books, no, nor for ever mealy-mouthed, nor pulling long faces like a Puritan eating cold porridge. We must have our pleasure; some will take it hunting, some drinking, some wenching, and some at all three. The Protestant clergy a'n't neither self-tormenting monks nor solemn Puritans, else what was our glorious Reformation for? I'll tell 'ee, Jack, Parson Beanes comes nigher the spirit o' the Church of England than do a mystical saint such as Mr. Herbert, or a fanatical ceremonial busy-body such as our Archbishop, or a great mighty learned preacher and poet such as Dr. Donne was."

"Like enough. Your Parson Beanes is doubtless the common sensual unthinking man, no better and no worse than the rest of us, taking his pleasures where he finds 'em, asking his God to forgive him when he's o'erstepped the bounds, doing his neighbours kindnesses when he's in good humour, and spites when he's in bad, and ever concerned to uphold the Church and constitution agen perverters and rebels, and to hunt down their enemies to the death. Such a parson you might be, Robin, if 'tweren't for your wit and your poetry and your heathen learning. By the way, what do Beanes and his kind make of your verses, with their flavour of the ancients and their heathen lore?"

"They like best my epigrams on the villagers. They can't have enough of those. For the rest, save where the verses concern persons and happenings as th'are acquaint with, my bucolic friends make but a poor dull audience, and, times, I can ill bear with them. Still, a man must have some audience; a man don't do well to shut up his verses within himself, to burn holes in his guts with longing. Hast learnt, Jack, that country-dwellers, when they hear of one among 'em as writes books, ever conceit as they are themselves the subject and matter of 'em, and read with no hopes but of finding themselves and their neighbours in the pages, for, think they, what else can the poor fellow have to write on? So they ransack the pages for such savoury passages, and pass by the rest with a yawn. At the least, I can tell thee as that's the way on't in Devonshire."

"And in Suffolk and Lincolnshire, too, Robin. And with some e'en in our blest and beloved Middlesex."

"I'll not grant that. Looking at London from here, I tell you it shines like the citadel of Jerusalem, all honey and milk, with angels treading the golden streets and bending their ears to hark to a poor poet singing, and then dropping bay-wreaths on his head."

"You've forgot your native city a trifle, Robin. But don't mind; think so and be envious with longing; 'tis as good a heaven as another, and one, to boot, as some of us finds more within reach. Look now, shall we follow the hunt and see what fortune they have at the medico's? I'll warrant he'll make a stand like an old boar and horn 'em out his lair if they try and thrust in."

"Aye, we'll go. Should they find poor Moll there and drag her off, we must do our most both to keep the doctor from the sin of murder and to console little July."

At that Suckling quickened his step, and in a few minutes they were among the crowd of horse and foot at the doctor's house.

Sir Ralph was at the door, speaking with Dr. Conybeare, who stood, angry and untidy, his horn spectacles pushed up on to his forehead, his grizzled black hair flaggy and wild, his great quill pen in his hand.

"You disturb me, gentlemen, you disturb me. My daughter lies in her chamber, sick with an aching head, and I myself am occupied in writing. I must pray you to go quiet away and leave them as like peace to't."

"We'll not discomfort you and your daughter for long, doctor," Sir Ralph Furze said. "But, in the cause of justice and the law, we must make search of your house. I have here a warrant for't, so I must trouble you, sir, to be so good to stand aside and leave my men enter."

The doctor, with a shrug, stood aside.

"Enter, then, fools. Search. Tousle my house about; tramp to and fro; fright my daughter and worsen her sickness and disturb my work, and then be off. But I beg you'll make short work on't, for I like you not."

At his compliance, Sir Ralph stared at him in surprise and some disappointment. However, he entered the house, his two men behind him, and set them about their business.

16

Lying stretched in the shallow space between bedroom floor and parlour ceiling, Mrs. Prowse, cross, stiff, fatigued and aggrieved, heard the heavy treading of the men above her, and muttered low to herself in her peculiar language her opinion of them.

"Dowl splet mun. Dowl fly away wi' mun. Vengeance rat mun, hey go, hey go. Gar! Chall be buddled i' this muxy quelstring hole. Doctor di'n't ought to let mun in. Should zem you'm paddled, Diccon Trant and Abel Dodds to Reddicleve, so betwattled troants as never a zee, plague rat 'ee. Lock, lock do pray dowl to vet ee an bren ee forever, so a do, ees fay. Aye, look zee in cupboard, and be hanged to 'ee; aye, aye, there ee go, muxy rats so ee be, roilying and tramping on ma head. Vor why a dowl did doctor let ee in to plague ma? Chaven't had no rest nor no comfort since doctor vet ma from ma bed. Aye, aye, there ee go, Diccon an' Abel, convounded trash, so ee be."

"Please t'ope thicky chest, doctor," the thick and certainly rather paddled voice of Diccon or of Abel was heard to say.

"Ope it yourself and be damned t'ye," the doctor's irritable answer came. "I'm not paid to do your dirty work. Go on; earn your pay, jackals; none's letting ye."

"That's tha way," Mrs. Prowse muttered. "Them's the words to gie'm, the trash. Doctor's a right rixy dowl-take-ee man. Vor why don't he gie'm a tack in tha muxy vaces? Lock, lock, chall be all buddled and vorspent; chall die here like rat catched in trap. Hey go, hey go, chall buddle and die."

Her bones ached; the sharp anguish of rheumatism shot up thigh and back and shoulder; she breathed dust and cobwebs; a rat scuffled and leapt over her face. Rats were, said her neighbours, her familiars, but she could not endure them on her face. With a sharp screech she raised her head, flung up her arms, and struck fiercely and repeatedly at the thin flooring above her.

"Plague take those rats," complained the master of the house, even as Sir Ralph Furze lumbered up the stairs from below, shouting, "By cock, a heard her creeking, th' old chun. Where from was it? Sikker out, lads, sikker out! She'll be shut in a cupboard i' the wall, by cud she will! Stand away, doctor, and don't let the officers o' the law. 'Twill stand ee in a pretty penny already, this gullery ye've put on us, so ye'd best not make matters worse by insolence. Be so good, Mrs. Julian, to stand away and leave us try that wall."

"Sir, 'twas from the floor under the bed as her yammered and tacked."

"I tell ye 'twas rats," the doctor asserted.

"Indeed," his daughter put in, "w'are plagued by 'em night and day, Sir Ralph, I swear we are."

"Very like, my dear, very like. 'Tis a plaguey rat indeed y'have here. Harky, there she goes again. Why, damme, she's creeking like she felt hell's flames already."

The old lady beneath the floor beat with clenched fists on the boards above her, crying. "Chall buddle, chall buddle, chall be ate of varmint and rot. Let ma voert, dowl splet ee!"

She hammered till her knuckles bled, raving and crying. The rats would bite her; she was nailed down into a living tomb, and would rot, forgotten and lost.

But no; they were prising up the floor overhead; crack, crack, the boards gave as the nails wrenched out; daylight and air rushed in; then a crowd of men darkened it, dragging her, lifting her, setting her in a chair, all shouting together.

"So we've got 'ee at last, y'old devil's chun. You'll not slip us again, I'll warrant ee. We'll soon prove ee, ye old chun, if y'are a witch or no. There's one below as'll prove ee."

"Damme, sir, leave her be. Can't you see as she's but a poor old moidered creature, beside herself with fear? Had she been a witch, would she have screeched out and bewrayed herself? In the name of humanity, leave her be."

"Indeed, sir, poor Moll's no witch, but only a silly crazed old woman, tormented till she don't know herself if she be a witch or no. Oh pray, sir, let her go!"

"Not I, my dear. In my view she's as muxy a witch as never I saw. But zart, I'm a fair reasonable man, with no prejudice, and she shall stand her just trial according to the law, I shall take her to Dean Court and she shall be questioned there by Mr. Witch-finder and stand her trial before the magistrate, and all shall be fair and square and in order. Aye, doctor, you can come and witness for her an you please, so let be your roilying now."

"As her physician, sir, I protest. She's extreme sick, and must stay in her bed."

"She a'n't so sick she can't be carried to the Court. Truss her up, men."

Diccon Trant observed that he felt considerably alarmed lest she should bewitch him.

Mrs. Prowse confirmed him in this suspicion by saying, "Aye, chall by-gage ee, chall rat tha kee, tha childer, tha vauther and thasel, hey go, tha muxy lollpoop, leave ma be! Dowl vet tha, Ralph Vuzz, dowl fly witha to hell."

Sir Ralph, though no papist, made the sign which his forbears had made against similar imprecations for several centuries, and would doubtless have paled had his complexion admitted of it.

"'Sbones, gag th' old limb, can't ee, and lin her devil's tongue from wagging."

"Fair and softly, man. I admire ye ha'n't more courage than to be frightened at the crazy flim-flam of such a poor old dwallying creature. Let be gagging her. Keep thy mouth shut, Moll, and no harm shall happen thee."

But Moll could not keep her mouth shut; still she dwallied and raved and cursed, until they gagged her toothless mouth and bore her away, bore her downstairs and out among the cheering mob, hoisted her on to the stout back of Diccon Trant's cob, and rode off with her down the lane to Dean Court, the neighbourhood running beside the horses with cries of execration and joy.

"Lord, what a nasty rout," Sir John Suckling commented. "Yammering like beasts for their prey. Do we go with 'em, Robin? As their pastor, you should do so, I think."

"Aye, to be sure. Where's Conybeare gotten to? Doctor,

you'd best let me take July home for my sister to mind; this is no scene for her."

"No. She's for coming to the Court to aid that poor creature so far as we can do't. At the least, 'twill be a friendly face for her to look on, and there's few enough on 'em, God knows."

"That's true. Still, my dear, you'll not like to see that canting witch-smeller at his nasty work."

Julian wore already a sick and curd-cream face; her heavy eyes were red with tears, and she twisted her hands together in front of her.

"You'll stop 'em, parson. Father, you and parson'll stop 'em hurting her. Mr. Yarde's kind, he's good, he'll not let 'em hurt her. We'll beg and pray him, by Christ's mercy."

"Christ's mercy, child? When have Christians e'er understood that? We Christians, God help us, are as bad as pagans in the black cruelty of our lusts and our fears. There go your Christian flock, Parson Herrick, yapping after blood like a wolf-pack, damn their filthy tongues and hearts."

"Damn them an you will; I'll not stint you. But they've a certain reason in their yelping; 'tis in part simply the cruelty of the beast, but in part a right wholesome horror of the works of darkness. Th'are maybe mistook in this old dame, but they howl against sorcery and the devil, and th'are right in that."

"Enough, enough. We think different, and there's an end on't. It's not the hour to brangle over differences, but for those few on us who are agreed at least in pity to stand together and try to save this poor creature. We both know she's no witch, and yet as that devil down yonder will prove her so, and as she'll then be tried, and lucky if not tortured, and if we can't save her, sentenced to hang or burn. There it is, and if we can't by any means let it, so 'twill be. This much at least I swear; she shan't suffer for long, for when I see as 'twill go agen her and there's no help, I'll despatch her myself with a quick poison and save her the rest on't."

"You'll run a grave risk yourself by that, my friend. You'd do well to keep on the windy side o' the law."

"Hell, do I care for the law? Beside, Yarde won't desire to inform agen me. He may be witch-mad, like the rest of you, and he's a stubborn old fellow enough, but he's a good friend and an honest kindly man. He may conceit it his duty to God and his country to sentence a witch to die, but he's no love of suffering and no malice."

"Aye, he's a just man enough, only when 'tis a matter of church government and the squire meddling with the parson's rights, and then he turns a very bigot. But the poor get justice from him, and when he deals 'em the whip and the stocks, they deserve it."

"That consoles 'em; cud, that must console 'em greatly," Suckling said.

"I mislike the whip and stocks," said the doctor. "Th'are the weapons of savages; but 'twouldn't come amiss to me now to see that bloodthirsty rout there get a taste of both."

"Yet when all's said and done, there's good in the mob," their vicar said. "They'll run yelling for blood now, but should any fall sick, there ne'er lack neighbours to sit with 'em, care for their children and their house, and give 'em alms they can ill spare. Look, they have more o' many o' the virtues Christ taught than have some of the richer sort. But they lack the gentle, knightly virtues; they be little generous to foes, they want valiancy and truth, and you can't hold 'em to their given word."

"They lack loyalty, honour and churchmanship," said Sir John.

"Aye, and they stink," said Julian, tearfully, diverted momentarily from her grief and fear by the ancient game of class abuse.

"So they do, surely," the vicar agreed, pleased to see his pet taking an interest in the conversation. "Aye, they do surely stink like brocks."

But the doctor angrily turned on his child.

"And wouldn't thou stink, if thou lived in some o' the hovels they live in, with no money to buy thee soap or a change of wear, and thy pigs and poultry scratting around thee? Ne'er let me hear thee speak o' the poor in the mass like that, for 'tis ungenerous and nit-wit." As a matter of fact, it reminded him of his wife, who had consistently done so, and he did not intend that Julian should grow up with any of her habits. She retired from the conversation, perceiving the justice of his rebuke. And as to that, plenty of people besides the poor stank.

"I would you could make 'em wash more," the vicar went on, riding a favourite hobby of his, and one on which he had written much verse. "And pull their rotten teeth out."

"I do my best," the doctor gloomily said. "But folk mislike to lose their teeth, however rotten. I look forward to a day when these miserable human teeth of ours be all removed as they come through and replaced by false. Nature's a very bungler in her trade, at the best."

"Not at the best, doctor." Sir John glanced at Julian, who, however, took no notice, for her thoughts had reverted to Mrs. Prowse, being carried to her doom on Diccon Trant's cob. In any case, she was in no mood for Sir John, and had decided that she did not care for the flattery of so philogynist a gallant, and, furthermore, that his nose was a trifle red.

"There goes that white slug to join the rout," observed Mr. Herrick, seeing Mr. Wilkin the witch-finder coming up the lane to meet the procession, a gratified smile on his face.

"Aye, there's the common pricker," the doctor growled. "Smirking to see his prey catched for him. But the squire don't like him; the squire'll not let him lay hands on her, if we put it to him as a matter of fair dealing. Question by torture a'n't permitted in this country more, and this pin-pricking and trussing-up's torture. We English are fools and brutes enough, but at least w'are less savage beasts, in these days, than the rest of Europe in the matter of legal torture."

"I fear we except witches from that humanity, my friend," Sir John said. "Witches is fair game everywhere. Any grace Mr. Yarde grants will be from his personal charity, or from his mislike for that nasty fellow yonder. Rat me, but a coystrell toad it is!"

The procession had passed Dean Burn, and were arriving at the Court. Dusk was gathering as Sir Ralph and his men clattered into the flagged courtyard, the people of Dean surging behind them against the iron gates that were clanged to in their faces by the Court stablemen, who had orders from the squire and his lady to keep the villagers without. Only the gentry were to be admitted. ("Gentry, forsooth! A rout o' country parsons, leeches and schoolmasters!" old Mrs. Yarde acidly commented.)

Julian, slipping out of the crowd in the hall, joined Meg, who stood throwing food to the dogs in a corner.

"Holla, July. So they ran old Prowse to earth in your house."

"Yes."

"Pity. I'd as lief she'd a-gotten away. I hate that witch-pricker fellow."

"Mr. Yarde mustn't allow him hurt her. My father swears it shan't be. Pray, Meg, entreat the squire to send the man off."

"I entreat my grandfather? Why, he never harks to me. Nor does my grandmother. And they both think 'tis only just and merciful as Moll should be examined for a witch by a man of experience afore she's tried, for she might prove innocent after all, and be set free without trial."

"But she won't. My father says the prickers always find

'em to be witches, for they receive twenty shillings for each witch."

"I'm sorry that toad will have twenty shillings. But old Prowse *is* a witch, Jule; we know that. She's overlooked all manner of folk and beasts. Aye, I know your father don't credit witchery, but then he's—July, shall I tell you what my grandmother calls your father?"

"No," said Julian, gloomily.

"Aye, but I will, for you should know. She declares he's an atheist, and don't believe on God himself, or on the Bible. That can't be true, can it? For there aren't no atheists, are there?"

Julian looked cross and embarrassed. "My father's an extreme good man, so he a'n't an atheist, for parson says atheists is wicked."

"Well," said Meg, tossing a scrap of meat to a wolf-hound pup, "it don't matter, and I don't care. But I knew Dr. Conybeare warn't an atheist. Some tell as he's a magician, with his potions and his pills, and that's why he don't come to church, but I don't believe that neither, for his pills did nought to cure me or Giles when we had the fever. I'll not admit any spiteful tales agen the doctor. Look, he's marvellous angry as he talks with Sir Ralph. Indeed, Jule, he'd best spare his breath, for he can't do nought to let the law, they say."

But Julian remembered that there was one thing he had sworn that he could and would do to let the law, if it should come to that; he could kill old Moll himself, and be tried for a poisoner. Her tears came again.

"Don't cry, July." Meg, with her rough girlish kindness, flung an arm about her friend's shoulders. "Moll won't suffer pain, for even if she be condemned to die at the stake, they'll strangle her first. Grandfather says he'll never let 'em burn her quick, witch or no. And she's so old and so poor, she's nought to live for. Lord, we can't cry for all the folks as get hanged, or we'd never be dry. Come, take heart and cheer, and throw Prince and Duke some biscuits, for I'm teaching 'em to sit up and beg. Th'are extraordinary ingenious in't already—see . . . Look, Sir John Sucklin's gazing toward you as if he would fain come and dry your tears. I think him a mighty silly fantastical gentleman, with his quips and conceits and flatteries. Lettice likes him; he's very well for her . . . See now, I believe th'are all going away. A'n't this the strangest uncomfortable day, nought but witches and prickers and grave talk and men brabbling in the hall from cocklight to cockshut."

Dr. Conybeare came up to them. Julian knew his angry white face, and how it boded trouble.

"Go home, child, with Mr. Herrick. He'll take thee to the parsonage, and thou'lt lie there to-night, for I stay here. I'll not leave Moll with that cursed pricker without I'm there to watch. Be off with thee, bud, and get a night of sleep, for thou wantst it."

But Julian did not get a night of sleep, for she lay with Mrs. Elizabeth, who snored, and with Tracy, who frequently and affectionately arranged himself on her chest, and over the parlour, where Mr. Herrick and Sir John Suckling sat until midnight, playing cribbage, conversing and quenching their thirst.

17

At six o'clock the vicar turned out into the still, dewy morning, pulled the church bell's creaking rope, and said matins in the apple-sweet, corn-decked church. He repented him of his night's excess; this morning he suffered from the ale-passion, a heavy head and an uneasy throat. God forgive me, he prayed, for I am fallen again into sin. Jack shall drink alone to-night, shrew him.

He said the psalms, and healing and comfort followed remorse. God was merciful, and would not chide a man too harshly for obeying nature. The punishment was an ill head, and that would pass as the morning wore on, and after the breakfast draught of buttered ale.

At the back of the little church knelt Julian, praying, numb and tired, for God's merciful pity, that he might perform a miracle and soften men's hard hearts. Aye, dear Lord, even if she be a witch, have mercy! And if she ben't, make 'em to know it and to set her free, for dear Christ's sake! And grant my father do no murder; oh, dear God, save him from that, for Christ's sake!

The sunrise gilded the apples and pumpkins, the earth-apples, sheaves of corn and golden sunflowers, and the twined branches of hop, as if the God of earth smiled on these gifts to him, even as he had smiled two thousand years since.

> " ut Baccho Cererique, tibi sic vota quotannis
> agricolae facient: damnabis tu quoque votis,"

the vicar murmured, having said the grace and risen to his feet. This harvest decoration he had devised pleased him greatly. He would surely repeat it in other years, unless it should be stopped by those cursed nosing beagles from the little man at Lambeth, who would not let a man alone to order his own church.

18

Each day the natives of Dean thronged to the Court, where, in the dark, armour-hung hall, the trial of Widow Prowse for sorcery proceeded before Mr. Yarde, the magistrate. Each day a cloud of witnesses appeared, were sworn, gave their testimonies and told their tales, in broad, burring Devon speech. Each day Dr. Conybeare rose to his feet and volleyed at them a fire of sharp ironic questions that pierced not their intelligences nor shook their certainties. The prisoner too was questioned; sometimes she denied, sometimes exultantly admitted, that she had worked the ills of which she was accused. Sometimes Dr. Conybeare shot his questions at her.

"Hark now, Moll. Did ye cause the death of old Jake Mudge by ill-wishing him?"

To that Mrs. Prowse replied, "Aye, that did I. Aye, chell warndy I wished him, th' old miching lollpoop."

The doctor turned, amid a murmur of surprise, to the magistrate.

"You hear, sir. She don't know what she says, or what she means. Jake Mudge stands in the hall at this minute, and has had not a day's ailing in years."

But after all, that only proved, as was pointed out, that God was sometimes too much for the devil and had protected Mr. Mudge from sorcery. Mr. Mudge uneasily crossed himself and muttered, and the squire said, gravely, "Even where a witch hath not power to harm, she should die if she hath the will."

"But by God, man, she's but a doting, dwallying old nit-wit, can't ye see it now?"

They could not see it; they saw instead the devil and his familiars in attendance on the wizened old lady who cowered maundering in the middle of the hall.

On the third afternoon, Mr. Harrison, the priest, gave evidence, as having attended old Hoon Miggle in his last illness. He was looked on by the magistrate and Constable without approval, as a popish spy, for the court favour to Papists had small currency in the countryside, and the squire was half inclined to arrest him for illegal saying of mass, only that he knew it would be useless, and that the fellow carried about with him a grace signed by the Secretary of State. His Protestant Elizabethan gorge rose against this licensed law-breaker, this abettor (doubtless) of popish plots who was permitted to move about the country as he would, working against the Protestant and reformed Church of England. Still, he took the fellow's evidence.

Old Mr. Miggle, said the young priest, had beyond a peradventure been bewitched and died of it. Yes, he knew sorcery when he saw it. Yes, he had seen much of it, both in England and abroad. It flourished everywhere, and was easily recognisable. The dying Mr. Miggle had exhibited all the symptoms of the bewitched.

Mr. Yarde inquired what these were.

Mr. Harrison replied, rolling of the eyes, foaming at the lips, writhing in pain, alternately sweating and burning, and wasting away.

"He had a fever," Dr. Conybeare snapped.

Further, Mr. Harrison proceeded, the dying man had declared himself bewitched, and could date his illness from the day the witch had been seen to put a curse on him.

"He had a quarrel with her, then?"

Yes, a continuous quarrel. The old woman, like Satan her master, had cherished a peculiar hatred against the Miggle family, for the flame of true religion that, with all their lapses and backslidings, they had kept alight.

"Enough, enough, sir," Mr. Yarde told him. "We wish not a discourse on true religion from you. The Miggle family are not generally credited to know much of that." (Murmurs from members of the Miggle family in court.) "All we desire of you, sir, is your sworn testimony in this matter of bewitchment. This you have given, and you may go. Mr. Herrick, have you any evidence to furnish? Be so good, sir, to step forward. You too was waiting on the old man in his illness; was he bewitched, think you?"

Mr. Herrick said he didn't credit any such matter. He agreed with the doctor that old Miggle had died of a natural fever, working on the weakness of age.

In his view, as a minister of God, was this old woman in league with Satan?

"I don't think it. In my view, 'tis but a poor crazed creature, with no power to harm."

"What makes you of that opinion, sir? Y'are a close judge of witches, belike?"

"Aye, tolerable close. I've seen a many of 'em in my time. They have more sense and understandings than old Moll Prowse, who's more fitted for Bedlam than for the stake, in my conceit."

"You know that the parish is full of those that swear themselves, their beasts, and their children bewitched by her?"

"Aye. The parish'll swear anything, pox take 'em for as oafish a crew of lying churls as never I saw."

"There he goes," his sister-in-law whispered to Mrs. Yarde. "He will roily and curse at 'em so, when he's in his moods. "But, lord, he knows well as the old lady's a witch.

Prue'll tell you that, and how he cursed her for setting her black cat on Tracy and nigh murdering him with poisoned claws. Aye, and she o'erlooked our hen, too, and let her in laying. But look, he's soft-hearted, and the doctor's talked him over, too."

"He shou'n't harken to that mad fantastical leech," Mrs. Yarde tartly returned.

Prudence Baldwin stared at her master with disapprobation, for she perceived that he forswore himself.

Such as they were, the vicar's were the last good words that Mrs. Prowse had on that day or the next. The parish came forward one by one, each with his or her damning, incontrovertible testimony. There was no doubt of it she was a witch.

On the fourth evening of her trial, the old lady, badgered and bullied with questions, burst into a passion, screamed, cursed, and when silenced, fell to whimpering like a frightened child. Dr. Conybeare muttered to himself, "I'll stand no more on't, nor she neither."

That evening, when the day's business was done, he went to see the prisoner in the closet where she was confined in chains by night, and gave her a draught from a phial. Shortly after, she fell into coma, and there was no more trial, questioning or testifying, and no gallows nor stake, for they found her a corpse.

"The dowl's took his own," said her guards, and reported it to the magistrate and High Constable.

But the Constable swore to the magistrate, "Rat me if 'twarn't that rookster of a leech that murdered her. First he seeks to hide her from the law, then he filches her from it with poison. Cock's death, but he shall swing for't. What a plague, sir, are we to let the poisoning of prisoners pass, and take no notice of murder because 'tis done by a leech?"

"We must not suppose any such business," Mr. Yarde

reproved him. "Dr. Conybeare attended her for colic and fits, and we must by no means charge him with her death."

"And I say we should by all means charge him wi't; aye, and prove it, by God; aye, and drive him from this place for a pestilent godless coxcomical knave of an atheist. Zart, sir, he should hang; he should stand in the pillory; he should lose his ears and have his tongue slit, he should——"

"Enough, friend Ralph, enough. There's no need of brangling and roistering. No crowner's sat on the corpse and pronounced it murdered, and we should by no means usurp his office."

"The crowner shall do so; 'sdeath, he shall sit on't forthwith, and the leech shall be charged. Damme, sir, if you are pleased to permit the murder o' prisoners and the defying o' the law in this hundred, I'm not, and there's an end on't."

"Peace, peace," said the squire. "We'll speak on't again, when you are cooler. For my part, I am not sorry the witch hath been took, for there was no doubt o' the issue, and 'twas a black ugly uncomfortable business. Now she's gone to pay her debts to her own chosen master, and we need have no further trouble of her. Please God we have no more witches discovered in these parts, for in truth th'are a most plaguey abominous pest."

"No question she should have hanged," Sir Ralph grumbled. "'Twould have been an example to others who may be minded to make such a contract wi' the dowl. Further, had we strangled her and burnt her body to ashes, she'd not have went again. Now, if in truth she's murdered, she'll walk. D'ye mind that old miser slain for's money up to Rattery four years since, and how he went again through a whole winter till his murderers was catched and hanged? No question but the witch'll walk, starkling all the countryside, and that'll make a pretty pudder."

"She shall be burnt to ashes," said Mr. Yarde, considering

this point, " and the ashes scattered to the winds by the parson, with bell and book. That'll keep her quiet, if Satan can't mind his own prisoners."

Still uneasy, Sir Ralph muttered, " She'll find a way; she'll by some means walk, pox take her, if we don't lay the leech by the heels."

19

The leech was not laid by the heels. The crowner decided that Mrs. Prowse was deceased of her own wickedness and the devil's finger; her ashes were scattered by the vicar with suitable ceremonies, and Dean Prior settled down again.

But many people looked askance upon the doctor, for rumour crept abroad concerning that last visit of his to the witch, and, though scripture said thou shalt not suffer a witch to live, it was not for private individuals, doctors or no, to step in thus. First he had tried to cheat the law by hiding the old woman in his house, then, when the trial was going against her, he had paid her a mysterious visit, and soon after she was found dead. Things looked queer, and Dr. Conybeare was received with suspicion by many of his patients. A doctor had overmuch power; he gave you a draught from a phial, and who knew what might be in it? If he had poisoned once, he could poison again . . .

" A pest on the churlish starkled nit-wits," the doctor muttered; and often fell to considering whether he should leave Dean and set up practice elsewhere, in some less bucolic spot.

" It might do Jule good, too," he thought. " The child's peaking and pining a trifle. I've a mind to take her away for a time to merry her humour and her health. This cursed business of poor old Prowse has been heavy on her; she's took it at heart. And no question we've gotten ourselves into the north of our neighbours' favour, and young folks care for that. Then, she sits too close at her books.

He looked from the table at which he sat with his own books and papers to his young daughter in her low chair by the hearth, her large forehead resting on one hand, her heavy eyes bent down to the lexicon on her knee. There was something listless, weary, dejected in her air, unlike her wonted diligent absorption. This her father noted; though he did not know that, between his child and her book, dreadful words seemed to hover—my father has done murder. Murder by poison. He is a poisoner; he has took life of purpose. They all whister and pister of it. Even Tib . . . One day they'll take him and try him for't, and perhaps he'll be hanged. He has done murder. . . .

"Jule," said the doctor (and at his voice she started with a violence that convinced him more than ever that she needed a change of scene), "Jule, how wouldst like to come away from here for a spell?"

She stared at him.

"Oh, father, I would like it extreme well."

"You would? Then you shall. You and I would both do well to leave this place for a time, afore the roads get impassable, and seek a change of scene. Where shall we go? Shall we visit your sister at Norwich? Or has your ladyship a gust to see London?"

"Yes indeed, father. Or——" Julian broke off.

"Or, bud? If you have another fancy, possess me."

"Cambridge, father, if you please."

"Cambridge! Y'are right; y'are very right, y'are extreme well-minded, bud. 'Tis very far, and the ride would stand us in considerable, but we could do't in a week or thereabouts.

We should be long on the road, but 'tis worth it. Aye, we'll go see Kit at Cambridge. 'Tis time as I looked into his studies and spake with his tutors. And there's a many of old friends there that I would gladly see. Books, too. Aye, Cambridge. Cambridge is going through stirring times presently, what with the noise concerning the etcetera oath, and quarrelling on church ornaments, and Dr. Laud's meddlings with University order, and Puritan factions and Papist conversions, and now the burgess elections coming on, and all the town and gown shouting for or against Oliver Cromwell and Nat Finch. Aye, at Cambridge we'll be in the heart of things. And I've a mind to talk with some o' the new men at Christ's, who are running after Plotinus and reading Descartes and setting up Plato against the Aristotelians. There's a deal of new thought in Cambridge since I was last in't. Look, chuck," the doctor was hurrying with his quick short steps about the little room, sawing the air with his hand and getting excited, "any new life that's to come into these dry bones of the Christian religion and of the education of the schools, that John Milton called a feast of thistles and brambles only fit for asses, will come out of Cambridge, mark me, not Oxford, maugre Mr. Hobbes that's now fled abroad from his own shadow, for Oxford's too straitly trussed about with Aristotle and Aquinas and the schoolmen to be loosed yet awhile. No, 'tis Cambridge winds as stir and blow the flame among the thistles and brambles, and may make us a reasonable educated country yet. Not as I'm much for this new Platonism, for it leans to the fantastic and windy, but there's a kind of rational moderation and light begins, aye, even among some o' the churchmen."

"Yes, father. And there's poets."

"Poets! Aye, perhaps. But you'll not find much moderation, nor much reasoning, among poets; moon's men all. Still, there's ever a plenty poets at Cambridge, for those as crave 'em; you can run after 'em, my chuck, to your heart's pleasure. That is, if Giles Yarde give you leave, for poets a'n't greatly to his mind, I think."

"No, 'tis pity. Giles his taste is all for games and sports, and he says his friends is the same, though his College has the most fame for poets in all Cambridge. But Giles don't matter. 'Twill be Kit as will show us the Colleges and halls and chapels, and the learned men in 'em. And he knows Mr. Cowley, and will perhaps quaint us with him."

"Why not? Whoever Mr. Cowley may be, if y'have a gust to quaint with him, chuck, you shall."

It has often been observed how ignorant of modern poetry are even the most intelligent fathers, and Julian thought that hers had better have a little instruction on it before he should disgrace himself, Kit, and her, at Cambridge, so she possessed him of something of young Mr. Cowley's achievements, which he sustained very kindly, pleased to see his child animated again. Possibly he was not closely attentive, for he broke in to say, "Well, since we mean to go, we'd best go suddenly. When canst be yare, child? Thou'llt want some gowns, perhaps?"

"Well, my cloes *is* all rather old. But it don't greatly matter; I can do."

"Oh, get thee a new gown and a new coat, or Kit will be shamed for thee. But get 'em suddenly; don't tarry, for what we can't take in our portmantles on the saddles must go by carrier, and will take longer on the roads."

"I think you want a new coat more than I do, father. All yours is extreme worn, and all over snuff, and the pockets burnt with your pipe."

"They'll do for Cambridge. I'll have 'em smugged up. Canst be yare in a week, dost think?"

"Aye, can I." Julian's cheeks had grown pink; her lexicon

had slipped from her lap, and she gazed out of the window, seeing not the orchard in the soft rain, but grey towers and great courts, and learned philosophers and poets strolling about them as common as bilberries in a furze patch.

"I'll write to Kit," she said, "and tell him w'are coming. And to Giles . . . I wish Meg could come with us, father. She would enjoy to see Giles. Then, if Meg and I was together, 'twould be less burdensome to you, for you could leave us more by ourselves."

"Aye, y'are right there. Not but what the little she-hoyden wou'n't get you in more trouble than ever you'd find out alone; still, I would like you to have her for company. Would they let her come, think you?"

Julian was doubtful. The doctor, she knew, was in poor favour just now with old Mrs. Yarde; she would surely never trust him with her wild granddaughter.

"You don't think it," her father voiced her thought. "And neither do I, for I don't stand well in that quarter now. So, unless the girl can herself fudge some exquisite reason why she must visit Cambridge and see her brother, we must do without her. Look, child, I have a notion; the parson shall entreat for her. Furthermore, he shall come with us himself. The project will be extreme cordial to him, for he escapes from his parish with greater content than a boy miching from school. Only we shall have some ado getting him north of London, for he'll be for turning off there and staying. But I'll tell him all Cambridge is dying to hear those verses of his that he carries about with him; that'll be to him as a carrot before a donkey's nose to coax him on. Aye, Parson Herrick shall come; his intellects fust, like mine, in this wilderness, where he hears nought o' the new theologies and heresies, that parsons should keep versed in to defend their flocks from 'em. Not that Herrick cares one scruple for heresies, nor theologies neither. Enough for him if he swears by the Protestant Church of England, her constitution and her tithes; damns Puritans and Papists, and can sit down and read of ancient gods and write of young goddesses. But, 'slife, th' old bawcock shall to Cambridge and furbish up his mind . . . Aye, bud d'you write to Kit and bid him look for us by All Hallows. But first I'll to the parsonage and speak with the parson, and pray him to entreat the old lady at the Court for that young limb, Meg."

20

Two days later the weekly post from Plymouth to Exeter collected as he rode through Dean Prior a bag of letters for Cambridge.

Dr. Conybeare wrote to his son Christopher, scholar of St. John's College.

"Child,

"When you shall receive this, y^{r} sis^{r} Julian & I, companion'd by her friend Megge Yarde, & by Mr. Herricke, soe you see we are a messe of foure, shall bee riding after it, bound for Cambridge, whither wee hope to be for All Hallowes. You'le admire that wee come thus on a sudden, without having wrote to possess you a great while since of our intencion, but I have bin something consarned for Jule, who hath bin out of tune this sennight past, no stomache to her vittels, & a heavie sadde languid aire, & I know not what physsicke to give her, beyond stiponie & possets, for 'twas her minde that was disordered, shee being extreme sadded by ye most hellish cruell hunting of that poore ould ooman Prowse, of wh: cursed newes I writt you afore this. So for physsicke more holesome then any rubarb or scamonie, I have prescribed a journey from here to a fresshe scene, to witt Cambridge; so cordiall to her has this proved that alreadie shee perks & bloomes agen, for, thinkes shee, she'le see not onlie her dere Brother, butt all ye larned world of Cambridge, & I know not what of philosophers, poets & schollers. Indeed, sonne, I'm of her minde, & look forward mightily to spaking with you & with many others, both ould friends and newe, for this rusticall life in Devonshire is the dullest uncomfortable tediose businesse, and fusts and sadds a man's witt & parts so as hee hath great envie for some ingeniose discourse & to larn agen how ye world waggs. I hope to heare good newes of y^r Burgess Elections, & that Mr. Cromwell & Mr. Lowrey bee well in, & not that time-sarving Nat Finch. But I forgott; yr College, Master & tutors is all of ye wrong color, & you perhaps for ye wrong men, pox take you. Wee shall lye at ye White Horse Inn in Kings Lane, where I have wrote by this same post to ye Host to looke for us on All Halowes E'en, so you need be in no case about that. Wee shall lye six nights on ye road. I heare ye small pox are greatly about the shires, & must take heed to chuse well our inns. Do you bee carefull, childe, & not adventure into ye more lewder quarters of Cambridge, lest you take them thus, though I have not hard if they be rife thar presentlie, 'tis more of ye ague as I've hard on thar of late.

"You have wrote little of late to mee, though more to Jule, who hath bin something private with yr letters, & discovers mee but a few newes from them. I hope you keep close at yr studies, & doe right well, & that Ile have a good report on you from yr Tutoure Mr. Cleveland, to whom pray commende mee with kindest resentments. We'le possess you of our arrival so soon as may bee after reaching Cambridge & you must ask permission of yr tutoure to wait on us att the inn on the following morning. Have to you, deare Boy.

"Yr loveing fr.

"Michael Conybeare."

Julian Conybeare wrote to her brother:

"Deerest Kitt,

"I have now to tell you ye plesantest chearfull newes in ye world. Ware comin to Cambridg, & shall bee thar by All Hallowes without ware held up on ye road by ill wether. Ant this extream wonderful goode newes. Mr. Herricke & Megge is comin beside. So Ile see you sudenlie, & wele spake on what you've wrote mee in yr letters of late, of all wh[ch] i have tooke noe notis to our Fr. as you bade mee. Indeede Kitt, hee woud bee extrordinarie vext & put aboute war you to doe any such thinge as you planne. But this you know very well, & Ile not spake on't more, for it shod not bee our cheefest consarn in this bisness of religion. Deere Kitt I doe hope as youle doe nothing rashlie, but will wait & talk with many good philosophers & clargie men, in wh[ch] Cambridg do soe abound. I wou'd talk with them too while I'm thar, & ask them a many things consarnin Philosophie & Poetry & Religione & else. Pray Kitt to let mee spake with Mr. Cooley, if it bee by any manes possible. I know he's of Giles his Colledg & not of yrs, but Giles don't fadge well with him, hee bein poetic & Giles all for games & sportes.

"I have much envie to see a Latin playe, & an Englysshe one too, also to here a Declamacion & Disputacion in chappel, particul[r] from you or Mr. Cooley, & to attende a Commonplace & a Problemme.

"I have wrote to Giles as w'are comin.

"Kitt, we have bin extreame sadd in Deane of late, &

are mightily glad to lave it. I woud I war yr Brothere & not yr Sistere, soe as I coud stay with you in Cambridg. I beginne to bee like Mr. Herricke, who doe ever rail on Denshire for a sadd dull tedoise countrie wh^{ch} he do loth but when ye sunne doe shine & ye floures bloome & wee goe a-mayin or a-primrosin, or sing harvist hoam, or revell att Church wakes & ales, then hee do like Denshire very well, & soe do I, when its fine & curiose wether & I can walke abrode in ye feelds & woodes & plucke floures. But yet I woud stay on at Cambridg for ever, for indeed i've small minde to returne to Dean, whar ye peeple is so cruelle, & reads nought niether, only Mr. Herricke & our Fr. doe, & th' are all agen him now & make havock of his name for y^{t} hee tooke part with poor ould Moll & don't allowe as there's wiches.

"But enough of this, for ye poste will suddenlie bee away. I have gotten mee some new cloes for Cambridg soe shall be verie smug & quaint, but our Fr. hant done soe, hele come in his ould, though I telled him as hee wou'd be a nay-worde in Cambridg & bash you. He says Larning shoud bee above such fripperies, & I am sure I hoap it bee so, butt none ye lesse have gotten you the culored hankerchers you writt on, & some frinjed gloves, & two culored weskits. I gott them in Dartmouth, what wee sailed down ye rivere t'other daye to merrie us but itt did not do so, for wee had not then conceited to travaile, & I was goin to sende yr thinges by Caryer.

"And soe goodbye, Kitt; my hart dances to see you soe suddenlie.

"Yr most luving Sis:

"Jukiane Conybeare."

"I have bin readin Mr. Cooley's Comedy *Naufragium Joculare*, y^{t} you saw plaied at Trinity last yeare. Mr. Herricke saies its poore stuffe, & indeed I dont thinke tis anything extrordinarie. Mr. H. bringes with him a packette of his verses, wch hee woud show to Cambridg. I hope they'le bee well thought on. Sir John Sucklin thought they was too much out of ye mode to-daie.

Julian wrote to Giles Yarde, at Trinity College:

" Deere Giles,

" Megge will have wrote to you to possess you of our cumin to Cambridg. I hoap y'are well. I have not bin very well, or soe my Fr. thinkes, but, I thank God, am now recuvered, & am marvaillose contente to bee goin travaillin. W'are left Rawley att ye Parsonage to bee cumpany fr Tracie & bee minded by Mrs. Eliza & Prew. Megge had noe minde to lave ye Dogges, & was for bringin one of ye newe lyttel puppes with her on ye sadell, to showe you, but Mr. Yarde wount lett her. Shee & I are minded to injoy Cambridg extreame well, & shall kip you busie showin us alle thinges, that is alle as Kitt dont showe us; you can divide ye burden, hee can showe us ye Libraries & Chappells & Colledges, and take us to alle ye larned diputacions, & youle take us to ye tenis courts & rivere & to see Cocks & bars fite & alle ye thinges you shou'd not, & we'le discover none on it to yr Granfr or my Fr, for you know w'are exceedin privit & discrete. And soe no more til wee meet, from yr luving shee-frind to sarve you,

" Juliane Conybere."

" Sir J. Sucklin left these parts since some daies, soe yr Sistrs & I are forsook, & must come to Cambridg to seek other gallant gents.

Meg Yarde (who spelt very vilely) to the same:

"Deere Gyles,

"Looke, ime cummin riden to Camebrij, with Jule & hir fr & ye Parsun & wele bee thar by Hallowes, wch plazes me beyonde meshur. Grann has bidd Nance make two gret pyes fr mee to bringe you, a massard pye & a kyd pye, both verie delcat & curiose. Wele ate em upp togither, fr youle sartinly bee obleeged to giv us sum intertanment & ye pize will spare yr pockitt. Theres a manie thinge I wishe to doe in Camebrij, see bars bated & cocks fite & menn playen tenis & bowles & roav aboute ye strits & goe a-rowin on ye Rivere, soe gett al redie to bee thus bisie when wee cum. From what Dr. Cunnibere ses it woud sim an eggstrordinrie tejiose dull towne ful of Politiques & relijun & larned menn brablin togither about bookes & lawes & church sarvises & nonsens, but you hant neer said its soe tejus, soe ile not beleeve itt. Pray tell mee whar in ye towne I can gett mee a Nife like thatt you have. Tis pittie Granfr wount lett mee bringe yu a lickle Pupp, Bess had six all doin well. Twas luckie Granmr lett mee cum, twas Parsun prevaled on hir, for shese tuk it verie hard agen ye Dr fr ye part hee plaied tryin to save ould Wich, & Gyles ye mussen saie itt to Jule but wee all conceet as he tuk hir lyfe with Poysin to save hir bein hangd & brent as shee wud of bin. If hee did soe twas noe harm, still hese then a merdrer as wells an aythist, & Gran dont like thatt. Shee was pruved sartin to bee a Wich, & had dun a manie to deth but ye Dr & Jule dont beleeve itt soe wee dont spik ont. But Jules bin soe caste doune wee conceet she doe suspishun as hir fr is a poysyinr. The villig dont like itt & itt sims as ould Wich walks nowe, tho hir bodie war brent & Parsun threw ye asshes about & praied but itt dint doe noe good for shee wauks still. Dont spik ont to Jule, who is now cum upp out of hir melanklie fitt & I hoap will staye upp fr pleashur of travlin horsebak & bein att Camebrij on wch hir hart is extream sett. I hav sum newe cloes, as Lettis ses my ould are a disgrase. Butt what's ye use since my cloes dont neer indure long, I bein egg-strordinrie unlukie with em. Still I shall luk fine & quent for a lickle spase & shal doe yu sum credditt in Camebrij.

"Yr sis:

"Megge Yarde."

PART II

ACADEMICK

Ye fields of *Cambridge*, our dear *Cambridge*, say,
Have ye not seen us walking every day?

ABRAHAM COWLEY

I

HAVING ARRIVED in Cambridge late on All Hallows E'en, weary from their long days on the road, the party from Devonshire were waked at six on All Saints' morning by a carillon and dashing of bells, from such an assembly of churches and of College chapels as the two young ladies had never beheld or heard before.

Meg, stretching and yawning in the big bed, mumbled, "Lord, to what a noisy religious city w'are come! Is the whole world off to its prayers?"

Julian was sitting up in bed, quickly unplaiting her two long pig-tails. "Get up, Meg, get up. This is Cambridge and past five o'clock, and a fine noisy All Hallows morning. We must up and out and about, and see the sights. Or at the least we must be up and dressed, for our brothers will be apt to wait on us suddenly, after chapel and breakfast. Beside, ha'n't you a mind to attend matins or communion in one of these fine ringing churches?"

"What d'you think?" said Meg, sleepily sardonic. "Matins and communion, forsooth. I can do that at Dean Prior, if I've a mind to't. Did I come to Cambridge to attend matins?"

"Will Mr. Herrick go to church?" Julian speculated. "If he do, I'll with him."

"He 'on't," Meg opined. "He's a clergyman of good sense, and he's on holiday. Depend on't, he and your father have both turned over and sleep again. And I'll not come with you, and you can't go alone, so you'd best bide quiet."

But Julian was out of bed, and at the window, flinging the

lattice open and looking out at the jumble of tiled roofs and grey towers and narrow crooked streets, already, though it was but the dark of the dawn, thronged with people hurrying to market or to church, and a few gownsmen in their round caps, and gowns of all colours, bound for the University Church.

Julian sighed, for she would have liked to go out to church at dawn on this magical Cambridge All Hallows morning. She washed herself and began to put on her clothes, her dark-blue gown and deep, lawn collar and white neckerchief that emerged a little crumpled from the saddle-portmantle in which she had carefully packed it. She brushed her blue cloak and broad black hat, and rubbed her neat buckled shoes until they shone; then she did the same by the slumbering Meg's, who would certainly do no such things for herself. After that she knelt by the lattice window and leant her arms on the sill and her chin on her hands and gazed at Cambridge, that home of learning, philosophy, and poetry, with its grey walls and towers, its courts and Colleges full of wise men. Where, she wondered, was St. John's, Kit's College, with the beautiful chapel he had told her of, its pictured hangings and painted roof, its candlesticks and gilded communion plate, its altar-coverings of velvet and silver, its organ and cherubim, its dove and glory, and the new east window that had been struck to show all these new adornments in a better light? And where was Trinity, where lived Giles Yarde and Mr. Cowley, and Christ's, her father's old College, and Mr. John Milton's College too, and now that of Mr. More, whom her father spoke of as a Platonist? Where was Peterhouse, that contained Mr. Crashaw, whose religious verses were, said Kit, though few as yet, the most lovely written since Mr. Herbert; and Dr. Cosin, the Master, the author of that book of devotions that Mr. Herrick said was unnecessary, since we have already the Prayer Book? Oh, there were a hundred of noble clergymen, Arminian, Calvinian, and Latitudinarian, who must even now be worshipping all the saints in church or chapel, and who would later be walking abroad, and might be catched sight on as they passed. There was Dr. Beale, who had so beautified St. John's Chapel; there were Dr. Whichcote and Dr. Holdsworth and Mr. Cudworth of Emmanuel, Dr. Fuller of Queen's, and a host more. Surely Kit could not go wrong in matters of religion for lack of guidance. . . . But, despite all this available guidance, Kit was inclined to become a Papist, and had been writing long letters about it to her which she had to keep very secret, since, if Kit's father and hers was to get wind of such a project, there would be such a praemunire and a pudder as to drive them all distracted. Julian hoped to be able, now that she would see Kit, to reason with him privately and dissuade him. He was three years older than she, but they had always talked and discussed and argued as equals. Julian had been brought up (as, indeed, had Kit) to disapprove firmly of Popery, which their father said was the most fanatical and cruel and superstitious of all the fanatical, cruel and superstitious sorts of religion that unhappily existed, and which had caused his own grandmother (among many other virtuous, stubborn, and unfortunate gentlemen and ladies) to be burnt to death at Smithfield. How Kit could think of embracing a religion that had burnt his great grandmother at Smithfield and was even now most firmly and efficiently burning Protestants and heretics abroad, confounded Julian. Besides, there were a host of arguments against it, many of them set forth by the Archbishop of Canterbury himself in a book; it was, as Mr. Herrick said, as much against reason, revelation, judgment, and the English spirit as were the un-English excesses from Geneva and Amsterdam. Could one imagine Horace a Papist, Mr. Herrick would ask; and would answer, By no means; Horace would have been a Church of England and Prayer Book man, had he lived in England to-day; his was that moderate and urbane spirit and sound, unfanatical judgment that distinguished Protestants as opposed to Puritans and Papists. So thought Mr. Herrick, but others, Julian knew (including her father), did not think so well of the Church of England's unfanatical sweet reasonableness, and would call the High Commission Court and the persecutions of His angry little Grace to witness.

It was all very difficult; and Julian would have been glad if people would not discuss religion, but would confine themselves to history and poetry. She thought, that if Kit had kept as closely as he should to his logic, his rhetoric, his history, his ethics and physics, his Aristotle, Ramus, Molineus and Gellius, he would not have been thus troubled with theological distractions.

Meg stretched and yawned again, and now fully awoke, sitting up in bed, her tousled red curls standing like a burning bush róund her small freckled face.

"Oh, gimmini! I must rise. Is't a fine morning, Jule? Will it shine? Oh, la, I hope 'twill shine, and that we can row on the river with Giles and walk abroad."

"It's as fine-seeming a morning as never I saw for November, and the sun rising through a mist. No question 'twill be fine this day, for it's All Hallows, and All Hallows always shines. And to-morrow 'twill rain, for All Souls. Mr. Herrick says as All Souls always rains, since the poor dead souls weep for their sins, and Hallow Day always shines, for the blessed saints do rejoice in their virtue."

"Aye, now I think on't y'are right, Jule, and Souls' Day *is* wet. So we'll go on the river to-day, while the saints smile. Is it salt, think you, the rain the souls weep on their day?"

"No. I think the tears the dead weep is fresh."

"Well, I would they ha'n't been so wicked, or wasn't so sorry for't as to plague us with their grief. Oh, y'ave been a good elf and shined my shoes. Will the boys come here early, d'you think?"

"If their tutors don't let 'em, and keep 'em at work. But no, it's a holiday. I expect they'll come instantly after they've breakfasted. I'm going to make sure my father's waked."

"Lord, those bells'd have waked the dead," said Meg, who had stripped off her shift and was rubbing down her long, slim, white-skinned body with a damp towel, as she had been taught by her grandmother to do.

2

Christopher Conybeare walked along the path through the river meadows from St. John's College towards King's Lane. He was a pretty boy, small and dark-haired and pale, like his father and like Julian, with the Conybeare grey-violet eyes, broad brow, and small thin mouth. He wore his straight dark hair undergraduate length, that is, cut round the neck to the lobes of his ears, for flowing locks were not encouraged at the Universities among those in statu pupillari. This mode, and his slender build and round cap and wide-sleeved gown, gave him something the air of a discreet page. His eyes had Julian's dreamy, speculative, brooding look, but his mouth was of a less fine and certain line than hers. He was happy to think of meeting his father and young sister, whom he had not seen since he had come to Cambridge a year ago, for Devonshire was too far for visits. He wanted to talk to Julian, and to show her Cambridge; as to his father, he was always good company and an affectionate parent, but Kit hoped that he would not talk very freely and at large in a manner that would discredit them both, for, really, he was *not* like most men's fathers, and did often make very strange observations very loud in public places, and, beside, had the most unseemly irreligious notions (like that of disbelieving in witches) which he aired abroad and which might make people marvel and frown. Kit also hoped that the doctor would not converse too closely with his tutors and masters, for, when he had done that at Blundell's, he had always been dissatisfied with Kit's progress and habits, and with the whole system of the education he was receiving. And he would never realise that to rail against Cambridge education to, for instance, Mr. John Cleveland, Kit's tutor, would be a monstrous impertinence, even though he was a Cambridge man himself. Furthermore, Kit had no mind that his father should hear any of the rumours that might be going about concerning his own association with certain Jesuits, and other practitioners of the Old Religion; or, for that matter, even concerning his ardent championship of the Laudian and Cosinist party in the perpetual quarrel between the ceremonialists and the anti-ceremonialists in matters of worship and doctrine. Though, as to that, thought Kit, it might be good for his father to learn a little of the good side of Arminianism, and to note how some of the best men in the community were for it; and to see how rude, uncivil, and ridiculous were the manners and ways of some of the Puritan party at worship (though the doctor held no brief for the Puritans, and, indeed, was the first to gibe at them; it was a great vexation to him that his elder son, Francis, now at the Middle Temple, had joined that party). But this matter of Popery was different; before anything could be discovered to the doctor concerning that, the ground of his somewhat vehement mind would have to be very carefully prepared indeed. It would carry no weight with him that conversion was coming to be quite a fashionable step to take; that at Peterhouse several of the Fellows and many undergraduates spoke of it, even preached of it, with sympathy; that Mr. Nichols, a Fellow of that college, had even suffered imprisonment last January for preaching a sermon seducing to Popery and speaking against the king's supremacy (though if anything could cause Dr. Conybeare, a naturally seditious man, to approve Popery, it would be this last).

It will be seen, therefore, that Mr. Christopher Conybeare suffered the usual doubts and tremors which afflict sons when their parents visit the places where they are receiving instruction. Still, he was an affectionate young gentleman, and, as he entered the raftered parlour of the White Horse, his heart rejoiced at the sound of the well-known voices from Devonshire raised in lively conversation from the oak table by the hearth, where the doctor, the parson, and the two young ladies ate manchets and caudle, and drank warm buttered ale.

Julian, her brother noted, had grown prettier than ever, and had a creditable enough dress, not so much behind the fashion as might have been feared. The doctor and parson were shabbier, and their clothes a trifle the worse for tobacco and snuff, but shabbiness was not amiss in elderly men, and often accompanied intellectual distinction; both appeared most animated and cheerful. As to Meg Yarde, that long, merry, freckled girl, Kit liked her, though he considered her rather too hoyting a tomrigg, and if she didn't grow more womanish she'd end a horse-godmother. It was very well in the country to run like a boy, and beat all others at barley-break, to chase a-foot after the hunt, and swing across country whistling her dogs to heel, but in Cambridge a sedater, more lady air was apt; unless she was careful, she would discredit her brother Giles, and be considered a ramp. Giles Yarde, though a duncicall hoyden himself, would prefer his sister to modify her striding rustic gait and free drolleries.

The Conybeare family embraced heartily.

"Y'are well, child?" the doctor inquired, his hands on his son's slim shoulders, looking with a delighted smile into the pale, intelligent face so like his own. " Y'are grown an inch; I'll swear y'are grown. So's July here, but she's more call to, at her age. Not that any of us Conybeares'll ever be of great stature."

" And none the worse for't," put in Mr. Herrick.

> " It is not growing like a tree
> In bulk doth make man better be.

" Though I must ask pardon of Meg here for saying it, since she's shot up like a young beech tree. Aye, a young copper beech, with that flaunting top to her. Here's a fine brace of young virgins w'ave brought to delight this sober University city, hey, young princock?"

" Come, come, parson," the doctor broke in. " Don't talk as w'ad brought mammets to a country fair. The girls are here to be delighted, not to delight, to see Cambridge, not to be seen by't. They a'n't queans looking for a hirer, but students seeking edification, hey, chicks? Meg desires nought so much as to be taken a round o' the Colleges, halls and churches, with a guide like her brother, who'll possess her of all the information concerning them, the dates of their building, the histories of all the worthies th'ave suckled, and of all the philosophies, theologies and heresies that have been argued in 'em. Do I speak truly, Mrs. Hoyting Tom?"

" I suppose y'are asking July, doctor, as that's no name of mine. At least, I'll promise as anything Giles is pleased to show me, I'll be pleased to look on, for he and I fadge tolerable well in the matter of sights; we both know what's tedious."

" And here the young bawcock comes to speak for himself."

Giles Yarde swung cheerfully in, kissed his sister and Julian, greeted the elderly gentlemen with warmth and Kit Conybeare with a grin, and said, " Y'are come in pudding-time. All the townsmen and gownsmen's astir with the elections, and with the new oath, and the new parliament to-morrow, and Lord knows what beside; we might see some sport in the streets this night."

"Aye, there was considerable brabble and junketing last night as we rode into the town," said the doctor. "So Oliver Cromwell won his seat. A lucky win, in my view."

"Lucky!" Kit exclaimed. "Mr. Cleveland says that by that vote Church and constitution are likely ruined."

"I must talk with that tutor of yours." Dr. Conybeare happily ruffled up for a fight. "He'll ruin the constitution himself with his mad monarchical notions, he and the rest of your obsequious College."

"Not a word against my first College, doctor." Mr. Herrick, having drained his mug, set it down with a thump on the oak table. "And not a word against your king, Church and country, in this loyal place, my alma mater and yours, and on a holy day of the Church, too. Further, not a word against John Cleveland, who's a very loyal ingenious gentleman, and writ some loyal honest verses about Ben, though, as to that, he didn't know Ben as I knew him, and why John Cleveland should be asked to write to his memory when I warn't, passes wit to conceive, and many have took notice on't to me. 'Tis I must converse with John Cleveland, doctor, not you, for I'll be bound he'd liefer talk of poetry with a poet and a friend of Ben's than of politics with a maggoty brawler such as you. A'n't I right, boy?"

"Mr. Cleveland enjoys to speak both of poetry and politics, sir," Kit discreetly answered. "But he most enjoys poetry as concerns politics."

Kit did not really believe that Mr. Cleveland, whose own verse was so conceited, metaphysical and political, would enjoy greatly Mr. Herrick's pastoral and rustic songs of flowers and fields. He did not like to wound the vicar by saying so, but in his heart he considered his verses old-fashioned, and not likely to be heard or read in Cambridge, at least by the younger set, with much esteem, and least of all by the ingenious, brilliant and witty Mr. Cleveland.

"Mr. Cleveland," he went on, "has a mighty witty broadside poem hot from the press about the etcetera oath. It's being hawked round the town to-day, as the oath is to be out to the University to-morrow. 'Tis called a dialogue between two zealots upon the etcetera in the oath, and it has some extraordinary stinging satirical lines. Mr. Cleveland is uncommon witty in his conceits."

"I grant, I grant. And he's mighty welcome to his wit and his conceits when he uses 'em to put the zealots in the pillory. I only would he could keep 'em in't, rat 'em for pestiferous canting knaves as all want their ears snipped."

"A damned unnecessary oath," the doctor said. "I'll ne'er sign it. Approve the doctrine, discipline and government of the Church of England as containing all things necessary to salvation, forsooth. It don't contain scarce anything necessary to salvation, to my mind, saving your presence, parson. But then you and I might not fadge as to the nature and meaning of salvation."

"Well," said Giles, perceiving that what with politics, and what with poetry, and what with the doctrine, discipline and government of the Church of England, he would soon be bored, "Shall we go out? What have you a mind to do to-day, sir?"

"Why, I shall go wait on some of my old friends at Christ's and elsewhere. I would like to see Dr. Bainbrigg again, and old Will Power, though he was wont to be a solemn, dull, learned fellow enough, and I'll wager his wits ha'n't been bettered by being Lady Margaret preacher nigh on thirty years. But I would speak with him and with the lot on 'em concerning this vile hollow system of education that they don't do a scruple to improve, for all Francis Bacon cursed it and young John Milton and all sensible fellows curse it too.

I want to know how much of Descartes has got over here; and what all this new Platonic philosophy comes to. Look, Kit, there's a young man, a tutor at Christ's called Henry More, as I must meet. D'you know him?"

"Yes, sir, I know Mr. More. He's a quiet man, very studious and ingenious and religious—goes little about. They call him the Angel of Christ's, for that he's so pious and so learned and so poetic, and wanders about with such a rapt air, as if he heard a quire of spirits singing to him. He's just completed a long poem on the soul—'Psychozoia,' he's called it. For a China orange, he'll read it out loud to you, so you'll have to walk warily and be discreet if you talk with him; unless you're so eager to be informed on the new mysticism that you'll willingly sit and harken for two hours. Every one likes Henry More. 'Tis rumoured he smells of violets and other sweet blossoms, so holy is he. I've never been near enough to him to get a whiff of that myself, but his friends say it's so."

"He can stink of a whole hedgerow of flowers for all I care," the doctor said. "I'll not hearken to his poem—that's more in your line, parson—but I'll wait on him and request him to possess me in prose of his views on philosophy and on the soul. If Plato's beginning to drive out Aristotle and the schoolmen a little, I am for Plato, though I would liefer more of Euclid and Archimedes than either. How much of mathematics do you know, boy? Scarce a demonstrandum or a faciendum, I'll be bound; and still less of science or astronomy. Nor will you know more on 'em when y'are through with your quadriennium, nor yet your triennium neither. Seven years I spent sucking the dry breast of my alma mater, and all she gave me for my pains was some scraps of schoolmen's logic, rhetoric and metaphysics, some Latin, I grant, a bare meagre scruple of Greek, a thousand commentaries on Aristotle, several tomes of schoolmen's logomachies and finical dry quibblings and dividings of straws, a smatter of Roman history, a mauseous surfeit of dead theology, and training in foolish disputations in the College chapel or the schools with such other young ignoramuses as myself. 'Tis something bettered here presently, they say, though scarcely so at Oxford, but I would know how far th'are gotten. What books have you been at of late, child?"

"Oh, Seton's Logic, and Aristotle's, with the commentaries; Keckermann, Molinaeus, Piccolominaeus; Florus; Ramus . . ."

"Enough, enough. It troubles me to hear the old stale tale of names. A pox on 'em, th'are so stale they stink like dead fish. Do you read M. Descartes any?"

"Not I. But Mr. More lectures on him at Christ's; he grows to be quite the mode here, particularly since Oxford damns him for being against Aristotle, Aquinas and the schoolmen. That puts him into good odour here with many, as you can guess. They've started a Cartesian Philosophical Society at Christ's, to which the Emmanuel men run, and some from Sidney. Mr. Cleveland don't hold with it, nor with Platonism. He judges it unsound, and that it leads to latitude in religion and fanaticalness in speculation."

"Both good things, chuck, both good things, so far as they go. I must by all means meet this Mr. More and his friends. But look, I would first meet Mr. Cleveland and speak to him about your work."

"Not to-day, sir; 'tis Hallow Day, remember, and we make holiday. Lord knows where Mr. Cleveland will be gotten to, for he's very busy and gay, and runs about with a finger in all pies. And this morning there's divine service in St. Mary's, where Dr. Power will preach his Latin sermon, and all the world goes there. I have permission to go anywhere to church to-day, since you are here. This afternoon you can, if you like, go hear Dr. Whichcote give his afternoon lecture in Trinity Church, or you can attend a tolerable ingenious commonplace in our chapel, between two reasonable learned lively fellows that will argue concerning the resolution of matter."

"Knowing nought on't, I'll be bound, except the Latin phrases for it. Still, I'll attend it, if only to make sure y'are so silly at this present as we was five and thirty years since. But I want none of old Will Power's sermons, Latin or English, god-a-mercy, so I'll not with you to church, either to St. Mary's or elsewhere."

"Shame on you for an atheistical recusant, man," Mr. Herrick said; "not to attend church on Hallow Day itself. Ne'er mind, young virgins, you shall come with me and with your brothers. And I'll wager as my pupil will understand more o' the sermon than either of 'em."

"And I'll wager," said Kit, "'twill treat more of the new parliament and our two new burgesses than of all the saints."

"Sit by me, July," said Giles, "and I'll promise to discover to you who are the masters and fellows, and learned doctors; yes, and even the poets."

Meg turned faintly pink with hurt feeling, because Giles was her brother and yet did not care if she sat by him or not. As to Julian, she would rather be informed on who was who by Kit, he being, she thought, more likely to be correct.

"I'll sit between you," she said, "so as you can each tell of your own College. And while Kit tells me of the learned doctors, you can be telling Meg of the great tennis players."

"No, July," Kit said. "Since to-day I can go where I please, come with me to Little St. Mary's, and let the others go to the University Church. I like better Little St. Mary's; it's smaller but more beautiful. Besides, I want to talk with you."

Julian, impatient to be alone with him, agreed. Disappointed, Giles said to Meg, " Then we'll not stay for all the service at St. Mary's, for it's extraordinary long and I find Latin discourses disgusting. We'll be in at the beginning, and before the sermon we'll out, and walk around the town. We'll down to the river, if you like."

The party thus divided, and, the bells being now in full clamour again, made ready to set forth to divine service, except for Dr. Conybeare, who, hopeless of finding any of his own acquaintances at leisure, betook himself for a solitary walk round the colleges.

As they left the White Horse, they met a gentleman that entered it; a small, slight man of somewhere round thirty years, fair-skinned, delicately and austerely featured, with long, smooth, chestnut hair on his shoulders. Mr. Herrick stopped and bowed to him. " Surely 'tis Mr. Milton. I recollect meeting you in London this spring, supping with my friend and yours, Mr. Lawes, after a performance of your *Arcades*. I am Robert Herrick."

Mr. Milton, a grave, distant and rather shy young man, bowed, while Julian gazed at him with open mouth, a lilt of lovely lines whispering through her head like a running brook.

> " The frolick wind that breathes the spring,
> Zephyr, with Aurora playing,
> As he met her once a-maying;
> There on beds of violets blue,
> And fresh-blown roses washed in dew . . .
> To behold the wandering moon,
> Riding near her highest noon,
> Like one that had been led astray
> Through the heaven's wide pathless way . . .
> Oft on a plat of rising ground,
> I heard the far-off Curfew sound,

Over some wide-water'd shore,
Swinging slow with sullen roar . . .
Far from all resort of mirth,
Save the cricket on the hearth,
Or the belman's drowsy charm,
To bless the doors from nightly harm . . ."

So this beautiful, elegant, noble-faced gentleman, who seemed to be a little bored, a little in haste to be on his way, even a little impatient, was Mr. John Milton, the one-time lady of Christ's, whom fortune had brought to visit Cambridge at the very same time as themselves, nay, even to lie, perhaps, at the very same inn.

"I am glad to meet you, sir," Mr. Milton politely averred.

"Do you stay in Cambridge?" Mr. Herrick inquired.

"Yes, sir. For the playing of my masque to-morrow night."

"*Arcades* again, perhaps?"

"No, sir. *Comus*. Good-morning." Milton bowed again to the clergyman and his party, and went into the White Horse.

"I should have telled you that, sir," Kit said to Mr. Herrick. "All Cambridge knows that *Comus* is to be performed to-morrow evening in the hall of Trinity. I'll warrant he was offended you di'n't know it, for they say he's an extraordinary proud man."

"Do him good," said Giles Yarde, who had noted Julian's gaping reverence. "All these budge poets and their airs . . ."

"Can we see *Comus*, Kit?" Julian asked.

"Why, yes. I had forgot to tell you on't, but I had meant we should go."

"'Tis a pretty piece," said Mr. Herrick. "An uncommon dainty pretty piece, but should be performed pastoral, not in a hall."

"Aye, they would have had it in the great Court, but for fear of rain and cold. And to-night (for y'are come in for the All Hallows' festivities) there's to be played in Trinity a Latin piece of Abraham Cowley's that was writ and played last year —*Naufragium Joculare*. 'Tis in part a droll on the schools and the disputations, and very ingenious and witty, and mimics some of the fellows and tutors. If you want to see Cowley, Jule, as well as half Cambridge beside, there's your occasion. But come, or we shall be late at church."

3

Kneeling in the little church, so dim, so charmingly aisleless, so reminiscent still of the college chapel for which it had served for three centuries until seven years back, Julian seemed to herself to have entered into another religious country from any she had trodden before. Here was a new Anglicanism, decorated with ornament, lit with tall tapers that flamed softly in brass candlesticks on the high-raised altar; a crucifix hung over the altar, and incense drifted faintly about the church. It seemed to Julian very lovely, and that if Kit could not stay in a Church where he could worship like this, he was indeed hard to content. How much seemlier was such a service as this than the communion service at Dean Prior, with the difference of opinion between the priest and many of his congregation as to whether they should come up to the chancel rails to receive or stay in their seats; with the determination of others to drink their full pennyworth of wine from the chalice; with the sermon that so often sent this or that worshipper marching out in umbrage. Here, all was quiet, all moved smoothly and in order, though there was a good deal of what Squire Yarde was wont to disapprove as " mopping and mowing " on the part of the clergy.

During the sermon, which was devoted to melancholy premonitions of the actions of the coming parliament and the mistakes of the Cambridge electors, Kit nudged his sister, and whispered, " D'ye see that man sitting in the chancel? That's Richard Crashaw of Peterhouse, the poet. He's the chaplain of this church."

Julian gazed at Mr. Crashaw the poet, whose name she already knew from Kit. He was in deacon's orders, it seemed; a pale, thin, dreamy young man, with visionary eyes.

" They say he watches and prays in the church all the night, sometimes," Kit whispered.

Julian was impressed. This was her second poet this morning; and who knew how many more would cross her firmament before night? Cambridge was indeed living up to its reputation and to her expectations. To-morrow evening, doubtless, she would see Mr. Cowley at Trinity, watching *Comus*, and Mr. Cleveland, Kit's tutor. As to Mr. Crashaw, he seemed to have watched and prayed something too long, for he had a wrapt, shadowy, almost emaciated look. If he was the chaplain of this church, it well accounted for its refined and exquisite grace. He read the gospel in the most mellifluous pretty voice in the world, contrasting very sweetly in its mannered cadences with the harsh, monotonous tones of the celebrant, and entrancing the ears of the young ladies of the congregation.

" It is not worldly to think on him," Julian decided, " for he seems not a man but a kind of angel, appointed by God to guide our souls upward. I am sure I think he is an angel, and ha'n't earthly parts. I wish he would help Kit."

She forgot Mr. Crashaw then, in prayers for her brother's

difficulties, for her father's scepticism and blood-guiltiness, and for her own worldliness and idleness and ill-nature.

When they left the church, Mr. Crashaw still knelt on in the chancel, a motionless, praying figure, as still as a stone effigy on a tomb.

"Have you consulted Mr. Crashaw on that matter, Kit?" Julian asked as they walked along Trumpington Street.

"Yes; I've very often spoken with him. He has been very kind, he and his friend Mr. Beaumont. He has a wish for me to go with him and visit Mr. Ferrar at Little Gidding, where he often stays—you know, Mr. Ferrar and his household live like monks, and pray day and night. But I don't know it would help me, for I cou'n't ever pray like that, 'twould be beyond me. Mr. Crashaw's extreme religious."

"But *he* don't think of turning Papist, do he?"

"He telled me he'd thought on't a many times, and I believe 'tis chiefly Little Gidding as has kept him out on't. That, and Dr. Cosin, the Peterhouse Master, he that built and decorated their chapel of late. Dr. Cosin's a great Church of England man, like the Archbishop, and follows him in order and ceremonial, and in making the university churches and chapels more seemly. People call him Popish, for his book of devotions and the rest, but he a'n't. He's for checking Popery in the University; all the same, there's been a many of converts of late, and several in Peterhouse. There was a tutor there, Mr. Nichols, sent for to London and shut in prison for preaching last January against the king's supremacy and for the Pope."

"Kit, darling, why *do* you desire to be a Papist?"

"Well, 'tis the old ancient church of this country, a'n't it? I know that Laud and Dr. Cosin and Mr. Crashaw and my Master, Dr. Beale, and the rest of the Anglican persuasion, do say the Church of England is the old church of the country, only reformed, and that it's the Roman religion has gone astray, but the Papists say t'other. There's some Jesuit priests in Cambridge, very learned, eloquent good men, and when I talk with them they make havoc of all the Anglicans say. And, as I see it, they have the right on't. Because look ye, Jule, there's no *authority* in the Protestant Church."

"There's Canterbury. Mr. Herrick says he's for ever putting his finger in."

"Aye, he *exercises* authority, but has he a right to't? . . . Oh, well, don't let's go over all those arguments and reasonings, for I have too much of 'em already. You know, Jule, what I fear, and what Mr. Crashaw and many men fear, is that the Church of England may go a-whoring after the Presbyterians, and fall all to pieces in sects, and that Rome will be the only safety. All this barbarous insolent Calvinian regiment—wou'n't you liefer have the Pope?"

"I wou'n't have neither," said Julian briefly. "I see no need. The Church is quite secure."

"It a'n't secure. Look, we'll come through this stile and walk on Coe Fen while we speak of how little secure the Church is. You should hear Dr. Beale or Dr. Cosin preach on Church disorders. Why even here in Cambridge we have the Geneva and Dort disease walking abroad, and men falling sick of the five points, though that affliction has been partly cured by the better discipline there is now than else. But you've but to go to the University Church during service to see the townsmen sitting about smoking and insolently doing God dishonour. What Popish church would permit such things? The Jesuits say none would. Yes, even in some of the college chapels—Trinity, for instance—half the men sit during the prayer, and some turn to the west door for the creed, and stalk in front of the altar without bowing, and behave in the most insolent barbarous manner."

"Well, that's for their chaplains and tutors to mend."

"Aye, but there's a great many of chaplains and tutors as approves 'em, and puts it into their minds to act so. Look, ours is a Church where one parson says bow, and another says, by no means, and there's no correct order. But the Roman Catholics have an order, and enforce it."

"But Kit, that's no great matter, since we can each go to the church that pleases us, and where they do the way we like. Even at Dean Prior, though it's not like that church we was in just now, Mr. Herrick makes the people act seemly enough, and turns 'em out when they don't."

"Aye, but if the Genevan party get their way with us, as there's a fear they may in this coming parliament, they'll out the Bishops and let all the seemly services we have now, and, some say, even abolish the Prayer Book. For they hate prelacy and the Bishops."

"If they should ever stop our church services, we should still be in no worse case than the Papists, for theirs a'n't permitted now."

"No, but to be proscribed is a better thing than to be poisoned and piecemealed, as the Puritan party would do to the Church of England. To be proscribed can be noble and grand . . ."

"Yes," Julian agreed. "And it can be extreme harmless and pleasant, beside, for, under Her Majesty the Queen and Sir Francis Windebank, they say as the Pope's party hold services openly in London, and the court ladies run after 'em, like to a new play."

"That's nothing to the case." Kit spoke crossly. "I'm no court lady to chase the fashions and make religion a toy and curry favour with the Queen. With me, it's a question of what's the truth. More and more, ingenious and informed men are turning to Rome, like to the only castle as is fortified against assault."

"Your Jesuits have telled you that," said his sister.

"Well, what if they have? Should they not know? I tell you, July, I'll listen no more to the flim-flam talked by Protestants about the Old Religion. It wearies me. The Jesuits know more of their faith, aye, and of religion, than do the Protestant clergy; and as for these cursed coystrell Puritans, they know not the first sentence on't, for all they cant and talk at length."

"You needn't hark to the Puritans."

"Needn't! When England's poxed with 'em. To be sure in the Universities th'are held well under in present, I thank heaven, but who knows how long that will endure? July, is our father extreme hot against Papistry?"

"He can't stomach it. He don't like the Protestant Church, but he hates Papists and Puritans worse, for he says as th'are both more fanatical, and Papists more barbarous cruel. He still has it in his head how they burnt his grandmother."

"Belike she deserved it. Anyhow, that's long since."

"Yes, but th'are still burning heretics abroad. You know how he feels on cruelty. He hates even the Protestant Church because of the Archbishop and his persecutions, and his pillories and his High Commission, and because, when he was a young man, he remembers three men being burnt in Kent for denying the Trinity. Indeed, killing by torture's most monstrous horrid; and you can't say, Kit, as the Papists don't practise and uphold that more than others do."

"May be. If so, 'tis because they know more of hell and its perils. . . . But look at witches; even Protestants would kill 'em by fire, or did so kill of late, for they say th'are apt to strangle 'em first now, in this country."

Julian refused to look at witches; she would never willingly look in that direction again. "Don't mind witches, Kit. Let's not talk on 'em."

"No, I'm sorry, Jule. I had forgot how you was catched in

that business of late. But tell me one thing"—he looked cautiously round him and dropped his voice, lest other walkers on Coe Fen should overhear—"do our father truly and without question deny witchcraft and sorcery?"

"Yes," said Julian uncomfortably. "You know what he is, Kit; all hot out after any scent he's on."

"But 'tis against everything—all religion and Church teaching and the Bible, and all the history of the whole world, as well as what's presently about us and beneath our eyes. How can he think so?"

Julian sighed. "He's most strange and unbelieving in all things. He even questions astrology. Mr. Herrick says he doubts everything but medicine, and there he's as fond as any necromancer, it being his hobby. Mr. Herrick says since father doubts his spells, and he father's, th'are well quits."

"July, think you he do truly question religion? For that would be atheism."

"I greatly fear he do, Kit. But perhaps he believes more than he thinks he do. That's what I hope."

Dr. Conybeare's two children walked for a moment in silence, troubled and confused.

People, thought Kit, seemed to have all kinds of fathers, and some of them were a great pity; but never had he heard of any one else having a father who was an atheist. That is, a real true atheist, not merely an atheist in the sense in which the word was flung about as a depreciatory term by members of all religious parties concerning the views and habits of the others.

"Well," Kit sighed, "it's time we returned to the inn and met them for dinner. . . . July, if my father doubts all Churches, I don't truly conceit as it concerns him greatly to which I belong. So I shall take no notice to him on't yet."

"Do not," said Julian, relieved. "And neither will I. But

pray, Kit, do nothing in haste but seek counsel with many wise advisers in the meantime. Perhaps you could wait until y'are finished with Cambridge, so as you can do your work here with the less interruption."

"Finished with Cambridge! I am only in the second year of my quadriennium yet. I can't wait a life-time to decide on my religion. And look, life in Cambridge a'n't easy; a man needs help from religion if he's to lead a decent godly life here. I tell you, 'tis no easy task to be virtuous in Cambridge."

"Nor elsewhere. Cambridge a'n't wickeder than Dean Prior, I'll swear. Nor than London, if Sir John Sucklin's in the right, for he says many live like hogs there, though Mr. Herrick runs it for first place after Paradise. For my part, I opine as it's the world that's wicked, and not one place in't nor another. Though Cambridge has no call to be wicked, having all these fine churches and colleges and pious learned men in't."

"That don't hinder wenching and dicing and taverning, and riotous living," Kit gloomily said. "All the churches and learning in the world don't let a man from living like a hog if he's the mind for't." Julian was grieved to hear that Cambridge so nearly resembled Dean Prior.

"Still, we can always pray to God for virtue," she suggested.

"Aye, but prayer's easier if w'are sure in our minds about the sacraments and other. And I like, beside, to pray to our Blessed Lady, and to practise confession to a priest."

Julian was shocked at such preferences, believing both these exercises to be superstitious.

"Not," Kit went on, "that I don't use—or did not till of late—to make confession to Dr. Cosin, who sits in Peterhouse Chapel on vigils to hear any who come. But Father Dell says as the Protestant clergy ha'n't gotten the keys, so 'tis of no use. He tells too that if I was to die on a sudden now, I should be lost, since I've seen the truth and not accepted it, and am yet in my sins. I've a great mind to going over, but very secretly from my father, till all's done and can't be revoked."

"No, Kit, pray wait. Have you spoken of it to your tutor, Mr. Cleveland?"

"He has spoken to me on't, for he knows I am much with the Catholic party, and seeing the Jesuits. He bade me be discreet and not fall under their influence, as many have done. But I di'n't tell him much of my mind, for he's not greatly concerned with religion. He's a loyalist and a Protestant and all for the king's supremacy, and he suspicions the Jesuits for Pope's beagles and believes on a Popish plot. But he's too busy drolling on the Puritans and on the Scots and on Oliver Cromwell and the new parliament to think much about the Papists. I like Mr. Cleveland very well; he's very witty and pleasant, but I can't talk with him as I can with Mr. Crashaw, for he's all of this world and ha'n't gotten a foot in t'other; he wou'n't understand. You'll know what I mean when you meet him. . . . I hope my father won't talk to him in any unseemly way, for he'd be amazed, and after he was gone he might droll on him to others. But I wish my father would tell him as I'm to have more money in my purse, for indeed I can scarce contrive on what I get now. What with clothes, what with books, what with everything, each week stands me in as much money as I'm given to spend in a month—or would, if I should pay my debts, Lord forgive me."

"I'll speak to father," Julian promised. "But indeed, he's gotten very little to spare, and now he's away from his patients, and lodging abroad, less. I think you'll have somehow to make shift, Kit. Is life in Cambridge very costly?"

"Wonderful costly," Kit sighed; and Julian once more concluded that Cambridge must be, in the important matters, very like the rest of the world.

"But look what you get for't," she added, sighing in her turn. "How I wish I was a man, and could stay up here and read and learn."

"Aye, 'tis pity, since y'are so apt and quick at books. You could be better employed here than Giles Yarde, who never willingly opens his books or attends his lectures, and has no more Latin than they flogged into him at school. Still, he enjoys himself mightily, and has more money to turn than I have, though he complains he's stinted and can't pay's debts. But then few here can do that, not even the rich. 'Tis opined to be the last extravagance."

They were now returned to King's Lane and the White Horse, at whose door their father and Mr. Herrick stood and smoked their pipes.

"Y'are late, chucks; 'tis past time we dined. Kit, you can stay and dine with us? Good. Well, I've been around the old place, and seen some changes. That's a fine new chapel Peterhouse has built itself. And John's Chapel, into which I looked after the service, is smugged up so you'd scarce know it. Your Master seems to have the measure of Canterbury's foot pretty well, Kit."

"'Tis very beautiful, sir."

"Oh, aye, 'tis very beautiful, 'tis very exceeding beautiful. Candlesticks and silver altar-cloth and paintings round the walls and all. I make no complaint on't; 'tis very fine, and will make Mr. Herrick here, when he shall see it, die of envy to have the like at Dean Prior. And then I visited Christ's, and stood under the old mulberry there once more. I see th'are constructing new Fellow's buildings in the Second Court, that'll look very well, as I judge from the designs. I made no visits, conceiting every one would be at church; but I swear I spied the Angel of Christ's, pacing up and down the Fellows' garden with his book—a spare young man, pale and olive, that slipped away as shy as a fawn at sight of a stranger. I must quaint with him later."

"Come, sir, 'tis time we quainted with our dinner," Mr. Herrick reminded him. "And I'll warrant w'are all sharp set, for if you saw the sights, we sat under as long an eloquent rolling *clerum* as never I heard. Old Will Power was in fine fettle, and thundered at us of doom and God's providence, sin and grace, the Divine Right of Kings and Bishops, and the Divine Order Ecclesiae Anglicanae, till you'd have wished all the new Parliament sitting in a row to hear him. But one of 'em, at least, was there, for I saw Mr. Cromwell sitting in front with the Master of Sidney, and hearkening most polite and attentive, and I hope it profited him. They say he's a fair Latinist, and can both talk and understand it nimbly, so 'twarn't lost on him, as 'twas on Giles and Meg here, and, I'll warrant, on half the congregation beside, for a very rabble of townsfolk lolled and behaved themselves unseemly at the back, the half of 'em only come there to gape at Cromwell, I'll be bound, and to show contempt for God's house and God's ministers. And as we came out, a mob of 'em lined up and shouted for Cromwell, and when Power passed by behind the beadle and mace they cried "A Pope, A Pope," like so many silly Bedlams, and he a staunch old Protestant of forty years' ministry, I think the popular party is beside itself with spite and unreason."

"They don't like the Latin sermon," Kit explained. "They've took to shouting at it of late. Yet none forces 'em to attend it, indeed none wants 'em at it. But they delight to speak spiteful things of anything that's too high for 'em, and will go out of their way and spite their own selves to do't."

"Aye, th'are a monstrous barbarous uncivil ignorant lot, pox take 'em and God defend England from their breed. Let's forget 'em, and eat and drink, a health to His Majesty, the Church and the State, and to the ancient Latin tongue too, hey, Giles?"

"Aye, sir, and let 'em all stay in the places heaven was pleased to appoint for 'em, and not stray out of 'em."

"If you mean, young dunce, as you think heaven di'n't appoint Latin for use in the University Church for an All Hallows' *clerum*, may God forgive ye, for I'll not."

4

Trinity College hall was full by half-past seven o'clock of a triumphant audience, hailing not only from Trinity, but from the university at large, and triumphant in that they had succeeded in rushing in and securing places when the doors opened, to the defeat of the large, noisy and annoyed crowd outside, in whose faces the guard had now locked the doors, opening them only for the entrance of such privileged persons as masters, doctors, and important guests, for whom places had been reserved. For the majority, seats were obtained not by ticket but by scramble and physical prowess. Giles Yarde had triumphantly, with the help of two other athletic Trinitarians, pushed his party in and seated them not too far down the hall. Having done this, he joined with his fellows in exchanging cat-calls and loud insults with the defeated outside. "Yah, you dirty Johnians," was a frequent cry from Trinity men; from which it appeared that many members of the society of St. John had failed to gain admittance. But when Trinity uttered this cry, the St. John's members of the audience, who seemed to be plentiful, made noisy repartee, alluding frequently and unflatteringly to discreditable events in the careers of Trinity men, and inquiring, when other matter failed, who had won the battle of the Great Gate.

"That's well said; aye, that's very well said indeed," exclaimed Mr. Herrick. "D'you mind the Great Gate fray, Conybeare? I was in the thick on't, being at John's at the time. They wou'n't let any Johnians in to Trinity for a comedy as was to be played there, and we fought 'em outside the Great Gate, aye, and drove 'em well back into their court and up against their college walls. Aye, there was a many broken heads that night and a many brought up afore the Vice-Chancellor's Court for't afterward. But we had the better of Trinity; aye, we had 'em well on the run, crow you as loud as you may now, young bawcocks. . . . In those days, I mind, we let no ladies in; and now here are several, and without a mask among 'em, so bold are females gotten to be, Jule, prinking it among the men. Come, let your bawling, boys, and resolve us who are the mighty, for I see proud creatures taking their seats in front there. Some I know; there's Whichcote and all the Emmanuels—no, not the Master; I don't see Holdsworth."

"No, sir," said Kit; "he'll come in later with the Vice-Chancellor. They'll sit immediately before the stage, next to the Master of Trinity. But look, there's our Master."

"Aye, there's Beale. Who is the tall young man he speaks with?"

"That's Mr. Cleveland."

"Oh, that's your tutor, is't? Well, he's a proper comely kind of fellow, and looks like he had a wit. I would speak with him, but I suppose he'll not come so far back in the hall as this; he seems properly busy with it all, and to be having a word with every one."

"He's to make a speech before the play begins."

"How does Trinity permit that, in their own hall?"

"Indeed, I hear they don't like it much, but the Vice-

Chancellor desired him to do so, he being Rhetoric Reader, and a very easy and witty orator, full of quips and sly turns, and better and more practised than Trinity can show. But there's some fear for what he'll say on politics, if he touches 'em, for Cromwell is to be here, and Mr. Cleveland loathes him like the devil. Some say as the Vice-Chancellor desired him to speak instead of a Trinity orator because he cou'n't endure to hear all the compliments and flattery that might have been poured forth on the new town burgesses, Trinity being in the main not over loyal to the King and Church."

"Y'are a liar," Giles remarked, truculently but something mechanically, for he was listening to the shouting without, and hoping that some windows would be broken, since they were only partially netted against assaults this time, not taken out, as was often done on these perilous occasions. He was also trying to catch the eye of a stage-keeper who was carrying mugs of beer about among the audience.

Kit, taking no more notice of this remark than it deserved, said to his sister, "If you want to see poets, there's a plenty here. Cowley's behind the scenes. He'll speak the Prologue and Epilogue of his play. So you'll see him suddenly, but masked. But there's Andrew Marvell; he's a Trinity scholar, that took his B.A. last year, and has wrote some pretty verses that he says he means to publish later, when he shall have wrote more."

Julian looked at this dark-haired youth with indifference, not deeming his poetic condition to be anything above her own. It was Mr. Cowley whom she was eager to see; Mr. Cowley, who had blossomed poetically (and in print) at the tender age of ten years, and continued to blossom ever since, and was now already an experienced and accomplished playwright.

The Master of Trinity now entered the hall, accompanied

by some of his fellows, little Dr. Duport, the learned Regius professor of Greek, trotting among them.

"Listen, when the play is on, to that small man laughing," Giles told them. "'Tis like a cock crowing, and he sends it forth all alone, when none else laughs, and sets every one in a roar. He'll do't in one of his own lectures; I sit under him on Theophrastus, and I swear many of us don't heed a word he says, but only wait his laughing, and then we burst out ourselves, as if we seed the jest he's made, and he's mightily pleased, not knowing 'twas but his screech that set us off. He thinks the plays should be neither in Latin nor in English, but always in Greek."

"I mind his father," Dr. Conybeare said. "He was Vice-Chancellor in my time. I hear this little fellow's a most obstinate Aristotelian, and all against the new Platonic studies."

But of this Giles knew nothing; he imagined that Dr. Duport would like any studies that were Greek.

"Look," said Julian, "here comes Mr. Milton." Mr. Milton was walking on one side of the Master of Sidney, and on the other walked the newly elected city burgesses, Mr. Oliver Cromwell and Mr. John Lowrey. Julian thought Mr. Milton and Mr. Cromwell a strange contrast; the one so neat, trim, elegant, fair, and austerely beautiful; the other a great sloven of a man, heavy-featured, red-nosed, and unkempt.

The passage of the burgesses through the hall caused a stir and murmuring, not, on the whole, friendly. Among a group of St. John's fellows and others stood the defeated Sir Nathaniel Finch, Mr. Cleveland's hand on his arm. This group looked coldly and disagreeably on the successful burgesses, registering a haughty distaste. The Emmanuel and Christ's undergraduates, on the other hand, raised a cheer, which might have been either poetic or political, for Mr. Milton or for his companions.

They all took their places. There lastly entered, with more of ceremony, Dr. Cosin, the out-going, and Dr. Holdsworth, the in-coming vice-chancellor. By this time the audience were stamping and calling for the curtains to be drawn. The guard, armed with cudgels and links, still kept watch on the doors, lest the excluded should attempt entry by assault.

"Now Mr. Cleveland's to orate," Kit told his companions, and Mr. Cleveland was seen to ascend the stage and stood before the black velvet curtains. A tall, vigorous, well-built young man was Mr. Cleveland, handsome, with short, satirically curled upper lip, full, firm, cleft chin, fine head of long, curling, brown hair. Julian thought that he looked a wit, and something contemptuous. He was popular, it seemed, for he was greeted with shouts and cheers, even from an assembly predominantly Trinitarian, but with the cheers were some hostile groans and derisive cries.

"He's always liked," Kit exclaimed, proud of his tutor; "but presently more than in general, on account of the pains he's been at during the town elections, to bring in the loyal members. He's been speaking in public everywhere for Finch and Meutys, and against Cromwell and Lowrey; and is in a great passion now, as are most of the university."

"Lord forgive him, he speaks in Latin," Meg sighed to her brother. "Is all Cambridge crazed with the Latin tongue, that it's forgot its own?"

"Yes," Giles gloomily replied. "But we need not listen."

Mr. Cleveland was a graceful and eloquent orator, referring only now and then to the paper he held unobtrusively in his left hand, and using his right for delicately emphasising his points. He began by complimenting the Vice-Chancellor on his much esteemed presence on this auspicious occasion, and made a pretty encomium on the splendour of his years of office, on the good he had wrought in the university by beautifying not only the chapel of his own college, but the services and discipline of all the churches; by restoring the University Church of St. Mary's to decency and seemliness, from the disorderly confusion and litter of recent years; by his labours towards the building of a University library and Senate house, by his generous gifts of books to the library of his own college, and finally by his unswerving and loyal upholding of the Church of England and the constitution against all malevolent attacks, from whatever side. For this, said the orator, he had been a victim already of persecution from spiteful, vindictive and irreligious fanatics—(" He speaks of Peter Smart and his complaint against Dr. Cosin to the April parliament," Kit whispered, " and in this parliament 'tis said 'twill be brought up again, and suddenly.")—and doubtless the persecution would now be resumed, in this present loyal and most religious Anglican Parliament to which the citizens of Cambridge had contributed, by their recent vote, two most loyal and religious Anglican members. (Groans and ironical cheers. The two members looked with interest round the hall.) Anyhow, Mr. Cleveland continued, there were two gentlemen present, Sir Nathaniel Finch and Mr. Meautys (prolonged cheers, and a few triumphant cries from the opponents of these defeated gentlemen) who had done their best that such a contribution should be made by Cambridge town, as it had in fact been made by the University in its election of its own burgesses, the illustrious Dr. Eden and Dr. Lucas. He would have them know that the good-will and support of the most loyal University of Cambridge was with them.

Mr. Cleveland waited calmly until the mixed, but mainly friendly, noises provoked by this statement had a little subsided, before proceeding to remark that, in whatever factious onslaughts might be made upon their illustrious Vice-Chancellor, even by this most estimable Parliament which was to meet in two days, he would have the support of his university; and finally, he offered his congratulations on his new preferment to the Deanery of Peterborough, a richly deserved addition to his mastership, for alas, college masterships were but meagrely paid. His last official function as Vice-Chancellor would be the administration of the new Oath of Allegiance to the Church of England, to which some discontented persons had taken exception, finding some strange cause of offence in the harmless word " etcetera " by which the framers had spared themselves the trouble of enumerating every order of the Church. (Cries of " Your verses, sir; give us your etcetera verses.") No, he would not detain the audience by reading any compositions of his own. He would only wish this oath a smooth passage down the throats of those who should swallow it, and that the indigestion of those with whom it should disagree might not prove fatal, for he wished no man ill. He concluded with some elegant compliments to the illustrious assembly of Masters, Doctors, Fellows, Tutors and Scholars, now gathered together to witness again this *Comedia Jocorum* by the youngest and one of the most ingenious poetic sons of Trinity (that illustrious College of poets). This famous poet, the prodigy of the muses, who had been delivered of poetry at the tender age of ten years, when most children were busy only with games and balls, who had been illustrious at thirteen years, and now, at two and twenty, had already a long life of achievement behind him (Julian sighed)—this prodigy of literature was waiting behind the curtains to speak the Prologue to his own play. Exit, then, the tedious orator and appear the playwright.

With which the smiling Mr. Cleveland stepped down from the stage amid applause and took his seat among the Fellows of his College, and there stepped before the curtains the slim figure of the poetic prodigy, violet gowned, a purple velvet mask over his forehead and eyes, revealing a thick nose, full mouth and round chin. Light-brown hair grew back from his high forehead and clustered to his shoulders. He was a handsome poet, and withal of a modest and even bashful demeanour, and lacking Mr. Cleveland's cool and practised self-possession. He began in clear and sweet tones his prologue:

"Exi foras inepte; nullamne habebunt hic Comoediam?
Exi inquam, inepte; aut incipiam ego cum Epilogo . . ."

and Julian thought, "I am hearing Mr. Cowley speak."

The play began, and the audience settled down to listen, to laugh, to talk and jest with one another, to smoke, to eat oranges and drink beer, according to its taste.

"Oh, I think a Latin play's tedious dull," Meg whispered, stretching in her hard seat. "Can't you and I slip out, Giles, and go somewhere more diverting?"

Giles was doubtful.

"We can't go out during an act. We might at the end of the first act. But we had best not, for we cou'n't come in again, and 'twill go on late. Beside, I must stay and get you all food and drink, as it's my College."

He could, thought he, at least play the host to Julian, and show her that he was a proper Cambridge man, even if he could not talk books and poetry to her, or do anything to make her gape at him as she had just now gaped up at that self-conceited fellow Cowley while he spoke his silly prologue, or listen in absorption, thin black brows drawn together, white forehead puckered, as she was now listening to this tedious comedy. If it had but been she that had whispered in his ear, "Can't you and I slip out, Giles . . ."

Poor Meg was weary of the sad stuff already, but poor Meg must sit it out and bear it, as must poor Giles.

5

Mr. Herrick was pleased with the comedy. It derived from Plautus perhaps too obviously; in fact, it derived from many sources, but it went well. It took him back to the old days, when he had been a young Johnian, and had sat at the back of this same hall with a friend—who had it been? John Weekes, was it, or Clippesby Crew—on the night when some German Prince or other had been there, and a dull comedy had been played and had lasted five hours, and the Prince had slept, and so, indeed, had many others.

But there had been a better evening later, when King James and Prince Charles had visited Trinity, and they had played *Ignoramus*, by Ruggle of Clare, and the King's loud guffawing had filled the hall. That had been a witty farce indeed; more witty and ingenious than this young fellow's, though this was well enough. But George Ruggle had been a wonderful droll wit; how angry the lawyers and the Recorder had been with him for the play!

There was more wit in Cambridge in those days, thought Mr. Herrick; aye, there was more wit everywhere. More wit and more poetry, and belike more learning. Cambridge had had a different look. The boys had worn their hair short, and the men had half of them worn beards, and some of them piccadillies. And they had been for ever in trouble for wearing over-large shoe-roses, ornamental cuffs, gay-coloured gowns, parti-coloured stockings, and long pipes, which they had smoked in the streets and even in chapel and church. What a pudder there had been about smoking the year King James had come! The young men still smoked and wore coloured gowns and gay stockings, but now half of them had long curls on their shoulders, though some, like Kit Conybeare, obeyed the university rule and wore their hair only to the neck.

Well, it had been a gay time, full of friendship and jollity, though notably empty of purse; he had been kept so short by his uncle that he could often pay neither for his books, his clothes, nor his tutor's fees; though life had been less costly after he had moved to Trinity Hall. With it all, ginger had been hot in the mouth, and ale had tasted good. Had they led a wilder life than these young men led to-day? Young Kit looked thoughtful and virtuous enough, with his pale, grave face, almost the spit of his sister's, only weaker about the mouth; but the red-headed Giles was probably a young rakel. Did the boys dice and fight now, go to cock-fights and bull-baitings, and visit the Rose, the Dolphin, and the Mitre, and make love to the town wenches? Did they hire horses from old Hobson—no, old Hobson was dead nine years since—and ride up to London in term-time? According to what one heard, rules were something stricter now, and harder to evade.

Not that life had been all play. He had been attentive at lectures; he had taken part in common-places and problems, read his rhetoric, logic, ethics, Peter Ramus, and Roman history, and worked for his degree. He had read Roman and Greek poetry, and written English poetry; he had belonged to a little circle of poets, who met in one another's rooms and read one another their verses. . . . A magical time, poverty and all. He had written some of his best verses then, even before he came up to London and joined Ben's circle; and knew Julia, aye, and knew Julia.

He dragged his mind back from its useless, straying dreams, and listened again to the boy's Latin play.

This boy, Cowley, was a famous poet at two and twenty; he had been a famous poet for years. Fortune had smiled on him. Other men had written verse since before his birth, were still writing verse, and better verse too, but had only been printed in collections, with the verses of others, and never yet appeared before the world in independent, separately published form.

"By God, I'll publish me," Mr. Herrick exclaimed to himself. "I'll languish no more in obscurity, while all the young apes leap over my head."

Having decided thus, he could listen with an easier mind to the adventures of Aemilio and Aegle, the pedantic buffooning of Gnomicus, the bombast of Bombardomachides, the fooling at the expense of the schools.

"Thin matter, but reasonable witty," he said, as the first act ended. "I've seen better, and I've seen worse."

"Well, Jule, is the play to your mind?" her father asked. "Y'understand it all, I trust?"

"Most on't, Father. It's not Mr. Cowley's best, I think, but it's ingenious and droll, and runs very smooth and quaint."

"It goes better in the third act," Kit encouraged them. "When he gets on to the *schola jocorum*."

"'Twould go better if we was all foxed," Giles suggested, and beckoned to one who passed by with a tray of drinks. So they all had canary, claret, or ale, and felt more able for the next act.

Mr. Herrick drank his canary, lit his pipe, put his feet on the seat in front of him, and settled down to enjoy the fooling.

The best laugh he had was at the song of Aemilio and Dimon at the beginning of the third act, which seemed to him excellently well aimed at the medical profession.

> "Purgate cerebrum, medici O insani,
> Nec sitis amplius mortis publicani . . ."

"Wait," Dr. Conybeare answered him; "Parsons'll get it next."

But parsons did not get it, only lawyers, alchemists, philosophers, and schoolmen. What the doctor regarded as the good ancient English (and, indeed, continental) custom of mocking in drama against clerics, seemed to him to be not sufficiently observed in the Universities to-day.

"Too many of 'em about the place," he decided. "The writers lack courage. They'll droll on Popish priests and Puritan pastors, but not on the Protestant clergy. Indeed, how could a young scholar do such a thing, before that grave and reverend row in the front? Beside which, their plays might not pass the licenser."

"No question they wou'n't," said Mr. Herrick, thinking of his old friend Mr. Weekes of Sherwell.

The play ended. Again the author stepped before the curtains, and said his epilogue.

> "Habet; peracta est Fabula; nil restat denique;
> Nisi ut vos valere jubeam . . ."

"But it's *not* good-bye," Julian thought. "For I know I shall meet him and talk with him."

A strange exhilaration possessed her; she felt a poet among poets, surrounded, for the first time in her life, by persons whose company she would like, whose conversation was (doubtless) what she held that conversation ought to be. She scarcely heard Giles at her side, saying, "God-a-mercy that it's over at last. Let's come out of our seats and walk and eat and drink."

"Lord, I could eat a whole basket of oranges, and drink a quart of sack," Meg said, "that play's drained me so dry. If this is what you call in Cambridge a merry evening, I shall wish no more I was up here."

" Kit," said his father, " you must bring me to Mr. Cleveland and quaint us. Look, he stands over there."

Kit hesitated from this forwardness.

" He's taken up with friends presently, sir."

" Nonsense, boy. The young man's not the Vice-Chancellor, that you should bash to break in on him. Come, if you won't bring me to him, I'll go alone."

" No, no, sir, that would look inconvenient. I'll quaint you suddenly, so soon as he leaves speaking with the master. . . . Now he looks this way; shall we come ? "

Mr. Cleveland greeted Kit with a smile, and, introduced to his father, the small and shabby country doctor with the fierce black brows and the clay pipe in his hand, was pleasant, but somewhat absent, with eyes that strayed about the hall noting friends with whom he would speak.

" I would have a word with you to-morrow, at your convenience, concerning this lad, sir," the father, like other fathers, was saying, and the tutor, like other tutors, perforce agreed.

" With all my heart, sir. Will you wait on me in my room at four, and you shall hear of your son's idleness or industry, virtues and vices, and the progress he makes with his books. I must tell you he disputed in a philosophical act in the college chapel with great credit last Michaelmass. Every one admired at his skill, for he all but unhorsed a most redoubtable antagonist."

" Indeed, I'm content to hear't. If Kit could not dispute with vigour, he'd be no Conybeare. Where his Latin faltered, his zeal would carry him on. But I have much to say to you, Mr. Cleveland, about this whole matter of university education."

Mr. Cleveland raised his eyebrows a little at that.

" As to that, sir, I fear I can do little, for the course is mapped, the books set, and there 'tis. Still, we'll talk on't, and of aught else you please. But I must leave you now, for I have to speak with Nat Finch. I see that bird of ill omen, Mr. Cromwell, is departing. He'll have to be away at cocklight to-morrow, if he's to take his seat in this precious assembly on the next day. I hope he found my harangue cordial to him, God rot him. Well, sir, adieu until to-morrow. Do you stay long in Cambridge?"

"Some little time, I think."

If Mr. Cleveland felt this to be a pity, his pleasant, ironic countenance gave no sign of it. He bowed with courtesy and took his leave, and plunged into more important affairs than those of a pupil and his father.

"You'll be particular what you say to him to-morrow, father?" Kit uneasily requested. "He's something impatient and mocking; and he don't like to spend time in discussing what is settled and can't be changed, such as University education."

"Can't be changed, ape? There's nothing can't be changed, and there's nothing an't the better for discussion. God help ye, child, any person hearing you would take you for the old man and me for the young. But don't bash for your father; that's to take needless pain on yourself. Where's your sister gone? Oh, she's with t'other children, sucking oranges. Mind her, while I go speak to some old friends, for I see plenty scattered about; aged beyond their years, too. I observe that other men change their appearance more than I do, so I suppose a country life, for all its trials, has its merits."

Mr. Herrick too, greeting his old friends, observed the same thing. The old friends of both, on the other hand, perceived that it must be a quiet life in college halls that kept men young, for Robin Herrick had grown stout and grizzled, and Michael Conybeare as grey as a badger. So every one was content.

6

Julian, too, was happy, watching the loquacious and learned gathering, observing celebrated figures strolling about the hall, Mr. Milton conversing seriously with Dr. Whichcote of Emmanuel, Mr. Cowley (less seriously) with all his friends in turn, being congratulated, one supposed, on his play, for he appeared gay and pleased. Julian thought him handsome and interesting, but that he looked self-conceited, and no wonder for that.

"Well, Jule," Meg said to her, "you may stare at your Mr. Cowley, but your staring won't make him aught but a sad tedious playwright. He's given me a cramp from sitting still all these hours that I'll not forgive him; I'm distasted against the man for ever. Lord help them, why can't poets and playwrights write in their own tongues?"

"He doth, Meg. He's wrote *Love's Riddle*, and all kinds. But doubtless they desire a Latin play for great occasions, when the new burgesses and the Vice-Chancellor, and all come to harken. It's your fault you won't learn your Latin properly, and are such an ignorant girl."

"Oh, I've better things to do than to pore over Latin grammars. Heaven knows I wish I was a man, but at least being a woman has spared me years o' that. They tried to whip lessons into me when I was a little maid, but when they found 't warn't possible, they renounced it and let me run my own way, though Lord knows they went on with the whippings on other counts. But Giles, who had no more head for't than I, went off to school and is still at it. And I warrant he understood not so much more of that nonsense play than

I did, for all his years of trouble and the rod. Did you, Giles?"

"I understood all I wanted on't. 'Twas a stupid thing. Try this burnt claret, July. And this almond cake is very sweet and curious. Nay, Meg, I got this for July; if you want some, I'll bring you another piece."

Meg wished that Giles would make Julian acquainted with Mr. Cowley or some other poet, for it was tedious and painful having her brother so absorbed and unfair.

Men and boys, Meg knew, were indeed unfair and unkind when they had a she-darling; far more so than women in the same case, who retained some sense of appearances, as of good manners towards others. To make things even, Kit should be pressing cake, wine, and attention on her; but she and Kit had little in common, and he, though friendly and polite, would rather talk to his sister or his friends. For the first time in her hoydenish life, Meg felt that she needed a squire. But it was Giles, her beloved, scapegrace companion in sports and adventures, whom she desired for this post. Why must Giles squander his affections on July, who thought nothing of him at all, whose eyes were roving round the hall after poets? On my life, thought Meg in sudden impatience, she shall *have* a poet. If these stupid lads won't get her one, I'll do't myself.

Bold girl, she moved from her brother's side, who was still plying his she-darling with unwanted wines and curious cakes, and advanced alone up the hall, a straight, long-legged, free-stepping girl, a flow of full brown velvet skirts about her ankles, her small bright head set on its long neck like a freckled golden apricock on its stalk, her red unruly curls straying from beneath their confining velvet hood.

Mr. Abraham Cowley, happening to glance up and see her approach, wondered at her bold, uncompanioned youth, wondered who she might be that moved thus alone through the hall of men.

"See there, Hervey," he said to his friend. "Is she some

one's wife, some one's miss, or a street quean strayed in? Nay, not that. Look how free and straight she moves—she brings to mind Ben's lines on the Lady Venetia—

"Not tossed or troubled with the light lady-air,
But kept an even gait, as some straight tree
Moved by the wind, so comely moved she.

She's like a lad in petticoats, Hervey—freckled like a lad, too. Look, she's like Yarde, of our College. And, 'slife, she comes toward us; the devil's in't if she an't going to speak with us."

The young lady had reached them by this, and, still untroubled by light lady-air, said abruptly in a small, deep voice, "Y'are Mr. Cowley, a'n't you?"

He bowed, a little puzzled, a little shy.

"At your service, madam."

"Well, sir, look, I've a friend envies extremely to speak with you, for she greatly esteems your verses and your plays. Y'are acquaint with Giles Yarde, an't you?"

"Indeed, mistress, I think, doubly so, now I'm so happy as to be acquaint with you."

She nodded. "Yes, I'm Giles his sister. He wou'n't bring you to speak with Julian, so I said I would. You see her? She stands over there with my brother."

Mr. Cowley looked down the hall to where Giles Yarde's tall red head gleamed, and by Giles Yarde stood a white and lovely girl in a deep-blue gown and hood.

"You see her? That's Mrs. Julian Conybeare, as desires speech with you. Will you be so good to come? 'T won't take you much time."

Mr. Cowley bowed again.

"I shall be honoured, madam. But, indeed, I take it ill of your brother to leave you go such errands."

"Oh, he don't know; I took no notice on't to him, or he wou'n't have had me go."

They were walking down the hall together, watched by curious observers. Mr. Cowley, who was rather shy with ladies, but flattered by their admiration, said, " I hope the play pleased you and your friend, Mrs. Yarde."

" Not me," Mrs. Yarde replied, " for I ha'n't gotten Latin, and understood not a word. Mrs. Conybeare liked it well enough."

" She has Latin, then ? "

" La you, yes, all the Latin in the world. Greek, too. She's a proper scholar. And writes verses, too."

" One of the learned ladies. They are all too few in these times, I fear."

But, really, quite enough, Mr. Cowley thought; who did not greatly hold with learning in ladies, believing it to give them, sometimes, a proud, equal, independent manner, and too high a conceit of themselves; besides which, it was but seldom that they were comely. They should know a little; know enough to appreciate a man's learning and a man's witty conversation; wit they should have, and quick parts, but not learning. For anyhow, Mr. Cowley reasoned, a woman cannot think or speak on a man's level, and can never know a great amount; so it were better that she should not enter presumptuously into fields for which it seems probable that God did not intend her.

Nevertheless, this young Mrs. Conybeare appeared, from a distance, to have so much beauty that she might, Mr. Cowley decided, have as much learning as she pleased.

The beauty did not lessen at a near view. She looked up and saw them approach, and blushed with surprise into a pale pink rose. Never, thought Mr. Cowley, had he beheld such great violet eyes, under such fine level black brows and broad white forehead; never such a fine, delicately turned mouth and jaw. He bowed low as Meg said, " This is Mr. Cowley, Jule. He would know you. Mr. Cowley, this is Mrs. Julian

Conybeare. She would know you. So now y'are quaint, and can talk Latin together." And, turning her back on them, she put out the tip of a pink tongue at her brother.

Giles had grown red and embarrassed.

"Did she fetch you, Mr. Cowley? You must forgive her rustical ways. She's up from the country, and knows nought," he said spitefully.

"Indeed," said Mr. Cowley, "I think she knows more than you do, for you knew not enough to know how it would please me to meet her and Mrs. Conybeare. You knew only that you desired to keep them both to yourself, as a miser hugs his gold. I take it ill in you, sir. Howbeit, your sister has atoned for your fault, so we'll pass it by. I am mightily content to learn, Mrs. Conybeare, that you took some small pleasure in seeing my poor jest played?"

"Aye, sir. I took great pleasure."

"A good jest, you thought? You found it ingenious and droll?"

"Ingenious and droll enough, sir. Though, indeed, I wished it had been *Love's Riddle*, for that's a play greatly to my mind; 'tis extraordinary elegant and quaint and full of pretty conceits. I love to read it."

"Oh, so you read my plays?"

"Yes, and your verses, too. Mr. Robert Herrick, who teaches me, has 'em all."

"Is that Mr. Robert Herrick, the country poet, that has verses sometimes in *Wit's Recreations* and elsewhere, and was else well known about town, they say?"

"Aye. He's a wonderful pretty poet, and has a whole book of verses that's not yet printed. He's with my father and me in Cambridge now. See, there he is."

"The parson, you mean, that drinks over there with the professor of Greek. He looks a fine merry divine. If I remember, he's wrote some pretty faery verses."

"He's wrote some marvellous beautiful poetry. Only it a'n't mostly printed."

But Mr. Cowley, regarding the merry clergyman, perceived him to be of the past generation, which, except for a few famous names, did not seriously count in poetry. His verse was, no doubt, hopelessly outmoded. It was probably fortunate that it was not, for the most part, printed.

"Still, he must print it," he kindly said. "My bookseller, Mr. Henry Seile, would perhaps print it for him. And you, too, Mrs. Yarde telled me, have wrote verses?"

"Aye, sometimes." Julian was suddenly shy. Was Mr. Henry Seile to print her verses, too? But it seemed that this was not in Mr. Cowley's mind.

"It's a sweet pretty pastime for ladies," he said. "I'm acquaint with a lady writes posies for rings; very elegant small verses, much meaning in little compass. Have you ever wrote posies?"

"No." Julian was a little offended. She no more, thought she, wrote posies for rings than he did. "I write sonnets, and epics, and plays, and Latin verses sometimes," she explained in proud and casual tones. "All kinds of nonsense."

"Very pretty nonsense, I am sure," said Mr. Cowley, graciously gallant. Then he changed the conversation, lest she should offer to show him some of it, which would be a disaster.

Giles stood by, uncomfortable and sulky, as they thus talked. It was turning out precisely as he had known it would, should July fall in with Cowley. Why, their very names rhymed; and here they were off on poetry together, and might talk all night, so far as he could see.

He turned away and took his sister's arm in hard fingers.

"Little toad, I'll punish thee for this," he muttered hoarsely. "I admire thou wasn't bashed, to walk alone up the hall and make thyself known to a strange man, for all the world like a quean at the Rose Tavern, and pray him to come along with 'ee. When did any one tell you you could do so in Cambridge?"

"I'll do as I like in Cambridge. You don't own Cambridge, however hard you pinch, you crab. Leave go my arm, or I'll pinch, too; yes, and kick your ankle, and I've gotten my sharp shoes on to-night."

"Making yourself a sight and a nay-word before all the University. I shall have my tutor sending for me, inquiring who was the bold-faced tomrigg I let loose in the College hall to plague the men. And that fellow of all, with half the world taking notice to-night of his comings and goings, and observing with whom he speaks. 'Slife, I may's well leave Cambridge to-morrow, as stay and be a laughing stock, the man as has a ramping sister pesters men. 'Tis pity our grandmother a'n't here, to give you one of the whippings you was speaking on just now."

"Twish! No one's whipped me in years."

"Then it's great pity, for you need it. For a little, the Vice-Chancellor'd send you to the spinning-house for a bold whore."

"Leave pinching my arm, I tell you. There; I telled you I'd kick."

Giles released her with a grimace.

"There you be again. Bringing your rustical tricks to Cambridge with you, kicking like an ass and fighting and hoyting as if we was in Denshire. Y'arn't fit to leave Dean, or to do aught but play at barley-break in the garden and hawk and hunt on the moors."

"You can say what you like; y'are jealous of July and Cowley fadging. July and Cowley, July and Cowley . . ."

"Will you be quiet, ass, afore I pinch you again? They'll hear you."

"Not they, th'are too occupied one with t'other. And if you pinch, I shall kick."

"Mule."

"Crab."

"Cat."

"Cat's don't kick, toad."

"And toads don't pinch, cow."

Dr. Conybeare, coming up to them and seeing the two red heads bent down together whispering, thought what a good thought his had been, to unite again this loving brother and sister. He had met a number of old friends, and was pleased with himself and his escape into this congenial atmosphere. And here was his child, having somehow got acquainted with the young poet of whom she was for ever speaking, so she too must be content. But it was time he took her and the other wench back home to bed.

"Why, Jule, bud, thou'rt in clover; I see thou'st gotten a poet to talk with thee. Mr. Cowley, sir, let me present myself; I'm this young lady's father. I was up at Christ's College years back, and am come here from Devonshire to visit my alma mater and see what she's at in these days. So far as I see 'tis the same old tale of Aristotle and all his commentators, schoolmen's logic, and theology, a little Roman history, a scruple of the Greek tongue, and these endless, wordy disputations you hit at so nicely in the comedy we've just witnessed. Though they say that at Christ's they've ta'en up with Plato and Plotinus."

"Yes, sir, they do study Plato greatly there now; and not only at Christ's, neither. Some men say the schoolmen's day is passing, but I doubt that. 'Tis attractive, this new Platonism; I am looking into it myself. Mr. Henry More of Christ's, who upholds it, is a very learned pious man; and is writing a wonderful great epic on the soul."

"More poetry! Well, my daughter here don't agree with

me, but I say as poetry's an escape from reason and clear thinking, and is best left alone by philosophers. 'Sdeath, man, what would be thought of a mathematician or an astronomer who worked out his notions in verse? I say, leave verse to those as feel but can't think, for 'twill vent their passions and assuage those of their readers; but don't bring it into learning and philosophy."

"You have the world all against you, sir," Mr. Cowley rather stiffly observed, and the doctor recollected that he addressed a poet.

"Why, God bless, ye write the stuff yourself; I had forgot; aye, on my life, I had quite forgot. I mustn't preach t'ye on your own profession; 'tis as if you took and telled me for what uses medicine should be kept; which, indeed, you very rightly might. Well, I'll bid you good-night, sir, and thank'ee for your play. We must meet again. Come, child; come, Meg. Where's Kit gotten to? Oh, here y'are, boy."

"Your brother," Mr. Cowley said to Julian. "That was why I felt your face familiar to me, for I've seen your brother often. Dr. Conybeare, will you let me have the pleasure to meet you and your daughter again. Perhaps you'll be attending *Comus* here to-morrow evening?"

"Perhaps, perhaps; if we can get into't for the crowd."

"Giles promised to try to get seats for us, Father."

"I will see to that," Mr. Cowley said. "If you'll let me know where you lodge, I'll send you a note to deliver to the doorkeeper when you come. Y'are at the White Horse? Good. Then I hope, Mrs. Julian, I'll see you to-morrow. And you too, madam." He turned to Meg with a smile. "For *Comus* is plain English, and you'll not be so fatigued by it as you was to-night."

"Is't a comedy?" Meg doubtfully asked.

"You don't know *Comus*?" Mr. Cowley lifted his brows in surprise.

"She don't know anything," her brother said, "only the puppet shows as trapse round Denshire with the fairs."

"Oh, but I mind now, I do know it, for Mr. Herrick had it played at Dean, and I played a reveller, and danced on the meadow with bare feet, and July played the lady. I had forgot the name on't."

"Well, 'tis a mistake really, to play a pastoral masque, within doors. The stage will be made to appear like a wood but some think it great pity to play it in a hall. However, Mr. Milton is here, and is arranging it all. 'Tis very beautiful verse, and the songs, sung by the College choristers, will sound well."

"Oh, I think they'll sound tedious. I think 'twill all be extreme tedious. The Trinity chairs is too hard and straight; I got cramp this evening. Still, I suppose if t'others mean to come, I must, since they won't leave me go about by myself. But la you, where there's a masque, I would liefer be in it than look at it, for then one can dance. Don't you dance in Cambridge at all, Mr. Cowley?"

"Peace, idle jackanapes," the doctor bade her. "Cease thy flim-flam and come away. Thou'rt not fit for this staid sober city of learning; thou'rt for ever upon the hoity toity and agog for a game of barley-break. Good-night t'ye, sir, once more."

7

Mr. Herrick, returning to his inn something after midnight, merry with wine, for he had been carousing with old friends, saw ahead of him in Trumpington Street the trim, slight figure of Mr. John Milton, who was walking alone. A few strides brought them level.

" Good-evening t'ye, sir. Y'are bound for the inn and bed, like myself, I take it."

Mr. Milton looked at him with his polite coolness and perceived him to be intoxicated. This rather boisterous and free-mannered parson-poet was not much to his austere, seemly and gentlemanly mind; still, since they lodged at the same inn, and had friends in common, he must show courtesy.

" Yes, sir. I stayed late at Trinity, arranging for my masque to-morrow night."

"*Comus*—aye, I shall like to see *Comus* again. I had *Comus* played in my Devonshire parish in a meadow, on a fine summer evening two years since. It went very pretty, in that green scene, with all the young wenches and lads, and my little pupil, Julian Conybeare, as the lady. Aye, 'tis an elegant pretty masque, though perhaps with two much of reasoning in it for some. For look 'ee, I think a masque should run quick and smooth, with music and action and laughter and love, but no more than a scruple or so of philosophy or grave talk. Indeed, we did cut out some o' the talk, for the two brothers, two young sparks that stayed at Dean Court, wou'n't get it all by heart."

"Indeed, sir." Mr. Milton spoke a trifle coldly. "Well, we shall, by your leave, play it in full to-morrow evening at Trinity."

"Surely, surely. Aye, 'tis fine pretty stuff, and a wholesome lesson for maids to cherish their virginity. What did ye think o' young Cowley's play, sir?"

"Good enough harmless fooling. But he is not accomplished Latinist enough to sustain a whole drama. He should write in English. This antique worn tradition in our Universities of despising the English tongue, whereas we should be employed in studying, polishing and moulding it to the uses of the noblest literature—did you speak, sir?"

Mr. Herrick had spoken; he had ejaculated, "Damme, as I live there's a fine quean." For they were now arrived at King's Lane, and as they turned up it there passed them, leaving the White Horse, a handsome young woman, in company with a slightly merry gentleman.

"Your pardon, sir," said Mr. Herrick, looking after the comely figure. "A handsome creature; she catched my eye. You were saying, sir?" She had not catched Mr. Milton's eye, and he looked bored and a trifle impatient, as if he did not think that the eyes of poets, clerical or otherwise, should be catched by anything of so small consequence.

"Well, as I was saying, in the two Universities we neglect the great heritage of our native tongue, which it should be our particular care to mould and polish to the noblest uses. We lend ourselves to the desiccation and sterilisation of poesy and thought . . ."

"To be sure, so we do. Aye, poesy grows monstrously desiccated and sterile, very dry and dismal indeed, since Ben died. Poor Ben, as should have lived on like some great oak, sheltering the little trees growing up in's shadow. Aye, there was a man."

"Nevertheless," said Mr. Milton, "there's plenty young

poets, and English poetry may do considerable things in their hands. 'Tis a wonder all joy in poesy's not ground out of 'em during these seven years of harsh, dry study of empty quibbles, this pushing through arid and thorny waste country, that the Universities still call education. Aye, 'tis a marvel that so many as do should find their way to Parnassus, through such choking nonsense thickets. At Oxford, they don't; at Oxford th'are even more bound in the rusted chains than here; 'tis even more of an Aristotelian lumber-room; besides which, Oxford don't make, and never has made, and I conceit never will, poets as Cambridge do."

"I grant, I grant. 'Tis something i' the air, belike. Not as Cambridge, too, a'n't a devilish miserable ill air, and as full of ague as my old bones grow full of gout. Shall we have a jug of sack to keep it out, sir, now w'are at our inn?"

"Thankye, no, sir; I have some writing to do before I sleep, and must up to my room. But as to Oxford, I take it it's no discrimination of air makes her an unfit mother for poets, but the closer devotion she's ever had to the chop-logic of the schools, and the old theologies, loyalties and traditions of thought. Cambridge is bad enough, indeed, but Oxford worse. And now she lives close under the gimlet eye of His Grace of Canterbury, which would, I take it, have let Leto from breeding Apollo. Parnassus must be free; it can't be scaled by climbers with chains clanking on 'em."

"Y'are right, y'are very right and true-spoke, indeed, sir. Hola, lad, a jug of canary sack, and see 'tis well burnt. Aye, and haste; see thou don't drop asleep as thou draw'st it. Aye, Mr. Milton, that was right well spoke, as Parnassus must be free. Chains kill poesy, and we all must wear 'em, in this wretched sad tedious life we live. For my part, I'm chained to Devonshire, and 'tis the saddest barbarous tedious country as never you saw. Still, I write; aye, I write verses, despite all hindrance. I have 'em with me in Cambridge, and 'twould be very cordial to me if you would cast an eye through 'em sometime when you have a spare hour, for, by God, I should prize your opinion, sir."

"Thank you, sir, but I must ask to be excused, for I leave Cambridge within a few days, and my time here is already too well filled."

"Then it can't be. Well. Here comes the sack. You 'on't join me, sir? 'Tis good, cordial stuff.

"If Spanish apes ate all the grapes,
What should we do for sack?

I know not, nor you. 'Tis a friend in need, and a kind mistress to warm and cheer us, better than any woman, or tobacco, either. You look, sir, if I may say so, as you'd be the better for more on't. More of all three, belike—women, wine and tobacco. Aye, th'are all good cordials to revive thin blood and drooping spirits."

"Very likely, sir." Mr. Milton bowed his rather aloof good-night, and left the clergyman sitting by the dying hearth, tankard in one hand, pipe in the other.

8

" He's gone," Mr. Herrick said, in some surprise. " Gone to his chamber to write. Aye, and I must to my chamber and write also.

" If all the world were paper," he gently sang, in his soft rich baritone,

> And all the sea were ink,
> And all the trees were bread and cheese,
> How should we do for drink?
> If all the world were sand-o,
> Oh, then what would we lack-o?
> If, as they say, there were no clay,
> How should we take tobacco?
> If all our vessels ran-a,
> If none but had a crack-a,
> If Spanish apes ate all the grapes,
> How should we do for sack-a?

He's a very fine poet, John Milton, but his blood runs too thin i' his veins. The lady of Christ's—aye, he colours up like a very lady at a coarse word. He could well play his own lady in *Comus*. He's something of a cold, distant, unfriendly man, with his mind all set fast on reforming education, and no time to stay and take's pleasure by the way. He was never one o' Ben's merry circle, nor could'a been. *We* never went to bed when we might 'a stayed up to talk and to drink:

> " Solebamus consumere longa loquendo
> Tempora, sermonem deficiente die.

Ah, those days, those days; they 'on't any more return to this poor old earth.

> " Soles occidere et redire possunt:
> Nobis cum semel occidit brevis lux,
> Nox est perpetua una dormienda.

Well, then, Ben, good-night to thee. But what do I say? Am I a heathen unbeliever, or do I hope for heaven? Here's All Hallows' dawning, and I swear I'll leave thee a manchet and a flagon, so thou canst refresh thyself when thou walk'st abroad; though why thou shouldst walk in Cambridge I know not, only that thy Robin's here, that's burned a lamp for thee each Souls' night these three years, and said a prayer for thee each Souls' morning at his mass. Aye, Ben, and I'll do't this day; I'll up betimes and hie me to Little St. Mary's, where they keep a decent Christian order, and say a mass for thee in my heart at the Eucharist. Sweet soul, thou shalt suffer no pain as I can rid thee on. Nay, I'll not to bed this night; I'll wake for thee, Ben, beside this lamp and this bread and sack, so, if you com'st, thou'll find a friend. John Milton can burn his oil at his books; I'll burn mine for my friend. Aye, and while I wake for him, I'll repent me of my sins, that I may come to my mass with a free heart. For I'm sure I'm so clogged and weighed down with wickedness that God 'on't let me to his table unless I repent. Sin, and repent, repent and sin; 'tis a tedious alternation, but better than to sin all the time, and more within a man's compass than to repent all the time."

His hand strayed to the pen and ink-horn that stood on a corner of the table; he drew towards him a sheet of paper, and began scribbling on it as he communed with himself.

> " God pardons those who do through frailty sin,
> But never those who persevere therein.

Aye, but I do persevere. I fear I'm the most persevering

sinner in the world, at least in thought. 'Tis all very well for thee, Ben; thou hast purged thy sins, where'er thou art now (and, God knows, I think they did need purging), and canst approach the Holy Table without fear; whereas I, each Sunday and feast day, must prepare myself and make my parasceve with tears and trembling. Yet God's kind, and I'll be there with thee this morning, never fear. W'are both invited, and we'll both attend. That's a good thought now for a verse." He wrote it slowly with the scratching, blotting quill.

> " To a Love-Feast we both invited are:
> The figur'd Damask, or pure Diaper,
> Over the golden Altar now is spread,
> With Bread, and Wine, and Vessells furnished;
> The *sacred Towell*, and the *holy Eure*
> Are ready by, to make the Guests all pure:
> Let's go (my *Jonson*) yet e're we receive,
> Fit, fit it is, we have our *Parasceve*.
> Who to that *sweet Bread* unprepar'd doth come
> Better he starv'd, then but to taste one crumme.

I'll write it out fair, and add it to my noble numbers. John Milton 'on't look at 'em, but others will. Happen young Cowley'll be pleased with the chance to see an older poet's work. Ah, were Ben here, he'd make me read 'em all out to him as he was used. I swear if thou walk'st here to-night, Ben, I will by all means tell thee out my recent verses. What's that? Did something stir?"

What stirred was the sleepy lad who had brought him sack, and who now stood at the door, tousle-headed and a-yawn.

" Be you going to bed, Mr.?"

" No, boy. 'Tis close on the dawn. I'll sit here to-night."

" Very good, Mr." The drowsy youth slouched off to his

bed, hoping vaguely and without confidence that the wakeful parson would, before he should fall asleep in his cups, extinguish the lamp, which would otherwise burn down in its pot and smell evilly in the morning.

"He's gone," Mr. Herrick murmured. "All are gone but I, Ben, and thou canst come an thou wilt." He sat alone among the flickering shadows cast by the dying fire and the floating wick in its pot. He sat alone, reclining back in the deep, oak chair, his chin sunk on his breast, and the wavering shadows made shapes and figures on the rough, timbered walls and the uneven stone floor, and the dying fire and the ancient house made whispering, creaking sounds.

Ghosts walked, doubtless, for All Souls. The ghosts, perhaps, of old Protestants, of dead reforming theologians, of translators of the Bible who had met in this room by night a century ago. William Tyndale; how often had he stolen here under cover of the dark to talk with other heretic scholars. They had sat whispering round this very table, afraid of their shadows, yet bent, with the obstinacy of scholars and of theologians, on treading to the end that strange road that would lead them to the fire. Did their ghosts, perplexed and restless still, whisper now in the old White Horse room beneath the low rafters? The vicar of Dean Prior heard them not, if so. Nor did he hear his dear dead poet. All he heard was a sweet, rich woman's voice that seemed to mock and caress by turns; all he saw in the twisting shadows was a full, swaying female form, a face of cream and strawberries, black eyes that laughed and glinted.

"Julia, my beautiful," he whispered. Yet why should she, who was not a ghost, who was not dead but only fled from his side long since, why should she be the only ghost come to torment him, to delight him, to come between him and his friend, between him and his God? How could he make his parasceve, be shriven for his sins, with that sweet ghost teasing him, that merry soul, that had never known the stabs of conscience, speaking to him, with her long, black eyes and her warm, white arms, of love, of past sin and present longing and desire? "Julia, sweet torment, go, for I would pray. . . . Nay, Julia, my beautiful beloved, stay with me, and I'll not pray to-night. *Vivamus, mea Julia, atque amemus,* and none shall break in and disturb us; nay, not Ben himself, for see, I'll pledge thee in his wine, and thou too, shalt drink, and I after thee, when thy lips have touched the rim and made it sweet. Thou leftst me, my cruel dear, but I'll not send thee from me while I breathe. See, mine eyes cry; kiss them dry. My heart aches; lay thy hand on't and ease it. Nay, Julia, say what thou may'st, there's never been a woman I loved but thee, sweet quean, nor never will. Robin's alone, alone for ever, since thou left him. What are the others to me? Toys, things of a dream and of an hour, flowers that die ere the day is told, the frail lusts of imagination, that I must toy with in my verses and in my fancy to save my heart from the cold grave thy going trod it into. All the years I wait for thee, against thou should'st return of a sudden, not in a dream but in the flesh, in the dear, warm, sweet flesh; and waiting I grow old and weary. . . . Aye, kiss them dry, my love, for they weep for thee. . . ."

9

Coming into the parlour at six o'clock on All Souls' morning, with the church bells of Cambridge clanging, the sleepy inn boy found the parson sprawled asleep in his chair, his head and arms across the table. The lamp had burned itself out with an evil smell; the empty pewter jug, overturned, rolled on the floor; the parson's clay pipe lay in two broken pieces beside it. The parson heavily slept; so sound asleep was he that not all the bells of Cambridge woke him. Only when the shrill loud Cambridgeshire voices of children sounded in the street outside, begging All Souls' fruit at the door, did he stir, disturbed from his sleep.

> " Soul, soul, an apple or two;
> If you ha'n't any apples, a pear will do,"

chanted the children, as they had chanted on this day for many centuries.

> " Soul, soul . . ."

Robert Herrick turned heavily about in his chair, and stared with dazed eyes at the twilight morning. The bells' clamour had ceased; only the children now spoke of All Souls—

> " If you ha'n't any apples a pear will do . . ."

But Mr. Herrick had not even a pear.

IO

Kit Conybeare, after reading Aristotle with his tutor from nine to ten on the feast of All Souls, said, as he rose to go, " My father, sir, is to wait on you this afternoon, I think."

" Y'are right. He desires to speak with me concerning your studies. Fathers do often so use. You must suffer it, and so must I. Indeed, I shall gladly talk with Dr. Conybeare, who's a very ingenious learned man, and will know of what he speaks. O *si sic omnes!* "

" Yes, sir, my father's ingenious and learned enough, and has a great many of bees in's head, which will buzz finely about yours, I'll swear, when he lets 'em fly. But that's no matter; that is, it's no matter to me. What I would pray you, Mr. Cleveland, is to be curious to take no notice to him that I've spoke to you sometimes of religion, and asked you your opinions on Papistry. I would not for the world have him troubled about me in that quarter, as he would be did I possess him that I had been considering conversion. For, if I should change my church, 'twould be then time enough to acquaint him on't, when 'twould be too late for him to let me. So I beg, sir, as you'll not resolve him of any such matter."

" You need be in no case about that, Mr. Conybeare; I'll consider as I had it from you *sub sigillo*, and be mum. Does your father greatly hate the Papists, then? "

" No more, sir, than other fervent sects. Indeed, he prefers 'em to the Brownists, and the other crazy sectarians, as being less noisy."

" He's right there. All right-thinking men is agreed on that. Then I take it he's a staunch Protestant? "

"Not greatly that, neither." Dr. Conybeare's son blushed a little for his father's very peculiar attitude. "The fact is, sir, that he's a philosopher, and all churches stand somewhat in the north of his favour. He don't object to the Protestant Church so much as to the others, for he thinks it less fanatical and firm-set."

"Aye, he's right there, too, as I've often told you. Arminian Protestant is the best thing a reasonable loyal gentleman can be. To desert the Church of our country is to play the traitor. There's too much presently o' this flying into Rome's arms, chiefly because a few idle persons at court have made it the mode, and because certain Jesuits in the Universities know how to work on you little apes of boys. I shall take it very ill in you, Mr. Conybeare, if you go that way; if you allow yourself be run off by the priests as was Mr. Marvell of Trinity, as there was such a pudder about two years back, when he was took up to London, and his father hunted for him for weeks and found him at last in a bookshop. But there's this about young Marvell; this adventure cured him, for he's now, I'm told, as sound a Church of England man as any in Trinity. All the same, I beg you'll try no such cure, but stay in the Church you was born to."

"A man a'n't born to any Church, sir. He's received——"

"Peace, peace, Mr. Conybeare. Keep your dialectics for a leisure hour, 'Tis time you was at your next lecture. You can be at ease; I'll say nothing to your father. But for Lord's sake stick you by all means to your studies, and leave religious disputings till y'are done with Cambridge and are better fitted to undertake 'em. And a word of advice, young man—be less frequent at Peterhouse. For, though Dr. Cosin's a very pillar of our Church and extreme loyal to King, bishops and etceteras (save the mark!) and stands manfully (whatever's said of him) in the gap between Puritan and Papist, 'tis not so with all the tutors there, nor yet with all the scholars. And the less you run about with 'em the safer you'll be from that infection."

Kit gave no undertaking to abstain from this company, but went off to his room to read Ramus.

His chamber-fellow, Mr. Drake, lay shivering in bed with the ague. "You've been out?" he inquired between chattering teeth.

"No, with Mr. Cleveland."

Kit settled himself at the table with his books.

The sick young man looked enviously at him, for he doted on Mr. Cleveland.

"Will he come to visit me to-day, think you?"

"I don't know. He made no mention on't. He is much occupied to-day with business. And this afternoon my father waits on him."

Mr. Drake turned his face to the wall, and drew the blankets up to his ears. He admired his tutor more than any one in the world.

"The devil take this fellow Ramus," muttered Kit. He did not care for Ramus; his thoughts strayed, as he stared out of the window into the court, where the mild November sunshine strove with rain. Julian was right; it always rained for Souls' day and shone for Hallows'. In chapel that morning they had prayed for the poor weeping souls. But only a little, only as Anglicans pray. His friends, the Jesuit priests, at their lodging in St. Edward's Passage had doubtless said their mass for the dead, in the tiny room they used as oratory. The romance of this secret oratory, these quiet hidden masses, said by priests who were (anyhow legally, even though it came to nothing in these days) in peril of their lives, stirred his heart to a kind of gallant adoration. Colour and beauty and history, and the high courage of rebels hunted but undefeated—these haloed the heads of the practitioners of the Old Religion, and called to his romantic spirit to join them. Yes; if conversion were a fashion just now, it was, he protested, these things made it so.

I must go over, he said to himself. Whatever my father feels on't. A man must decide for himself. I shan't be at rest till I do it, for I know I have to do it. John's and Peterhouse chapels, and Little St. Mary's and a few more like 'em, a'n't the Church of England, only one small part of it. Most of the Church is dull and cold, and all is torn by faction, and now this parliament will put down the Arminian bishops and clergy, and the Calvinists may prevail. I wish I was already gone over.

He saw himself stealing out to mass in St. Edward's Passage; telling his confessor, Dr. Cosin of Peterhouse, that he was going to be received; hinting to the people he met that he, for his part, was a Papist. . . .

Meanwhile there was Ramus to be tackled before dinner, and after dinner he was to meet his father and Julian, and show them the College and chapel.

II

Kit left his father and sister at four to attend a lecture, while they waited on Mr. Cleveland. For, said Dr. Conybeare, Julian might as well come too, since there was nothing else to do with her, and since he did not suppose that Mr. Cleveland would object to her sitting in the room while they talked, she being such a quiet good wench. Now, had it been Meg, who could not sit quiet for five minutes, would not read a book, or listen patiently to the conversation of her betters, it would have been another matter. Or had it been Lettice Northly, or many another vain young tit, who could not be in the company of a personable man without endeavouring to attract his notice and conversation to herself—but, as it was Julian, she had best come. Julian thought so too, for she could have lingered in this College for ever, and was pleased to see Mr. Cleveland's rooms. In Kit's room she could not remain long, since his chamber-fellow, Mr. Drake, had the ague.

Mr. Cleveland rose to greet them as they entered. He wore a black velvet coat and an embroidered orange-brown waistcoat, collar and cuffs. There was a kind of graceful, careless ease in his presence and manner; his brown eyes laughed; his fine, full mouth curled often in a half-smile; he waved his large, long white hands to emphasise his speech. An impatient man one guessed, sarcastic and somewhat masterful, but withal courteous, until he was annoyed. He offered Julian stiponie wine and cake as apt to her years and her sex, and gave the doctor a glass of canary.

"Your brother's shown you our College and chapel," he said to Julian. "I hope they pleased you."

"Very greatly, sir. The chapel is so beautiful, I never saw the like."

"Aye, 'tis very beautiful and well ordered. The most of it is Dr. Beale's work; he caused to be put in the new panelling and the painted curtains, and the silver cloth, and the crucifix and candles and the altar, and the dove and glory. Our College chapels are much more seemly and fine of late years, as is the worship in 'em, and in the town churches too. Dr. Cosin has done a great work in his Vice-Chancellorship. And now this new parliament, save the mark, will call him up to answer for't, and question him as to how he dares to prefer seemliness and beauty and reverence to disorder, plainness, and indecent incivility. 'Tis for that, if you please, that this country elects its representatives. Dr. Cosin has turned Great St. Mary's from a lumber house and a chattering-hall into a seemly church, and has endeavoured to enforce in the Lord's house such civility as men would show toward any common host, and for that he'll be called to account by these apes in office. We shall be fortunate if they don't send commissioners down to take away our altars and ornaments and turn our chapels and churches into barns. . . . But I mustn't plague you and heat my own temper with these digressions. We'll speak of your son, Dr. Conybeare, if you please."

"Aye, sir, surely. To be brief and not to waste your time, I would know of his studies. Does he do well?"

"Very tolerably, sir. He hath quick parts and good intellects. His declamations and disputations are well executed. He is still a trifle backward in his Seton, Keckermann and Ramus."

"Let him be so; I don't care if he be so. I care nothing for Seton and Keckermann, no, nor Ramus neither, for all he's spoke of as something new. They tormented the life out of me when I was a little ape myself. These fooleries and bickerings of the schools don't do a young mind no good, but only serve to entangle, perplex and cramp it."

"Nevertheless, sir, th'are part of the University course, and must be learnt."

"No must, sir; I admit no must in education, but what is for the scholar's own good. Look ye, Mr. Cleveland; here's a lad of good parts, as you say, as'll have shortly to battle with the world and make what he can on't, and how do we equip him for life? By teaching him for seven years the outmoded logomachies of quibbling old men, splitting hairs, quartering straws, striving for victories in the air, poring in books that should have mouldered long since, as the notions inside 'em have. . . . Look now, sir, do they read Descartes' his *Discours de la Méthode* in Cambridge?"

"He begins to be read. But he's not well considered academically, for he would upset Aristotelianism and its commentators, on which our schools are based, and we can't have that. Oh, he's a very pretty philosopher. They fond him at Christ's and Emmanuel, for, think they, he's on their side against the schoolmen and would fling Aristotle, Aquinas, Peter Lombard and John Calvin from their thrones. Hence the old school think he's the devil. Canterbury has pronounced against him, though not, I conceit, greatly understanding him. And in truth, he's a something dangerous fellow, for though outwardly a Christian and Catholic, some of his theories of motion would seem to sap the notion of God's being its perpetual cause. Or so I am told, for Lord knows I'm no philosopher. Mr. More and his Platonist friends swear by him presently, and exalt his doctrine of the immateriality of the soul, and approve his opposition both to the Hobbesians and the Aristotelians, but I fancy he won't endure with 'em, for he's more mechanical in his theories than they know."

"That's as may be, and I don't give a fig for the immateriality of the soul, or for Mr. More and his friends who appear to me to have their heads in the clouds. But I would have Kit read the *Discours* for I would get some rational philosophy, mathematics, and science into his head."

Mr. Cleveland shrugged his shoulders.

"'Tis no part of his course, and wou'n't well fadge with it. Your son a'n't naturally a philosopher or a scientist; whereas he has a tolerable good bite on divinity, history and rhetoric."

"What of his geometry?"

"I don't teach him that myself, and, as you know, it's but weakly nibbled at in the schools. When Mr. Seth Ward, of Sidney, discovered some mathematical books in his college library some few years back, there was not one there could make either head or tail of 'em. But w'are improved of late, greatly owing to Mr. Ward himself. However, I don't take it as your son will ever be a very ingenious mathematical, and he's best not devote over much of his time to't. Nor to astronomy neither, in which I'm told he's weak."

"Then he's weak at the things best worth his attention, and I'm very sorry for't. Look ye, Mr. Cleveland, my boy is by nature something of a dreamer, a bookish poetical lad, and his roaming fancy needs curbing and directing, and the punctual discipline of the mathematical and exact sciences would greaten his intellects and regulate his mind, and help him, moreover, to understand better the world as he lives in, and that's an office as the quibbling definitions of the logicians, the metaphysicians and the schoolmen will never perform for him. Look, sir, I left Cambridge myself dried and staled and perplexed with the chop-logic they'd caused me to spend those good years at (I read much divinity, and they turned me out a parson), and thirty years later I send my son, and, ecod, 'tis nearly the same old round, the same old stale fare. *Occidit miseros crambe repetita*, as the poet says. And this after all the war that's been made on it by Lord Bacon in the cause of history and science, by John Milton in the cause of English history and literature——"

"John Milton be—sent to the place as he belongs to," Mr. Cleveland acidly interrupted, a glance towards the listening maiden in the corner deflecting his sentence. "I beg, sir, as you won't speak to me of John Milton. For all his poetry and his scholarship, he's a pestiferous, arrogant, self-conceited precisian, and lent his support to that hell's scrich owl, Cromwell, at the election; for which I'll not readily forgive him. He's of the wrong colour, and grows to be a damned disloyal troublesome man, and this at a time when all loyal university men should stand fast for Church and King."

"And constitution, sir. What of standing fast for the constitution? Lord knows, I don't give a China orange for it myself, 'tis such a damned silly one; but you must give leave to those as hold by it to oppose a king, ministers and bishops as don't."

"I'll not give 'em leave to no such impudence, sir; by God, I won't. Cud, sir, d'ye want to hand England over to a set of canting hypocritical knaves? The bishops may be often enough at fault—they're human sinners and fools like the rest of mankind—but at least they stand for the ancient order of our Church against a set of un-English fanatics who'd pull it to the ground. For look ye, sir, these tedious Calvinistic prating predestinating Puritan fellows who strive now for the upper hand in our Church and Parliament are foreigners in spirit; they derive from Geneva and Holland, pox take 'em——"

"Jacobus Arminius," the doctor interpolated, "being, in course, an Englishman born and bred."

"And are trying their alien excesses," Mr. Cleveland went on, undisturbed, "in a country hath no mind to 'em. They'd take the maypole and the church ale, the playhouse, the Christmas pie and the Twelfth Night dance, from a people as has ever loved 'em, and give 'em long sermons instead. As go our University-bred Puritans, these grave budge scholarly gentlemen, as bait the bishops in Latin too hard for the poor bishops to comprehend, like busy Mr. Prynne now in jail (and God keep him there), yes, and like learned and poetical Mr. Milton, who knows better, for he has wrote some of the finest beautiful poetry on Christmas and on Church music and on country feasts, as any man has—but look now how he lends himself to the aid of the wrong side. No, sir, don't talk to me of John Milton, or I must open the windows and cleanse the air, and then the November fogs would enter and make us cough."

"All I was saying of John Milton, sir, was that he's been pleading for a more liberal and humane university education. He may be as wrong as you please in's politics—I won't argue for or against them, for I've no mind for either King or Parliament as tyrant—but he's right on education in my view, and the University should hark to him."

"Well, I won't say he's so wrong on education as on politics, and for my part I read more English with my pupils than is well thought on by most, who say I am wrong not to keep wholly to the ancient tongues. 'Twas poor Tom Randolph, who was at Trinity when I came first to Cambridge, who started me in that way. As to classical history, they learn quite enough on't. Some say too much, and that it turns 'em republican, but indeed, I conceit that English history is more like to do that, seeing we've always had sovereigns and yet have done no better than we have. As to the mathematical sciences, they begin to be taught and studied more, as I said, but they'll ne'er agree with your son. What do you intend to put him to, sir?"

The doctor shrugged his shoulders.

"Indeed I don't know. If he's no head for natural science, he won't make a physician. He might read for the law, like his brother." (At the mention of Kit's brother an expression of amused distaste passed over Mr. Cleveland's features; he and Francis Conybeare had been contemporaries at Christ's.) "I should be sorry for him to turn parson. Has he any mind that way, think you?"

"I don't think it," said Mr. Cleveland cautiously. "Not in present. He's ingenious at his divinity disputations, and knows his Aquinas and Lombard well, but I don't conceit as he's any mind to be a parson."

Happening to look at his pupil's sister, he met her eyes fixed on him in a wide and grave anxiety.

"The girl knows the lad's leanings," he said to himself. "Questionless he's telled her, and she's frighted I'll drop a hint on't to her father. I can read it in her eyes—and Lord, what eyes the pretty elf hath!"

He looked into them for a second; long enough to convey, he hoped, a message of assurance.

"God-a-mercy for that," said Dr. Conybeare. "He seems mightily taken up with chapel ornaments, and to 'have himself very pious and clergy in a church, bowing and scraping and ducking, as made all of joints, as the poem hath it. I feared he had it in's mind to become one o' 'the times' new churchmen, a new churchman o' 'the times.'"

"There's a great many of laymen, Dr. Conybeare, like a seemly habit in church. We enforce it in this college; unlike Trinity and some others. You should have sent him to Emmanuel if you wished he should be of the other colour. Not that Emmanuel's what it was in old Chaderton's day; 'tis riddled now with the heresies of Whichcote and the Latitude men, and the Five Points are gotten blunted. In fact, 'tis at Emmanuel and at Christ's that the war against Calvinism's most vigorously waged, though from another angle than from the Arminian. The Mad Puritan's song wou'n't be apt for Emmanuel in these days, for now 'tis all of Plato and the inner light you'll hear there. You mind old Dick Corbet's song?

"In the house of pure Emmanuel
I had my education,
Where my friends surmise
I dazzled my eyes
With the light of revelation.
Boldly I preach,
Hate a cross, hate a surplice,
Mitres, copes and rochets;
Come, hear me pray,
Nine times a day,
And fill your soul with crotchets.

But I fancy you'd have been no more partial to that way than to t'other. If a man has religion, let him carry it like a gentleman, say I, and not lose his manners over it."

"Oh, a pox on your gentlemen; I don't give a fig for 'em. Let a man use his intellects, say I, if so be he have any. I've no patience with a man wastes the short time he hath here in this bad world hating crosses and surplices or loving 'em; for look, his mind should be bent on something more useful. But I've spent enough of your time, Mr. Cleveland, and will take myself off. I must to Christ's, to wait on Dr. Bainbrigg. He has promised to quaint me with Henry More."

"Yes, well. You'll like Mr. More. He's a most eximious learned pious fellow, though with his head too much in the heavens looking for spirits. And 'tis pity he thinks he smells of violets."

"Why is it pity?" inquired Julian, for the first time so forgetting herself as to interrupt, for she was interested in Mr. More.

Mr. Cleveland turned on her his amused, indulgent glance. "Why, only because he don't, so far as anyone would notice it. But never mind. You'll like Mr. More very well. Do you meet him, as well as your father?"

"I should greatly like to meet him, sir, for I've heard much of his great poem on the soul."

"You have?" Mr. Cleveland looked still more amused. They were on their feet now, and he bent his handsome head down towards her, as one might to a pretty and intelligent child.

"Mr. More's poetry's not for you, I fear, little madam. 'Tis too hard, and full of learning, and deals with high philosophical matters that young ladies comprehend not, and find sad tedious dull stuff."

Julian coloured. Mr. Cleveland thought it made her pale skin like a pink sea shell. She was much too pretty a little miss to be troubling herself about philosophical poems, he thought. As if, too, she could understand anything about them!

But her father said, "Why, Julian's a fine forward knowing little scholar, a'n't you, Jule? She don't find poetry tedious stuff, nor philosophy neither. I warrant she'd sit so still as any image, were Mr. More to start reading out his poem; she'd drink in every word, and at the end, when the rest of us was nodding, she'd be able to tell us all about it. She's a better head than her brother, and that's a fact."

"Indeed? It seems I've wronged you, mistress." Mr. Cleveland smiled down at the grave, blushing young lady. "We must start a College for ladies in Cambridge and let you teach at it. You must attend Mr. More's philosophical lectures for ladies. He expounds the universe and the Platonical soul to 'em in St. Clement's Church of a Tuesday afternoon. Perhaps you have Latin and Greek, also?"

"Aye, she's a proper Latin scholar, and Greek too," the complacent parent answered for her. "Talks Latin like a Roman virgin, and writes verses in't as readily as in English. Parson Herrick's well taught her, down in Devonshire."

"Parson Herrick's fortunate," said Mr. Cleveland pleasantly, "in having such a pupil."

His merry eyes on her made Julian feel shy and abashed; she wished that her father would not thus boast of her before those who knew so much more, who thought nothing of her learning, and cared less.

Yet she liked his eyes as they looked down at her; they laughed and teased, but kindly. She thought it would be very agreeable to be Kit and have lessons from this brilliant tutor, who could orate so fluently and wittily in Latin.

"I must meet Mr. Herrick again," he added. "He and I have had common friends, in poor Tom Randolph, Tom Carew, and others. He used to have a pretty wit in his verse.

'Tis pity so much talent and beauty should be buried in remote Devonshire. I hope you'll stay in Cambridge a while now y'are here."

" Aye, we shall do so. I am writing a book that will progress better in Cambridge than in muddy Denshire. Faith, 'tis good to be in reach of books again, and of men as read and converse. A history of human credulities, sir; that's my subject."

" A mighty large one, sir. You may say an endless one. You have my sympathy, and I wish you luck."

" Thankye, thankye. It will go apace, now I can run about and free my mind from country loam and country bumpkins. Not but as what Denshire's a right good place in which to study credulity. But so's Cambridge, for that matter."

" So's Cambridge, indeed. Cambridge, where any day another fish might be catched with his belly stuffed with books, to foretell all the country's ills. *Vox piscis, vox Dei*, as they say. Aye, human credulity'll never fail you, wherever you seek it out. They say as even in Oxford there's a trifle on't; while in London they'll believe anything. Well, I must not keep you gossiping here. I shall see you perhaps at Trinity to-night? *Comus* is a pretty masque enough, though should be played pastoral, but those two prating, preaching brothers in't do greatly fatigue me; the saddest tedious pair of budge cockets as never I saw. They'll weary even you, Mrs. Julian."

" No, sir; I like the brothers."

" Oh, so y'have seen *Comus*? You seem to see and hear everything in Devonshire; I swear I must visit there. Farewell then. Be curious not to stumble on the stair; it's something dark."

He watched them descend, before returning into his room with a smile.

" That's an extraordinary little pretty solemn virgin. Fresh as a blossom from the country, and yet with a *je ne sais quoi* about her. . . . A skin like lilies, eyes like pansies, a brow like alabaster, a dimple that plays peek-bo in her cheek, and, cud's life, she must needs prate of books! Some young spark will teach her better than that ere long. He'll be a happy man as enjoys her. . . . Well, I must go wait on the Master about the administration of the oath in the College. A pox on these parents, they'll keep a man all day with their 'my son this,' 'my son must learn t'other.' Did they but know it, what their sons have every one of 'em to do is to follow the course set 'em, keep at their books, and do what they can at 'em. No young bawcock's going to have a particular course of study planned out for his peculiar benefit. Ah, did parents but know on what stony ground do fall their words of wisdom, and what hard hearts and rigid souls do College tutors have, for all the honeyed and cheverel speech they may affect. . . . Ne'ertheless, I like the little doctor. I swear I'll bid him and old Robin Herrick to a poets' party. Young Cowley shall read his latest verses, and I mine, and Mr. Herrick shall pipe us some of his pastorals, and Dick Crashaw shall give us an ode, and that little Marvell from Trinity, who turns as pretty a verse as any lad of his years, shall come; and Henry More, only I'm damned if I'll let him read out much of that tedious great poem of his, that he calls a private record of his soul and to be seen of none, but that seems to be seen or heard of all in turn. 'Tis pity I can't have the little maid too, to listen with those great eyes of hers, but that can't be. I'll bid her brother come, to keep company with his father. Aye; I'll ask 'em for Friday evening, and we'll forget our country's horrid state and this misbegotten bastard of a new parliament, and sit on Parnassus like the gods."

12

On Friday evening, the 5th of November, Kit called at the White Horse inn after supper, to conduct his father and Mr. Herrick to Mr. Cleveland's party at St. John's.

" 'Tis pity Jule can't go," Meg said, " since it's a party for poets. And 'tis pity I can't go, since it's a party of pleasure. But there, the wrong persons is always bid to diversions, while the right ones have to go to bed. 'Tis fate. And we mayn't so much as walk abroad in the town, since it's Guy Fawkes his day and there's merriment and bon-fires. What make you abroad, Kit, for Giles telled us the scholars might not stir out this night for fear of embroilment with the townsmen and their roistering and roilying? He said as it caused much discontent, not only for that they want to see the guys and the roistering, but for that it's a Friday, and fish day in College, and on that day all who can do so get their supper-money from their tutors and eat in the town."

" Aye, they do, the hogs. Most particular in Trinity. I am very glad they must stay in to-night and fast, and can't join in the guying. I got permission from Mr. Cleveland to come here and back, for he knew that I wished neither to eat flesh in a tavern nor to shout and burn guys."

Meg primmed up her mouth and folded her hands before her. Kit reddened, and thought what a tiresome girl she in some ways was.

" We had best come now, sir," he said to his parent. The girls watched them go, and Julian sighed.

" So many poets at once, how fortunate Kit is! Yet he don't care near so much for poets as I do."

"Ne'er mind," Meg cheered her, "we'll play mumchance in the ladies' parlour with the door wide, and perhaps, who knows, Mr. Milton will pass by and you'll see him. Why, perhaps if you speak him pretty, and tell him how you wept at *Comus*, he'll join our game."

"You know he won't. He never will say a word to us. He don't hold with females. I don't want to speak with him, neither; I should never dare, knowing how he scorns us. Why do men scorn women? 'Tis great pity."

"I don't notice as they do, so much. Giles don't."

"Oh, Giles."

"Well, you needn't say his name so scornful. Giles is much better than all those poets of yours. Y'are growing cocked up because Mr. Cowley talks t'you."

"I'm not cocked up."

"Y'are. But no matter; let's come and play at mumchance before we go to bed. Lud, how tedious 'tis to be females and to stay in, with all the fun without. Hark to 'em shouting down the streets."

"I don't like it," said Julian, and frowned. "People is terrifying when they shout together. Come upstairs, Meg, and we'll shut the windows and keep 'em out. They'd shout out in the same way if they had catched a live man and was carting him about the streets, instead of only mawkins. Rabbles are dreadful and horrid and cruel."

The cries and laughter and torches swept up from the market-place as Dr. Conybeare and his son and Mr. Herrick walked along Trumpington Street. Merry crowds jostled them, bound for the market-place bonfires, carrying guns, faggots, and flaring links. Broad Cambridgeshire voices chanted happily,

"Please to remember
The fifth of November

Gunpowder treason and plot,
I see no reason
Why gunpowder treason
Should ever be forgot.
A stick and a stake, for King Charles his sake,
A stick and a stump, for Guy Fawkes his rump!
If thou won't give me one I'll take three
The better for me,
And the worse for thee.
Holla boys, hollo boys, holla!"

"'Tis in the market-place we should pass the evening, and not within a College room," Mr. Herrick said, "I like these merry Bacchanalian frenzies and fires. Mr. Fawkes, godamercy for thy gunpowder, that's made for the English people so much honest mirth. 'Tis a finer show here than in Devonshire, for there are more guys, though less wood for the bonfires."

Cries arose behind them.

"A Pope, a Pope, a Pope! make way for his mammetship the Pope!" And, bearing a chair in which sat a mitred figure with upraised arm and black face, four stalwart youths marched past.

"Hellish uncivil vulgar hoydens," Kit commented, loud and scornful. "Bringing the Pope into their hoyting too."

A stout young apprentice, hearing what he had been meant to hear, turned about and struck the undergraduate in the face with his open hand.

"That for a Papist, and hell roast the Pope. Lads, here's a Pope's boy; shall we chair him for a guy?"

Kit had shot out his fist, but was jerked back by his father.

"Let be, let be, and don't brawl. Must thou be mixing up with a louts' brabble when given leave out and put on thine honour to keep out on any such doings? Cock's life,

I'll not stay and help thee, but will proceed to thy tutor's and tell him I've left ye brawling i' the streets. And you there, y' uncivil brocks, take shame t'ye and be off with your mawkins and mammets to your bonfires, and say godamercy to me that I don't haul ye up before the courts for assault. Why, a pox, a'n't speech free? Mayn't a man say what he please in the open street without being struck i' the face?"

This rhetorical inquiry, to which the answer was plainly in the negative, was addressed to the backs of the Pope-carriers, who had by now forgot the trifling incident, since it was apparently not to lead to a fight, and were marching off.

"Damn their eyes for blasphemous foul-mouthed coystrells," Kit angrily observed. "You should not have let me from punishing 'em, sir. I hate such nasty sort of impudent rabble. What are they, to be permit openly to insult His Holiness thus?"

"His Holiness! The Pope of Rome a'n't in your keeping to defend, my lad, that you need wax so hot on him."

"Why, sir, at the very least he's a renowned foreigner, and the head of a great Church, and our Queen's Church, too, and we owe him civility. Then, there's a many of Papists in Cambridge, and some even of priests, and are they to see us use such rude bawdry towards their Holy Father?"

"If they use their eyes, boy," said Mr. Herrick, "they could see such rude bawdry used even toward our own Holy Father; for there goes His little Grace, mitre, crozier, and all, and shears in his hand ready to lop the ears off the Leightons and the Prynnes. Pox take the louts for their impudence, they have given the mawkin Canterbury's very eyebrows and turn-down mouth. I warrant there'd be trouble did that come to the notice of Cosin or Beale, or any of our other Canterburians. What do they sing?"

They appeared to be singing,

" Canterbury too,
Let him now rue
How with his shears
He cropped English ears,
Bowed low to a cross,
Ducked down before dross,
Tie him up with the Pope,
Swing 'em both to a rope.
There's a new Popish plot
Ere the last is forgot.
A pox on Arminians!
Sing hoy for Calvinians!
And tonnage and poundage and free will be damned!
With a hoy, hoy, hoy! "

" Sad beggarly doggerel stuff," said Mr. Herrick. " I could have wrote 'em something better than that."

" 'Tis as good as they want," the doctor said. " It says what they want said. But I admire if one on 'em knows the meaning of either tonnage and poundage or free will."

" They all want whipping," Kit pronounced, and so disposed of the coystrell rabble as they reached St. John's gate.

13

The room was full of the voices of poets, the smoke of their pipes, and the fumes of their drinks. They sat or lolled about in agreeable ease, most of them with manuscripts in their hands, and expressions either expectant or already gratified, while they listened with varying degrees of inattention to Mr. Henry More, who, sitting, as his wont was, straight and upright in a hard chair, was reading aloud from a manuscript, his pale olive face illumined by an eager comprehension and sympathy with his own meaning which was not shared by quite all his audience.

" But yet my Muse, still take an higher Flight:
Sing of Platonick Faith in the First God;
That Faith which doth our Souls to God unite
So strongly, tightly, that the rapid Flood
Of this swift Flux of things, nor with foul Mud
Can stain, nor strike us off from th'unity
Wherein we steadfast stand, unshak'd, unmoved
Engrafted by a deep Vitality.
The Prop and stay of things is God's Benignity. . . .

At this point, Mr. Herrick was conquered by the immense yawn that had been tormenting him for some minutes past like a gagged giant who now spewed the gag forth and freely and convulsively respired. Mr. Herrick uttered a hoarse cough of camouflage, and Mr. More's sweet and even voice read on.

" It may be very good platonicks," Mr. Herrick whispered to the doctor; " but 'tis confounded sorry stuff as poetry."

"He shou'n't write it," the doctor agreed. "His meaning, granted he have one, would appear more plainer in prose. But hark, here's a piece on astronomy, as might hold more of sense. Or, as likely, less."

> "Blest souls, first authours of Astronomy!
> Who clomb the heavens with your high reaching mind,
> Scaled the high battlements of the lofty sky,
> To whom compar'd this earth a point you find."

"Aye, truly," Dr. Conybeare muttered. "'Tis truly but a point, and so much for Ptolemy. Hark now, while he has at the Ptolemaists."

> "O you stiff-standers for ag'd Ptolemee,
> I heartily praise your humble reverence
> If willingly given to Antiquity;
> But when of him in whom's your confidence,
> Or your own reason and experience
> In those same arts, you find those things are true
> That utterly oppugn our outward sense,
> Then are you forc'd to sense to bid adieu,
> Not what your sense gainsayes to holden straight untrue."

"He thinks of Galileo," Dr. Conybeare whispered. "Galileo's 'him in whom's your confidence.' That's a good hit, a monstrous shrewd sharp hit at the Ptolemaists."

"It a'n't poetry," returned Mr. Herrick, uninterested, and plainly now perceiving that Platonism was not enough; though he did not get so far as to arrive at the dictum that good philosophy makes, as a rule, bad poetry. "Using Spenser's noble stanza too, for his pious painful conceits," he muttered.

Looking round at his fellow-listeners, he saw young Mr. Cowley's fair, square-chinned, high-browed face turned on the reader in frowning attention, and inferred that Mr. More's poem on the soul would probably have on this brilliant young man's verse an unfortunate influence; for Julian had said that he was himself engaged in a long religious epic.

"Which, doubtless, we shall suddenly hear in part," the clergyman sighed to himself. He considered long religious epics a mistake; it was so very few poets who wrote them well. Mr. More, he had by now decided, might almost as well be writing that kind of verse as any other, but this lad Cowley was an ingenious poet in his way, and had written some tolerable matter, and doubtless would again, when he had gotten his epic off his chest.

From Mr. Cowley the vicar looked at his friend, Mr. Crashaw, sitting next to him. Mr. Crashaw's sensitive brows were drawn a little together; probably this was not his notion of poetry either. Neither, for that matter, would the appreciation of Plato, of Galileo, or of the Copernican system be particularly pleasing to his Aristotelian and even Ptolemaic spirit. Kit, too, looked impatient at this wordy astronomical good sense.

As to their host, his face was impassive, polite, and a trifle amused, as he leant back in his chair, puffing at his long pipe, and listening to his friend from Christ's. He was thinking, "At what point shall I stop him? We can't have the whole that he's wrote of his *Psychozoia Platonica*. Lord, I di'n't know the dear fellow'd wrote so much. We shall have Robin Herrick breaking in in another minute. He's all on the hoity-toity to read his own verses, and he don't think much of these, and small blame to him. These Platonists are very amiable learned good creatures, but poor and heretical theologians and monstrous dull poets."

Mr. More, a modest and generous, but somewhat absent-minded, poet, might have continued reading for some time longer, but Mr. Cleveland, when he paused at the end of a stanza, said quickly, "Thank you, sir; w'are greatly obliged t'you. Y'have given us much profound curious matter to ponder and discuss."

"There is more yet," said Mr. More simply, marking his place on the page with one slim white hand as he looked up.

"I hope much more," Mr. Cleveland heartily and hastily rejoined, "so as we'll be entertained by't at some later date. But now, as the night wears on, I'll ask our friend and guest, Mr. Robert Herrick, as many of us have known by name if not in person, since he was one of our late loved master's, Ben Jonson's, circle, and one of its merriest blithe lyrical poets —I say, I'll ask Mr. Herrick to read out to us some of his country verses."

Mr. Herrick did so, in his rich, fine, resonant voice. He read them poems of flowers, of barefoot girls that gathered them, of country feasts, of fairies, elves, and weddings; then to please the loyal society of St. John's, he read his good wishes for the most hopeful and handsome prince, the Duke of York.

> "May his pretty Duke-ship grow
> Like t'a Rose of *Jericho*:
> Sweeter far, then ever yet
> Showrs or Sun-shines co'd beget.
> May the Graces, and the Howers
> Strew his hopes, and Him with flowers:
> And so dresse him up with Love,
> As to be the Chick of *Jove*. . . ."

And this was so unlike anything that Mr. More ever wrote, that he gazed at the loyal clergyman as from another planet.

Mr. Herrick was well away now, among Antheas and Corinnas (but of Julia he read nothing), daffodils and primroses, meadows and music, gilly-flowers and sack, hock-carts, weddings, births and deaths. He was transported with the sound of what he read.

Looking up, as he pronounced the title "Divination by a

Daffadill," he met the grave, attentive, politely appraising eyes of young Mr. Cowley, and for a second he paused, checked, as it were, by the impact of a cold wave. The first wave, was it, of the rising tide of a great, approaching, ineluctable sea, the sea of the next, of the younger, of the coming generation? What if the coming generation, who would decide a man's fate, did not admire that poetry which was his heart's blood, his life's vocation and employ?

Slowly, and rather low, Mr. Herrick read his "Divination by a Daffadill," and the words dropped on his soul strangely, like passing bells.

> "When a Daffadill I see,
> Hanging down his head t'wards me;
> Guesse I may, what I must be:
> First, I shall decline my head;
> Secondly, I shall be dead;
> Lastly, safely buryed."

Aye, that was it. That poem was an omen of his decline and death. His verse would be passed by, made nought of, by these new young men, with their elaborate, involved conceits, their scorn of forthrightness. He was too old to learn to Clevelandise, did he wish to—and, God knew, he did not wish to; he preferred his own style, and that of Ben, his master. These involved, these conceited young men, would never write like that . . .

> "Yet, when one of them I see
> Hanging down his head t'wards me;
> Guesse I may, what I must be:
> First, I shall decline my head. . . ."

He jerked it back instead, in petulant defiance, and challenged young Mr. Cowley directly.

"Do my verses please you, sir?"

"Why, yes, sir, greatly."

But young Mr. Cowley's slight hesitation, his faint embarrassment, betrayed him.

"But th'are not in the newest mode, y'are thinking," said the parson.

"Indeed, sir, verses a'n't obliged to be like cloes, all cut to the latest fashion. There's a dainty rustic simplicity in your country verses, as very well pleases me."

"Aye, w'are all agreed there," Mr. Cleveland said. "One wearies of elaborations, twists, and conceits. John Donne was a very fine poet, but his weren't the only way to write poetry, though 'tis now so much the mode. Yours, Mr. Herrick, if you'll let me so say, smacks of the English meadow and the Roman vineyard in very nice proportion, and falls extreme sweet and tuneable on ears grown used to epigram and to knots and twists of thought and speech."

"Aye, d'ye find 'em sweet? But I can write epigram, too, that's not so tuneable nor sweet. How's this, gentlemen?"

Stung by the hint of a civil indifferent patronage that he fancied in the polite faces round the room, he flung at them a rude and dirty quatrain that he had made on a Dean Prior cottage woman to avenge himself for ill-washed shirts. He would show them that he was not merely a sweet singer of bucolics, a hymner of flowers and maids.

As he declaimed the uncivil lines, he saw the sensitive face of Mr. More wince, stiffen, and then grow blank, as if his spirit withdrew to some inner fastness where foulness could not touch him. Mr. Crashaw leant his forehead on his hand, as if abstracted in thought; Mr. Cowley listened in polite attention, Kit in cross discomfort, wishing that Mr. Herrick knew better how to conduct himself in modern Cambridge, which was doubtless better bred than the Cambridge of his own days. Coarse jests enough passed, and none but the precisians and the pious cared, but who wanted dirty doggerel about an old Devonshire washerwoman flung into an assembly of scholars and philosophical poets?

Mr. Cleveland politely smiled.

"Y'are right, Mr. Herrick; that's not near so sweet. If y'have many more such, your flock in Devonshire must have you in a wholesome fear. And now, Mr. Cowley, perhaps you'll show us what the youngest poets is writing to-day."

Mr. Cowley, blushing a little, began the epic, *Davideis*, on which he was engaged.

> "I Sing the *Man* who *Judahs Scepter* bore
> In that right hand which held the *Crook* before . . ."

Mr. Herrick sat and listened, but, running beside the story of David like a thin, cold, singing brook, he heard:

> "First, I shall decline my head;
> Secondly, I shall be dead;
> Lastly, safely buryed. . . ."

He noticed that Mr. Crashaw, Mr. Cleveland, Mr. More, all of them, listened attentively to *Davideis* as if it were something of importance; not with that polite, tolerant civility which they had shown (he saw now) towards himself. Let a poet be but a young ape of two-and-twenty, and his fellows will hang on his words, seeing in 'em a portent and a sign of the times. Let him be nine-and-forty, greying on the head, writing as he wrote in his youth, and the world will pass him by with a half-kindly, half-impatient nod; he is safely buryed. But he would show them yet; aye, he could write 'em all down, and he would.

As to this *Davideis*, it was tedious dull stuff. Fortunately, Mr. Cowley had not so far written a great deal of it, so could not continue reading it for very long. When he stopped, an interested discussion arose on it between him, Mr. Crashaw,

Mr. John Austin, and Mr. More. Mr. Crashaw and Mr. Austin then each read, shyly and not very well, a few brief and charming devotional verses, and Mr. Cleveland, not shyly, and very well indeed, some droll satires, a rather complicated poem on a Hermaphrodite, and his new skit on the Etcetera in the Oath.

Dr. Conybeare, meanwhile, had been stirring restively under this torrent of poesy. It was more than time, thought he, that they ceased to read aloud and fell to talking. When Mr. Cleveland seemed to have finished, the doctor quickly broke in with conversation, lest young Marvell, or Mr. Crashaw's friend, Beaumont (or whatever his name was), or even Kit, might be asked to oblige. He addressed Mr. More who with grave civility bent forward to listen to him.

"Now, what I would learn, sir, is, what, to your thinking, most nicely discriminates this new Platonism of yours from the old beliefs—that is, how 'twould affect, did it spread, the common man's view of his standing in the universe?"

Mr. More's face lit up at such welcome inquest.

"Sir, your question is most apt. I would answer by repeating your own last word. This new learning we urge lights for man the very universe itself. It gives infinity to his conceits, eternity to the smallest living being. It teaches him the infinity of worlds, the pre-existence of his soul, and its present nature of a Deiform seed, an immaterial soul infinitely perfectible. It reveals God not as rigid task master, but as the Absolute Idea of goodness, busy ever in his world to perfect it. It shows man that he has but to open his soul for the everlasting and absolute light to flow in; or, if you will, that he has but to dive deeply into his own spirit to find and cherish the springing fountain of everlasting life. And this light of life springing ever within him (as, you will recollect, Origen and Plotin speak) will burnish all the universe for him, and brighten every star. His enlarged world, seen through the mystic eye of purity and faith, will shine again. The vast spaces of infinity which he has newly apprehended will awe but not alarm him; rather, he'll see in them the measureless wisdom of the God who shines also in his own soul. Aye, and he'll know that God hath peopled this planet of ours with his aetherial beings, so that we have among us not only our ministering angels, and not only the seven kinds of angels or spirits which Gregorius Tholosanus reports, according to the number of the seven planets, but angels and spirits everywhere about us, to be beholded of our very senses if we so purify and master them as to bestow on them that vision."

Angels! That was tedious, thought the doctor, if he was going to run after those flighty angels, as indeed he looked like he might well do, his eyes wide opened, yet not seeming to see aught in the room; doubtless they were turned within, gazing at his deiform soul, or into infinity, spying angels.

Dr. Conybeare quickly called him off this chase.

"But I take it, sir, as a man needs not to see spirits because he reads Plato, Plotinus, Tully and Origen."

"Indeed, sir, you are right. A man will see no spirits unless he fits himself for the sight. For they lie leaguer, not to be spied of the gross senses."

"Maybe. For my part, I don't credit 'em and don't desire 'em. See here, sir, speaking as a man as don't greatly believe on angels, nor on gods neither, so setting these, for the occasion, aside——"

"An atheist, Dr. Conybeare?" Mr. Cleveland blandly inquired, while Kit hotly blushed.

"Aye, if ye like. The name's no bug-a-boo to scare me. There'll come a time when men will be able freely to profess their disbelief or their belief in any gods they choose."

"That's as may be, doctor, but that time a'n't here yet, and I fear you implicate us in misprision of heresy by your frankness. Meanwhile, since you are my guest, I'll not recall to you the horrid deaths Providence in's wisdom hath meted out to atheists, that our good Dr. Fuller speaks on in his latest manuscript I have here—how Diagoras was burnt, Pherecydes devoured of lice, and Lucian of dogs, and so forth; but will only hold out hope and cheer to you, as the reverend doctor also does, by reminding you that *nullus in inferno est Atheos, ante fuit*; on earth were atheists many, in hell there is not any. So, though some may deem it a woeful thing to be hell's convert, you should rejoice as there's yet religion in store for you."

"Thank ye. I'll wait patient for't, and not forestall Providence."

"Since hell," Mr. More said, "is, like heaven, first a temper, then a place (as you may hear Dr. Whichcote preach in Trinity Church of any Sunday afternoon, and as Dr. Browne of Norwich also saith in his most eximious and curious as yet unpublished treatise, *Religio Medici*), I would suggest that we none of us need wait for it, but that we carry both tempers about in our breasts. I am very sure, however, that Dr. Conybeare hath in his more of the heavenly than of the infernal temper, whatsoever he may conceit that he do believe. Is there much of atheism in Devonshire?"

"Not a scruple," Mr. Herrick answered for the country of his ministry, "now as this physician's took himself away to Cambridge. Devonshire'd be all with you, Mr. More, concerning your plurality of spirits. Scarce a soul took its leave of my parish these ten years but it went again. Not to speak of all the elves, fays, pigsies, pucks, goblins and dowls as walk i' the woods and moors. I don't know, though, as to angels; angels is scarcer visitants, at least in the Dean neighbourhood. But look'ee, ye'll ne'er convert this doctor, since he's lived among the rustical apparitions these four years, and don't believe on 'em yet."

"Ah," said Mr. Cleveland, "another characteristic of the

atheist. 'He loveth to maintain Paradox, and to shut his eyes against the beams of a known truth.' Dr. Conybeare, we must see you hear sermons in Cambridge; you must sit with the Latitude men beneath Dr. Whichcote and hear of the Platonic soul; beneath Dr. Cosin and hear of the ancient and Catholic order of the Church of England; and beneath some of our Calvinists and hear predestination proclaimed. All these learned preachers of an undivided Church will mayhap convert you where the ghosts of Devonshire failed."

"By all means let 'em do so, if they can. In the meantime, I would inquire more closely into this new Platonism. How, *exempli gratia*, do it fadge with the Copernican astronomy, and with Descartes his theories?"

"Excellently well, sir," Mr. More told him, "with the Pythagorean astronomy, as it is better called than Copernican, to my mind, since Pythagoras first discovered it. Platonism must lead men to the study of knowledge of truth in science, as elsewhere, since it acknowledges the guidance of the inner light that leads man on toward truth. If your dogmatic Aristotelians lost their Ptolemaic universe, they would lose their God, since their creed is that God has anciently revealed to them all his truth, and, if it prove to be error, what then? But Platonists, led by the light of wisdom, are ever ready to replace one order by another, should the former prove erroneous. Aye, and they'll treat the divine scriptures so too, granting 'em the human element of error; whereas the schoolmen and priests, Catholic, Protestant and Calvinian alike, have so tied men to the literal word that they've lost God's sense that lit it; look how the story of the Creation, because insisted on as literal by the Catholic Bibliolators, has fostered atheism in the world, and made profane men swear the whole business of religion a fable. Yet to suggest latitude and allegory in scriptural interpretation vexes the dogmatists more considerably than atheism itself. But I stray from your point.

You speak of M. Descartes, and I take it you will agree with some of us in Cambridge that he's an extraordinary great subtle philosopher, a greater than Lord Bacon, and will come to affect our thought here beyond guessing, as he grow more known. His doctrine of the incorporeal soul is very admirable, and strikes both at the Epicureans and the Peripatetics. Though, indeed, he is of a somewhat mechanising humour, and the hypothesis of the plastic medium, which begins here to be put forward, finds no favour with him, and squares not with his doctrine of occasional causes. But, indeed, sir, you doubtless know M. Descartes his theories full as well as I do," the young man added, with agreeable modesty.

"Why yes, I've read the *Discours*, and do greatly esteem it. What I would know is, what influence he has, and will have, on English thought. What you call his mechanising humour I consider a mighty wholesome good antidote to the spiritualising angelical humour of you Platonists."

"They are both in the wrong," Mr. Cleveland pronounced. "For my part, I'll have none of 'em. Neither will Mr. Crashaw, Mr. Beaumont, Mr. Austin, nor, I trust, Mr. Herrick. Will you, sir? Don't Ecclesia Anglicana spew 'em out, both mechanisers and spiritisers? What do she want with 'em, having the Prayer Book, the Bible and the sacraments? A'n't it enough, and these men must go a-whoring after fantastical notions of deity, natural law, and plastic mediums? For look ye, I keep my Church and my religion, as it were, here, and my scientific researches and notions there, so as neither need mell with or do hurt to t'other. But you Platonists, pox take me, you let your religion spill over into your science, and your science into your religion, till both are a kind of mystical mixed brew, as like one another as two bowls of caudle, and like to nought else that I know on."

"'Tis the Christian Church first mixed them," Mr. More said. "If the Church will burn men of science for declaring opinions concerning the planets, you can't blame us for mixing science and religion. Though, for my part, I follow Plotinus in regarding religion as no matter of science, but as God's life in the soul."

"Aye; God's life in the soul, fed by devotion, meditations and sacraments," Mr. Crashaw amended; and Mr. Herrick, Mr. Austin and Mr. Beaumont approved him, but Mr. Austin very naturally and properly believed, though he did not mention it, that no one present except himself had his soul fed by devotion or meditation to any good purpose, or by sacraments to any purpose at all, for he had, discreetly and unostentatiously, lately become a Roman Catholic.

All this religious chatter rather fatigued Mr. Cleveland, and it was, after all, his party, so he changed the subject to politics, and they discussed the iniquitous doings of the new parliament (which, early as it was, had already begun misbehaving), and how that vindictive, fanatical jackanapes, Peter Smart, formerly Prebendary of Durham, and Dr. Cosin's old malicious foe, would next week present again his petition against the doctor for the practice of Popish ceremonial, and it might be a serious matter, for the parliament was speaking spiteful things not only of ceremonial, but of the barest Church order and seemliness. They were even accusing Dr. Cosin, that great devout Protestant Anglican, of seducing to Popery. Dr. Beale, too, would probably find himself arraigned again.

"And my Lord Strafford has been sent for from Yorkshire," said Mr. Cleveland, "and 'twill go very ill with him, for they all hate him like the devil, and, I do believe, more for his seizing of tobacco than of the people's liberties. 'Tis the first as they call hellish, and would like his neck for, more than all his misdoings in Ireland. A man few love; 'tis pity. They say 'twas the same with him when he was up at John's. A proud, high, haughty man, whom some few would die for, and the rest loathe. Pym and his merry men are out by all means for his blood, there's no doubt on't. Though how they have the impudence to charge him with treason, when themselves are fonding the army of the rebel Scots as you'd cocker a savage dog, passes the wit of the sane man to conceive. 'Tis they are the traitors, treating brotherly with the king's foes. I hear they'll have a great debate on Monday, and discover to the house this marvellous Popish plot of theirs. Now, I wonder, what's the truth of that? There's doubtless something to't, but how much?"

"Not a word," said Mr. Austin. "Questionless, the Catholics and the Queen would wish to see England reconverted, but not by treachery nor force. Conn and Rossetti made no plot, nor the Queen nor her mother, neither. And as to Canterbury, as you well know, he's as stubborn bigoted a Protestant churchman as never breathed; as Anglican as our Cosin, whom they charge with converting to Popery. The Catholics have no hope there. But this damned parliament will work it up against 'em, and use it for a stick to beat the Queen's party with, and to make the poor Papists' lot harder."

"Ecod, Jack, my poor Papist, you can't wave your plot away so easy as that. What of the Spanish negotiations. What of the appeals to the Pope for money?"

"Well, what of 'em? The King had no money, and desperately required it to pay off the rebel Scots. He had to try all quarters, before he was drove to summon and milk this savage kicking cow of a parliament. Can you blame him?"

"I never blame His Majesty. Save, perhaps, for a trifle of indiscretion here and there. And if there were a Popish plot, 'tweren't his, for all the world knows he's a firm Canterburian Church of England man, and distastes Her Majesty's religion and priests. But your legates and your Jesuits and your Windebanks—I don't trust 'em, nor do any man."

Mr. Austin said, "In that case, you had best go out and shout with the street rabble and their guys. For my part, I'll leave you, gentlemen, and go to bed."

"Good-night, sweet Jack. I love you, for all your false superstitious religion. As these Latitude men say, 'tis the life counts, not the doctrine. Why, he's gone, and can't be teased more. Cud, I love to droll on the dear solemn fellow, going about so pleased with his secret Popery that all his friends know on and that none will take cognisance on officially because they all love him so well."

Mr. Crashaw said gently, "A man's religion's but a poor occasion for drollery, in my view."

"Nonsense, Dick; 'tis the most savoury curious good occasion in the world, for the graver the theme the fairer the jest, you know. Lord, if we mightn't jest and droll on the Puritans and Papists and t'other godlies, what in life could we do with 'em? What d'ye say, Dr. Atheist?"

"Why, I say that religion, whether the Puritan superstition, the Papist, or the Protestant, is past a jest. To jest at it is to condone it, and I'll be no party to that in principle, whatever my weak human nature may entice me to in practice."

"And I say," said Mr. More, "that to jest at the light in men's souls, whether it be the true light or the *ignis fatuus*, is a scurvy trick, and advances neither the cause of truth nor of charity. You droll overmuch, Cleveland."

"Lord, 'tis one's only comfort, these bad times. I'll warrant Mr. Herrick agrees to that, and has a store of comical facetious tales he could tell us if we would harken. Have you not, sir?"

"Yes, well; a tale or two, belike."

"Look, gentlemen, now our poetical readings and budge discourses is over, we'll begin, if you'll give me leave, with one of John Milton as I heard yesterday."

The tale of John Milton bore an unveracious air, and Mr. More dismissed it with a smile.

"John Milton could invent likelier tales of thee than that, Jack Cleveland. And I dare say that he do, for he hath a very satirical malicious wit."

"I grant, I grant. Rat the fellow, he's all the gifts, set aside the right politics and a trifle of pleasant friendly levity. Now, Mr. Herrick, pray divert us."

Mr. Herrick, a clergyman of florid and witty discourse, proved so competent to do so that they kept him at it for some time, and Mr. Cowley and Mr. Marvell had departed for Trinity, and Mr. Crashaw and Mr. Beaumont for Peterhouse, before he was finished.

"Soft and fair, sir," Dr. Conybeare said at midnight; "we must lin this parson, who's apt, once started, to continue all night long. 'Tis past time we relieved you of our company, and that this lad of mine went to his bed. Aye, boy, get you gone forthwith, having thanked your tutor first for bidding you here." Really, thought his son, he was a somewhat annoying father, and left the room in embarrassment.

"I thank ye, sir," added the doctor, "for a very cordial agreeable evening. Do you go our way, Mr. More, for I would have another word with you?"

"With all my heart, sir. Cleveland, did you hear his physician say that Dr. Chaderton can't last a week more?"

"Aye, I heard. I fear he'll not touch a hundred and four; he'll stint of it by ten days, unless God's good to him. I writ my elegy t'other day; 'tis all yare for the funeral. Cad, to think as he was helping to translate the Authorised Version, as a hoar old gentleman of seventy odd, before either you or I was born. One of the few Puritans I ever esteemed, even though he begat a mischievous progeny. But Puritans were different, I take it, in his young days—if he ever had young days. He must have been zealous for't, for he was thrown out of his father's estates for deserting the Old Religion. Aye, some of Queen Elizabeth's Puritans (not as Queen Bess had any gust for 'em, for she was ever a good ceremonious Protestant) were a fine upstanding sort; not like this generation of whining, snivelling hypocrites. Though even they have a good man here and there, like my old schoolmaster Vines, as beat Latin verbs into me when I was an urchin and he a young man."

"There was also one's parents," Mr. More said.

"Aye, true enough, One's parents was Puritans. 'Twas the mode in those days."

"Mine was very Calvinistic, and reared me to predestination. But I never could swallow it down. I mind, as a young boy at Eton, disputing earnestly against it with my eldest brother, and being threatened by my uncle with the rod for my forwardness in so doing. I had an aversion to the doctrine from the cradle. 'Tis strange, the hold it hath on so many minds."

"'Tis un-English," said Mr. Herrick. "Its mean injustice smacks of foreign parts. Unless we purge our land of these wild alien heresies, our English temper will be quite destroyed. Calvin was a fanatical fierce Frenchman, and Luther a turbulent fierce German, and the Pope's a bigoted obstinate Italian and, say I, none of the three's any good to England, as hath her own Church and doth very well without any of 'em."

"Hear, hear, parson. You and I are well met, and must talk further on the things of the spirit. Farewell, and give my resentments to Mrs. Julian. Alas, that propriety forbade her attendance at my little gathering! Dr. Conybeare, More, hath a most exquisite lovely daughter, who is, further, a lover of poetry and learning, a maid after your own heart, who would have hung on you, all attention, while you read and expounded—would she not, sir?"

"Aye, no question she would. Indeed, Mr. More, it's of

my daughter I would speak with you as we go, if you will be so obliging to walk with us."

"And believe me, More, 'tis a marvellous pretty theme, and should bring even your luciform soul down to earth. Except that the young lady's doubtless a luciform soul herself, so should soar easily in the empyrean with yours. There, that's a pretty compliment to you both, and so good-night."

14

"Look 'ee, Mr. More," Dr. Conybeare was saying, as they strolled along through a still crowded and rejoicing Cambridge, which had not yet seen, nor would for some hours see, any reason for forgetting gunpowder treason. "Look 'ee, sir, I have a daughter, as Mr. Cleveland says."

"Y'are fortunate, sir, since I infer from his merry words that she has graces both of mind and body."

"Aye, has she. She's a tolerable ingenious knowing maid, quick in her parts, and fonds on learning like a spaniel on bones, or a babe on dolls. Don't she so, Mr. Herrick?"

"Aye, Jule loves her books. She's a studious little maid, and learns apace. I've taught her of late years, and ne'er had a more ingenious or diligent scholar."

"It's an extreme pleasant thing," said Mr. More, "to find a young female thus. For I ever maintain it that women have parts such as men have, if not so robust and well formed, and should be well instructed young, as have many of our learned ladies been, both else and presently, but the generality of maidens is not. For the most of human kind to-day is so fast-set in prejudice that it can't believe on the good of learning to a woman, be she never so naturally ingenious a bibliophile and scholar. For my part, were my destiny other than it is, and should I choose to marry and rear children, I would give the boys and girls the same teaching."

"Indeed, there'd be fewer female fools abroad if all parents so used. 'Twas my theory, too, but I had a hard contest to rout my wife in the matter, who was determined her daughters' learning, after they had mastered their horn-hook, should go little further than the still-room, kitchen, and embroidery-frame. She almost got her way with the eldest, for the girl proved a dunce, and could neither swallow nor digest the least scruple of Latin, history, or algebra. So I married her off young, and gave my attention to the youngest, who showed some intellects from the time she could first diddle across the room. I had my way with her, though not without pudder and wrangling before her mother died, and she's been well grounded and taught in the mathematics by me, and of late in the classical tongues and English literature by Mr. Herrick here. She's in a fair way to become a woman of sense and learning, if she don't get falling into love or marriage too soon, which is a disease brings destruction to a wench's intellects while it endures, though they sometimes recover from the fever later, if by that time th'are not too fully occupied in breeding and rearing to give a thought to knowledge. I'd as lief if my girl stayed a maid—or, at the most, did so until past twenty years, or even twenty-five. She's but fifteen now. Well, sir, to come to the point, I'm telled you have a philosophy class for females, and should greatly like my daughter to attend it, if it were possible."

"With all my heart, Dr. Conybeare. I hold the class in St. Clement's Church of a Tuesday afternoon at two o'clock. 'Tis a kind of lecture, but if any of the pupils desire closer instruction and to consult me concerning the difficulties they encounter in their reading, I see them in the church vestry after. Often I have two or three there for half an hour or thereabouts, when I run through with them the theses they have wrote, and expound difficulties in the books I set them to read. My mode to prove my pupils is to inquire of 'em, '*Quis dubitas?*' and, if they have no doubts or difficulties, I take it they have no benefit nor comprehension neither of what th'ave read."

"What books do you read with 'em?"

"In present we read Plato, Plotinus, Origen, Tully, and Clement, and that eximious little book, *Theologia Germanica.* I hope suddenly to bring them to comprehend some of Descartes his *Discours de la Méthode*, but none are yet sufficiently forward for such difficulties."

"Well, I would you'd teach my girl the Frenchman; I'd liefer she had him than the Platonists. She'll be apt for him, and he'll give her what she needs, something to bite her teeth into. The luciform seed and the plastic medium and the inner light are very well, I dare say, but more airy, and the girl's enough of a dreamer already, and over inclinable towards pious meditations. Indeed, she's of a something phantastical enthusiastic complexion, and wants to be bedded more firmly into the earth."

"Bedded," said Mr. Herrick, "Aye, that steadies a wench."

"The luciform seed, Dr. Conybeare," Mr. More went on rather quickly, fearing that Mr. Herrick intended, and might even utter, an unseemly jest, "the luciform seed is not airy. 'Tis the germinal part of man's being, and joins the earthly with the heavenly, giving the soul exquisite and curious pregustations of what it will one day be. That is by no means to be called airy, or enthusiastical phantasy. Still, I will gladly assist your daughter to study also M. Descartes. It will stand her in ten shillings for a course of ten classes, which I call tolerable reasonable."

"'Tis well enough, for the inner light, the plurality of worlds, and the theory of motion, all thrown in together with a quarrel between you and the Frenchman on the impenetrability of matter. Julian should by the end on't have her intellects much greatened. But tell me this: D'you go into the arguments concerning the existence of God with 'em, or d'you let 'em take him for granted? Possibly, though, you admit no argument or uncertainty in that matter yourself?"

"If you mean, sir, do I *feel* uncertainty, I do not. The sense of the Divine Presence has always been too strong with me to admit that I should doubt it for long, even in my youthful days, when I sometimes *believed* myself to doubt. I would say to myself, in a melancholy fit, those verses of Claudian—

> "Saepe mihi dubiam traxit sententia mentem;
> Curarent Superi terras; an nullus inesset
> Rector, et incerto fluerent mortalia casu.

But some innate sense which was mine from birth forbade doubt in me to become more than these poetical dubitations. As to my lectures, the only arguments I use in the matter are the reasonings from nature and the life of the soul."

"Well, well; so long as you don't batter and load 'em with disputations. But what sort are your other pupils?"

"I have only five. Two are the daughters of Cambridge parsons, two the wife and daughter of one of the Masters, and one the daughter of the secretary of the Cambridge Press."

"And are they ingenious? Do they learn well?"

"Only tolerably. They are somewhat easy fatigued, and don't show, in what they've wrote for me, much comprehension of the thesis. Singularly is this so with the Master's wife, who is firm set to attend the classes, but I think understands nought either of what I speak or what she reads. She's greatly took up in the notion of the deiform seed, but what she conceits it to be, I know not, She's a most diligent enthusiastical gardener, and much inclinable towards seeds, and, while I lecture to her on the soul, I take it her mind's roving away among her garden beds. Still, she calls my lectures beautiful, and tells her husband I have shown her the earth and the fulness thereof, not to speak of the heavens, so I should not complain."

"Ah, I know those women," Mr. Herrick said. "All tongue and eyes, to chatter and gaze, but no intellects to receive and digest. Poor, pretty fools. *Nam muliere inepta res ineptior nulla est.* Unless, indeed, 'tis a foolish man. But here we are at our inn. Good-night t'ye, sir; your philosophical poem greatly interested me."

"You are very obliging, sir. 'Tis in truth a very private and secret record, too intimate perhaps for such public reading, and I doubt I shall never publish it. But if you have a gust to it, I must show you the major part, that I read not out to-night."

"I'm damned if you shall," said Mr. Herrick to himself, and, after waiting a moment to see if any favourable comment was to be made on his own verses, he bowed and turned into the White Horse with his friend.

"And yet mine was the best verses," he said. "Wasn't mine the best melodious sweet verses, doctor, for all the others conceited 'emselves so quaint, out-fantasticating their master, Donne, with only a scruple of his wit? But I forget, you've no mind to poetry. Well, now for a tankard and a pipe before we go to bed. . . . All this new, modern verse—prickling with conceits and bloat with philosophy . . . it needs a tankard to wash away the taste."

15

The doctor and his party, since the poor cannot lodge for long at an inn, found rooms in Petty Cury, above a bookseller's, and transferred themselves thereto very shortly. For the doctor, now that he had tasted Cambridge again, had no mind to leave it as yet, so congenial did he find it to be within reach of books and scholars. He felt that the history of Human Credulity would make much better progress here than in Deancombe, and medical research had also a better prospect. As to his practice, he wrote to the Ashburton doctor who was carrying it on that he would not be back at least until the spring. For himself, he found more than enough of occupation without practising, and could get along for a while without earning; or so he told himself, with the determined optimism of the author.

As to Mr. Herrick, it seemed to him that Parson Beanes of Brent could very well continue until Christmas to take such services at Dean Prior as seemed necessary, in addition to any that he might elect to have, in the intervals of hunting and shooting, in his own parish. He heard from his sister-in-law that she and Prue were

> "busie maken appel jellie & damsen, & i am senden a pipkin on't to the Court. We have made 2 keggs of syder, but they as cum upp sumthing ower swit, ye appels was riper then they shd a bin. Y^{e} fysshe marchant at Dartmouth hath sent stinken coddes; I am senden em back by ye bote with a mitie sharpe messij y^{t} i admire hee shd playe you such a trik. Thar's bin 2 Bastardes born this

sennite, to Pegg Turvie & Joan Leeke; tis said one o' ye fatheres is a sojer, t'other's Will Grene, Sir Rafe Furze his cartere. Sir Rafe hadd Will whipt, & sweres if hee had's way hee'd doe ye same to ye 2 wenches for Strumpetts. But Mr. Yarde on't say yes to yt. I hoap Brothere as you is in hailth & Cambrij to yr minde & yt you on't tarry long away. I have hadd ye bone-shave, but, i thanke God, am bettere. Prue is wel. She has a trifle of bone-shave too, but lesse severe then myne, tho sayen more on't. Beanes gave Communion here on All Halloes & ould Andrew Vynes when hee'd gotten ye Challis ins hands, hee bein first att ye raile, supt upp alle ye wyne, for it sims as hee'd sworn as for once hee'd drinck well, you not bein thar to lett him. Parson B. gat it from him with a great pulle, but thar was scarse a droppe remanen & Parson sweres at him for a hogge & hath him run out o' churche by Joe Bell. You'de admire how an ould fellowe soe nere his grave wd bee such a hogge in ye House of God & befor ye naybors, butt truelie rusticall lyfe is a sadd shocken bisness. Doubtless in Cambrij peeple 'haves 'emselves more simly, butt i here ye ague thar is parlose bad, & i hoap Brothere you kips warm & drie. Heere t'has raned alle ye wik, & ye mists are shoken. A lad from Ratterie was pigsy-led on ye moores & drown'd in Grene Hole. Well Brothere ile say god b'w'ye. Comend mee to ye Dr & ye yonge maides. I hoap they alle kip well & yt ye wenches 'have 'emselves & injoye Cambrij. Farewel.

"Yr luvin Sis:

"Eliz: Herrique.

"Ye ill newes last—i admire how i cd have forgott. Kitkin hath ate upp littel Phil! Shee catch't him on ye windo sille, while hee pickt his crummes. Wee have buryed ye remanes (fetheres) in ye corner bye ye lupin bedd, whar rests ye last Phil, as Tracie cach't. Prew bate Kitkin soundlie as shee desarv'd. Howbeit shee hath done shrewde worke among ye myse of late. Tracie misses his maister, but is well, i thanke heaven. Piggie pynes a scruple, & sayes Noe to his drincke."

This budget of news from home Mr. Herrick read out over dinner. "A woman's postscript," he said, embittered. "All that matters tucked away in it as if 'twas of no account. I'd not have lost that sparrow for a whole keg of cider, or a hundred pipkins of jelly. Piggy pining, too. A man can't leave his home, it seems, without all goes wrong."

"Oh, I would like to have been in church on All Hallows," Meg said. "Wou'n't you, July?"

"No. I'd liefer be here."

Cider kegs, stinking cods, bastards, old men misbehaving in church, pixie-led lads on the moors, sparrows and pigs—they were half the world away. Here was a magical, enchanted city of towers and courts, philosophers and poets, lectures and books. On Sundays all the churches of Cambridge ringing their bells, summoning people to lovely, sweet-quired liturgies, to learned and pious sermons from great preachers; on Tuesdays the wonderful, the most eximious, angelical and learned Mr. More lecturing at St. Clement's on philosophy, and holding afterwards his little class in the vestry, expounding one's difficulties, criticising and commending one's thesis, pouring light into one's brain as if he lit a dozen candles with a word. And, on the other days of the week, always some interest and pleasure. Kit would come and talk, or she and he would go walking by the river, or riding over to Madingley, Trumpington, or the Gogmagog hills. Once or twice they met Mr. Cleveland out riding, and then he would ride with them and talk. But Julian was shy of Kit's tutor, who, she was persuaded, looked down on women; it was easier to converse with Mr. More, or even with Mr. Cowley, who had come with Giles three times to wait on them and pay his respects, and who, now that he was growing used to her, had left off some of his shyness, and talked with her of all manner of things, and particularly of his own poetry. She liked and admired Mr. Cowley greatly; he had even consented to see her verses, and had read them and written to her a most interesting letter of criticism.

Yes, the popular, the admired, the adulated young elegant, Mr. Abraham Cowley, Cambridge's darling poet, had deigned to be her friend, even if a friend something reserved, shy and remote. Giles said he was afraid of women, and not at his ease; if Giles thought that this would lessen her pleasure in his company, he erred; on the contrary, it implied more of compliment that he should break his habit for her, talking with her as if she were a poet of his own sex, discussing some point of literature with her as he might with his friends, Mr. Hervey or Mr. Crashaw, doffing at times, but not always, his stiff embarrassment in his zeal to make her see the meaning of his quiddities, and never wearing the remote air that enveloped Mr. Crashaw on the rare occasions that he chanced to meet her with Kit.

"Do Mr. Crashaw think women wrong?" she asked her brother.

"In part that," he admitted; "but more that th'are not there. Except they be constantly at prayer, like his friends at Little Gidding. Mr. Crashaw lives so much in prayer and meditation himself, that I think the world outside seems to him something shadowy. And as to women, he's partly in the right, for all Christians have held 'em as a temptation, not lightly to be played with."

"But, Kit, so are men a temptation not lightly to be played with. That is, th'are so to women. Women might as truly say that men is wrong as men women."

"I suppose so. Perhaps each is wrong to t'other. But Mr. Crashaw, you see, is a man. And a man at Cambridge, and in Cambridge men don't meet a great many of women as equals."

"'Tis a very tedious way of regarding men and women," Julian said, vexed. "Th'are both human creatures, and God made 'em, and they should not shun and fly each other as if they was the smallpox they feared to catch."

"They don't, in general," Kit dryly reminded her.

"No, indeed they don't. In the world at large it's always love, or playing at love, as th'are after together when th'are young, and that's tedious too. Why can't young men and women talk together reasonable, of life and philosophy and books and such, as if they was of the same gender?"

"Because th'are not," Kit with finality replied. "And when a man has a mind to talk of such matters, ha'n't he a world of men to choose from, particularly if he be at Cambridge? He'd be a fool if he went to a woman for such talk."

"He wou'n't be a fool. Y'are silly, Kit. You know you talk to me."

"That's different; w'are brother and sister. But in Cambridge we lead a life that's something monastical, and we have the habit to talk only with men, and indeed, 'tis true as men talk the best. We forget 'tis ever possible to talk with a woman save of nonsense and compliment. Indeed, with most women it a'n't, for they have nought in their heads; they've read nought and know nought and think nought, so what's the use in talking? Now a man, unless he be a dunce or a fool, will know what you mean, and you can discuss and dispute over an idea."

"So will a woman, unless she be a dunce or a fool. Still, I allow she somewhat more often is so. Well, 'tis ill fortune to be a woman, and despised."

"Nevertheless, there must *be* women," her brother explained, "for marrying and breeding, and minding a man's house and children. So, Jule, you don't ought to rail against the Lord for making you one of 'em."

"I don't desire to marry and breed, and mind a man's house and children, godamercy, brother. I don't intend to wed at all."

"What shall you do, then, when as y'are older? Enter a nunnery?"

"Lord, no. I shall live in Cambridge, and read and write books, and be a learned lady. Poets and philosophers will come flock-meal to my house."

"Why?"

"To talk of poetry and philosophy, in course."

"I don't see why they should need to come to your house for that. They can do all they require of that in their own chambers, or in the town taverns. If the philosophers wait on you, 'twon't be for philosophy, but for dalliance."

"Nonsense. I shall be old then. An old poetess respected of all."

"Then they'll not wait on you for aught. Now enough of your philosophers and old poetesses, for I wish to speak sense. I saw Father Dell yesterday and he counselled me to say no word to my father of being received, lest he hinder me, but to be all-thing secret on't until after reception."

"I've telled you, Kit, you would vex and hurt him thus greatly more than by reasonably and patiently speaking with him on't. He would endeavour to dissuade you, but he wou'n't hinder you, for he believes on liberty of conscience for all."

"I know he thinks he do, but he don't, for he would pester and pray me to stint from following mine, or, at the least, to wait for years; and how could I flout him to his face? I should want both the heart and the courage for't. Beside which, he would speak spiteful bitter things of the Catholics, and that would anger me, and I should huff him back, and we should wrangle."

"I wish you would call them *Roman* Catholics, Kit, at least until you be one and can't. Mr. More says 'tis an extreme arrogant assumption they make, to be the only Catholics."

"Oh, I know that. I hear it from Dr. Beale, and Dr. Cosin, and Mr. Crashaw, and all the devout Protestants. 'Tis old stale stuff, and Father Dell says 'tis they make the arrogant assumption, leaving the Church and retaining its name."

"Well, you have the Puritans, the Brownists, and the Anabaptists on your side in the matter if you'd liefer fadge with them and with your Jesuits than with the Protestants. For my part, I would liefer speak the tongue of Dr. Cosin, Dr. Beale, and Mr. Crashaw."

"There; you see even you and I fall a-brangling when as we talk on't. How would it be with my father then? Religion's a topic breeds more bitterness and wrath than any, therefore I conceit as each man should go his own road, obeying his conscience and desire, and take no notice on't to others save where he can do good by discovering it to 'em. So can we live in peace and amity instead of in anger, spite and dimification. Look, July. I'll not possess my father of my intention, for I cannot. I cou'n't say out the words, for very fright. 'Tis different with you; you are a girl, and his nestle-chick, and he fonds you. He'd never arunt you so bitterly as he would me."

"He fonds on you too, Kit; y'are his very he-darling and his hope and pride. And after a brief while of wrangling and vexation, he'd accept and forgive you, whatever you became, if you could expound it to him reasonable and cause him to see that you but followed that which Mr. More calls the light of reason in your soul. I wish you would talk with Mr. More on't."

"He don't like the Roman Church. I could never talk with a Latitude man."

"'Tis true he don't like it, for he thinks 'tis closed against new light, and intolerant. But he talks very calm concerning it."

"Well, I do not. I can listen to Beale and Cosin and the high sacramentary Protestants, and not grow vexed, for till of late I was of their colour myself; but the Platonists and the Latitude men do anger me, playing hocus-pocus with God's word itself, doubting on the truths of scripture, and setting up their own judgments above those of the Church. 'Tis they, together with the Puritan destroyers, drive men to Rome. Father Dell says they build on shifting sand, and will be swept away with the first wind and sea. The very atheists and profane are less perilous to religion."

Julian sighed. She was beginning to see that her brother was not to be stayed; he was destined for a true Papist, and must go his way.

16

Giles was depressed. He experienced strange, unwonted feelings of inferiority, envy and dislike. His work bored him even more deeply than usual; he sighed over his Seton, cursed his Keckerman, quailed from Aquinas, and started from his Aristotle in disgust. He would, had he been acquainted with them, most fervently have endorsed Mr. John Milton's diatribes against the scholastic grossness of barbarous ages—"this dull and weak subject-matter which creeps along the ground, this dry and dead style so punctually suited to its barren subject." Giles too, could have cried with even more of pathos, " When I go through these vain quibbles, it seems to me that I force my way through stony, arid wastes, desolate wildernesses, and steep mountain gorges. These barren bickerings please none but those of a rude and churlish temper, loving quarrels and disputes, praters, that hate sound wisdom. Let us then exile such a one with all his quibbles to the Caucasus, or wheresoever blind barbarity reigns. There let him torment himself to his heart's content with questions of no importance."

And yet good and honest young men, such as Giles Yarde, were forced to keep company with these barbarians, forced so to master their horrid, their contemptible quibbles and questionings, as to be able to dispute one with another on them in their College chapels or in the public schools, making a show of themselves before their teachers and companions. Never had any youth performed this office more execrably than did Giles Yarde, who had hitherto failed with a most admirable and cheerful indifference. But it so happened that he was due for another of these horrid exercises shortly, and Julian had expressed a desire to come and look on. He had told her that this would not be permitted, but her father had undertaken to get leave to bring her, and come they probably would, unless Julian should forget, or something more entertaining should arise to distract her attention and employ her afternoon. She had already been to Great St. Mary's and watched Mr. Cowley common-place with another young Master of Arts; what a display of nimble wit, eloquent Latin, and shrewd thrusting dialectic had been there! What a contrast to the lame stumbling performance that Giles put up on these occasions! Giles felt, as he thought of it, a keen desire to alter the field of contest, to challenge Mr. Cowley to a duel at tennis or bowls, and to invite Julian to watch it.

When this notion entered his mind, he pushed back his chair from the table and flung his Keckerman on the floor.

"Fair and softly, what's a-foot?" enquired his chamber-fellow, a cheerful young man, who was reading for Holy Orders.

"Why, nought. I was but thinking how bowls is better than books."

"That's not so new a thought as you need leap up like a started hare and all but knock the table over. Y'have all-to spilt my pack of cards and spoilt my game. Get you off to your bowls, then, and leave me in peace."

Giles took no notice of these remarks; he was pacing up and down the room in thought. Bowls: tennis: skittles: fencing: boxing. Aye, boxing and fencing, those were the sports. To overthrow publicly the smart and courted poet at these masculine feats of skill and strength, would be in some measure to redress the balance that now stood so high in his favour. For Julian, even though she had the perverse twist of mind that induced in her a preference for feats of the intellect, could not be so apart from the rest of humanity as not to admire also bodily ability and skill. The girl was human. He would challenge Cowley to a contest in any of these sports he chose, and then, when the time and place were fixed, he would get Kit to bring Julian to watch.

He looked happier when he had thought of this, and sat down again to his disgusting books.

"Oh, I had hoped you was gone," his companion said. "Y'have took air and exercise enough by your walk around the room, perhaps."

"Aye, for a moment. And it wants but twenty minutes of the dinner bell."

"What do you do after common-place this afternoon? There's to be a cock fight at Saunders his ordinary at three o'clock. We could steal there secretly after common-place, and be back within two hours. They say th'are extraordinary good mettlesome birds, and Jack Joyce possessed me which to back. Art for't?"

"No."

"Y'are useless at all in these days, and for ever trapesing off on your own devices. What's come t'you? Y'arn't sickening of a melancholy fit by reason of the wicked doings of our murnivale of knaves at Westminster, as the dons is so glum over?"

"Not I. The dons is a-feared for their posts and their livings, and that the Commons will stick their noses into Cambridge and make havoc on 'em. They've hauled up Cosin already for Popery, and all Peterhouse and John's is afrighted. Serve em right, I say. But politics is all moonshine to me. I've better matters to think on."

"You should care. My father writes as 'tis the beginning of ruin and devastation for the Church, and that the Brownists and Separatists will come to reign over us, now the cry against the bishops is so loud. Not as he likes the bishops, for he says th'are chosen wrong, and only the Laudians have in present a chance of preferment, but 't is Episcopacy itself as the more clamorous now cry down. And what right have they, a pack of Puritan separatists, yapping agen our Church?"

"Well, let 'em. Th'are forced to attend it, after all. They used to sail to America to escape it, but they ar'n't permitted to do so no more, so, in a manner, it is their Church, and they should have a voice in it. My grandfather says they should, and that the Puritans in the Church should be extreme useful in purging it of the ceremonies and abuses have growed in it of late. But then he's of the old school, and likes both Church and State at all as they was in his young days. He conceits the clergy have all-thing too much power presently, and he don't like that, nor do I. What, am I to be ruled over by you? I'll see you poxed first. 'Tis for me to rule over you, 'tis clear, since y'are paid out of my lands and pockets."

"You forget that I'm your spiritual pastor and master, and that the soul's above the body. You and your grandfather's in error, and most likely heretical. The Church can excommunicate you, remember, and that's more than you can do to the Church. Now, pray don't lurch on the table—you'll spill the cards again."

"Excommunicate! I should dearly like to see Mr. Herrick try to excommunicate my grandparents. . . . But 'tis like you clergy to think of nought but Church affairs, when what's afoot is the liberty of the subject and of the subject's pocket, and the subversion (so says my grandad) of the English constitution and laws. Th' old gentleman's wrote me three pages on't; I had to run through it, seeking what he might, or so I hoped, have to say in reply to my letter to him concerning money. He hath a scurvy trick of squeezing such important matters in betwixt pronouncements on affairs of State by which he thinks to benefit my understanding. . . . Look, I shall row to Chesterton this afternoon."

"With your sister?"

"I suppose she'll come. She and her friend, if th'are not else occupied. Wilt come with us, and take an oar?"

"What, and miss the cocks? Well, since your sister'll be of the party, I'll oblige you, for she's as pleasant jolly a romp as never I met, and I've took to her mightily. She stands higher with me than do your dark-haired miss, for, though less handsome, she's merrier, and a man can talk with her at his ease. T'other's too learned grave and puritan a maid for a common dunce like myself. 'Tis well enough for you, as are long quainted with her, but me she frights, as 'twere some sprite or changeling from another world, come to warn me of my sins, with her white nun's face and the great eyes of her. Give me Mrs. Meg, for she's warm flesh and blood like ourselves, and, besides, ever up to a jest or prank. Tell me, do I please her?"

"How should I know? You'd best ask her yourself. If you come with us to-day, you can put to her any quaeries you please."

"Well, I'll with you. Though mind you, I shall be something out of pocket, missing what I thought to make on the cocks."

"You'd as like to be catched going there by the proctors and mulcted. We'll have a game at bowls at Chesterton. That's a more savoury innocent good diversion for us both than wagering on a cock we neither on us set eyes on afore. There goes the dinner-bell, I thank God. I'm damnable hungry; this cursed logic ever makes me so."

17

November crept on. Julian felt herself wrong to be so happy. On the 17th, which was proclaimed by parliament a public fast, she prayed and fasted, and heard two sermons. Dr. Holdsworth preached in the morning in the University Church, bewailing the evil plight into which the Church, harried by maligners and scandalisers, was like to fall, the persecution to which their loved Master of Peterhouse and late Vice-Chancellor was even now subject, and which was being prepared for the Master of St. John's, and doubtless for others of the University; and the rebellious treachery of those who sought to coerce their sovereign by parleying with a rebel army in the north. In the afternoon Dr. Whichcote preached at Trinity Church, deploring the ill-conduct of those counsellors of the King's who had brought into jeopardy the ancient liberties of Church and State, and exhorting his hearers to a firm and manful following of the light of conscience and reason in their souls, wheresoever it might lead them.

Obviously, whichever way you looked at it, to fast was an appropriate gesture, to pray no less. Mr. Richard Crashaw spent the whole night (as he was wont to spend a considerable part of each night) on his knees in Peterhouse Chapel, beneath the glorious flock of angels and cherubim, praying before the altar with its lit tapers and its great crucifix, offering prayers for the Master who had helped to make this beauty and was now in peril; for the Church which, if the efforts of such as Dr. Cosin were brought to nothing, would walk bare and unadorned, stripped of loveliness, mutilated in liturgy and life.

Julian, kneeling with Mr. Herrick at the early Eucharist in Little St. Mary's, where Mr. Crashaw also knelt in the chancel, haggard and white after his vigil, thought, if prayers such as his fail, if the Church be seized and spoiled by rude and barbarous hands, if all this beauty should be let and hindered, what would happen to " the daily sacrifice and the eternal fire of devotion that went not out by day nor night? " Could they subsist, that had had their being in beauty, dignity and grace? And, if they should fail and perish, who could blame such as Kit, who would go and seek them in Rome? Mr. More would blame them, Julian knew, seeing, as he did, in the Roman communion such monstrous fetters of blind and cramping error that no ritual beauty, no fire of piety, compensated. Dr. Whichcote would blame them, for not trusting better God's light and seed of reason in the soul. Yes; all the Anglican party in the universities, and His Grace of Canterbury himself, would blame them, for deserting the ancient ship of the English Church for that of an arrogant rival, whatever stormy seas might for a time beat on, even submerge, their own vessel, whatever strange unlawful pirate crews might for a time board her and set the course.

Julian spoke of this to Mr. Herrick as they walked back to their lodging after church.

" If the Puritans get their way with the Church and Prayer Book, what then ? "

" They 'on't get their way at Dean Court," said Mr. Herrick, grandly. " Whilst I am vicar, no parliament mells with my church or my services."

" But they say these committees of inquiry as th'are setting up mean to put down all superstitious ornament and make our services bare and Genevan at all, as the Puritans desire. That will be hateful."

" God will mind his own," said Mr. Herrick, a little too easily, thought Julian, considering that he spoke, as it seemed to her, in the teeth of all experience and all history.

" Howbeit," the vicar went on, " if they do put down some o' these duckings and doppings and bowings as now go on in some places, and a scruple o' the dainty wardrobe as some priests affect in church, no great damage is thus done to religion. 'Tis all very pretty, and like to a fairy's mass. As good Dick Corbet sang, the fairies

> " Were of the old profession;
> Their songs were Ave Maries,
> Their dances were procession.

Indeed, I like to watch it well enough, but 'tis not necessary to the Church's order. 'Tis not ' a wicked wardrobe,' as busy Mr. Prynne and his crop-eared friends term it; but 'tis a wardrobe something childish and extravagant, to my mind, and more gratifying and cordial to women than to the most of mankind. Trifles, child, pretty trifles. If the Puritan rabble, having lopped 'em off, then stinted, 'twould be no great harm done. But the trouble is, they'll not stint there; they'll proceed in their cursed barbarous insolence to more and worse, assaulting our Prayer Book, and endeavouring to force on honest moderate English churchmen the excesses practised in Scotland, Geneva and Amsterdam. But Englishmen will be too strong for 'em; mark my words, we shall ne'er set Calvin and John Knox on thrones this side the Tees. Nor the Pope neither, nor yet His proud little Grace."

"We must pray and keep fast to-day, that all come well."

"Fast? Oh, aye—well, I suppose we must fast."

"And for my Lord Strafford. For they say he's in the most sorrowful peril as never was, now he's before the Commons, and they crying for his blood."

"Oh, they can have his blood, for me. He's a plaguey tyrant, and has gone far to ruin the country with his monopolies and his debasing of the coinage and his tricks in Ireland, and then threatening us with foreign levies to subdue us. He's done the King and country great disservice, and th'are in the right to down him."

"But he's a great brave noble gentleman, even if he has made mistakes. Mr. Cleveland says he is like a stag at bay, with the hounds barking and leaping at him. Oh, they should send him into exile, perhaps, or at least deprive him of his offices, but they shou'n't try him for his life, for he's far greater than they."

"Aye, and they know it. Too great to be safely let live, think they. And too close to the King's ear. He's their foe, is Black Tom, and they hate and dread him like the devil. For my part, if I must be ruled, I'd near as lief be so by such as he as by our Westminster rabble of budge lawyers and country gentry; but the country thinks other. 'Tis a strange thing in the English; they reverence this assembly of theirs so greatly as tyranny from it don't seem to them tyranny at all, whereas if the King or his advisers do so much as lay a tax of fourpence on 'em, th'are all on the hoity-toity forthwith. And here's parliament cockering the Scots rebel army, for all the world as 'twere a pack of pampered hounds, flinging 'em meat and patting 'em on the head, saying, ' Good dogs, good dogs, hold yourselves yare to spring when we give the word, and meanwhile here's your dinner, good hounds '—and no word may be spoke in the House agen 'em, His Majesty himself being let from calling 'em rebels, and half London yammering and clamouring to have a Church and service book such as theirs (bless the mark!); whereas, if the King, who'd have the greater right, was to treat a rebel army so, the whole country'd be up about it. Why, our very army's faint-hearted and sullen, and loath to be used against such an excellent worthy covenanting foe—more particular, I'll allow, since no man pays 'em their wage. Th'are plaguey bad times w'are fallen onto, and 'twill take aplenty of prayer and fasting to set 'em right."

Yes, they were plaguey bad times; Julian knew it, for all Cambridge so said; except, strangely enough, the Cambridge that had elected Mr. Cromwell and Mr. Lowrey. She herself could weep for my Lord Strafford, that noble gentleman at bay, and be troubled for her mother Church's plight, and for her brother's desertion of it.

Nevertheless, she was happy. She trod the Cambridge streets light-footed, with soaring heart and singing soul. She sat beneath Mr. More of a Tuesday afternoon and grappled with the philosophic system of M. Descartes, and absorbed the inner light that, filtering through Plato, Plotinus, Tully and Mr. Henry More, seemed to flood her own soul with radiance, making of it a veritable luciform seed. She was reading, in her private classes with Mr. More, Plato's *Republic* and the *Enneads* of Plotinus in Greek, a language in which Mr. Herrick was less strong than Latin, and had imparted to her much less instruction. For Mr. More she entertained that kind of reverence which one feels for a philosopher at once mystical and rational, and that kind of affectionate gratitude which a female pupil must feel towards a master who at once imparts the knowledge she would have, and bends an attentive intelligence to her own inquiries, difficulties and endeavours. Mr. More believed that women should be scholars, as men should. He was one with Dr. Conybeare in that; only, having been neither married, nor having had to minister to female invalids, he had more faith in the female understanding. It was indubitably gratifying to be taught by a learned master who believed in the female understanding. As it was, also, gratifying to converse occasionally with a famous young poet and find that he was not unwilling to discuss with a woman his verse, nor, even, to read and criticise hers. In fact, Cambridge University proved itself, in the main, not unkind to young females, whether or no it thought much about their intellectual accomplishments. Part of it definitely thought little of these. Mr. John Cleveland, for instance.

"If I were Kit," Julian would think, "if I were Kit, he would teach me. . . . Lucky Kit." Why lucky Kit? Because Mr. John Cleveland was witty, was handsome, was brilliant, wore an air of easy, careless grace, could rise to his feet at any moment and deliver an oration in graceful, pointed Latin, in which accomplishment his only superior, they said, was Mr. John Milton. For Mr. Cleveland's English verse, Julian did not greatly care; to her mind it was too elaborate, too often also political and satirical, with overmuch cumber of notions and conceits; it lacked the sublime noble cadences of Mr. Milton's, the fresh charm of Mr. Herrick's, the serious beauty of much of Mr. Cowley's. And his poetry on women was at times somewhat coarse. No, she did not care greatly for his verse, and he cared nothing at all for hers; the compliments he paid her were not addressed to her mind. He even mocked at her philosophy lessons, calling her Mademoiselle Descartes, or Mrs. Platonick, which she found tedious in him. If she had been Kit, he would not have found it droll that she studied philosophy; he would have taken it for granted, and helped in her instruction.

He was a strange, derisive, pleasant gentleman, and looked extremely well in his violet gown and cap and white bands, when he waited on Dr. Conybeare or Mr. Herrick in their lodgings, as he not infrequently did, having taken a liking, it would seem, both to doctor and parson. He would sit for a while and drink a glass with them, and entertain them with his talk, and perhaps speak of Kit's studies, or give them some invitation to a College function. Then he would take his leave, and sometimes either Dr. Conybeare or Mr. Herrick would walk out with him, talking still on politics, for every one talked of politics now. With the two young ladies, Mr. Cleveland exchanged pleasant railleries; that is, the exchange was only with Meg, for Julian was little use at that pastime. He jested with both of them, was answered by one, and looked at the other.

"He's a pleasant droll, and a tolerable handsome man, but proud," Meg said one day. "He's mighty ingenious, but not more ingenious than he conceits he is."

"Aye, he's something self-conceited," Julian agreed.

"Still, God made him, so let him pass for a man," Meg kindly dismissed him, as she set up her skittles again.

18

The day of fasting and prayer had, it seemed, been better observed by the friends of this great and happy parliament than by its foes, for nothing fell out as these last had desired. The Master of Peterhouse was put into the custody of Black Rod, to be charged later on with his crimes; my Lord Strafford was committed to the Tower, there to await impeachment for his. And the great, the portentous Popish plot swelled to terrifying proportions in the minds of its believers.

Kit Conybeare, on the day that the news of the regalvanising of the recusancy laws reached Cambridge, went to see his Jesuit friends in St. Edward's Passage. He found them, as usual, calm and unperturbed. There lived in the passage, above a barber's, a group of four priests, two English, one French, and one red Perthshire Highlander. When Kit went up to their rooms, he found Father Dell and Father Mackay sitting together smoking, with the cat purring on Father Mackay's knee. They were dressed, as usual, as laymen.

"Here comes our catechumen," Father Dell, the elder, said. "Well, young man, you come in a good hour for the Church, for we may all be apt to suffer for our profession presently, now th'are becoming so sharp on the laws again. You'd best give us a wide berth, or you may find yourself in a sad praemunire."

"Father, my mind's made. I desire to be received suddenly; so soon as may be."

"God bless thee then, my son, and grant thee perseverance in't. Aye, thou shalt be received, and that suddenly, for th'art already well instructed. Come to the oratory and make thy general confession next Friday afternoon, and on Saturday thou shalt be baptised, and on Sunday morning—'tis Advent Sunday—make thy communion. What of thy father? Hast possessed him of any hint on't?"

"No. I can't. I must be received first. Then, maybe, I shall take courage to discover it to him."

"Or, maybe, ye'll no need to do any such thing," observed Father Mackay, stroking the cat behind the ears. "Maybe 'tis a case of least said soonest mended, and that whisht and the rose is the way. For look, ye'll mebbe make our poseetion here awful deeficult and undo all our work, gin ye go rinning around telling of Jesuit priests in St. Edward's Passage as have baptised ye. There might be complaints from your guid father to the Vice-Chancellor, and we might be sent packing, and there'd be an end to our work in Cambridge. So haud thy whisht, man, and go thy ways mum."

"The Father's right," said Father Dell. "We don't need to wear our religion on our sleeves, before the hour's ripe to witness for't. Don't trouble your father, but set this step secretly."

"Am I not to tell my College on't?" Kit was disappointed at this secrecy.

"Best not, in present. You don't desire to be sent from Cambridge, do you? Mr. Austin says he's to depart forthwith, for Dr. Beale hath now been openly informed of his conversion, and can't wink at it more. You must remember that the Colleges have been captured by the Protestant heretics, and those whom their founders meant 'em for is cast out. So the wise and rightful plan's for Catholics to stay in the foundations created for 'em, but in such manner as not to draw the enemy's fire, always save it become necessary to witness."

"Aye, whisht's the word," Father Mackay agreed.

"Very well, father. But I may tell my sister? For she knows it all, and how I have been on't for months past. We talk on't often, and she's vowed to keep it secret from my father, until I tell him myself."

Father Mackay lifted sceptical blue eyes to heaven.

"Ye'd trust a lassie! The Lord help ye, lad."

"Indeed, father, she's as mum as if she had it *sub sigillo*. Julian would ne'er break a promise, though she is a girl."

"If ye ask my opeenion, there was ne'er a woman yet. . . . And forbye, I've seen your sister walking with ye, and she's too sonsie a lass not to have gallants around her, and, if she's secret with her father, she'll no be secret with her suitors. There's a long, red-polled lad as I've seen often in her company."

"Oh, yes, Giles Yarde. She'd never say nought to him, or to any other."

"Can you win her to the faith, my son?" Father Dell asked.

Kit looked doubtful.

"I don't think it, father. She's firm Protestant, and hangs on Mr. More's lectures, and loves the English Church very greatly."

"If your Puritans get their way, there'll be little left of the English Protestant Church to love. I hear they'll aim sharply at the service book, when they've done with the bishops. What can good Protestants do then, but come to us? We may get our Canterburian foes, Dr. Cosin and Dr. Beale, yet; even, who knows, Canterbury himself? But I don't think it. Your high Protestant Churchmen are as bitter against us as soldiers that fight in a beaten cause. The more Catholic they incline in ceremony and doctrine, and the more painful they are to prove as they can do't as well as we, and have never ceased in't, the more they discover 'emselves as impostors. The poor blind gulls, they cling firm to the shadow and mind not as they have long since let the substance go. They ignore that we, saying mass in a garret, with nought but a stole to mark our office, do offer the Holy Sacrifice and feed our people with Christ's body, and that they, saying their communion service in a rich church or chapel, caparisoned with ornaments and sweet with incense——"

"An abominous horrid smell," Father Mackay interpolated.

"——do offer nought save their own vain emptiness, for they have no power for other. What do they call Dr. Cosin? The seven-sacramentary man; but he should be called the no-sacramentary man, for he hath never administered or received a sacrament since his baptism, and most like not then, so careless are Protestants in that. And 'tis your Cosins and your Beales, your Canterburians and your sacramentarians as set 'emselves up to be of a purer Church (bless the mark!) than true Catholics. If your Canterburians did but know how all-thing we scorn 'em! Th'are deceived at times, in that we speak soft and fair to 'em to entice or persuade 'em; they dream we prefer 'em to the Puritans as howl against us and them together, but, God's life, we'd as lief have a Brownist as a Canterburian. They'll both lie in hell, but the one will burn for a fool as well as for a heretic. . . . When will Mr. Crashaw join us, think you?"

Kit shook his head.

"I don't know, father. He kneels in chapel all through each night presently, I'm telled, and prays for Dr. Cosin and the Church. But there's those think he a'n't far off conversion, and that if this parliament goes farther in its ill work against the Church, he'll be so distasted shortly as to turn Papist."

"A rare soul. He's of the stuff mystics is made on. I have more hope of him since Nicholas Ferrar died. Little Gidding had him, heart and soul. That's a Protestant community extreme dangerous to us, for it offers such mystic and prayerful souls fare as they couldn't get elsewhere outside the Catholic Church. And yet some say it helps us, by leading men and women part way along the road. Now, my son, you must go. Christ and his Holy Mother and the blessed angels attend thee, and bless thee in thy ways. Return to-morrow at this hour."

Kit knelt for a blessing, and departed.

19

He walked on air. The bells that rang were the very chimes of Paradise. He sang beneath his breath, as he walked to his College by the green lawns that sloped down to the slow, full river:

" Thy vineyards and thy orchards are
Most beautiful and fair,
Full furnished with trees and fruits,
Most wonderful and rare.

Thy gardens and thy gallant walks
Continually are green;
There grows such sweet and pleasant flowers
As nowhere else are seen.

" There's nectar and ambrosia made,
There's musk and civet sweet;
There many a fair and dainty drug
Is trodden under feet.

" There's cinnamon, there sugar grows,
There nard and balm abound:
What tongue can tell, or heart conceive
The joys that there are found?

"Quite through the streets, with silver sound
The flood of life do flow,
Upon whose banks on every side
The wood of life do grow. . . ."

"Oy!" a voice interrupted these charming heavenly speculations, and Giles Yarde came up from behind, very wet and muddy, and carrying in his arms a draggled spaniel pup.

"See here, Kit. I have just now saved this pup; it was chucked into the river by some louts, and was a-drowning. 'Tis a good pretty little pup, or will be when 'tis dried and combed and smugged up. I should like to give it to Jule. Would she take it, d'you think?"

Kit, a clean and dainty youth, looked without much favour on the draggled and muddy little object, that smelt of the Cam and of all the experiences of its brief pre-Cam career.

"Oh, Jule would take any live thing. But, if you should show it him as it is in present, 'twould stand somewhat in the north of my father's favour, I fancy."

"Well, fool, I shan't. I shall wash it, dry it, comb it, scent it, and bedizen it with scarlet ribbons, before any Conybeare but you sets eyes on't. Meg will help me. Only if Meg sees it, she'll covet it so as I shall have some ado giving it to Jule."

"Then why not give it to Meg? She'll return to the country before Christmas, and heaven alone knows how long my father and Jule mean to stay away, for my father seems settled at all in Cambridge, and a spaniel pup's apter for the country than for Cambridge lodgings."

"I grant. But I wish to give the pup to Jule, if she'll have it. Meg has a plenty dogs at home."

"Well, you'd best approach my father first, before Jule lose her heart to the little beast."

"Not I. Jule shall lose her heart, and persuade the doctor. Don't he so fond on her as to grant her anything in reason?

. . . Will they truly wait in Cambridge the whole winter through?"

"Aye, and longer, it seems, for my father swears he'll finish here that great learned heretical book he's so busy on, that'll do none of us no good, should it e'er come to be printed."

"Books do no one no good," Giles gloomily agreed. "There's too many of books in Cambridge, and in the world, hell burn 'em."

"My father's book stands to be burnt not only in hell but in England, should he print it. And did he live in another country, he'd be thrown on the bonfire with it himself, for, so far as I can make out, 'tis an outrageous presumptuous heretical atheistical work, as brings all things in question, and treats all religions as so many human superstitions. W'are grown tolerable free in these times, God knows, but not so free as to let that pass. Canterbury would gladly have a man's ears for less. But my father ne'er thinks of consequences; the more perilous is a road, the more jot set he'll be in't. A book like his is not only dangerous and against law; 'tis against all religion and truth beside."

"Aye, in course 'tis so," Giles agreed, wrapping his shivering pet closer in his gown.

"And yet," Kit sighed, "my father's the best honest charitable man as e'er breathed, for all he's thus blinded and in error. I don't know what to make on't; but I wish to God he'd think better of his rashness and write instead only of medicine and surgery, as won't get him into any trouble. 'Tis hard for July and me, as our father should scandalise religion and act so odd."

"Fathers do act odd," said Giles, commenting without surprise on a fact of nature. "Look, will Jule be at home at three to-morrow?"

"I don't know. She may be anywhere, she gads so. And

that's another oddity of my father's, to let her and your sister run about the town unaccompanied, taking the risk of being spoke to or of being suspicioned for queans. It a'n't seemly."

"No, and so I've often telled 'em. But Cambridge is grown used to 'em by this, and they don't seem to come to harm, though I don't like it. But I but seldom find 'em home when I wait on 'em, and when I do find Jule, she's deep in a pile of books, and can't be troubled, for, says she, she writes her thesis for Mr. More, or has to finish some verses she's on, or to get by heart a piece of Greek. She's far closer at her books than you or I. So off I have to go with Meg, leaving her at it, for she'll have none of me. I conceited, if she took the pup, as she and I could walk it out in the meadows sometimes."

"So you might, to be sure. Well, try it with her."

Kit spoke without conviction, knowing his sister's mind in this matter of Giles; how she liked him, was fond of him, but at present somewhat bored by him, her head being in the clouds; turned a little, so Kit considered, by the notice taken of her by ingenious Cambridge men; somewhat tipsy also with philosophy and the new learning she was so enthusiastically acquiring. Kit did not approve much of this learning, nor of Mr. More and the Platonical Latitude men. Still, he hoped that these were balanced, and his sister kept rooted in sense and religion, by her acquaintance with Mr. Cowley and Mr. Cleveland, both sane men. He had no desire to convert her to his own new faith; one in a family, and particularly in the family of Dr. Conybeare, he considered enough for that. Girls had best not share in these adventures, he told himself. Then, it was more interesting and grander to be alone in his conversion.

Giles had left him, going into Trinity, concealing his rescue under his wet cloak.

An honest, good, merry fellow, though duncical, Kit

thought him. Julian might do worse than marry him, later, if he could persuade his grandfather to allow the unequal match. She would then have a good safe position in the country, whatever might befall. Yes, Julian might do worse.

But Kit had of late come to think his sister less level-headed than of old. Had he considered, he might have remembered that no Conybeare had ever been level headed at all.

20

The Master of Peterhouse returned to Cambridge, released on bail, the while the parliamentary committee appointed to investigate his case prepared its charges against him.

"And to all Peter Smart's old Durham charges," he complained in the senior common-room, "and to those of making seemly our own chapel, they have now added, if it pleases you, encouraging in Popery our late good friend Mr. Nichols, as I made recant that sermon of his and expelled from the University myself last year. The Reverend Mr. Norton, too, was up before the committee, making fresh trouble concerning that son of his as we offered a fellowship to, complaining we tried to seduce him to Popery. Th'are run anti-Popery mad, and bite, like mad dogs, the very hands of them that have served 'em, for, though it distastes me to think it, the truth is that they and I have always fought the same enemy, but in different ways. 'An Arminian's the spawn of a Papist,' cry they, never marking that Arminians are, if that be so, abominous parricides, and the sworn foes of those that gat 'em. This rabble here, that cries 'a Pope, a Pope,' after Dr. Beale and myself in the streets—if I scorned not to spend my breath on such inconsiderable insects, I would turn on 'em and expound to 'em punctually what the Pope thinks of me, and I of the Pope and his, a matter on which those Jesuits in St. Edward's Passage could enlighten them somewhat. But they'd not understand. They argue, 'The Pope's men burn incense and candles and set up images and altars; you do the like; ergo, you are a Pope's man.' Aye, I could answer them, and here in Cambridge we read Latin and Greek, logic and metaphysics, and so do they at Oxford (after a manner), but do that make us Oxford men? God forbid it should. But there's no reasoning with the great vulgar, nor yet with those are tipsy with their own opiniastry. Let 'em cry 'a Pope,' then, and much good do it them. As you doubtless heard, there's a hot Papist-hunt afoot, and Windebank's letters of grace to the priests is all revoked."

"Windebank lies hid, they say?"

"Aye; he's for France, I hear, so quick as he can get a ship. But Rossetti stays. The Queen's had the order from parliament to dismiss her Papist servants, but she's firm against that. And they say she's been praying Barberini and the Pope again for money, to be used for her friends; but she hath gotten none, nor will. There's no doubt the Queen's been little wise, and did truly conceit as she could turn this country Papist, and she and her favourites have done the King's fame much harm. He takes a high tone in present, and speaks he'll protect Lord Keeper Finch, but 'tis useless, for Finch hath the whole parliament agen him, even the moderate men and the loyalists. Mr. Hyde and my Lord Falkland are as hot on him in the matter of ship money as is Pym himself. Finch telled me he would ask to be heard in his defence before the Commons, and if it go against him, His Majesty hath a ship ready to take him to the Hague, for he'll not stay to be impeached. But Canterbury won't flee, and my Lord Strafford can't, and 'twill go ill with both, I fear. 'Tis hard, for, though both may have overturned some few laws in the interest of

King and Church, th'are guiltless at least of part or lot in the Popish plot."

At these words, Mr. Crashaw moved his head impatiently.

"That Popish plot!"

His Master regarded him with a little severity.

"Mr. Crashaw, we may not dismiss it for a moonshine notion. I have heard too much on't of late for that. When a queen parleys with foreign potentates and with the head of a foreign Church for help against the King's subjects, and when all the laws against the free and open practice of a forbidden religion are put to sleep, and the court is filled with its adherents, and the country swarms with its busy priests, there you have a good suspicion of a plot. But His Grace and my Lord Strafford are staunch Church of England men as e'er breathed, and know nought on't. I truly believe Dr. Laud would die for our Church, to defend it alike against Papists and Presbyters."

"'Tis not the Papists are our most deadliest enemies in present," said Mr. Crashaw. "'Tis the Papists have sent in a petition to abolish Episcopacy, fifteen thousand strong. We had best make common cause with the Papists against the Presbyterians and Brownists."

"Mr. Crashaw, I've heard you speak in that sort a scruple too often, and, to be round with you, I've no mind to it. Bethink you as you are Fellow of a Church of England society, in a Church of England University, and take heed to speak according."

Here the Vice-Master changed the subject, aware that the Master and Mr. Crashaw were apt to disagree on this matter.

"You know, sir, that Little St. Mary's was mobbed t'other day by a rude rabble during communion service? 'Twas a near thing they did not get to the altar and desecrate the sacrament. The congregation fought 'em out, but the door must in future be locked."

"Well, God will punish 'em in his own time and way," observed the Master; but Mr. Crashaw, who found him optimistic, sighed.

"Keep your heart up, Mr. Crashaw," Dr. Cosin admonished him. "We must not show poor faces to the world. I am a prisoner, and the skies are black enough, but they shall not see me quail. Let Peterhouse be the cheerfullest merry society in Cambridge, and return our enemies jest for jest." He tore across a squib that had been sent in to the college that morning. "No sense, no taste, and no wit to't. If we could write a reply no better than that, we should deserve to perish. But no; we'll let such vanities be. Bugs of a day, that sting and die. And now, Mr. Vice, if you will withdraw with me to my room, we will transact some business together."

21

Both Mr. Herrick and Meg were rather dejected, for they had been summoned back to Devonshire. Meg had received a letter from her grandmother, and the vicar from her grandfather.

Mr. Yarde wrote:

"Deere Sir:

Questionless you will suddenlie bee returning to yr Duties, since X^{t}mas draweth on, & there is none to take ye sarvices in church. Wee shall expect you so soone as you can gett heere; you shd sett forth earlie, as ye roades will be dirty for going, & ye daies short & ill. Wee admire somwhat as wee have not hard afore this from you as to yr comming, as I writt you some time since on it. Wee wish our Gerle Megge to ryde with you; pray minde as shee do noght ventursome on ye Roade, & do not ryde her Mare into a swet. Y Mare shd not do ower 40 myles in one daie, & that not each daie. At Exeter, you shd lye att ye Ould Boare, & not at ye Lion, as you did going, for Mr. Swire mine hoste of ye Ould Boar owes me for a briding Bull & hath paid noght, so Megge's chamber & board thar will bee to his cost; see she pay noght for't. Yr owne bille will not bee consarned in this, but betwixt yrself & yr hoste. Thar hath much fell out heere since you went, ye which Ile tell when as I see you agen. In London too it seems much hath bin a-doing, both good & ill. This Parlament doth tolerable well, but grows something immoderate. 'Tis well they have cach't my Lord Strafford by ye heeles, & I hope they will suddenlie bring Maister Laud to book. Yr frind Dr. Weekes of Sherwell rid ower to wait on you three daies back, & was vext not to finde you. Hee admired somwhat you was from ye Parysshe thus long, after being from it thru ye Springe, but hee hopes to wait on you agen about Twelfth Night. He layed with us the night, & wee had much talke of affares. That foolish gent. his nayboure, Mr. Francis Rouse of Barnstable, seems to bee uncommon busie in Parlament, & to have bin sett to looke into Dr. Cosins his follies & those of t'other Arminian clargie; a taske, we thinke heere, for a wiser noddle then his. Thar is talk they make him Provost of Eaton, an extream fine office indeed for a gent. of his trifling understandings. But it seems as a dunce in Devonshire passes for a wise man in London.

"Farewell. Commende me to ye Dr. & his lyttle maide. 'Tis strange they stay on at Cambridg. Theyle miss ye X^{t}mas and Twelfthnight mumminges, & the ball.

"Yr friend to sarve you,

"Geo. Yarde."

Mrs. Yarde had written to her granddaughter:

" Megge.

Deere Childe:

'Tis ower time thou came hoam. What, dost thinke as thou canst gadde abrode for months, & noe cloes with thee nither? Soe thoult ryde hoam with ye Parson, who thy Granfr has wrote to cum forthwith, for hee doe negleck ye Parysshe shamefulle. 'Tis pittie thy Brothere can not cum with thee; i hoap hee doe not wast his tyme a-dancing after you & Juliane. We don't desire hee fonde too gretly on Juliane, for shee growe too ould, they ant no more childer, & noght can never cum on't. You shd give him a hynte afore you lave, tellin him as how it ant right toward ye Gerle herself. Megge, you must ryde quiet & simly, & not to plaie ye hoyden. Yr Granfr. hoaps as youle well heede ye Mare, not to swett her or toe bringe her down lepen gates. Remember Childe what a gret Gerle yare growne & act accorden. Att Shaftsburie wait on thy Ant Mrs. Hestere Corbett at ye Manor & lye thar y^tt^ nite. Despach thy Chest by ye Caryer instantlie thou receive this, for 'twill bee longe on ye Rodes in this ill sayson. Fould thy cloes careful in ye Chest, y^tt^ they bee not too spoyled travellen. Is ye Dr. & Juliane to bide from hoam alle wintere? None admires as ye Dr. bee loath to returne, after ye odde singuler part hee plaied consarning ould Prowse, ye which is still much spoke on here. Thar's none to minde ye sicke now, onlie ye White Wich to Rattery, who cures & kills they say as manie with her simples as Dr. Cunnibere with his pills & bloudings. I hoap to see thee a weeke this side X^t^mas, but thoult bee too late to stirre ye Puddynges or helpe mix ye mins. Y^e^ Balle's Twelfnite Eve. Thoult bee gladde to get hoam after soe long from it.

"Commende mee to Mr. Herrique but not to ye Dr. tho you may give Juliane a kinde worde from mee. Assure yr Brothere Gyles of our continued affeccions & hoaping hee kips harde on his Books,

"Yr Granmr.,

"Christiane Yarde."

"I have the lamentablest tedious letter from my grandmother," Meg complained.

"And I from your grandfather," Mr. Herrick gloomily said. "It seems w'are to get us back to Devonshire forthwith. Well, 'tis duty, and in the last ten years ne'er do I fly from that tedious country, but I have to fly back again, like one of Mr. Davenant's Barbary pigeons homing."

"Well, you chose the Church," Dr. Conybeare unkindly reminded him.

"Aye, and you chose physic. But it seems you can run and leave your patients when you please, and none's the worse for't, indeed doubtless the better; whereas, there's none can mind poor Robin's few sheep in the wilderness for him while he's from home. I save souls, while you do but kill bodies; that's the difference 'twixt you and me. Well, child, we must shortly bid Cambridge good-bye and get us on the roads again, and extreme dirty riding 'twill be. But look ye, I had meant to return by London, to see some friends there and feast my eyes once again on its blessed streets. Would that be to your mind, my merry maid?"

"Oh, yes, parson. I've been to London but once, two years back come June, when I lodged with my Aunt Greville by St. Paul's. I would enjoy to lie in London again, and see the unicorn's horn in the Tower, and the shows in the streets—oh, and the plays! Real true plays, Jule, not tedious plays in Latin, acted by stupid lads at Cambridge. Can we stay several days in London, pray, parson?"

"Aye, surely can we. If w'are home by Christmas Eve, in time to watch the pie, 'twill be enough. My sister and Prue can twine the font with holly and set out the little mammets in their stables in the church. Elizabeth writ me as Peter Scat is already carving a new ox and ass, the old ones being stole last Christmas by those Miggles. Aye, they'll do without the parson, till Christmas Eve."

"And Gran will have to do without me. She'll be angry, but no matter."

"Will you get the rod?"

"No, I'm grown too big for the rod. No one's whipped me these two years back."

"'Tis pity, jackanapes, for you want it. Still, you may get bread and water for your Christmas fare."

"Not I, for I shall lay it all on you, and say I pined to get home quickly, but you must needs tarry in London with your friends. 'Twill be you gets the rod and the bread and water. But if 'twas I, I should care nought, for London's worth it. I only wish as Giles could come with us."

But well she knew that Giles would not come with them for all the plays in London town, all the horns of all the unicorns in the world, so long as Julian stayed in Cambridge. Warn him not to fond so greatly upon Julian? Where would be the use of that, when he was plunged already fathoms deep in love, and had no eyes nor ears, in the beloved's presence, for any other? Meg had wept a little over it, from jealousy, love, and loneliness, and from having, for so it seemed, lost her darling playmate brother. But now she was resigned to it, and wished that Julian would make him happier, so that they could all three be jolly and merry together as of old. But Julian, always full of books and dreams, of her brother and her fine new friends, had little thought for Giles, though she had been pleased with the spaniel pup he had given her, which Meg coveted for herself and would have dearly liked to carry home to Dean Court on her saddle-bow.

But life was like that; and the long, exciting journey and London lay ahead, and Dean at Christmas was merry, and Devonshire country better than Cambridge streets; and Meg, never meant for a dweller in academic precincts, rode forth on her chestnut mare along the Trumpington Road in the dark of a still December morning, with the bells ringing for matins behind her, and the wide pale-brown country stretching ahead, to right and to left, like a sea, and was so glad to be out on the open road that she stretched her mare at a canter over the chalk hills of the Gog Magogs, crying, "Tantivy, tantivy, tantivy! A hunting we will go!"

It was Mr. Herrick who rode more sadly, for he was bound again for dull Devonshire, and his poems were still unprinted in his wallet, and he was not quite sure that they had been a great success in Cambridge, a place where every one was much too full of his own concerns. Still, they would lie in Bishop Stortford that night, and be early next day in London, and beyond that Mr. Herrick would not now look.

22

Cambridge lay shrouded in winter mists. Not the wreathing wind-blown mists of Dartmoor, wherein ghosts and pixies glided, but still white fen and river mists, dank and dense, filling the town with ague and the physicians' purses with fees. In Christmas week it was a silver city, and the trees along Trumpington Road and in the college gardens heavily and slowly dripped. Through the mist, fires blazed in the market place, warming and lighting the stalls where turkeys and geese, boars' heads and quarters of beef, puddings and pies, holly, mistletoe, rosemary and bay, were cried and sold all day.

Christmas Day broke through the mists, a clear, white, frosted morning, merry with carols and bells.

Kit went to mass at six in the private oratory of the Jesuits, and, returning into College, met the Fellows, tutors and undergraduates coming out of chapel, in time to join with the stream. But his tutor, having sent for him after breakfast, said, "You was not in chapel, I believe, Mr. Conybeare?"

Kit agreed.

Mr. Cleveland put out a hand to prevent his saying more. "That will do. Don't tell me why, nor where you were. I'll not hear. But I'll say this to you, young man. Should any evidence of disloyalty to the Church of the foundation y'are on come to the knowledge of the College, you would have to leave it forthwith. At a time like this, Dr. Beale can't afford to wink at Popery in the College; he'll have to face his own troubles before this plaguey House of Commons, before long, and must have a clean conscience for't, so I can promise you Popish perverts will be treated with the most punctual firmitude and no grace. I warn you, once and for all: if y'are joined that erred Church, or if you still think on it, take no notice on't to any. And for the Lord's sake stay not from chapel. Nay, not a word; I'll not hear it. Would you make me guilty of misprision of Popery? Resolve me aught, and I'll not lift a finger to save you packing. You young fool; aye, I'll call you so, even though I know nothing. . . . D'you tell your sister all your business?"

"Not all," Kit sulkily said. "Some on't."

"Aye, and I can conceit what, for I've seen her to look at you most sorrowful and anxious, with those violet eyes of hers. . . . Well, I've warned you, my lad, and there's an end on't. Do you spend the day out?"

"Yes, sir; with my father and sister."

"They come to our mummings this evening, I hope?"

"No; they go to Trinity, with Giles Yarde."

"Trinity! Faith, that's a pity; they should come here. Bid 'em here, for our revels will be better than Trinity's."

"I'll ask 'em, but I think th'are all fixed for t'other, and have engaged themselves to Yarde and to Mr. Cowley."

"Cowley! Pox take Mr. Cowley. Well, if they must go to Trinity, they must. But bid 'em, bid 'em; give 'em at least the chance o' the better College. Tell your father I've a thing or two I could tell him of Christmas mummings in the past, as might edify him. Though, faith, they'd not edify madam your sister; I pick my words with her as I was a cat walking on eggs. Well, begone, and mark what I've telled you."

Julian said, when Kit gave her the invitation, "I'd liefer come to St. John's with you. But w'are pledged to Giles. Will he be vexed?"

"In course he'll not," her father said. "He'll come with us to John's. I should like John's better myself, for I would talk with Mr. Cleveland, though mumming is much alike wherever you get 'em. John's be it, then. Do you take Jule to church now, Kit?"

"I am to go to church with Giles, father," Julian quickly put in, to save her brother embarrassment or deception. "And after church, we shall take the pup to walk on Parker's Piece."

So Giles and Julian attended the communion service at Great St. Mary's and heard a sermon from Dr. Holdsworth, the Vice-Chancellor, and were rewarded by a brawl, for directly the liturgy began a group of townsmen at the back began to sing the metrical version of the psalms to drown it, and desisted not until driven out by the beadles. The Vice-Chancellor added them to his sermon, reproving those who spoke spiteful things of our Prayer Book and behaved themselves unseemly at God's sacraments. They must see to it, said he, that Cambridge did not sink to the level of London, a notoriously ill-behaved city.

But, after the service, when the Vice-Chancellor and his train had departed, the brawlers returned in force, surged up the church, overpowered the sidesmen, and hacked at the chancel rails with knives and sticks, crying out, "Down with the rails! Table in the middle!" and other vulgar expressions of preference in the matter of church worship. Giles and Julian stayed to watch the performance, and the scuffling and fighting that accompanied it, before they took the puppy walking on Parker's Piece.

"Th'are grown uncommon impudent and bold," Giles said.

"Barbarous insolent hoydens," said Mr. Cowley, who had also stayed to watch, and was standing with his friend, Mr. Hervey, and young Mr. Marvell. "Damme, how I do detest a Puritan! If these had their way, they'd hack to pieces all the chancel rails in Cambridge and drag about every altar, and would all-to destroy every beauty in our churches. Th'are like so many hogs gotten loose in a vineyard, snorting and breaking. Damn set o' drunken Brownists, tipsy with religion and ale, straight from the Rose or the Dolphin, where they cheered 'emselves after their poxy heretical meeting in some cellar in a back street. I'll swear they meet secretly for worship (save the mark!) somewhere in the town, and could we but lay hands on 'em at it and hale 'em before the magistrates, they'd sing out with t'other side o' the mouth."

"I'll swear the Papists here meet for worship too," said Mr. Marvell.

"Well, you should know, my bawcock, seeing they took you off with 'em to London last year."

Mr. Marvell blushed; he was now ashamed of that impetuous and brief excursion of his into Papistry, and, having been rescued from it, had settled into a firm Protestant Anglicanism.

"I've no love for the Papists," continued Mr. Cowley; "but, to give 'em their due, at the least they don't run ranting and roaring into our churches breaking 'em up. Look, we should be helping to fight 'em back, not standing idle here, as if they was the Christmas mummers mumming for our mirth."

"Then come on," Giles Yarde cried. "At 'em, lads. Come, all on you, and we'll show 'em what Trinity can do."

He pushed forward, looking to Mr. Cowley, Mr. Hervey, and Mr. Marvell to follow. But only Mr. Marvell, ever pugnacious, did so. The other two young gentlemen, more given to controversy of words than of blows, and something mindful of their dignity as Bachelors, remained where they were. Mr. Cowley moved nearer to Julian.

"If your bold companion's going into the wars, you must let me stop with you, Mrs. Julian. 'Tis foolish, for he'll do no good and only get himself a bloody nose. Besides, 'tis against the rules that we brawl with the town."

"But Giles does right," Julian assured him. "It a'n't brawling, to drive wild animals out o' church. And it's the better on Giles his part to do so, for he cares nothing at all for the altar and the rails and the ornaments."

Mr. Cowley slightly shrugged his shoulders.

"So I should guess. But he enjoys to use his fists. He's one of the hoydens. A born man of action, whereas I and Mr. Hervey here are men of repose. There's a great many of hoydens in Trinity presently. Th'are useful for fighting John's; th'are the army we send out to battle for us, while we sit at home at ease. Splendid fellows. But I fear they'll do no good to-day."

The University contingent was, indeed, being overborne

and defeated, for the town mob increased each minute, surging into St. Mary's with shouts of Christmas joy. The emotions and desires of the populace appeared to be mixed, for some cried, "Down with the rails! Table in the middle!" some, "Give the parish back its church!" alluding to the appropriation of St. Mary's to the University and the exclusion of the town from the middle aisle, a deed performed by Dr. Cosin a few years back; while others, of more wide and general interests, shouted, "Down with the bishops!" or "Burn the Prayer Book!" or "Crush the Canterbury wasp!" And some again, more laconically, merely observed breathlessly, as they struggled and swarmed, "A Pope! A Pope!"

"Poor fellows. Their minds are truly extreme confused," Mr. Cowley pityingly remarked.

"I hope Giles won't get hurt," Julian said.

"Indeed, I hope not. Your brother's not in it, is he?"

"No."

"Well, here come the watch, so there'll soon be an end on't."

The watch pushed their way among the crowd, charged stolidly into the church, beat the rioters impartially with their staves, arrested some, and drove others helter-skelter away. The fight was, in face, over, and the onlookers departed to seek some fresh entertainment. The Proctors were also by this time on the scene, calling to order the combatant gownsmen. Giles pushed his way back to Julian, out of breath, with torn gown and no cap, and mopping a cut over his eye.

"Quick, Jule. We'll away before I'm catched and fined. A box of these meddling watchmen and Proctors. We'll haste back to Petty Cury and fetch the pup, and I'll smug myself up a trifle before we walk."

"I see you bleed for the good cause," said Mr. Cowley.

"It a'n't a very good cause," Giles said crossly. "And I

don't bleed much. For my part, I think the townsmen is in the right on't, and that the table ought to be in the middle, for 'tis easier to reach it so. But I'm hanged if I care. And, anyhow, these damned coystrells shan't have the shifting on't, and shan't call St. Mary's their church. Come on, Jule."

They walked off together across the crowded market place.

"*He* di'n't seem to have much envy for a fight," Giles spitefully remarked.

Julian cast him a thoughtful sidelong look. "No. He telled me he weren't a man of action, and loved not a fight."

"No more he do. He telled you true."

"Are you hurt much, Giles?"

"I'm not hurt at all."

"Y'are in a sorrowful pickle, though."

"Well, I shall help that suddenly, shan't I? Are you too quaint to walk with me till I'm smugged?"

"Don't be stupid, Giles. You used not to be so foolish to say such things to me."

"You used not to be so finical to make me think 'em. You and your fine Cambridge friends. . . . Well, no matter."

"Giles, let us lin quarrelling. We'll not fall out on Christmas Day."

"Hell, July, I've no envy to fall out with you. But you scarce let me see you now. And you swear to spend the evening with me at Trinity, and then you will go to John's."

"'Tis Kit's college, Giles."

"Kit would have come to Trinity. And you'll go to John's for the Founder's Day revels two nights hence, beside. . . . Well, I care not. . . . Is the doctor home?"

"No, he's gone walking with Mr. Lilly, the astrologer. He's gotten to astrology in his book, now he's done with apparitions."

"He don't deny the stars, do he?" Giles was by now

prepared to learn that this wrong-headed doctor denied anything.

But Julian said that he did not go quite so far as that.

"He believes on the stars, in course, but he thinks men have laid over much on 'em, and it should be more curiously examined. But he don't believe on apparitions. Not though they walk all around Dean, and nigh every person we know has seen 'em; aye, and they walk in Cambridge too. Mr. More says his eyes is holden so as he won't see, and his mind so as he won't believe. Mr. More, you know, conceits spirits to be everywhere, and to walk all about us. When he goes off into an ecstasy he sees 'em by the shoal, and they talk to him of holy or of evil things, according to their nature."

Giles thought there might be a happy mean between Mr. More's experiences and Dr. Conybeare's.

"You don't need to see 'em to believe on 'em," he said. "I've ne'er seen a spirit myself, nor you."

"Oh, yes, I have. I see them at home sometimes, walking at cockshut in the mists."

"Well, I shall go upstairs and clean myself," said Giles, whom spirits bored.

23

Christmas passed, and Twelfth Night. That part of the University that had left Cambridge for the vacation reassembled; and term began. Men came back with tales of the army everywhere rioting for want of pay; of officers murdered by their men; of Presbyterians and Separatists meeting unlawfully to worship where they pleased and coming to no harm for it, even being visited and prayed with by the Lords

Saye and Brooke; of riots against the churches everywhere; of the Scots rebel army that lay on the north like a great thunder-cloud, growing more insistent, more enormous, in its demands to a parliament which would refuse it nothing; of the navy and coast fortifications falling into decay for lack of means; of petitions from the Root and Branch party in Kent and Essex against the Bishops and the Prayer Book; of a sub-committee of the House sitting to consider religious and civil abuses in the Universities, of the King refusing the Triennial Bill and swearing to uphold the Bishops; of Oxford placed before Cambridge in the bill to exempt the Universities from the army tax.

"At the beginning," said Mr. Cleveland, who was just returned from a week in London and had called to see Dr. Conybeare, "they placed Cambridge first, but the Oxford men cried against it, so they formed a committee to consider the matter of precedence, and Sir Symonds D'Ewes, formerly of our College, makes, they say, a braver fine oration on't than you'd ne'er think to get from such a solemn Puritan pedant as he. Look; 'thas been already printed as a broad sheet by Daniel—I have it here. Cambridge, says he, is a renowned city at least five hundred years before there's a house in Oxford standing, and whilst brute beasts feed and corn's sown on the place where Oxford now stands; aye, Cambridge is a nursery of learning before ever Oxford hath a grammar school. And back he goes to the ancient catalogue of British cities, where Cairgrant precedes London in the list; he brings up Gildas and Nennius, and proves by 'em as Cambridge was an ancient renowned city in the days of Penda; he talks of those who studied here under King Alfred, and how King Henry I. is sent here by his father to learn, and so gets nicknamed Beauclerc; and, when he has all-thing proved his case (only he makes Pembroke the eldest College, save the mark), 'tis voted down by all the silly cocket burgesses as was reared at Oxford, and Oxford gets placed first on the Bill after all, a pox on its damned vainglorious envy. But 'twas a good fight Sir Symonds put up. I only wish there was some in that assembly who would speak as ardently for the Church. But the best they can say for the Bishops, even if they don't join the fifteen thousand and cry " down with 'em even unto the ground," as do many of our stubborn, obstinate burgess squires, the best they can say for 'em is, clip their claws, chain 'em up, and put 'em firmly under parliament."

" Well, sir, and what more d'ye wish said for the Bishops? "

" Nought, nought. Peace, doctor, and make not ready to wage a third Bishops' War against me, for I'll not defend 'em. All I'll say is, that I'd liefer have 'em to govern our Church than the Presbyters, pox take 'em. They may have been over-busy, and sheared a few too many ears (as was too long, so why mourn 'em), but t'others would shear away our Prayer Book, our altars, our very Church itself, and fatigue us with sermons longer than their ears and prayers wagging straight from their own silly tongues, Lord help us. Give me the Bishops any day."

" Well, you need give me neither one nor t'other. I'd as lief be ruled on by the astrologers."

" Even after talking with Mr. William Lilly? There's a lamentable silly ignorant fellow for you—knave or gull, I know not which. Astrology's a fine ancient science, and we should do well to take more heed in't, seeing as w'are all under the stars for good or ill—except w'are the moon's men and our fortunes ebb and flow with the tides. But I take it as Mr. Lilly's a quacksalver, and sells more knowledge than he do possess."

" Aye, he's a most pestilential eloquent quack. But he served my purpose, so let him pass for a man."

Julian sat silently by as they talked. Life was more interesting, amusing and exciting, now that Mr. Cleveland was returned to Cambridge. They had not seen him for a fortnight. He had had his hair cut and curled in the newest mode while in London, and looked very elegant and well. There is that about a modish man which appeals even to bookish and philosophising young gentlewomen; and, indeed, this might also be put the other way round.

" Well," said Mr. Cleveland, rising. " I'll not waste more of your time, doctor. I should be back in College before this, seeing my pupils."

" Aye, and I would you'd cause that boy of mine to work harder this term. The idle lad's seemed in a dream of late; I know not what's come to him."

" He shall work," said his tutor grimly. " I'll see to that." And to himself he added, " Lord, if the doctor did but know what the dream he walks in is, what a pudder and a dimification would there be! "

PART III

ANTIPLATONICK

Love thats in contemplation plac't
Is *Venus* drawn but to the Wast.
Unless your flame confess its gender
And your parley cause surrender,
Y'are Salamanders of a cold desire
That live untouch't amid the hottest fire.

What though she be a Dame of stone,
The widow of *Pigmalion*,
As hard and un-relenting she
As the new-crusted *Niobe*,
Or (what doth more of statue carry)
A Nunne of the Platonicke Quarry?
Love melts the rigor which the Rocks have bred;
A flint will break upon a Feather-bed.

For shame, you pretty female elves,
Cease for to Candy up your selves;
No more, you sectaries of the game,
No more of your calcining flame!

. . .

Love's Votaries in thrall each others soul,
Till both of them live but upon Parol.

Vertue's no more in Woman-Kind
Than a green-sickness of the mind;
Philosophy, their new delight,
A kind of Char-coal Appetite.
There's no Sophistry prevails
Where all-convincing Love assails.

JOHN CLEVELAND
The Antiplatonick

I

" LOOK, CHILD, is your father home? "

A wave of pink colour flooded the child's white face, as, looking up from her book, she saw her brother's tall tutor stoop his head at the doorway and enter the parlour where she sat.

He smiled as he bowed, pleased at the power he had to turn this white lily into a pink rose.

" No, sir, he's at Christ's library this afternoon."

" All the better, for I wish a word with you alone. It concerns your brother."

She had cleared a chair of books, that he might be seated. What with the doctor's books and papers, and what with hers, the little room seemed perpetually in a litter. She began to beg Mr. Cleveland's pardon for this.

" Faith, where else should books be but lying about a room, all yare to a man's hands when he needs 'em? Your father's a greedy scholar, and likes his dishes all around him, not kept in the larder where he can't reach 'em when he has a mind to."

" Some of 'em are mine," Julian pointed out; but he took no notice of this.

" What of Kit, sir? " she asked then, rather anxious.

" Why, this. I take it as you and I both know something he keeps secret from his father. Is that not so? "

" Aye; he telled me. And he telled me too he conceited as you knew it, although he had not telled it you roundly, for you refused to hear it, and bade him be extreme secret on't, on pain of expulsion from Cambridge."

" That's the truth he telled you. But, plague take the vain

cocket, I doubt he's not near so secret as he should be, but is grown high and flown with pride, and flaunts and vaunts it around. He comes into chapel enough to make up his bare tale of attendances; I supposition his new pastors grant him that much of indulgence, for security's sake; but he's ceased to bow reverentially to the altar, as he was ever wont to do, and as the Master has most strictly enjoined; he'll give it now the paltriest trifling dop o' the head, as if to show the world what small conceit he holds it in, and how, for his part, he deems it, for all its crucifix, candlesticks, and golden ornaments, the merest plain table, such as the Puritans like to call it, and that it might as well, in his opinion, be fetched down from the chancel and placed where they desire it, in the middle of the church. Aye, he looks on it with as spiteful a proud scorn as any Brownist might, and, in course, approaches not the sacrament, which has not been marked until this morning, but, this being Candlemas, the most of the Fellows and scholars were curious to observe it, as is the custom, by taking communion. And your brother was of a something religious pious habit; he was but rarely absent from his duties until now, which makes it the more observed. I reprimanded him later; but, says he, 'tis against his conscience, and, though he has leave to attend chapel in so far as he must, he has no leave to make a false communion and 'twould be to tradition his faith so to do. Then, he don't go quiet about it, but must needs draw attention on himself by his words and manner, being in his heart puffed up with vanity in his new profession (how a change of Church breeds pride!) and, in brief, he's playing the fool, and may suffer for't, which I should mislike to see, for I'm fond of the little jackanapes. He has wits and good 'haviour, and is a fine pretty spark of a lad, if he had not been thus seduced from his proper tasks. He might do something good here, did he but keep hard at his books, and 'twould be very lamentable if he were sent away for a Papist, as John Austin was. And, if the Master finds him out, he'll go packing forthwith; let him make no error as to that. Dr. Beale is himself in peril of accusation and trial before these gulls at Westminster, for using the decent seemly ceremonies of the Church of England, which the gulls term Popery, and he can't afford to wink at Papists in the College."

"No. Indeed, I see that." Julian sat looking melancholy, her hands clasped on the table before her.

"I can't do much with Kit, now he is gone Papist, but I will pray him as earnest as I can to be secret. . . . Sir, is there danger in't aside from expulsion from the University? Kit says the priests have changed their lodging, for the justices have been bid to be very sharp in future on the recusants, now the graces Sir Francis Windebank granted 'em is all revoked, and he in discredit, and the Queen no more able to protect 'em. If they should be betrayed and surprised one day at worship, and if Kit should be there, what would they do to him? They wou'n't put him in prison, would they?"

"Why no; but they might fine him for a recusant, and bind him over, and the fine would come on your father, who would not be best pleased, though what would vex him more greatly would be the lad's being sent from Cambridge. 'Twould be a pretty praemunire, and you and I must try by any means to avert it. Aye, you and I must put our heads together, and save the boy from his follies. What say you, shall we be fellow-conspirators, and work hand in hand in this business?"

"But what can we do?" Julian anxiously and frowningly wondered. "He *would* go over and now he's gone, we can't pull him back, not yet let him from worshipping as he conceits to be right. Oh dear, how I do wish as he'd stayed till he'd a-left Cambridge, if he must needs turn Papist."

"Aye, I wish it too. But don't take on too heavily, child. We'll wish and hope the best. Sometimes these excursions to

Rome are but brief trips. Young Andrew Marvell of Trinity was back from his after a few weeks. We must try and work on Kit's mind with a battery of arguments. You and I together should be able to do something. In the meantime, be secret; but that I know you will. We must meet often, to talk on't. W'are fellow traitors, you and I, being both guilty of misprision of treason, and we must comfort one another. What! won't you comfort me, little fellow-traitor? Nay, don't shrink back, pretty bud; give me your hands. There: w'are hand in hand at last, as I've oft desired to be. Hast not ever desired it? Never? Come, speak truth. Lord, 'tis like holding a snowflake, as may drift away any moment. But snowflakes melt . . . Don't snowflakes melt, bud? Shall I melt thee, little flake? For, by God, I believe I can."

He had drawn her to him; he held her two hands close against his breast; he looked down on her pale face with a tender smile.

"I do verily believe I can," said he. "Can I not?"

She shivered, strange tremors running through her, as if strong wine were being poured into her body and soul. So did Semele feel when Zeus came down to her from Olympus; so Psyche when Eros clasped her.

"Can I not?" he repeated; and she gave him a faint, troubled smile, her heavy lashes dropped over her eyes that could not meet his.

"My beautiful," he murmured, and his lips touched her broad white forehead, where the dark hair strayed over it. Tilting up her pointed face, he pressed his lips on hers.

So they stood, clasped together, his hands behind her shoulders pressing her soft slimness against his firm strength, his mouth hard on hers. She had not known that a man's kisses were like that, bruising the lips, stifling the breath. Was this, then, love? On her side yes, a thousand times yes, since she long worshipped the ground his foot pressed. On his side, what other could it be, that held her in this strong and tender embrace, that fonded her with such honied words? Yet the great, the brilliant Mr. Cleveland, Kit's magnificent and witty tutor—could he indeed stoop to love such a little nothing as she, without position, rank, money, fashion, or (to speak of) clothes? Just for her face and her intellects? Though, as to the last, he had never seemed to take notice of her parts, only to look with approval (that one could scarcely have missed) at her person.

But she did not speculate as to the reasons of his love; she did not, in fact, speculate at all; how could she, while she was held thrilling in his arms, and could scarce even breathe?

He lifted his lips from hers for long enough to remark, "My honey-pot, my almond-blossom," and fell to it again, having given her just time, as it were, to come to the surface and take breath before dropping down again into the sea.

"Dost like it," he inquired, during the next interval.

"Aye," said Julian, a truthful and literal girl. "I think I do," she added, with a touch of perplexed doubt. She was, indeed, surprised that she liked it, for she did not really like kissing much, nor being handled, nor stifled, nor cuddled. And she felt, faintly, that Mr. Cleveland had in some measure fallen from Olympus in thus stooping to handle, stifle and cuddle her, and, with her mind, she was not sure that she did like it, except in so far as it seemed to indicate his preference for her. But her body liked it, for it thrilled and quivered like a fiddle-string that is played on. So, "I think I do," she said, after a pause.

He laughed, and cupped her face in his long white hands. "You think you do? Y'are not sure, then? Shall I continue till y'are sure, sweet doubter? Aye, I'll do so. I'll not lin until you swear you do like it. Thus—and thus—and thus——"

"Pray . . . Oh pray, sir, 'tis enough," came her small panting whisper.

"Enough, is it? Enough to make you own you do love it? Aye, and that you do love me too? Say it, bud; say 'I do love you,' before I kiss you again."

"I do love you, Mr. Cleveland." The tiny whisper stroked the air like a falling snow-flake.

"Mr. Cleveland? Y'are very cool and finical. Is that all the name you have for me? Though I'm near twice your years, you must do better than that to show you like me."

"Y'are too high and great," she told him. "Y'are the Rhetoric Reader, and Kit's tutor, beside a famous poet . . ."

"Aye, truly, so I am Kit's tutor, and now thy tutor beside, I think, for I've taught thee something, and will teach thee much more. So call me tutor, if thou wilt, and I'll call thee pupil. How is that, little pupil?"

"Very well, tutor."

Julian remembered how she had, from the first hour in which she had seen Kit's splendid tutor, wished that he might also be hers; wished that she too might go daily to him and learn and read and be instructed and corrected. The name came easily to her lips, and with it a hope that, if he really liked her so much, he might indeed teach her much more.

"Will you truly teach me? Will you help me with my Greek?"

At that he laughed out.

"Greek, didst say? Lord help us! I knew not thou wert such a little jester. No, little pupil, 'twon't be Greek as I'll teach thee. But never fear; there's a plenty beside, that both Greeks and English and all other men have known, as thou'llt learn from me. Greek, forsooth! Stint thy prating, my pretty, and throw aside those books of thine, and ape not dull men, when heaven has made thee a lovely maid. All thou and I have to say one to t'other will go into English; and what won't go into English will go into no words at all, but must be said thus——"

He was at it again, stinging her lips with his, dropping lighter kisses on her eyes, forehead, cheeks and chin.

"Th'art such a curious lovely sweet piece, I could all-to devour thee, leaving not a scruple on the dish," he observed. "Oh, rare nymph . . ."

His passion surged up like a wave, at the sight of the very young face, so beautiful, so flushed with his usage, close to his.

He released her.

"There: I'll not devour thee yet; not all at one sitting. We have time . . . Look, chuck, we must meet again suddenly. You must ride out with me to-morrow. We'll ride to Madingley, and walk there in the woods, for 'tis mild sunny weather in present, more like spring than winter. Canst come?"

"To-morrow, no. To-morrow I go to Mr. More's lecture in St. Clement's church."

"You go *where*? What a pox, will you go to other men's lectures when your tutor demands your company? Plague take Mr. More, I'll give you all the lecturing you require."

"But w'are reading the *Enneads*, and I've wrote a thesis, and must take it him to correct. Indeed I wou'n't miss a Tuesday afternoon, even——"

"Even for your new tutor? We'll see to that. Did I hear you say you loved me, or was I mistook? Indeed, 'twas so small a voice that I may have well been mistook, and I now see as I was. Go your ways, then: 'tis Mr. More is your tutor, not Mr. Cleveland."

He was laughing at her, gently, yet with eyes that commanded and prayed. She heaved a small sigh and gave in. He was her tutor and her lover, and could command her anything.

"Very well; I'll come riding."

"Sweet chit, in course you'll come riding!" He had her in his arms again.

"And I'll write to Mr. More and pray him to let me show him my thesis at another time," she added, wrinkling her forehead a little.

"Mr. Cleveland smoothed away the pucker with his finger.

"Plague take your thesis, my sweet. Your new tutor's changed your course of study, and you'll not need to write theses more."

"But I *like* to write 'em."

Strange, that he could not understand that, and he so clever and so erudite.

"Oh, we'll soon cure that. 'Tis a disease, a green-sickness, as my tutoring will mend. Philosophy, is it? Why a pox, what can maids, or women either, learn of philosophy? Henry More's a moon's man."

"But why shou'n't women learn philosophy? My father says they all ought."

"Your father's another moon's man, sweet chuck; a near-Bedlamite."

"He a'n't." Julian drew back from him, indignant. "You know as my father's an extreme learned ingenious man."

"Aye, to be sure he's a learned ingenious man, but a moon's man for all that, for he don't believe on Almighty God, or on the Church and the Bible, and he do believe that women should get more learning than's good for 'em. Whether of the two is the madder I'll not try and judge. But I'll not let my little pupil be led astray by him, no, nor by Mr. Henry More neither. In future, I'm thy only tutor; wilt mark and mind me?"

"Aye, if you'll learn me what you learn Kit and the rest."

"I'll no such thing, and there's an end on't. Give me no more of thy pretty nonsense, elf, for I'll not listen. Here, hand me thy thesis, so called, if that's it lying on the table there."

Julian collected her neatly written pages and gave them to him. He would read it, then; he did not mean what he said; he had been but jesting.

Mr. Cleveland took the sheets, glanced over them with a smile, tore them across, and dropped them into the fire.

"And so much for philosophy, sweet bud. See how it flies a-flame up the chimney, set a-fire and consumed by love."

Julian had started forward to save her philosophy, but too late.

"Nay, child, burn not thy pretty hands—it's all-to consumed. Come, kiss me; learn thy new lessons and forget thy old."

She was kneeling on the hearth, looking up at him with bewildered, indignant eyes, over which the thin black brows were drawn in a frown that kept back tears.

"But why . . . why . . . Oh 'twas my thesis, and had took me hours to write, and 'twas on Pythagoras his theory of souls, and 'twas for Mr. More . . ."

"Oh, a pox on Pythagoras his theory of souls, and on all the Platonists too. I must give thee some verses I writ for thee t'other day. A nun of the Platonic quarry—is that what you crave to be?

> "Love melts the rigour which the rocks have bred;
> A flint will break upon . . .

Well, the rest will keep a while, till y'are further on in your lessons. Y'are not *crying*, little one? Not weeping for your burnt philosophy?"

"No."

Julian got up, still frowning tears back from her eyes. She stood, her hands close locked behind her, looking at this strange, laughing, masterful man who had burnt her thesis and bade her forget philosophy. She was sharply, deeply hurt; she felt cold and bewildered with pain. What did he desire of her, then, if he did not desire her mind, her very self, all she cared for? He could not, in that case, desire her at all—or only for kissing, and such, as if, thought she, she had been a kitten or a babe. Her eager and unfolding mind, expanding so wide of late to new learning, as it had been a flower opening to the sun and air, shrank back on itself, as if a sudden frost had shrivelled it. Mr. Cleveland did not wish her to learn. It was like a hard pebble flung at her heart. What then of love, the love with which she brimmed so full that she could scarce contain it, that, for many weeks past, the sound of his voice, his approach in the street, the kind, tender glancing of his eyes on her, had set her heart shaking and leaping as if it were in an ague? What now of love, that had to endure this hurt? And what of his love, that could give it, that loved, but cared nothing for the interests and pleasures of what it loved; that was so ungentle, so cruel and so blind?

So she stood, a pale, pondering, resentful elf, her great eyes beneath drawn brows staring up bewildered at this strange, difficult lover, her hands behind her, clasped together that he might not take them, her slim taut body bent a little back from him, as she took stock of him and of her, and of the odd plight in which she found herself. She was like some small wary nervous bewildered animal, that has walked unawares into a trap, and now sees the trap-door swinging to, yet still ajar, still open for its flight, could it but take a step backward, push the door and run—or no, not run, but limp, dragging injured limbs and a fainting, desperate heart.

But she could not, would not, take that step, since the door would then close behind her, shutting her outside, in a waste country lit only by the frosty stars of liberty and resolution. Her lover had her proud, twisting, crying spirit in his hands; however he might assault it, and however she might struggle and strive, it was his.

"But," she said, slowly, in a small, remote voice, as of a

bewildered child, that seeks to understand, "but it was *my* thesis. Why should you wish to burn my thesis? It did not harm you."

He laughed, but half impatiently.

"Let be the thesis, bud. Thesis me no theses. I burnt it because 'tis a foolishness in you to be reading and writing of such dry hard matters, when there's life to be lived, and ginger's hot i' the mouth, and y'are my young she-darling and as lovely as the moon on water. Look in my eyes—there, so—and tell me if you conceit yours to have been made by the Lord to peer into dry tomes, or if this white brow was e'er meant to be wrinkled with hard problems of philosophy or the Greek tongue."

"Why not?" she asked, leaning back from him, her hands against his chest, as he would have enfolded her. "If I were a lad, if I were Kit or another, you'd not speak so."

"No, sweet protestant, y'are very right; I would not. But then, y'are not Kit, nor another. Y'are a maid, and formed for sweetness and love, and not for learning. As to that, in my view no woman's formed for learning, even be she ugly. If she be ugly, let her practise virtue and be good; if she be fair, let her give delight to mankind and walk in beauty—and, to be sure, practise virtue beside—if she can. But let her by all means refrain from seeking more learning than is apt to her sex, for no man asks that of her."

No man asks . . . this was strange language.

"But if she loves books for themselves? Why should she have ever at mind what men ask of her? Mayn't women please themselves ever, then?"

"If they please men, they'll best please themselves thus, my dear. Come, a truce to argument, for I must away. Here endeth your tutor's first lesson. And now he asks his fee for't."

He took his fee many times.

"There. Art melted again, little snow-queen? I swear I

have as much trouble thawing thee as thou wert cased in ice. Dost forgive me my auto-da-fé?"

She shook her head.

"No. For I must re-write it, and 'twill take much time."

"You'll do no such matter. I swear I need a ferule to teach thee with. But look, I must be gone. One thing more. Best take no notice to your father or brother of what's passed between us. Be very secret on't, and let it be, in present, between us two alone. I have good reasons for this. Have I your word on't?"

Julian looked doubtful.

"But is it right as I shou'n't possess my father forthwith of—of such a matter as this?"

"'Tis right in this case, believe me. Indeed, child, you must trust me in this. Come, your word."

"I promise, then."

"That's my bud. Faith, there's few men's word I'd more readily take, and very surely no woman's at all. Come, let's seal it—there—and now I must truly be away. Say to your father, if you say aught, that I waited on him but stayed not, finding him abroad."

"But that would be a crambe," she protested. "Indeed I'll say nought, but I pray you won't desire me to speak crambes."

"Nay, then, crambe not, little saint, if it distaste you. There, I leave all in your hands, only be prudent and secret, an you love me. Till to-morrow then."

2

He was gone, and it was as if a torch had been extinguished in the small dim room, which now held only the grey February cockshut light and the red smouldering of the burnt-out logs on the hearth.

Julian knelt by the dead fire, huddled over it, as if it could give her heat that could replace the ardent warmth which had lately held and burnt her. Burnt her thesis, burnt her face, body and heart, and all-to consumed her life, She did not conceit that any one had ever loved her so ardently as she loved Mr. John Cleveland, for no such ardent love could be possible but for him.

"He may command me anything," she thought, and sang whisperingly Mr. Herrick's song to Anthea.

"Bid me to live, and I will live
Thy Protestant to be:
Or bid me love, and I will give
A loving heart to thee . . .

"Bid that heart stay, and it will stay,
To honour thy Decree:
Or bid it languish quite away,
And't shall do so for thee.

"Bid me despair, and I'll despair
Under that Cypress tree:
Or bid me die, and I will dare
E'en Death, to die for thee.

"Thou art my life, my love, my heart,
The very eyes of me:
And hast command of every part,
To live and die for thee."

"He loves me," she whispered then. "He kissed my eyes, my cheeks, my chin, my hair, my mouth . . . He, whom I thought a Prince—who *is* a Prince . . . He loves me. But he'll not look at my writings, and he burnt my thesis, and he bids me not read nor learn. Oh, I don't understand . . . Dear Lord, pray tell him that I *must* read and learn and write, that, if I stint to do that, he'll be fonding an empty shell, not me at all . . . My verses: I'll show 'em him. If they please him, won't he desire me to continue to write? But perhaps they'll not please him; perhaps he'll cast 'em in the fire and laugh. His own verses is so ingenious and conceited and quaint, he might scorn mine for simple and old-fashioned; though indeed, of late th'are less so. Oh, I should die of sadness if he di'n't gust 'em. Bid me despair, and I'll despair under that cypress tree . . ."

She shivered, crouched over the grey soft wood-ash, wherein fragments of burnt black paper were bedded, like truffles in liver. She would burn down and die, she thought, like the fire, if he should kill her poetry. But what if he killed it and bade her burn and live? Bid me to live, and I will live . . . Or bid me love, and I will give a loving heart to thee . . . Thou art my life, my love, my heart, the very eyes of me . . .

A long curling brown hair glinted on the bosom of her blue dress; dark brown, but not so dark as her own straight smooth locks. She plucked it off and wound it round her fingers. Was it scented? Or was it her dress and person that were impregnated with the wholesome, astringent, masculine scent that he used? And would the doctor observe it, or would he be too snuff and tobacco-bound to smell anything? What deceits were these, that she must now begin to practise? Oh, she could never carry it through: his kisses burned on her face for all to see; she was new and changed and made over, and gladness and love must beam out of her eyes and ring in her voice. She must look down; she must be stooping over the fire to make it up, to conceal her strangeness.

She was so doing when Dr. Conybeare came in.

3

"What, the fire gone out? Well, 'tis so mild a February day we scarce need it. Don't trouble with it, child."

"I'll kindle it again, father, for 'twill grow cold in the evening."

"As you will. I'm warm enough, and your face is pink as a daisy. . . . I've brought in with me some books will interest you too; little Seth Ward of Emmanuel lent 'em me. Here's one concerns the magnetisers, and Paracelsus his stone, and cure by transplantation, and Kircher's magnet-swallowing cure, and touches on Hermes Trismegistus his medicine, that Mr. More was speaking on to you. Faith, were I to practise some of these recipes at Dean, I should have a rare success. They'd gust the magnet cure and the weapon-salve as much as they distaste my physic—more particularly since Parson Foster declared 'em to come from the devil."

"Aye, Dean would believe on 'em once they heard that. Mr. More says, father, as Sir Kenelm Digby believes on the philosopher's stone, and the elixir of life too, and endeavours to persuade M. Descartes to take it up."

"Aye, so he do. Digby's a strange great believer on marvels, for so ingenious a man. He maintains he cured Mr. James Howell's wounded hand by soaking in water and vitriol powder a garter as had his blood on't, without e'er touching or viewing the wound. I've heard him relate that wonderful likely tale to a gathering of physicians, and I'll swear he believes it too, and so do Mr. Howell himself. And they don't call it a miracle, but medicine, save the mark, yet 'tis as odd miraculous medicine as any cures by relics told in the Acta Sanctorum. . . . I've some very pretty tales of demon lovers here too, as thou'llt enjoy to hear. Mr. Cleveland was to show me a book of demons he has, now I think on't; I must wait on him to-morrow."

"He came this afternoon, father, while you was from home."

"Did he so? I'm vexed I missed him. Did he leave me a message?"

"Only that he was sorry . . ."

"He di'n't say when he would come again?"

"No."

"I like to talk with Cleveland, for he's a mighty ingenious wit, and full of tales and drolleries."

Dr. Conybeare seated himself by the kindling hearth, and lit his pipe. "He likes to talk with me too, I take it, for he seeks me out. . . . Aye, I like Cleveland, for all he's a damned subservient loyalist and would give the King all he asks and set up Black Tom again to tyrant it o'er us. There's overmuch of such short-sighted, foolish loyalty in this University and t'other. They ha'n't looked into politics close enough nor deep enough, or they'd not clamour for the continuance of methods as would rivet chains on us for good and all, and enable the King and his ministers to turn out our pockets when as they had a mind. Th'are carried away by a fine rush of loyalty to the head, and by their rage against those they call rebels, and by their love of their Church, as they truly see's in peril, and by their distaste for the Puritans as would stroy it, and so, oblivious of all other, they cry, Down the Parliament! Up the King and the King's ministers! like any rabble of unthinking, silly vulgars as ha'n't the power o' thought."

"But the differ is," Julian argued, "as they *have* the power o' thought, and have considered it well and throughly, and have chosen to stand for the King and his party because they deem it the true patriot party, and that the extreme men, if not checked and let, will make shipwreck of both State and Church."

"Oh, I see th'ave made you an all-thing loyalist between 'em, miss. So's your brother. Lord knows 'ta'n't my fault; I've done my best to put sense and justice and independent thinking into ye both. But the odds was too great, with Kit sucking in obedience and loyalty at Winchester and Cambridge, and you put to learn with a parson that breaks into obsequious fulsome odes to this and that princeling; calls that little ape the Prince of Wales the sun and the creator of his verses, and his little brother the nestle-chick of Jove, and feigns to be Venus-struck when he writes o' that little silly fool of a queen, that is her husband's bane. Aye, y'have had the wrong tutor, so far's his politics go, though he's well enough for learning. And so to this new tutor of thine—what is it, child? You start."

"Oh, Mr. More. He don't speak to us on politics, only of books and learning and philosophy."

"Aye, and I take it he don't think greatly on politics, neither; his head's up among the stars and the angels, and he don't take much notice on earthly kings and parliaments, and that's not too good for thee, neither, little dreamer. Still, he well advances thee in thy Greek, don't he? Hast finished that thesis of thine?"

"No, father. I must write it anew, for by mischance it was all-to burnt in the fire."

"Why, that was a mischance indeed. I was intending to look through it to-night, to see what Mr. More is now teaching thee. Write it anew, then, bud, and don't stay idling. I can help thee, perhaps. 'Twas on Pythagoras, I think?"

"Yes. His theory of souls."

"Souls, bless the mark! When you telled me Pythagoras, I had hoped it concerned his theory of numbers, or of squares and triangles, or else of the planets and the universe. Souls, forsooth! Well, you must write it, ne'ertheless."

"He telled us too of the Pythagorean astronomy, but bade us write on this. I like the stars better; but some of the pupils say they'll not write on the heavens, for th'are too high for the understandings of ladies."

"Ladies the devil. If ladies, or gentlemen, either, don't learn of matters above their understandings, the intellects th'ave got will fust away in 'em for lack of use. Never thou harken to such foolish talk, child."

"No, father." But his child looked into the fire and spoke without spirit, for what had she been harkening to only half an hour since, but just such foolish talk?

"Father," she said, "there be some speak as women shou'n't learn aught, nor read, nor write." Her voice rose in a question.

"Fools," her father succinctly replied, re-lighting his pipe.

"Fools?" she repeated, as if doubting whether this were the apt name for these erred beings.

Her father had no doubts.

"Aye, fools. For if women learn nought, they'll know nought, but stay as great sillies as God was pleased to make 'em. And he was pleased to make the most part on 'em greater sillies than he made most men; though, as to that, 'tis a near point. So, this being as I say, women have the greater need for learning, that they may become, if possible, rational beings. Not as most of 'em will; nor, for that, do most men. But we should all do our best in't, and not sit down hugging our ignorance. Faith, I lived with a female fool twenty years, and should know what I speak on . . . but there, don't heed me, for I should not be saying that to thee. Still, I do know. . . . There be some men as don't ask any intellects or any knowledge or wit in women, but only quite other matters, but we need not to consider such as they."

"No, father. . . . Perhaps they learn different, in time."

"Aye, perhaps. By living with a fool, belike; that teaches a man a many thing. . . . Now, child, th'art idling; get thee to thy books and thy thesis, or the man that weds thee will find he's gotten a fool. Be thankful I began on thee young, and set thy feet on the right road near as soon as thou couldst diddle across the room. Well, I mind setting thee to thy horn book and pointing out great A to thee, and thou with thy great solemn babe's eyes saying it after me. And, later, setting thee to thy first Latin book, and thy mother crying out against teaching a little maid what could ne'er be of use to her. . . . It shan't be my fault, said I to that poor soul, if our little Jule grow up a nit-wit. She shall get some learning into her, says I, if I have to whip it in all the way with the rod. Better a few tears now than ignorance all her life through. But faith, there was seldom need for the rod with you. 'Twas Kit needed more of that. And as for Doll, I soon gave her up, perceiving 'twas of no use and that she must go her mother's way and her own. And sure she has, and she's grown such a fool I can scarce talk with her when we meet. Howsoe'er, her husband seems content enough, and 'tis he has to hark to her. But a man wed with a fool don't hark to her greatly; if he's wise, he learns to think his own thoughts and turn a deaf ear, and take her chatter as what Solomon said it was, water dropping on a roof, and no more. . . . And now we'll both to work."

4

Spring came early this year. February, generally in Cambridge an even sorrier month than elsewhere, was pale with faint sunshine, and on the bare black boughs of the river meadow trees, thrushes and robins sweetly fluted.

Mr. John Cleveland had had a happy thought. He waited on Dr. Conybeare and requested leave to act tutor to his daughter.

"For," said he, "under Mr. More she is like to imbibe some maggoty, fantastical, irregular notions that will do her no good. With your leave, I could advance her learning with more of system than can he."

"I doubt not," said the parent. "Ne'erth'less, Mr. More expounds Descartes to his pupils, and I would fain she got some notion of his system into her head. I've been pleased to mark that she's gotten wonderful interested in Descartes."

Mr. Cleveland looked as if he thought this a pity.

"The Frenchman's somewhat stiff, dry reading for young ladies," he ventured.

But he perceived that he had made a mistake, for the doctor looked at him sharply.

"Young ladies? My daughter's not a young lady, sir, while she's learning; she's a scholar to be taught, the same as any lad, and with a quick, clear head too. Don't you be young ladying her over her studies, or telling her this and that is not for her, or you'll undo all my pains, and affront her into the bargain. But I see no reason why she should not continue to read Descartes with Mr. More, and Greek and Latin with you. I'm too much taken up myself with my own book to give an eye to her studies, and indeed, sir, I would thank you, and so would she, if you had indeed time to give her an hour now and then. She can't well go to you in College, since I must mind at times as she is indeed a young lady, so you would have to attend her here, which I fear will be troubling you."

"Not a scruple, sir. I shall be glad to do't."

"And your fee?"

"Nothing in the world, but the reward of adding to the attainments of so gifted a pupil."

"That's uncommon civil in you, sir. I'm sure y'are monstrously civil and obliging to make such a proposition, and Jule will be greatly obliged and pleased. . . . You could take her and her brother together, perhaps, sometimes."

But Mr. Cleveland did not think well of that notion.

"Th'are at different stages, and on different lines of study. Your son's working for his Bachelor's degree, and, as you know, reading a mass of stuff that's more necessary for the schools than for general education."

"Aye, y'are right enough there. You can read with Julian Lucretius his *De Rerum Natura*, that, when I was at Cambridge, and now too, is shunned like the devil by the schools, as is most other literature worth the reading, as John Milton so sharply complains. Kit will have to wait for his education, as I did, till he's done with the schools. His sister has better fortune there, for she has all the great books of the past open to her at fifteen years of age, when, were she a lad, she would be put to dry logic and scholastic commentaries."

Perceiving that the doctor was launching himself with vigour on a pet theme, Mr. Cleveland soothingly returned, "Aye, we'll see Mrs. Julian gets a more liberal humane education." And took his leave, having arranged his business to his satisfaction.

And, since Tuesday was one of the afternoons when he

was pleased to come and instruct his new pupil, she attended no longer the lectures of Mr. More in St. Clement's Church, nor wrote any further essays on Pythagoras his theory of souls, nor yet his theory of the heavenly bodies, nor on the philosophy of Plato, Plotinus, Origen, Tully, or M. Descartes. All this her new tutor waved aside, and read with her, when they read at all, English poetry and plays, and a little Latin drama and love poetry, for, thought he, the girl must have something to tell her inquiring parent. Never before had he known so sinisterly, awkwardly truthful a maiden; he was teaching her (among other lessons) discretions and guiles, and she had a store of silence and reserves on which to build, but to make her lie was a hard matter, and, when persuaded to deceive, she turned on him her great, startled, melancholy eyes and brooded over it as if she strove to resolve some paradox in her universe and could not.

A strange, lovely, enticing maid she was, but shy and remote, like a visitor from another star; and with her pretty head stuffed with maggots derived from her father about learning and books. Mr. Cleveland kept a firm hand on this nonsense, teasing it out of her with raillery and kisses; he knew, he could not but know, that she adored him, and that she would, in the end, do what he wished in each matter that arose between them, but she gave him, at times, some trouble, and even at times almost bored him, when she began about books, about astronomy, even about politics, questioning him, giving her own views, forsooth, or her father's, or some other, trying to induce him to discuss the affairs of the realm with her, as if she had been a man. He would tell her sometimes that she knew nothing of such matters, and should not talk of them.

"But," said she, "I do not think I know about 'em, and that's why I like to talk of 'em, that I may know more."

"Why should you know more? 'Twill never be your

concern to order the affairs of state, since women a'n't yet made Councillors."

"No, but I live in the State, and should know of what passes in't. My father says that if I do not I should be shamed, and count myself most ignorant, and not fit for a citizen."

"Oh, your father. Deuce take him, what's he about, to bid you regard yourself as a citizen? See here, my bud; women may have wit, and, for my part, the more on't they have the better I'm pleased, for I love a shrewd gay tongue in 'em and a quick answer, but let 'em leave politics, as is a dull silly business enough, to men."

"But that's nonsense." Since he loved a quick answer, she gave him one. "Why shou'n't I desire to know of the Episcopacy Abolition Bill and how it fares in the Commons, and what they all said in the debate, seeing 'tis my Church is concerned? And why can't I read Bishop Hall's *Remonstrance of the Liturgy*, since 'tis our own Prayer Book is in danger? Indeed, I think women are as closely concerned in these matters as are men, and, should we have a Presbyterial Church put on us, we shall suffer more, for we are the more ardent and constant church-goers. And why shou'n't I be curious to mark what the King do, and what the Queen and the Papists, and what measures parliament do take agen 'em, and what shall be the fate of Dr. Goodman, and if the King can save my Lord Strafford, and how goes the case agen him, and if the Archbishop shall be imprisoned, and what the Scots do, and——"

"And, and, and! You talk like a little news-sheet, my love. Well, you shall know all that, for I'll tell you on't. I'll even read you the squibs I write on affairs and men. But *your* tongue was ne'er made to chatter on such business; for look, chuck, you know too little of affairs to speak on 'em with knowledge, and what can be more tedious than political chatter without knowledge? So mind not what the Scots do (as to that, what do they ever do, save to behave like Scots and demand more money?). But tell me instead of what *you* do, and how you feel, the folk you meet and the things they say; tickle me with merry tales, and warm and delight me with loving ones; but leave politics, the Prayer Book, and all other books, save such as contain romances, plays and pretty verses, to men, and to old women as can no other converse, for thy converse, my sweet dear, is in pretty looks, great eyes in which love drowns, a white neck soft as a swan's, a bosom like. . . . Ah, no, shrink not. Mayn't I caress thee, who art my lovely love? Do lovers stand apart like marble statues, conversing but with eyes and tongues? A'n't I thy tutor, to teach thee languages, and must I not teach thee the language of caresses? Aye, I will teach it thee, little image, little Galatea that my embracing can warm to living flesh. Dost not know, has not all that reading of thine telled thee, that love makes all things right for lovers, that where love and beauty are, no shame is? If thou'st not learnt that, so much for thy book-learning. Kiss me, sweet child. Lord, thou'rt as a willow-wand to hold, so slim, so supple and so frail. A willow-wand as I could bend and break with my one hand, I do believe. But I'll not; I'll cherish thee like a flower, and thou shalt come to no ill with thy tutor."

And this was the manner of their lessons.

5

Once Julian laid before her tutor a sheaf of manuscript, tied up in white covers with silk strings.

"What," he exclaimed, "a thesis? I trust 'tis on all I've strove to teach you these past weeks."

"No. They are my verses, that I've wrote for many years past, since I was a child, and some of 'em just now, since we was in Cambridge. Will you take 'em back with you and read 'em sometime, and tell me if you think any on 'em is good verses?"

Mr. Cleveland regarded the pile with brows lifted in whimsical consternation.

"Faith, child, I've little enough time for reading verses." He flicked over the pages with his long, slim fingers.

"Shrew me, but y'have been a monstrous plentiful poet. More sins lie here to your charge than I've committed in twelve more years of living. Y'have had a busy fifteen years on't, young lady."

"Yes," the young lady agreed.

"Well, don't stare on me with those solemn, questioning eyes, or I shall weep. I'll take thy verses back with me, and look at 'em when times serves."

"But not if it shall trouble you. I would not cause you trouble, to read that as shall fatigue you and be tedious."

"Leave that to me, child. Be sure I'll not fatigue myself o'ermuch, nor let you fatigue me neither. I'll take the verses, and one day I'll possess thee of how I find 'em. But should I find 'em paltry matter, of small or no moment, why look, I'll love thee none the less, but rather the more, for an innocent sweet maid as wields a pen sinisterly when as she comes to rhyme. Lord bless thee, do I want a young Abraham Cowley to my sweet heart, as can run out the lines of an ode and rein 'em in like horses exercising, and turn out ingenious witty plays for our pleasure and his own ambition, or a Dick Crashaw to pen prayers in verse, or a little Andrew Marvell to write impudent partisan squibs on matters of which he'll know more when his beard grows? What does a lovely maid with rhyming, pray?"

"It makes no differ, being a maid," Julian told him, frowning and near to tears, which he detested, for they marred her eyes, but when he spoke in this manner, her very heart seemed to weep. In one moment, he would thus trample and bruise her dreams, striking at that self she had which lived among the stars, beyond the battlings and the ecstasies of sex; in the next he would, with the honey and wine of his charm and his love, cause her to exile and forget that troubled, star-haunted self, and drug her into a wild heaven of rapture. She knew that in a brief space she would be so drugged, but for a moment she fought and frowned, and stammered out, "It makes no differ. Men or women, if we crave to write verse, we must write it, and write it the best we can."

For the first time in their intercourse, he turned from her impatiently, and she knew herself a bore in his laughing, quizzical eyes. A prating, self-conceited, solemn maid, who must stand up to her lover and argue with him, when he supposed that he had concluded the matter by his firm words.

Whether he would have spoken further words to cut and hurt her, or turned on her his teasing merry smile, or taken her in his arms and stopped her mouth with kisses, seemed uncertain, and so stayed, for, while he was still silent, the door was flung open and Kit walked in.

His face and clothes were wet, for it was a soft and dripping day; he flung his cap on the table and pushed back his damp hair from his forehead, looking at his sister and his tutor with strange, unseeing eyes.

"They have took the fathers," said he. "The justice and his officers catched 'em at mass this morning early. Some one must have traditioned 'em. I was there, and several more. They sent us away, taking our names first, that they might inform our Colleges. But they marched the fathers off to be tried before the magistratees next Monday, and they'll most like be given a term in prison, and then sent overseas; and they'll be by all means let from ministering again in Cambridge. The justices were saying they'd had their orders to smoke out that vipers' nest and have a care it returned not. So—so——"

He sat heavily down in the rush chair by the hearth, and rested his head on his hands.

"You young fool." Mr. Cleveland spoke sharply. "I telled you how it would be, with this new rigour th'are practising of late to extirpate Popery. You must needs choose just this time to turn Papist. And now you'll be expelled the College, if the justices inform on you to the master. Here's pretty praemunire y'have gotten yourself into by your stubborn folly."

Kit looked up at him dully.

"I think 'tis you they'll write to, sir. They asked me for my tutor's name. I looked for you this morning after breakfast to speak with you on't, but you was lecturing."

"Oh, so they'll write to me. Well, what of it? I must resolve the Master on't, as you know. 'Twill come to the same end."

Two pairs of violet eyes were on his face. He met the boy's with unrelenting impatience.

"Aye, young man, you'll have to leave your studies and go. I am sorry, but there's no help for't. St. John's can't harbour Papists, least of all at this dangerous moment, when the Master's at bay against these Westminster asses for imputed Papistical leanings. There'll be no hiding this business of yours; the justices will put it abroad, with the name of your College and all, and we shall have it bruited in parliament."

"Can't you do something?" Julian asked, and, turning from the boy, he met the eyes of the girl, and no longer were his own eyes hard.

"What d'you think I can do?" he asked her. "Wink at Popery? Say naught and let it be discovered to our busy parliament by those meddling justices? Would the matter be bettered so? The only differ would be that I should then be charged with condoning it."

"I thought," Julian suggested, "that if you should see the justices, and beg 'em to take no notice on't to any one, but to overlook it this time——"

"That Dr. Beale need never know, you thought? 'Tis asking me something, to shoulder such a matter, and to sue to those poxy justices for secrecy. Still, yes, it might be done. Only," he added, more sharply, turning to Kit, "I should have to promise for you that there should be no more on't."

Kit looked sullen and proud.

"I can't recant, sir."

"Recant! Lord, 'tis no such heavy great matter as that. Who cares if you recant or no? But you must attend chapel and church, and renounce these conventicles. Indeed, if I understand you rightly, the conventicles in Cambridge has been ceased, by these arrests, so you can't attend 'em if you would. If I give the justices your word as you'll keep, while at Cambridge, within the communion of your College and University, I may perhaps persuade 'em to o'erlook it and let it go no further."

"But the others," Kit said. "There were two from Peterhouse and another from John's. If they are expelled, I could not stay."

"The Peterhouse gentlemen must contrive their own business with their own tutors and Master, whom heaven help. As to t'other, I suppose 'tis that little fool Gryce, and I'll not lift a finger to save him expulsion, for he can't construe a line of Latin without a score of errors. Indeed, he does little good here, and had best go, and be prenticed to his father's linen shop. But you, my young fool, are a different matter. If you'd but keep at your books and work steady and forswear a-whoring after forbidden religions, you could achieve something. Oh, not a vast deal, perhaps, but something. And I should be extreme loath to vex your father so sorely as he would be vexed by your expulsion, and on such a ground as this. Look now, I'll do my best for you in this matter, but only on the stock of your promise to keep clear of open Popery while you remain in the College. What d'you say?"

Kit brooded frowning over this.

"'Twould scarce be honest——" he began, but his tutor impatiently silenced him.

"Honest, forsooth! What honesty is there in taking education and learning, and holding a scholarship, as you do, from a University sworn to loyalty to King and Church, the while you practise a faith that undermines both? The less you Papist undergraduates prate of honesty, the better, for to tell the difference between your kind of honesty and fraud would be to discriminate as nicely as Thomas Aquinàs himself. . . . There, boy, be not so foolish. Hear reason, pocket your scruples, and wait to serve the Pope, if serve him you must, till you be free of Cambridge. Life's long—or so, anyhow, we hope—and 'twon't harm you to stay a while from your chosen Church, if indeed you do choose it when as y'are older and wiser. Your sister is with me in this."

"Yes, Kit. Oh, Kit, think of our father, and don't so hurt

him. Say you'll attend chapel, and Mr. Cleveland will see all's well. Why, I know not how you can endure to seek out bare conventicles, when you can pray in St. John's Chapel, beneath that glorious roof and paintings."

"That has naught to do with it. No beauty can make the true and real, when it a'n't so."

"Oh, pox take your theology, you cocket jackanapes. Back with you to College, and read Bishop Hooker, and get some sound Church learning into your head, afore you dare to dispute concerning the validity of the sacraments. Look, leave us now, I pray, for your sister and I have a lesson in hand, and would finish it undisturbed. Wait on me in my chamber after supper, and we'll discuss your matter further."

Kit went out. The masterly way Mr. Cleveland had with him prevented his thinking it hard that he should be dismissed thus peremptorily from his father's and sister's lodging while his tutor remained there. It was the way of things. Mr. Cleveland gave orders; others obeyed them.

Kit, who had been seized of wild, high thoughts of sailing for France and serving his queen overseas, joining his spiritual pastors in their exile and bearing high the standard of English Catholicism abroad, realised, as he walked back through the light, soft rain, that it would be far easier to stay at Cambridge and finish reading for his degree; play tennis and bowls, row on the river, sit and talk far into the night with his friends, if this could be done without too downright a jettisoning of his faith.

He wished he could see the priests once more, to consult them as to what he should do, whether he should play the stubborn martyr and be flung out into the world, with his College's and his father's curse, to seek new adventures, and make his own way; or if he should compromise with truth, bow down in the house of Rimmon, please his family and tutor, and work for his B.A., and perhaps do the more good to the cause later on.

His father's pale, fighting, ironical face and fierce blue eyes came before him, and he knew that he could not stand up yet to that alarming and shattering battle.

It occurred to him that he would seek the counsel of his former confessor, Dr. Cosin. He had not seen him to speak to since his change of faith; indeed, he was afraid to, knowing his stern views on that subject. But at least he would have an opinion, and would give it in no uncertain manner. Yes; he would go to Peterhouse and see Dr. Cosin after evensong.

6

In Trinity Street he met Giles, who stopped and spoke.

"Have you been to Petty Cury to-day? Is July home? I would see her."

"Yes, she's home. But Mr. Cleveland is with her; th'are having a lesson. They dismissed me, to be undisturbed."

"Oh." Giles turned to walk with Kit towards St. John's. He looked gloomy. Kit, seeing him suddenly, as sometimes he saw his friends at odd, unexpected moments, as a stranger, a new person, registered on the sensitive tables of his appreciation the tall, graceful, strong young man, his short russet gown clinging, dark with the rain, to his shoulders, his fair-skinned, freckled, handsome face (much like his sister's, but of late grown harder, clearer, more aquiline) glistening from out the unruly crop of red hair that, ringing strongly at the ends, curled about his neck beneath the round black cap. Giles was grown very comely, thought Kit, half-envious of his friend's greater stature and strength, and looked at him through a girl's eyes. Then remembered that there were girls and girls, and that some few set store by wits and learning, and of these poor Giles had somewhat short commons.

"Mr. Cleveland's for ever there now, a'n't he," said Giles, his indifference but a poor feint.

"Yes, he's often there. He likes teaching July, it seems."

"And she likes him very well, don't she?"

"Yes; he stands in the sun of her favour. As to that, all his pupils like him well; he has that way with him. He wakes a man's mind. Then, he's so full of wit. He makes dry books live. I'd liefer have an hour's reading with Mr. Cleveland than three hours with any other."

"Three hours!" That seemed to Giles a stupid comparison. "Than ten minutes" would have made more sense. "Aye, he's ingenious enough, I don't doubt."

They were now at St. John's gate.

"Stay a moment," Giles abruptly bade his companion. "I would know a thing. Does Cleveland begin to love July, think you?"

Kit looked at him in surprise.

"Lord, I don't think it. Why should he do any such thing?"

"Why? Because July's the most loveliest pretty maid as he, or any of us, have e'er seen. That's why."

Hearing the note of emphasis in his own voice, Giles blushed and turned away. Never had he spoken to Kit like this before.

"Well," Kit said kindly, seeing his embarrassment, "that's as may be. She so seems to you, perhaps. But not to most. Yes, I think July's pretty enough, to be sure, but there's a great many of pretty maids, and prettier than she. Mr. Cleveland's had a plenty of experience, they say. I conceit he's too much a man of the world to lose his heart to Jule, when, men say, he's fonded in London by grand ladies, and has been to court, and quaints with the high gentry round about Cambridge. And, since Fellows can't marry, he'd be a fool to lose his head over a maid as he knows would grant him no favours. No, no; July's his pupil, and he likes her, and doubtless finds her pretty and likes her the better for't, but I should much admire if he should go beyond that."

"I shou'n't admire at any man loving Jule." Giles impatiently told him. "Even though he mightn't think to throw up his fellowship to marry her. It's ne'er been said, of Cleveland nor any other man, as he can't love without thinking on marriage. If he fell into love, and she . . ."

He broke off, half-ashamed of that romantic flight of fancy.

Kit looked at him with compassion and irritation.

"Men don't bring honest virtuous young gentlewomen to love 'em, having no intention to seek 'em in marriage. Cleveland's a gentleman; he would seek his light pleasures among queans and courtesans, not among sober young gentlewomen of honour and virtue. I admire as you conceit such impropriety in him."

Giles, who could conceit any impropriety in any one, if it should consist in excess of love for Julian, lacked words in which to convey this, and, with a curious, hopeless gesture of the head, turned away, walking back towards Trinity with the cold, thickening rain blinding his eyes and shrouding the city in a silver mist.

What he thought, but had not said to Kit, was that this Cleveland, this brilliant, famous, disarming, witty, handsome tutor—a poet, too—might win the heart of any maid; might win and keep Julian's—aye, might win and keep Julian herself. For Giles did not credit that any man, looking on his Julian to love her, could forget her and pass on. To him, the love of these two seemed all but inevitable. Could a man, seeing

Julian so often and in such a manner, forbear to love her? Could Julian, her heart being free and disengaged, her mind all for learning, her eyes and senses those of other young females, forbear to love such a tutor, if he should love her? The only question to Giles was, what could come of it? A lover who was not likely to desire a permanent alliance; a young gentlewoman high of heart, deep of love, pure in honour; if these should meet, what would occur?

Giles did not know. He only knew that anything which should occur would be bad for his own hopes.

7

Kit slipped into Peterhouse Chapel at the end of festal evensong (it was the feast of St. Matthias) when the Fellows, bachelors, and undergraduates were filing out, bowing to the altar as they passed it, in the old reverent manner to which he had been used, and which he now, for courtesy's sake, still practised, though bowing to empty altars was, his new spiritual counsellors told him, merely bowing down in the house of Rimmon.

Knowing that the Master of the College, when he took the service, was used to linger a while in the vestry for any to speak with him that would, Kit repaired thither, and found the Master standing cassocked within.

Dr. Cosin was thinner and more worn than before the attentions of the House of Commons; on bail now, he was daily expecting impeachment and the loss of his Mastership; already they had taken from him his new Deanery of Peterborough, and left him with but his master's stipend of forty pounds a year. Undaunted by threats, he still filled the chapel with incense, burnt the excessive number of tapers which Prebendary Peter Smart and Mr. Francis Rouse of Barnstable so greatly deplored, and ducked and bowed and crossed himself as firmly as ever, and, in short, made not the least concession to his foes.

He looked up as Kit entered the vestry, turning on his one-time penitent an eye somewhat cold. He knew what this fickle and self-willed youth had done, while he himself was in London defending his Anglican principles. Few things angered Dr. Cosin more than this all too frequent desertion of his beloved Church.

"Well, Mr. Conybeare? You desire to speak with me?"

"If you will be so obliging, sir." Kit felt and looked nervous.

"Not, I take it, in confession?" his former confessor, with a hint of cold irony, inquired.

"Sir, no. But in privacy and secrecy, and on a matter in which I sorely need help."

Dr. Cosin gave him none yet, but to seat himself in one chair and motion Kit to another. He then waited, in a silence which Kit rightly diagnosed as disapproving.

"Sir," Kit stammered, forcing his speech, "Perhaps you know . . ."

"Yes, Mr, Conybeare? Perhaps I know what matter?"

"Well, sir, that I have, now near three months back, joined the Catholic Church."

"I had always supposed you baptised into it, sir. I have certainly given you the sacraments on that stock. But, if you desire to reserve for the particular Roman Church that great name, I would ask you to do it elsewhere, not in this chapel. I have no doubt there are those in Cambridge, not far from here, who would gladly hear you do it. But in my presence it shall not be done, if I can by any means hinder it. . . . Yes, Mr. Conybeare; I had reason to believe that you had joined that erred Church. I deplored it deeply. As you will questionless remember, I did my best to let you from it, in the days when you was used to consult me on't. I expended on you all the arguments I had; I stinted not to assail both your reason and your loyalty, I urged on you prayer and meditation, and besought you to consider and stay at least for a year afore you should decide. But you thought better on't. I returned from my own business, wherein I had attended, and do now attent, and so will until I die, to keep high the banner of our assailed and threatened Ecclesia Anglicana—I returned to find that you, that had been a loved son in Christ to me, had let fall this same banner in the hour of our Church's need, and had fled to the ranks of her bitter foes. 'Twas a most lamentable traditioning of honour, my son—nay, no longer my son, the old use betrayed me. . . . And now, what came you here to say to me?"

Having delivered his reprimand, he looked less sternly on the downcast face of the recusant. After all, the lad was young, and might yet be reclaimed, and should not be too sharply dealt with.

"Sir," Kit faltered, "I feared that you would so look on't."

"Feared? You knew it, for I had often telled you."

"Well, yes, sir, I knew it. . . . But indeed, I acted from conscience, and did what I conceited to be right."

"You acted from impulse, Mr. Conybeare, and did what you conceited to be romantical, modish, and gratifying to your self-esteem. These may seem hard words to you, but, believe me, they are the truth. I know much of these conversions; perhaps one in twenty may be from cause of conscience; the other nineteen are from less noble cause. God alone can see the heart, and I pray Him I do you injustice in so speaking, and that your fault was rather that of strayed and misled intellects than of erred conscience. In either case, you have betrayed your Church, but the one is the more readily atoned. And now, what would you?"

"I would ask your counsel, sir. . . . The priests were took, while at mass this morning. I was there. The justice writ down my name and College, with intent to lodge information on me to the College. I telled my tutor on't after."

"You telled Mr. Cleveland?"

"Yes, sir. Mr. Cleveland said he would be the one to receive the information from the justice, and that he would take no notice on't, nor resolve the Master on't, if I would renounce the practice of my faith the while I was at Cambridge, and attend chapel and church as a Protestant, and tell none that I am other. Sir, what should I do?"

"And why do you ask *me*, Mr. Conybeare? 'Tis the priests of your own persuasion you should inquire of."

The young man sat silent, shame-faced, unwilling to say that he knew well what these gentlemen would bid him do.

"I have come to you, sir, because you were else wont to instruct me in matters of conscience."

"Aye, I was so. But to such scant effect, I fear, that you are now fallen in this sad predicament. You know my advice before I give it. Use no practices and deceits and half-measures, but renounce the Roman communion flockmeal, and return to your mother Church, giving me, if you will, your oath not to look back, now nor at any time. That is your one course, and your one atonement for your straying. Believe me, my son, you may live all your days the better Anglican for this brief and foolish lapse of yours, if you now do firmly resolve so to do. Play no more with a Church as is very well for those born to it, and for those not subjects of our King and State, but is a treachery for such as you, born and nurtured in the goodly and lovely heritage of our communion, used to the noble beauty and seemliness of our liturgy and our mass. What would you better than Ecclesia Anglicana can offer, hath ever offered, since the days of Augustine, but more plenteously since she purged herself from the errors, accretions and corruptions that had grown up in the universal Church after its primitive purity had decayed? 'Where was your Church before the Reformation?' the Papists used to think to daunt Dr. Mede of Christ's by inquiring of him. To which Dr. Mede made answer, 'Where was the fine flour before it went to the mill?' Shall I speak to you again of the Sacramental Presence, of the spirituality of the mode of it we confess, of the grosser mode the Transubstantiationists believe? No" (Kit gave a small sigh of relief); "for all this I have urged on you before, with but small effect. Your eyes were blinded by your vanity and the credulous superstitions of men that flattered it, and you took your own foolish way. But now I bid you, since you come to me for counsel, retrace your steps. Go now; consider this matter with prayer, and return to me a penitent, to make your peace with your betrayed Church."

Kit stood up, alarmed but vocal.

"But, sir, I should thus betray the Church I have joined, to desert her when as danger threatens. How could I face the priests after such an action as that?"

The Master of Peterhouse looked coldly on him. "Is there need you should face them? I understand they are took from here and will not return."

Kit became confused.

"Aye, sir. Aye, th'are took. That is, three on 'em is took. There's the fourth, as comes and goes . . . he is still at liberty . . ."

Dr. Cosin raised his hand to stop him.

"Tell me no secrets, Mr. Conybeare, for I would not know. Remember that it is my duty, as a Church of England priest, to assist the law to lay hands on these Jesuits. I would not do so, for I believe many of them to be excellent men, and to be going quiet about their business with no rebellious or seditious intent, though a danger to our own Church, but I will not hear of them. My reply to you is this; if you needs must face any Romanist priest, do so boldly and forthwith, and possess him openly of your resolve to leave his erred Church and return to your own. There must be no compromise; no attendance at the Anglican communion with reservations of faith, and the allegiance of your soul elsewhere, for you would be acting a lie at the most solemnest grave moment, and would scarce find pardon. Abjure Popery allthing, my son; do whatever penance may be laid on you for your errancy, and live forthwith a pious, zealous Church of England man, That is my counsel to you. And now farewell. I look to see you here suddenly again, penitent and resolved. . . . One last word. You incline to talk overmuch, my son. Keep all this, and your present plight, to yourself; much harm may come from spreading these news. I shall say nought to Mr. Cleveland on it, for the more we in authority here are thought by our foes to know of and to countenance such matters, the more fuel they will have to feed the fires of their malice agen us. Already, as you know, the feet of some of us are caught and entangled in their snares, and we live under the shadow of their vengeance. Farewell. May God bless you and lead you into the right ways."

8

Kit went out into the dripping night.

He did not know what he would do. Mr. Cleveland bade him compromise and dissemble and finish his Cambridge course, caring nothing for his conscience, or for what road he might take after that course was over. Dr. Cosin bade him abjure his new faith, and return to the Anglican fold as a penitent. His Jesuit advisers would bid him, he believed, uphold his faith and face the consequences; face being thrown out of Cambridge into a world for which he was not ready, to sink or swim as he could; face disappointing and angering his father, and having to earn his bread, possibly, at some tedious drudgery of apprenticeship to a trade he hated. Unless, indeed, he could go up to London under the auspices of a priest, approach the Queen, and join her court as page, sharing later the visit abroad for which she was, it was said, preparing. That would be good; to go abroad in a Queen's train; to see France, to travel, to become a Catholic man of the world, such as Sir Kenelm Digby, perhaps. He could surely live on something, find some paid service, even in France. At least there he would find many fellow-Catholics, and priests pursuing their ministry unhindered by the pestering English laws. And thus he could keep his self-respect.

He would seek out Father Weld, the Jesuit they had not taken, and consult him.

He was sorry that he could not oblige Dr. Cosin. The habit of obeying this firm and stern divine, even when he thought him unjust and unreasonable, was so deep rooted in him that he could not withstand him to his face; he could not return to Peterhouse Chapel. And he was sorry that he could not oblige Mr. Cleveland, whose easy, persuasive charm, even when he was impatient and angry, as he had been to-day, wrought so strongly on him that he could not withstand him either; he would, when he had found the means and the way, steal secretly off to London, telling no one. Not even Julian, for she would entreat him, and he did not care to face that. He would act as other martyrs for the faith had to act, and slip secretly away by himself, without a word to any one.

London; the Court; a ship for France. Through the dark dampness of the Cambridge February evening, stole the stirring breath of adventure and romance.

9

"Deere Father,—I praye you will not bee vext & angrie for y^{tt} I am laving Cambridg & ridin up to London this daye earlie to seeke my forchunes thar awhile. I must possess you of ye Truthe, & feere extreamly y^{tt} 'twill much grive you, which is why you have not had it from mee afore this. I have latelie joined ye Catholickes; 'tis a matter of Conscience, & I cd nor can noe othere, so praye Sir thinke nott too hardlie of mee for't. Being catched t'other daye at Mass, & ye Priests tooke, ye Justices did threten to lodg informacion on mee to ye Colledge, wh: they did, & wh: Mr. Clieveland saith hee will suppresse, from kindnesse to mee, did I consente to worshyppe Protestant whilst I bee here. This I cannot doe, itt being agen my Conscience to Looke Backe, soe I am resolved to lave Cambridg for London. I have ye companie & aid of a very excellente good Preist who rydes with mee & who will quaint mee with sartain frinds of his in London, y^{tt} I may not bee without frinds. Indeed I believe I shall fare well enough, & may obtane some small post to sustane mee til better may bee. I shall not waite on my Brothere for hee wd not approve mee. I shall wryte suddenlie & quaint you with my welfare. Do not seeke to finde mee & dragge mee back, as for Conscience sake I must goe & may not looke back, & am ever, Sir, your most loving sonne to sarve you,

"Christopher Conybeare."

This letter Dr. Conybeare received late in the evening, it being delivered at his lodging by young Mr. Drake, his son's room-fellow. There was also a little note for Julian.

The doctor perused his epistle with bewildered ejaculations.

"What the pox! What the devil! Ridden to London! Matter o' conscience! Joined the Catholics! Cannot look back! 'Slife, the boy's out of's wits; moon-struck; a Bedlam. Seek his fortunes in London, forsooth! Fine fortunes they'll be, for a young bawcock as can no trade and has no favour anywhere. And to throw aside Cambridge, his education, his degree, all things, to chase up to London after fortunes, as fortunes did lie in the streets for his gathering up! Well, he must be pursued and brought back forthwith; I'll after him myself, at dawn to-morrow, and will soon find where this Mr. Priest will have took him. Turned Papist, has he? The boy's more of a fool than I conceited. Didst know ought of this, Jule? Ye stand there mumchance; what saith he to you?"

"Only good-bye and his love, father."

Julian's voice was startled and quivering; she had not expected this. For once, Kit had not made her his confidante.

"Well, speak up, child. Didst know aught, suspect aught, of this Popery of his?"

At this moment Mr. Cleveland came in, disturbed and annoyed.

"Your servant, sir. I hope I don't intrude."

"No, faith, you come in pudding-time, for perhaps you can throw some light on this fine escapade of that young ape of mine. Y'ave heard on't?"

"Yes. I received a note from him but now, saying he was off to London. And his room-fellow confirms that he did ride off at dawn this morning. I much regret it. I did my best to settle him, but it seems failed in't. Here's yet another scurvy trick of those cursed Papists. Believe me, sir, I would have gotten him out of that snare if I could. Indeed, I had supposed him more amenable and reasonable, but once Popery or Puritanism seizes on a man, reason goes by the board. And so the young cocket has flown off to London, and what he thinks to do there, his new pastors and masters may know, for I don't. When young Marvell of Trinity performed the same feat, he was found by his father a month after lurking in a bookshop in Southampton Row."

"I'll find him, no fear. And he'll be lucky if I don't flog him soundly when I do, the young micher. Return to Cambridge he shall, and if they'll not keep him without he acts Protestant, then act Protestant he shall. Aye, I'll to London to-morrow, to lodge with my son Francis, in the Middle Temple, who's so firm and zealous a Puritan, pox take him, that he'll eagerly aid me in hunting down Papists. I'll possess myself before I leave Cambridge, if possible, of the habits and haunts of this precious priest of his, that I may know where to seek. . . . You should have telled me of his Popery when first you was informed on't, Mr. Cleveland. Since how long time has it been toward? I take it ill in you as you did not possess me."

"Indeed, sir, I but hoped to spare you pain. There was, thought I, no case why you should ever know, if he had acted in a tolerable reasonable manner."

"Did you know on't, child?"

"Yes, father. But I had swore to be secret."

"Oh, you had? It seems I alone, his father, was to be kept in the dark and to have this gullery put on me. Well, no matter of that now. Papist, forsooth! I had thought too high of the boy's understanding for that. It seems he had more on his poor mother in him than I had suspected. Aye, poor thing, she'd turn to anything, hark to any one, and could swallow more fooleries at a gulp than any creature I e'er met. The lad's his mother's son, it seems; for I'm damned if he's mine, save that I don't doubt I got him. Well, I got a fool, and there's an end on't. Aye, three fools, for the eldest's gone Puritan, the second's a woman without a mind, and the third's turned Papist. The fourth's the only one as is my child, it seems. But return and complete his studies a shall. They may be to little purpose enough, but shrew me if a shan't continue 'em."

"You ride to London to-morrow, father?"

"Aye. You heard me say so. I must leave you in the care of our good landlady here, for it's of no purpose to take you with me. I hope to be prompt in the business, and should be back in a few days at the most; but I'll send you news. The devil's in't that such a matter should happen now, when as I'm most busiest in my book. But there 'tis, and can't be helped. And I shall find some pleasure in visiting London just now, though Francis will weary me with his Puritan flim-flam."

"I would I could come with you," Mr. Cleveland said, "for I believe I could be of some small use in tracking him down. But my time's full here, and I must not leave."

"No, no, why should you? It's a father's business, not a

tutor's' to find a strayed son. I'll make shift for myself, never fear."

The eyes of his two companions met, and both sent the swift, involuntary message, "We shall be alone together."

10

Searching for his truant son in London, and staying with his Puritan son in the Middle Temple, Dr. Conybeare found some interest, pleasure and profit by the way. He looked up some old acquaintances, made new ones, discussed politics with the Templars and in the city, and picked up the latest rumours concerning Lord Strafford's trial, the Root and Branch party, the greed of the Scotch army and the menace of the Irish, the negotiations for the Dutch marriage, the Queen's appeals for money (only it seemed that she never got any) to France, to Holland, to the Pope; the city loans for the paying off of the Scots; the King's vacillations, overtures, withdrawals, and deceits, the committal of Dr. Laud to the Tower; and the rest of the current excitements.

"These interfering jackanapes, the Scots," Dr. Conybeare wrote to his daughter, "have gotten most insolent and high, and beginn to be resented here, even by their sarvents the House of Commons, who protest 'tis growne more then they'll endure. But Francis swears they doe right well, since they support his side. Their newest impudence is to drawe up a Declaracion yt they will see Episcopacie abolished in England as well as in their owne savage lande, and this Declaracion, being hawked about for sale, hath much offended many, who, whatever they may wish consarning ye Byshoppes, do nott desire their affares resolved for 'em by the beggarlie sucking

Scots. But you should have seen Canterburie's coach mobbed by ye people in Hobourne as they transported him to ye Tower the day I rode into London; but for his guard, he shd have bin torn in pieces. If they won't have the Scots for their maisters, much less will they have this little man. The order is gone forth from the Lords as all the communion tables is to be moved back agen from the east wall of the churches, so here'll bee a plenty worke for parsons and vergers. I hope Mr. Herrique will see to't. But, Lord, these Scots! The city marchants have a lampoon on 'em as th'are like to new-born babes as cry aloud to be fed each two hours, and Parliament, their nurse, has to give 'em suck to quieten their dimificacion. Never afore have wee bin so humbled and dictated to by furriners. . . . No newes yett of Kitt. Doubtless hee lies hidd somewhere along with some priests or other. I am inquiring into their haunts, and becomming quaint with so many of Papists as they must be getting hopes of mee for a convert. Never feare but I'll finde thy Brother suddenlie. I have come on Sir John Sucklin, and did sup with him and plaied a game of cribbidge. Hee was very instant in inquiring for you, and railed on mee ytt I had not broght you to London along with mee. Take heed to thyself, child; I am loath to leave thee this long time, but I trust thy friends doe care for thee well. Greet Mr. Clieveland from mee, and tell him I hope he keeps thee close at thy lessons."

"Aye, then, greet him," said Mr. Cleveland, when his pupil had read this epistle aloud to him. "Greet thy tutor, sweet chuck, as thy father bids thee."

"With great pleasure, sir. My father bids me give you his duty, Mr. Cleveland."

"So you mock me, demure Mrs. Mischief, do you? Three kisses in pay for that, beside the one that is your father's greeting."

"I've never marked as my father is used to kiss you, sir."

"Well, now you learn that he is. That is yet another lesson for you. Do I keep you close at your lessons, as your father hopes?"

"Exceeding close . . . So close as I can't scarce draw breath, sometimes . . ."

"Well," Mr. Cleveland presently said, "it seems as your father is having a mighty agreeable diverting time seeking your erred brother. And we two are having a mighty agreeable diverting time, a'n't we? A'n't we, little July?"

"Yes," said the truthful girl, and dropped a light, soft kiss on the white hand that cupped her chin.

"So w'are all happy," he concluded.

"If only Kit be so," she conditioned.

"Kit does very well," his tutor lazily assured her. "You can be very sure that Kit will come to no harm."

"Oh, well," she sighed; and fell from demure mirth into a frightened sadness, at the thought of Kit lost and alone in London, having given family and friends so great content by his flight thither.

"My dearest heart," said Mr. Cleveland. "Sigh not so, or you'll break your tutor's heart. Smile."

At that she smiled at him, in sweet, adoring derision, and Kit was forgotten by both of them.

And so, very pleasurably, the days, the weeks, slipped by, in London and in Cambridge.

II

Dr. Conybeare said to his son Francis, " I would meet Sir Kenelm Digby, Frank. I hear he's now in town, conducting his experiments in his house in Holborn. I would fain look into some o' these quacksalveries of his, this sympathetical powder and the rest on't, for, though th'ave small bearing on medicine, th'are of import to my book on Credulities. Beside which, I hear he hath many choice and curious recipes in physick and chirurgery. Aye, I would enjoy to talk with the age's Mirandola, the magazine of all arts, the ornament of his nation, and the Pliny of our age for lying, as his friends is pleased to speak of him."

Francis, the austere young lawyer, looked contemptuous.

" A Papist and a mountebank, and some say worse. Aye, some say a traitor to his country, and in truth he is so. He'll not easily put the world out of mind of his appeal to the Papists to furnish the King with monies to war on the Scots two years back. That was a scurvy trick; a very exceeding scurvy trick, and the knight is like to pay for't. The Commons is set to make the King remove him from his counsels, with the other recusants. He'll not long enjoy the favoured place he now do."

" Well, I care nothing for his treasons, if traitor he be. 'Tis his chemistry, physics and astology as concern me, and I would meet him. I have heard him speak to an assembly of physicians, but had no speech with him. Canst find me among your friends any that knows him and will acquaint us? "

" I will inquire. But in truth, his friends are scarce like to be mine. Mr. Selden doubtless knows him; indeed, I heard one day Selden call him the greatest magnificent liar and lunatic as ever he knew. But an introduction from that quarter would commend you little to Sir Quacksalver at the present, they being so opposed politically; though Selden's all too kindly disposed towards the Papists, being himself something of a Gallio and an indifferent."

"Now I think on't, Sir John Sucklin can quaint us. I'll wait on him and desire him so to do. Then, beside telling me of his experiments, Sir Kenelm can perhaps tell me something of his Jesuit friends, and where they'd be like to take and hide our young gentleman."

"Yes, he'd likely enough know that. He has himself, or had when I was at John's, friends at Cambridge as well as at Oxford, and has acted patron to sundry on 'em, for the fellow has a kind of generosity of temper, it's said. He has been extraordinary good to young Cowley, amongst others. Cowley hath a play dedicate to him, in gratitude."

"Aye, so hath he. *Love's Riddle*, or some such. I mind it, for July speaks on't, having some regard towards that young man. She even reads a religious epic he is presently engaged in and hath shown her a piece on. Jule has her fill of poets and philosophers in these times, and enjoys it greatly."

"Such flighty stuff will turn her head," Julian's elder brother feared. "Plays and poems do young maids small good, nor men neither, for that matter. Nor will heathen philosophy make her any better a wife when her time for marrying comes."

"A tush for marrying. Belike the girl will stay unwed, and companion her father. And if she do wed, she'll make the better wife and mother for what she gets now into her head. She's a judicious grave wench, and not all the poetry and plays in the world will make her flighty."

"You say John Cleveland's teaching her. I am sorry for

that. He is a very notorious corrupt Arminian, for all his learning in Latin and rhetoric, and a vain, atheistical, rakehell fellow, that hath done great harm to the godly party by his malignant lampoonings, and will do more. I mind him well at Cambridge, where he was cried up for a wencher and a most flibberty dandical spark. I admire, sir, as you let Julian have him to her tutor, and that without vigilance, as now."

"Pish, boy. John Cleveland's a mighty witty learned ingenious fellow and a very elegant scholar, and highly respected in Cambridge. His private virtues and vices is his own affair, but you may depend he'll not behave himself unseemly to your sister at any time. Had he attempted it, Jule would have been offended at him afore this, and have telled me, for she is the shyest modest little maid, and stands no freedoms. As to vigilance, our good landlord and landlady are in the house, and Cleveland comes but twice in the week. You precisians make yourselves foolish with your suspicions and scandals, seeing evil where none is."

"Since y'are pleased to make a tush of all suspicion, sir," Francis returned, with a shrug, "I'll say no more. Only this—that if your she-darling become also John Cleveland's, never say I warned you not."

"Your conversation don't please me, Frank. I pray you, change it."

"Very well, sir. Indeed, I will cease it, since I must now read."

"Aye, read thy law books. And I'll out and purchase the latest Speeches and Passages of this Great and Happy Parliament, save the mark. A great parliament it may be, and so it do appear to conceit itself, but ne'er saw I a parliament as wore a less happy air, save when 'tis rejoicing in the downfall of my Lord Strafford. 'Pon my soul, I don't like the king's ways, and those of his counsellors much less, and his bishops least of all, but I'm damned if this murnivale of sour country gentlemen and lawyers, with its pampered, greedy pack o' wolves up in the north there, do please me much more."

With this, and without giving his son time to retort, the doctor went out. His son Francis annoyed him at times so greatly that he almost (but never quite) turned loyalist and Arminian.

" The sooner I find Kit and hear him speak his nonsense, the better for me," he told himself, " for that will side me against the King's party again. And when I get the two lads quarrelling together, I can be properly impartial and angry with both parties at once, as is right and fit in a reasonable man."

12

Sir Kenelm Digby was in his laboratory, mixing, for reasons clear to himself only, mercury with vitriol powder, sulphuric acid, spirit of rum, and the blood of a mouse, when his man brought him a message that Sir John Suckling with a friend had called.

" Then bring them to me here," the busy knight bade him; and a minute later Sir John and his friend were shown in.

" Your servant, gentlemen." The knight, turning from his savoury mixture, bowed. " Y'are very welcome, Jack, though, as ever, you find me among my messes, which I trust this gentleman will pardon, for I fear this concoction of mine hath a most vile stink. But make us known, pray."

" Surely." Sir John spoke with his silk handkerchief held to his nose. " This is my good friend Dr. Conybeare, a highly learned physician from Devonshire, but now sojourning in Cambridge. Let me present you, doctor, to Sir Kenelm Digby. Dr. Conybeare, Digby, is greatly interested in such experiments as yours, for he writes a book on—what is't called, doctor—Human Quackery, is't not, or some such title. And it seems we are come in pudding-time, for we catch you red-handed at your business, and making, as you say, a most abominous vile stink."

"Dr. Conybeare? Did I hear right? Y'are welcome, sir." Sir Kenelm, not heeding his volatile friend, bowed courteously to the little doctor from his great and handsome height, after a moment's pause of scrutiny.

"Y'are curious in potions, sir? Perhaps you too are a chemist?"

"Of small skill enough, sir. My patients are easily content with such brews as I mix 'em. Indeed, I am less concerned with potions than with the belief on 'em. The human mind and its beliefs—that's the theme of the book I write, and I find it most devilish engrossing."

"Aye, truly, 'tis so. The human mind had ne'er yet learned to believe enough; 'tis that has held it back. Did men but have the imagination and faith to experiment more boldly and more widely. . . . Did ingenious minds such as that of M. Descartes, for example, devote themselves to following new roads, what might not be achieved? The elixir of life itself might be discovered, as I was urging on him but t'other day. Are you curious after the elixir, sir?"

"No, sir," Dr. Conybeare with decision replied.

"Not? Strange! To me the finding on't is the very goal of man's ambition."

"If 'tis that as y'are mixing there," Sir John put in, "I will die after my three score and ten years, for I'll on no account drink the stuff."

"Nay, my poor Jack, this is but a cure for wounds inflicted

with arrows. You take the arrow that has caused the wound and soak it in this concoction three days. As it soaks, the inflammation leaves the wound, and by the end o' the time 'tis sweet and sained, and the poison all drawn from it."

"Indeed, sir."

Really, Dr. Conybeare thought, he might as well be in Deancombe, hearing one of his old wives talk. Learned virtuoso and simple rustic—in superstitions they all met.

"And what's this nasty looking mess here, my poor chymist?" Suckling inquired, sniffing about the pots and pans with interested disgust.

"That? 'Tis a salve to anoint swords to heal the wounds they have given. For metal weapons need a different treatment from others. Y'are acquaint, Dr. Conybeare, I don't doubt, with Paracelsus his cure for sword wounds?"

"I have read it. 'Tis something odious, if I mind it rightly. Is't that you have there?"

"So near as I could get. Some ingredients had to be omitted. But it serves, for I have tried it. As you doubtless know, the sword is dipped in blood from the wound and then smeared with the salve and put in a cool place, and very presently the wound cools and heals."

"Extraordinary knowledgeable and ingenious of it," said Sir John.

"But you forgot to add," said the doctor, "that 'twas part of the old chymist's treatment to wash the wound each day with a fair linen rag and water. Paracelsus neglected nought, howe'er busy he might be with his magnet."

"I fear, doctor," Sir Kenelm said, "that y'are something of a sceptic in these matters, like Sir John here, who makes a tush of all healing. If so, y'are come to the wrong man, for 'tis one of my great passions."

"Healing, sir, is one of mine. But I can't pretend to much concern with magnetic or sympathetical cures."

"In that, doctor, y'are devilish unreasonable," Suckling told him. "For th'are as good cures as your own, any day in the seven. Or as bad, should I say? Lord help me, here am I shut in this evil-smelling chymist's shop between an alchymist and a medico, and the devil knows if I shall come out on't alive. Well, no matter, such curiosities serve to distract our minds from politics, hey, Digby?"

"I have no envy to think those now, Jack, so don't speak on 'em. We must each serve our King, Queen, country and Church, as best we may; but I, at least, am happier when as I am shut among my books or my potions. Alas, that can't endure, for this barbarous insolent House of Commons will see to't I have no peace, and, if they should have their way, no liberty. But I go shortly to Paris for a spell, if I can get a ship."

"Aye; w'are both full of affairs," Sir John rather moodily said; then glanced at the doctor and checked himself.

It was at this moment that there was a knock on the door, and Kit Conybeare came in.

"Sir," he began; then stopped short as if he had been struck, and gaped at his parent, the blood surging in his startled face.

"The devil!" was all Dr. Conybeare found to say, staring back at his offspring.

Sir John Suckling let out a whistle of surprise, and Sir Kenelm turned with courtesy to the doctor.

"Your son lodges with me presently, sir. I should perhaps have mentioned it to you in the beginning, but I conceived it to be your son's secret. Howbeit, he has now discovered himself, as you perceive."

"Aye, he hath," the doctor grimly said, "though all unwitting, I take it. What dost thou here, boy, if your father may ask?"

"Why, sir," Kit faltered, "Sir Kenelm has given me leave

to lodge with him for a while, and to wait on him, and help him with his potions."

His admiring glance up at his tall master showed him in the early stages of hero-worship.

"Sir Kenelm has been wonderful good to me, father," he added, "and he says he will take me to France with him when he go. I should greatly like that."

"Doubtless, son. But what is writ in the stars for you is that I shall take you to Cambridge with me when *I* go, and perhaps you will like that less. Like it or not, it's your fate. You'll resume your studies forthwith and crave pardon humbly of your college, should it be so good to let you stay, after your impudent escapade. If they flog you for't, 'twill be no more than you've earned. Go to France, forsooth! Sir, I take it very ill in you, to steal and hide a lad 'scaped from his College thus."

"I make allowance, doctor, for your anger; 'tis natural enough. Give me leave to explain to you how it chanced. Your son came from Cambridge with a Jesuit priest, who would have spirited him off to a seminary in Antwerp, only that he waited on me seeking my advice, and bore a letter from my gifted young friend Mr. Cowley, and so I offered him a place, for the nonce, in my household. In part, I own it, I did it to vex my friends the Jesuits, who lose no occasion to speak spitefully of me."

"Nor you to do the like of them," Suckling put in. "You give as good as you get, Digby, in that quarrel as in others."

"I trust so. I do my poor best. But that was not, in course, my chiefest reason for taking charge of your son, Dr. Conybeare. I took a great liking to the lad, and conceited he would learn with me much that might benefit him. Further, he is a young and new convert to the Church, and I should be loth to see them turn him into a bigot after the hard and narrow pattern of the seminarists. A Catholic gentleman can and should, to my thinking, keep his mind a wide, open, and polished mirror to all new learning and discovery, and 'tis there the Catholics too often fail. When as I see a young convert has parts and aptitude, I like well to set his feet on the right road. I like to give protection and opportunity to a homeless young wanderer who has joined our great Church in ardour and hope."

"Church be damned. I don't give a China orange for any of your churches. A plague on all of 'em. The boy has to complete his education."

"I grant, sir, I grant. But what we have to consider is, how will he best do it? At Cambridge, studying logic, metaphysics, and the Latin text books, and practising declamations in the schools against other schoolboys; or seeing something of the world with a man who, whatever his faults (and, God forgive me, they are many) doth know a little of his world, and a few of its tongues, and more than a few of its books, and can show him courts, kings, cities, life and letters."

"And a hundred serviceable potions to boot," Suckling put in, glancing round the shelves. "If I may make so free as to offer my opinion, doctor, I say, let the boy go with Sir Kenelm, and give thanks for the chance. What would I have given for a like chance when I was a little ape? For in truth these universities cram learning into our heads, but teach us little enough of life."

"So I am to let my son go with you and learn to mix those salves and potions of yours," the doctor said; "and to mix with courts, and travel fro and to across the seas to France, to smug up his intellects. And how, if I may ask, is all this to set him in the way of earning his livelihood?"

"I will look to that," Sir Kenelm replied. "If the boy is of the metal I conceit him to be, I shall have no difficulty to set him in the way of an occupation, later. I have many friends in high places; though, as to that, they may all soon find themselves in a sad pickle, if matters proceed as presently they do. But never fear, sir; I will look well to your son, if you'll entrust him to me."

"And if I won't, sir?"

Sir Kenelm made a courteous gesture.

"Then I should, I fear, accept the charge of him all the same had he a mind to stay with me. He is turned eighteen; a man, not a child in leading strings, to be ordered by his father. I have seen o'er much of that in my time, and all too many young lives spoilt. In the name of liberty, I would reason with you and plead; and, did that fail, should not feel myself bound to obey your wishes. Forgive me, sir, but I take it you would have the truth from me."

"Aye. The truth."

The doctor stood in silence, looking darkly from his son's protector to his son.

In the name of liberty. These words had stung him like a sword-prick in his vitals. By them, he was discovered fighting on the wrong side; fighting for tyranny and tradition against liberty, his goddess. After all, had he the right? . . .

"You desire to leave Cambridge for ever, abandon your education, and to go with this gentleman?"

"Yes, sir. I do greatly desire it."

"You have no envy to read for the law, or for medicine?"

"No, sir. I would fain travel first, and see the world, before I choose what I would do."

"And y'are set on staying Papist? Y'are quite resolved in't, so that you'd not delay it until y'are done with Cambridge?"

"I am resolved in't, sir. I shall never look back."

"Then I take it you would openly profess your creed to your college, and not deign to attend its services, is't so?"

"Yes, father," Kit nervously assented, and prepared for an explosion of wrath.

But the doctor took it quietly. He knew when he was beaten.

"Y'have gotten the better of me betwixt you. Cambridge won't receive you back as a Papist, as well you know. . . . Then go your ways and find your own troubles. At least 'tis better thus than if they took and made a seminarist of you. If you must be a Papist, endeavour to be a Papist of parts and sense, and acquire such knowledge and science as you can. I ask you, sir, to look to that while my son is with you. I'll say no more; liberty shall have her head, though 'tis rhubarb unto me to give it her. But the lad will get no money from me, until he require it to stablish himself in some sound calling. I'll not give him money to trapse about Europe with."

"None is needed, sir. I will supply his needs while he stays with me. He will act as my secretary and scribe. And set your mind, so far as you may, at rest concerning the matter of religion; I'll see he don't turn fanatic, and will preserve him from the Jesuits. You'll mind that 'twas in Cambridge that those gentlemen made their assault on him."

"Those gentlemen, sir, are now clapped in gaol. But I don't doubt he'll meet a plenty on 'em while roving about with you, and if he should take up with 'em, why, I shall be very sorry, but he'll be in not much worse case than his brother of the Temple, who's ta'en up with the Puritans, and cants the Bible at me. I seem fated to see my children the gulls of this, that, or t'other folly, so, since I can't defeat fate, I must e'en accept it, and swallow my rhubarb down. Kit, thou'rt a young jackass and weather-cock, and want beating and sending back to thy books. But there, go thy ways; I'll not let thee. Thou and Jule have ever been my prize chicks, and now there's but Jule left, and lord knows what *she'll* fly off to next. . . . Have you children, sir?"

"Yes, sir, some young boys. In wedlock and else. How many, I do forget. Th'are away at school."

"No doubt but later they'll turn Protestant on you, or grow to be stupid oafs, or play you some trick else. Ne'er hope naught from your children. Well, I'll be gone."

Kit stepped forward.

"Pray, father, let me come out with you, that we may talk. Indeed, sir, I love you, and owe such duty to you that I hate to vex you. I would see you so much as may be while w'are both in London, for 'twon't be for long. And I would I could see July, to tell her good-bye."

"You'll not do that, for she's in Cambridge. You should have thought to tell her good-bye afore you rode away."

"Then I'll not see her till later, on our return from France. I would send her a letter by you, father. May I come with you now?"

"Aye, come, then. But I surmise you've no gust to wait on your brother Frank? No, I thought as much. And 'tis for the best; there'd be such a brangling and roilying did you two get together, I'd liefer attend a dog fight. You'd best come to a tavern with me, and we'll dine there, if you crave my paternal viaticum and benediction before you take your wilful way, and don't shun to be seed about with a leech in an old coat. For I perceive y' are risen in the world. Good-day, t'ye, Sir Kenelm Digby. I'll not bless you, but I'll not curse you neither, for you intend, I believe, kindness to this young princock of mine. Only for the lord's sake, teach him not your magical salves, for he's all too phantastically inclined and hare-brained already."

"As to that, Dr. Conybeare, I believe, with the Danish prince, that there are more things in Heaven and Earth than are dreamt of in your philosophy or mine."

"Doubtless y'are right, sir, though the Danish prince never said so. 'Twas of his own and his friend Horatio's philosophy he spake, not of yours nor mine. Well, good-day t'ye. Come, boy."

12

Giles Yarde and Julian went riding together over the Gogmagog Hills on a March day of wind and sun. Their horses scampered over short, chalky turf, and bore them up the smooth slopes, by beech coppice and dell, where catkins danced on the wind and velvety palm buds shimmered silver in the soft brown shadows of bare woods, and pools of pale gold and deep blue were splashed delicately in the brown heart of the coppices.

"At home they'll be a-primrosing," Julian said, seeing in her mind swelling banks of birch coppice and pale blossoms, and girls with wicker baskets plucking, and Mr. Herrick looking on with a smile and making verses on how violets came blue, and why primroses weep.

"There's no such flowers here," she said, and had a pang of home-sickness for wood, meadow, lane, and moor, for the Dean country in the exquisite spring.

"D'you wish you was home, July?" Giles asked her, as they reined in their horses on the smooth curve of the hill-top and stood to look across the wide, windy sea of pale chalk country, green pasture and brown plough, to the far huddle of spires and towers to the north that was Cambridge.

"Sometimes," she answered him, absently and gently, as if she spoke from far away.

It was thus that he knew her in these days, as a girl moving in a dream, scarce seeing nor hearing what passed without her, but with mind turned inward on its dreams.

"Oh, yes, sometimes," she said again, and sighed, a tiny whispering breath, that he barely caught.

"When do you go back?" he asked her moodily.

"Go back . . ." She looked round at him, as if his question perplexed her. "I don't know. . . . Perhaps never at all." She added that after a moment, and the low words dropped whispering down the wind.

He looked at her, searching with his very blue eyes her dreaming, lifted face, that gazed so distantly over the March landskip to Cambridge towers.

"What d'you mean, Jule? Never at all? Is the doctor minded to stay in Cambridge for ever, then? Has he all-to renounced Dean?"

She shook her head, as if she did not know how the doctor was minded, or how she herself.

"I don't know, Giles."

So they sat together, saddle by saddle, while their horses cropped at the short turf, and the sunshine and cloud-shadows raced across the downs, and the girl stared still at Cambridge, and the boy at her.

"If you should stay here till August, July," he said, "we could ride down to Denshire together, for I go then. You'll be home by August, at furthest, won't you?"

"I don't know," she said again, and as if she scarce heard him.

"But, July, you will. You must be home when I am. If you don't go, I shan't go neither, but shall spend all the vacation in Trinity."

"That would be great pity," she murmured.

"'Twould be greater pity to be home and you not there. More particularly if you was here in Cambridge. At the least, if I was to stay, I should see you sometimes."

She looked round at him then, and it was as if she dragged her gaze from far Cambridge and focused it with difficulty on his face. Blue eyes met violet-grey, and searched their deeps for what they would never find there. What they did find was the troubled shadow of a dream, like the purple cloud-shadow, that, moving across the sky, now held them in its cool shade.

"No," she said. "You mustn't stay here for me, Giles. Indeed, you must not."

"But look, July, I must, for you know I love you, and nought without you is worth a fig to me. What would I be doing in Dean without you? July, sweetheart, dostn't thou wish to climb again up the wood and the burn with me, and come out on Lambs Down, and ride over the moors along the Abbot's Way, and catch the moor ponies, as you and I and Meg did use to do last summer?"

"I would like to, Giles." Suddenly it seemed to him that her voice was full of tears. "You know as I would like to. For I love the woods and the moors and the ponies, and Meg, and you . . . and do dearly like to play and walk and ride with you. . . . But I must stay in Cambridge now, indeed, I must. . . . My father desires to stay, to finish his book. Then, they mistrust him in Dean, since the witch hunt. . . . Dean is grown dreadful, Giles, since then. Cambridge is better."

Of a sudden his anger and his pain broke loose.

"Cambridge is better—aye, Cambridge is greatly more to thy mind. For why? Dost think I don't know? Cambridge pleases thee by reason John Cleveland is in't. Aye, he's thy tutor and thy darling gallant, for all the world to know."

She stared at him with wide, blank eyes.

"Aye," she whispered. "Aye," and no more. He felt ashamed, before that wide, dreaming gaze, that assented to part of his statement, but ignored and heeded not his last words.

"He is, then?" The pang of certainty that stabbed him was like a sword in his breast. She did love John Cleveland, then; and loved him blindly, wholly, as one tranced, that saw nothing else in all the world.

"Aye, he is," he answered himself. "I knew it. You love him, and he you. . . . Does your father know it?"

"No, Giles. And you must keep it secret from him. We would not have him nor other know."

Giles looked darkly down at his horse's ears.

"July, doth he say he would wed you?"

"Aye." In the word there was an undercry of protest, and of doubt that would not let itself be doubt.

"And he a Fellow?" he flung at her, cruel in his own bitterness. "You know they can't wed."

"He'll not be a Fellow always," she quickly returned. "One day he'll renounce Cambridge, and go to London, and live as a poet."

"One day!" he repeated. "Which day will that be, I wonder? And in the meantime, why goes he not to your father, momently he return from London, and ask to be affianced to you? That is what gentlemen do. They don't pay court to young maids under the rose, and bid 'em be secret to their fathers."

They? She looked at the word from a distance, as if it had no relevance. This was John Cleveland; not any general gentlemanly herd of "they," but the particular and most gallant gentleman, John Cleveland, who knew the way of the world far better than did she or Giles.

"Mr. Cleveland knows what 'tis right to do," she said.

"Aye, I'll wager he knows. But 'tis a matter quite else if he do't. Look, Jule, Mr. Cleveland's very well; he's witty and ingenious and handsome, and a gentleman, and a man of the world, and a famous Latinist and Rhetoric Reader, and much looked to, and men like him (set aside his foes); but he's a known rake, and has had a dozen of women; aye, he's had many misses and cast 'em, and took others, for he sips where he likes. 'Tis known."

She looked at him still remotely, in distaste at the coarse crude words, and at his malice in saying them to her.

"Aye, call me tell-tale if you will; I am so, and will be. I mean Cleveland no harm; he's a good enough man, and he but comports himself as many do, but he'll not hold to you only, even should he e'er wed you, and July, that would vex and hurt you, though there's a many women don't heed. So, sweetheart, pray be said by me, and tell the doctor on't, and let him speak with Mr. Cleveland and inquire what he intends toward you. Pray be wise while there's yet time, July, and give him not all thy heart to play ball with."

"I have given him all my heart," she said, levelly. "Nothing can take it back, for I love him. So no more, Giles, I pray. . . . If he play ball with my heart, he must do so. I think that lovers must each play ball with the heart of other. We love each other so much that I can't tell it you in words, 'twould fill a many books. Let us not speak more on't, please, Giles."

The little quiver in her voice filled his eyes with tears.

"Oh, God, July, but I love you so much. Am I to stand back and watch another man sad you?"

"Yes, please, Giles." She gave him a smile, and winked back the tears that beaded her lashes. "And if it sads me sometimes to love, it glads me far more," she added. "Love is like that, a'n't it—sad and glad?"

"Between two that love," Giles returned, fiercely confident, "it should be all glad. If you was to love me, July, as I love you, there'd be no sadness."

"Aye, but there would," she told him. "For there *is* sadness in love. Always, always. For no two that love can feel alike in all things, and that hurts 'em. They'll desire different things, and think different thoughts, and love makes 'em give way though 'tis agen their reason and their wishes, for they desire love more than all else. They must renounce being themselves and lay by their wills, and deny their whole lives, just for love. 'Tis what Dr. Donne and Mr. Herbert and St. Thomas à Kempis and all great Christians else have said of religion, that we must deny all for't and lay down our very lives. And so 'tis with love."

"D'you talk thus to Cleveland?" Giles sombrely asked, for he was wondering what, if she did so, would be Mr. Cleveland's reply.

But she looked away from him and said nothing, and he guessed that she did not talk like that to Mr. Cleveland, for Mr. Cleveland would not listen if she did. Quite rightly, thought Giles, for it was sad tedious talk, not such as he would care to encourage himself.

"Come; we'll ride on," he said, and gathered up his reins, "for I must be in college by four."

They put the horses at a canter, and lilted in silence through the pale green country towards Cambridge.

Giles had an answer to his questioning, and the bitterness of it was as wormwood in his soul. Julian rode as in a dream, and he knew her heart had flown, more swiftly than their horses took them, to the city of towers in the level plain below. Why did not Dr. Conybeare return, now that he had found Kit, fiercely wondered Giles. Was there another father in England who would thus leave his young daughter unprotected and alone in a lodging in Cambridge, or any other town? The doctor was mad, a very moon's man, as had no business with a daughter.

14

Dr. Conybeare wrote his daughter letters, full of news of London doings, and always said he was to return in a few days, when he had seen this or that person, spoken with this or that printer about his book, read this or that in some one's library, and heard further news of the Army Plot, which George Goring had just revealed, and concerning which he and Sir John Suckling and others had been so occupied of late. "I conceited Sir John had something toward," he wrote, "for hee was so busie and so secret and so puffed up with important designs when I saw him. This same plott hath, all say, sealed the fate of my Lord Strafford, on whom Mr. Pym now presseth more hard than ever. His trial goes apace . . ." And, indeed, the doctor became so much interested in the trial, and found it so exciting to be on the spot and hear its latest news hot from Westminster, and to discuss it among the Templars and in the city, that he did not leave London until the trial was adjourned for three days on the 10th of April. Then he bethought himself of Cambridge, and of his lonely (but, he was sure, studious, cheerful and well-conducted) little daughter there, packed up his books and clothes to go by the carrier, bade his son Francis farewell, and rode down to Cambridge on the eleventh day of April.

He had sent warning of his coming the day before, and Julian was awaiting him when he walked into their lodging at eight o'clock in the evening.

Having embraced her, he held her at arm's length and looked at her.

"Why, chuck, th'art grown very handsome; aye, more

prettier than ever, this month I've been from thee. Thou'rt blossomed up like a flower. . . . I swear I've seen none so pretty in London, I should have took thee with me, to ravish the Templars. Even solemn Francis would smile kindly on so fair a little sister. But there, 'tis ill done in thy father to flatter thee. . . . Hast been lonely, child? Has good Mrs. Speedy companioned thee well?"

"Well, father, Mrs. Speedy was called to Norfolk, to a sick sister, and has spent the most of this month there."

"What! Called away? Dost mean, child, as thou'st been all alone here, without our good hostess?"

"I have had my friends, father. They have been extreme kind. Mr. and Mrs. Allen invited me to lodge at their house, but I liked better to stay here. Indeed, I have never been lonely."

"Thou shouldst have wrote to me of Mrs. Speedy." The doctor tardily and partially woke to the proprieties. "'Twas not seemly thou shouldst lodge alone in Cambridge without a hostess. I warrant Cambridge talked, for 'tis an infernal tittling tattling town. Did it not talk, and tell thee thou shouldst not be alone, and that thou hadst the unseemliest heedless father as ever maid had?"

"Very like," Julian admitted. "I di'n't pay heed, and don't know what any said."

"Well, well, that's well spoken; aye, that's spoke as my daughter. Ne'er heed wistering and pistering, and ne'er change thy ways to suit fools. Look, if thou hastn't been lonely, no harm's done."

"I have not been lonely, indeed. But Kit, father; tell me more of Kit. I had a letter from him from Paris only yesterday. He and Sir Kenelm lodge near the court, and he sees the king and courtiers often, and grows quick, he says, at French."

"Then you've heard later news than I. He writes to me

with difficulty, embarrassed with his knowledge of my opinion of his doings. I know not how long Sir Knight will stay in in France; he is the flightiest errant gadabout. The boy has chose an uncertain restless life of pleasure, and turned his back on the good solid years of learning that should have fitted him for the world. It shows a weakness in him that I lament. I suppose they'll turn him out a courtier and a do-nothing. But leave him be; he must make his own life, like the rest of us. We all disappoint our fathers. I vexed mine by cutting loose from the Church; mine vexed his by starting his own school instead of living and dying an usher at Eton; and so wags the world. And here's Frank gone Puritan on me, and Kit Papist, and Doll born and bred a fool, and you grown such a pretty chick that I suppose all the lads will give you no peace till y'are off with one of 'em. Nay, there's no satisfaction for a father in this world, that's clear. Still, he can always eat and drink, and that looks a good pasty enough on the table. While we eat, you can tell me of Cambridge, and of your doings and studies. Have you been to Mr. More's classes?"

"No; I had not the time."

"What! Does Mr. Cleveland keep you so close at your work for him? I am sorry for that, for he won't teach you Descartes, and I desire you should go forward in that philosophy. You must resume again with Mr. More. There's time for both, and the one tutor's a good balance to t'other. What have you studied with Mr. Cleveland?"

"Many things, father." Her face from across the table looked palely at him; it wore a kind of baffled, bewildered look, and her voice seemed oddly to entreat him.

He looked sharply at her. "Too many, belike. Thou'rt fatigued, child. I must speak with Cleveland, and bid him go easy. We'll not talk of work to-night; thou shalt tell me on't to-morrow. Does he come to-morrow?"

"Yes."

"Two afternoons in the week, is it not?"

"More, when he has time."

"Well, I suppose all the old women in Cambridge, and men too, have been saying 'tis most bold and unseemly you should receive a handsome tutor alone in your lodging without a duenna. I can hear in my mind what your mother would have said, and I thank God she's gone to a place from which no voices descend to earth. I hope, child, they make not havoc of thy name in Cambridge for't. Cleveland should have seen to't a duenna attended his classes; aye, I blame him, for he should certainly have seen to that."

"I thought, father, as we weren't never to heed tattlers and their tattle."

"No more we are, bud. But their folly and their spites and their jests can make a young maid's life devilish discomfortable. Oh, they can perstring *me* all they will, but I'll have no word said of you."

"Well, sir, I don't see as you can let 'em speaking of me when they meet together, if they've a mind to. But why should they trouble to? I am of no consequence, and 'tis most like they don't even know as I've been alone here, or that Mr. Cleveland has waited on me in your absence. In Cambridge, th'have better things to think on than that, and presently they talk of nought but political and church matters, and my Lord Strafford's trial. Anyhow, we need take no notice on 'em, for what we don't hear don't hurt. . . . Tell me, pray, father, of my Lord Strafford, and how it fares with him."

"Well, the Lords and Commons came to blows, and they broke up the trial yesterday *sine die*, but no doubt they'll be at it again very suddenly. His case worsens; one thing after another comes out agen him, and the inflexible party in the Commons grow more fierce. Jermyn and Suckling and the army officers have done him ill service with this plot of theirs. His foes were hammering again on the tack of his violence to the city, monopolies, and the forcing of ship-money, but 'tis the matter of bringing over the Irish army will drive the nails of his coffin home, and there they are sure they have him trapped, for they have a copy of notes took by Vane reporting his words on't. He swears he meant nothing of the sort, but quite other, but none believe him. Indeed, he is a most eloquent persuasive pleader of his cause, but they all fear and hate him so, it doth him little good. They swear if they can't find him traitor, they'll make him so, as, in the civil interest, he must die, and Pym hath his teeth in him like a hound on a bayed stag. They say they mean to bring in a Bill of Attainder forthwith, and get him so. For my part, I hold no brief for the earl, who is a most plaguey mischievous fellow and has nigh ruined the king with his counsels, but I wish they may send him to exile and not take his life. As to treason, what of their own, keeping the Scots army at their back to coerce the king? Damme, I talk like a man of t'other party, but this brave, arrogant earl at bay, with the Commons seeking his life and the mob yammering for's blood as if they'd tear him in pieces without trial, moves me extraordinary much. Then, Francis his bitter narrow talk ever drives me to see right in what he perstrings."

"Mr. Cleveland thinks the king may yet save him, and will scarce let him be executed at the last."

The doctor shrugged.

"Mr. Cleveland thinks better of His Majesty than I, as we already know. The king's so arrant shifty a coward as was his father, and will save no man at a risk to his own security. I don't blame him for not being of valiant metal, and he's further unnerved by that plaguey silly fool of a queen of his. My Lord Strafford's a better servant and a nobler man than either on 'em deserve. He stands for monarchy; he's lived for't, and will most like die for't; he deserved a monarch of steel, but has had one of straw. If he die, he'll die a great man in a bad cause, as others have before him, but to set the forces of the law and constitution on him like a pack of hounds, and then, if they can't by any means get him, call 'em off and try another pack, swearing all the while that if the matter can't be lawfully contrived it shall be so unlawfully, such cruel, malignant hypocrisy makes me sick."

"I'm glad, father, as y'are returned from London a Straffordian, for so you and I shall better agree. But, if you speak like that of the king to Mr. Cleveland, there'll be a sad dimification, for you know he's all loyalty."

"Faith, yes, I know't, I'm used to these ode-writing poets, that say their prayers to King Charles as he was Jove, hymn the queen as she was Venus or the Virgin Mary, and dub the young princes rising suns and chicks of Jove. 'Tis the road to advancement in the literary firmament, and few on 'em leave it untrod. Very surely Parson Herrick do not. There's times, bud, when I decide as there's more of the serpent's wisdom in the world of literature than in any other. Aye, serpent is good, for I think the men of letters have, beside, more of the serpent's gall than have others, even the politicians; aye, even, maybe, than the theologians. Spite, envy, back-biting, using the pen for a lance to prick with, and ever an eye to the main chance—there are your poets and writers, bud, that y' are so in love with and would fain take a place among."

"I would not, father. I envy no more to write books."

"You don't? And why not?"

"That's all ended. Now I'm grown I have no wish to write."

"Grown, forsooth? Who telled thee thou wert grown? I hope thou'lt grow a scruple more, my dandiprat, before thou stint. And as to writing, if thou'st no envy to't to-day, 'twill return to-morrow. Belike 'tis the spring weather, and thou wantst a pill."

He was looking at her anxiously.

"In course, sir, if you do desire me to join the band of malicious venomous time-serving serpents, I must study to oblige you," she said.

"Aye, that do I, little snake, for I believe 'tis your fate, and that you'd only miss it by denying your own nature, and that I should lament to see you do, for 'tis blasphemy. If there be a God, he made us to tread one road, and if we turn our back on't and take another, we'll rue it and it can't come to good."

Julian smiled at him and his inconsistent journey into theology. Sitting with him like this, talking freely and at random, she felt herself again; she could say what she liked, whatever came into her head, and he would take it up, reply, argue, discuss, treat her as a companion. Uninformed and dull as she was, he would talk to her, tell her of politics and life, spread his opinions before her, seek hers, bid her tread the road she was made for. Had he been like that, she speculated, in an access of grateful affection, as a lover? Had he spoken so to her mother—and if so, how had her mother responded? Within her own memory, he had not spoken so to her mother, but been cynical and sarcastic and aloof. He had perhaps learnt early that it was useless to talk of politics or life to her mother, who would have replied, doubtless, on some other topic.

As her love went out towards him sitting there in his riding-suit, lighting his great pipe and speaking to her of blasphemy, she felt free and disentangled, clear and light and of undivided purpose, as she had felt as a child. The next moment her other love, her dark, difficult, rapturous, tangled love, surged in between them and caught at her heart, and she thought, now my father's back, I shall not see him so easily alone; and her father became, from a companion and a release, an obstruction to let and hinder love.

Her smile died on her lips, and she gazed at him widely and darkly, like an animal caught in a trap.

15

John Cleveland received next morning a call from Dr. Conybeare, and the official intimation of the withdrawal of his son from the College.

"'Tis great pity," the tutor said, "for he was a lad of promise, and might have done well. But, as he's catched Popery, he's best away. Sir Kenelm Digby is a fine noble gentleman, though maggoty as the man in the moon. Your son will be apt, with him, to be whirled from one city of Europe to another till his head's more turned than already 'tis. But, at the least, he's no religious fanatic, and will keep the lad from the hands of the seminarists. Well, I liked the boy, and am sorry we've lost him. You would desire his books to be sent to your lodging, no doubt, and such clothes as he took not with him."

The doctor, feeling as if Kit had deceased, agreed that he would desire this.

They spoke of the news from London. Mr. Cleveland said, "We shall not long be secure here from these meddlesome coxcomical jacks-in-office, who would change the very order in our college chapels, and displace our heads. Aye, I see it all coming, rolling on toward us like a flood, this tide of disorder and perversity as threats to drown the country. If they kill Strafford, 'twill hearten 'em so as they'll be perked up to do worse. Damn them all to hell, say I, and let 'em lie and rot there for the foggy mean insolent traitors they be, bloat with their own coystrel arrogance."

"You swear uncommon devilish well," said the doctor admiringly.

"Yes," Mr. Cleveland complacently agreed; "I believe I do."

"But to step to another theme," said the doctor, "I've been something put about, Mr. Cleveland, to find as Mrs. Speedy, my landlady, has been from home these past weeks, and that you have waited on July many times all alone in the lodging, set aside mine host and the chambermaid. That's a thing makes talk in a place, if it get to be known, and I fear the girl's name may have been uncivilly handled for't."

"By no means," Mr. Cleveland said. "I am sure not. I have possessed no one of my visits and no more has she. I assure you, sir, I bore the matter well in mind. But faith, she's such a discreet good maid, and I known as a tutor and not as a gallant, that I decided 'twas no harm to continue our classes. I believed, sir, that you would be with me in this."

"Well, I don't know. Aye, I wou'n't have had you lin the classes, but you might perhaps have done well to secure a duenna to sit with you while they proceeded, that idle tongues might be bridled. Still, since you say it a'n't gotten abroad, there's no harm. I hope your pupil does well. What have you read with her of late?"

"Very well, indeed. W'have been reading Shakespeare, Jonson, and Beaumont, and some of to-day's English and French comedies."

"English and French? I had thought 'twould be Greek."

"No, doctor. To my mind, she has already all of Greek that a young gentlewoman needs to possess. But her French I found very trifling and poor, and that is a tongue gentlewomen should know well, since we now have much traffic with Paris. So I took leave to instruct her in't. I speak it tolerable well, I believe. Look, Greek and Latin do small good to women, and your daughter should, in my view, proceed no further with 'em."

" Sir, give me leave to tell you you speak nonsense. The girl's but fifteen, and her Latin's most imperfect yet, and her Greek backward, for Mr. Herrick, that tutored her, don't know it so well himself. She's a long way to go before she's a good scholar, though she's very well for her years."

Mr. Cleveland knew it was of no use to argue with the doctor concerning what young gentlewomen should know. So he only said, " Give me leave, doctor, to carry on in present the instruction I am now giving her, in which she makes good progress and finds, I think, entertainment. Later, she can betake herself to the dead tongues once more."

" Well, have it your way," the doctor grudgingly consented. " But at least, if you read French with her, you might let it be Descartes, not comedies."

" God forbid it. Your daughter don't want to converse in France, nor with the mounseers over here, concerning the extension of matter, nor to open an elegant conversation with '*Je pense, donc je suis.*' All I'll read with her of M. Descartes is his railing on those that study the dead tongues."

" You talk uncommon strange, for the eminent elegant Latinist y'are, Mr. Cleveland."

" Perhaps." The Rhetoric Reader shrugged his shoulders. " Say, if you please, that familiarity breeds contempt; or that I drub Latin into too many stupid boys to desire to teach it to a lovely maid. Indeed, you must give me my way in this, doctor."

" Since you make a present of your lessons, I see that I must. And, indeed, I am glad the girl should better her French. 'Tis a trouble to me I know not more on't myself, and now, what with Jule learning to gabble it, and her brother who'll come back from Paris, I suppose, high and flown with his own fluency, I shall cut a sorry figure. D'ye find the girl spack to learn?"

"Very apt, indeed. She's a pupil after my heart."

The doctor took his leave, and walked on to Emmanuel to see Dr. Whichcote.

He liked John Cleveland, but he was a devilish decided obstinate fellow. However, let Jule improve her French. The trouble was, life was so infernally short, and there was not near enough time for everything. He himself felt only at the beginning, standing on the lowest rungs of the ladder and looking up. Here he was at fifty, and might be took any minute and flung into a grave, where no new knowledge was, and lie there mouldered and unknowing through the ages, saying to himself, *Non cogito, ergo non sum*; and so an end to all learning and all knowledge—and see what little way he had yet gotten.

"For a dandiprat, I'll believe religion again and hope for immortality," he muttered, turning his back with a little shudder on his blind and ultimate bed. "I must take a lesson from Parson Herrick, who believes that the good and he (he makes that modest and delicate discrimination, if I remember rightly) will dwell in Heaven eternally. That's a better credo to give heart to an ageing leech."

He quickened his steps, eager to talk again with his learned friend Dr. Whichcote.

16

Though Dr. Conybeare had left him five minutes since, Mr. Cleveland still sat, unwontedly idle, in his chamber, his head resting on one fine hand, the other hanging loosely at his side.

He brooded wearily on love, and the snares with which it entangles a man's feet; on honour, and the discomfiting shame of its betrayal; on passion and desire, their ardour, enjoyment, satiety, and ultimate ineluctable end; on this eager little doctor who trusted and liked him, and whom he liked; and on his only she-pupil, whose lovely face floated in mists of longing before his mind's eyes. She was so irresistably, inevitably, hazardously desirable, in her young, white, starry beauty. She was like a nymph, fragile and remote, unearthly like the moon, elusive in his arms as a wraith. Yet her love for him gave him the power to charm her into what he would, as if he held Comus his wand.

" If I but wave this wand
Your nerves are all chain'd up in Alablaster,
And you a statue; or as *Daphne* was
Root-bound, that fled *Apollo*."

What had that very chaste and somewhat budge lady answered?

" Fool do not boast,
Thou canst not touch the freedom of my mind
With all thy charms. . . ."

Aye, she might have said that, his little sweet, with that

dear little eager mind of hers that she and her father so cockered and cried up, and that, to tell the truth, fatigued him somewhat when she would show it to him. But he had almost taught her not to do so; no longer did she try to hold bookish or political conversations with him, or show him verses she had written. He still had those verses of hers, but had not had time to look at them. Doubtless they were like the verses of other maids and boys; it was a disease that passed, if not encouraged. Yes, he had touched the freedom of her mind, and taught her not to irk him and make him impatient with her intellects, but to be to him what he desired of her, his lovely and yielding nymph. Blinded and transported by passion, he had not looked ahead nor counted the cost to both of them. When he began to desire the lovely child, he had not meant that love should reveal herself as one of the few, the rare, the embarrassing, who might live and die for love. Her very youth entangled and ensnared her, for she had known no other man's love, and had enshrined him as her God. As surely as the son of Bacchus and Circe had done to Milton's Lady, had he immanacled her corporal rind while Heaven saw good, or even longer.

What now to do? For all wisdom and discretion dictated, what love so clamorously denied, that the thing now must end. Here was her father back again, and to go on with their lovering would be to court discovery. How could they sit together, making a pretence of lessons, with that inquiring parent of hers looking in on them, perhaps sitting with them, making close inquest into what they read and how they fared? A pest on all fathers; they ever obstructed love. Yet take her from her father he would not, since he could not wed her, and would not abduct her to make havoc of her name before the world.

The thing must end. Familiarity had blunted passion's edge enough to enable him to reach this resolution to be wise for himself and her. After all, she was not turned sixteen; she would forget, and he. Time would cure their fever, and their love would be as if it had not been, or, at most, a lovely memory. It must be so, he told himself. Love burgeoned, bloomed, went over, fell like a dead flower; or else was cut in its bloom before it fell.

> "Like to the grass that's newly sprung,
> Or like a tale that's new begun,
> Or like the bird that's here to-day,
> Or like the pearlèd dew of May,
> Or like an hour, or like a span,
> Or like the singing of a swan. . . .
> The grass withers, the tale is ended,
> The bird is flown, the dew's ascended,
> The hour is short, the span not long,
> The swan's near death. . . ."

Even such was love, more brief than brief life itself. Indeed, far more brief, as he had ever found.

He would set this child free. He would tell her father that he had no more time to teach her, and would bid her farewell. Such pain as they both would have was the payment one made for love's pleasure; it would pass.

Had he, he wondered, done an unpardonable thing by her? He had his own code of honour, gallantries and sins. His loves had been frequent, but light; he had never before encountered so serious and intent a grave maid, whose love was all as hungry as the sea, and could digest as much. His own, he knew, might be called appetite, that suffered surfeit, cloyment and revolt. He desired and enjoyed; with a like-minded partner in pleasure there was an end of it, and no harm done. But love seemed to strike a deep anchor in the soul of this pale nymph, and, were it to sail away, might tear up the soul itself in so doing.

But no, it should not be so. He would speak to her with reason and sense, explaining why it was best for both to part. He would end it gently, and both their hearts would heal, and later she would love and wed some youth; perhaps that red-head young Yarde, from her own county, who was so lost in love for her, and who scowled so darkly at himself.

For his own part, he would lose his nymph and his pleasure, when pleasure was still keen, and had only begun ever so slightly to tire. Though he foresaw in the future of their love, had it been permitted a future, a time when strain might assert itself, when his grave immanacled Lady, the freedom of her mind growing proud and restive again under her father's unwise stimulus, might turn difficult, and tire him with her questionings, imaginings, and thoughts, when all he desired was to hold her in his arms, and all the words he wanted of her were love's tender or merry retorts. Of merriment, thought he, his nymph had something too little, though he could stir it in her by his jests. By nature she seemed a trifle solemn, somewhat sicklied o'er with the pale cast of thought. It was his pastime and his humour to make her laugh, but there were times when he felt it her turn to make *him* laugh, and at this she was not apt. Mr. Cleveland was partial to a merry rogue, a she-wag. At times he had ruefully told himself that Henry More, the angel of Christ's, would have found her a more apt pupil at the game of love than he. Then she had overmuch of conscience, scrupulosities, fine niceties of honour. To lie, hurt her; she was, in truth, he said it with a rueful smile, a most rare nymph, this lady he had enspelled with his love, and must now set free. That other nymph, Sabrina fair, should be summoned in this hour to their aid, to unlock the clasping charm and thaw the numbing spell that bound them both. For her beauty had such power over his senses that he could scarce find strength to look into her eyes and kiss and part, shake hands for ever, cancel all his vows, say, I have done, you get no more of me.

"Love's the very devil," said Mr. Cleveland, and rose to his feet to receive a pupil that knocked on his door. How simple, thought he, would the world have been had all pupils been of the male gender!

17

For half an hour Mr. Cleveland and Julian read *L'Amour Tyrannique*, while the doctor bustled in and out, read his news-letter, sorted the disorderly sheaf of papers he had brought back with him from London, and from time to time paused to give an ear to the rubbishy French play which his daughter and her tutor read in duologue, he correcting her accent.

"Why not practise some conversation more like to be of service?" the doctor inquired. "Lord grant you mayn't e'er desire to say such things as those to any mounseer. Look, you should learn instead to ask your way civilly about Paris, or to inquire when sails a packet for England, or to wish any French gentleman you may encounter over here a prosperous voyage back again, or ask him what is his opinion of M. Descartes his philosophy, or of Queen Henrietta Maria's good sense. Something to the point, such as that. I think nought of these phrases of M. de Scudéry's; you'll never require any such matter in this life, or so I trust."

"Well, sir," said Mr. Cleveland, wishing that the doctor would go out, "neither man nor woman knows what the chances of life may require 'em to say in the course on't.

However, we shall now practise letter writing in this same elegant language."

"Do so, do so, and I'll out. I shall be back within a half-hour, Jule, and we'll go walking."

Left alone, Mr. Cleveland pushed his chair back from the table and drew his pupil to him.

"Faith, sweet heart, these be lessons under difficulties. If your father had not then gone, I should have been obliged to write my message to you in the garb of a French epistle. For in truth, I have particulars to speak on with you, little one. First kiss me; there. Now rest close in my arms, aye, against my heart, the while I say what 'tis very gall and bitterness to me to speak. Look, bud, we can't continue on this manner; it's too difficult and parlous. Your father will mark something. Indeed, 'tis not acting just nor right by you. Sweetheart, I blame myself for thus entangling you—only that I can't find it in my heart to blame myself for what's been so sweet. But look now, I must set you free; I must not ask more of you, or I shall imperil your fair name. Would to God I could take you clear away and hold you in all men's sight. But that can't be; for I am bound to my College and can't wed, perhaps not for many years; and, bating that, I won't do you hurt before the malicious world. So our lessons must end, little pupil. For I'll not come here and sit and read French or Latin with you like a solemn budge schoolmaster. Perhaps sometimes you'll come out with me, and we'll snatch an hour alone together in the meadows, but I daren't do that over often in this devilish public gossiping University city. Come, look at me, and tell me I am right."

The face he tilted up with his hand was pale as his cambric bands, so that he feared she was about to faint.

"Oh, my sweet," he cried, shocked, "what is't? Look not so, dear heart, for I'm not worth it. See, 'tis harder for me to leave you, having once enjoyed you, then for you to leave so poor a thing as me. But believe me, child, 'tis best, and we must face it. . . . Look, then, 'tis but our lessons must cease; we'll meet still and love. Aye, we'll meet often."

This he said hastily and earnestly, looking down into her face to see if its faint natural colour would return at his words, for this waxen hue affrighted him. He had been too abrupt, he saw; a conclusion long by him foreseen had broken on her like a sudden great wave, smothering her heart's pulse. He had known many loves and many ends, she but this.

"You said you must set me free," she whispered, like a drowner whose feet, fumbling and unsure, again find earth.

"Aye, and you are free. I do set you free, my dove. But we can meet and love. I did not mean never to meet more. Look, we'll steal out and go a-paigling in the water-meadows, and I'll wreath the paigles in your hair, and you shall be my lovely Chloe, and I your Daphnis. Is it well so? Wilt smile at me now?"

But his nymph's smile was faint and uncertain, her voice troubled.

"But can we not have our lessons? If we do but sit good and discreet at our books and read French or Latin, I'm content with that. Indeed, 'twould be very cordial to me, for I like to learn from you; and as to courting, 'tis not necessary, since we know we love. So that it would not really matter if my father were present in the room or no."

"Nay, nay, my flower. I can't sit cold as a judge and teach you languages, when the only language I desire to teach you is that of love. You know I have no envy you should learn aught; I'd as lief have you a sweet ignoramus, and you'll get no tongues from me. Let it be, child; I'll tell your father I've no more time for pupils outside my College, and you and I will meet elsewhere. And look, go not about with that white and starkled look, or the doctor will think he must physic thee. Thou'lt still be all-thing secret? Aye, I know thou wilt.

Now I should go, for your father will be suddenly back. Kiss me this once, and then God b'wi' you, my sweetest dear. There, show me thy dimple, that's my sweet chuck."

He was gone, and she stood alone, looking after him, her hands clasped before her.

She was dazed and confused; she felt as if some one had pushed her suddenly into deep water to drown her, and then had quickly pulled her out again. What had he said to her? What had he meant? More than that the lessons must end but not their love, which was what he had ended by saying. He must set her free . . . he blamed himself for entangling her . . . he would not imperil her name . . . Oh, God, what echoes were these that drifted back to her? He had meant, then—what had he meant? That they must part? Part, and cease to love?

But how could she cease to love, having given her heart, her soul, her body, into his keeping? She was not a light lover, to give and to take back. Was love, then, like that, to men? A fleeting pleasure to be enjoyed for a while and left?

Remembering her lover's passionate embraces, his sweet words and ardent murmured vows, she cried in her soul, Oh, no, no, it cannot be. He loves me still. It is but the lessons he would end, not love; and the blood began to flow freely again through her body, and she thought, We shall often meet; we shall go and gather cowslips in the meadows, as he says. He is not casting me off at all.

The doctor returned, and said, "The lesson's ended? Then come, chuck, and we'll go walking." And they went off to stroll by the river.

18

In truth, Mr. Cleveland had more important matters than love to engage his thoughts in these troubled days. He was busy assembling a society called the Cambridge Straffordians. The members were many of them of St. John's College, and Mr. Cleveland, their president, composed a petition to be signed and sent to Westminster on behalf of the great imperilled Johnian so unconstitutionally, so illegally, being hunted to his death. In tone it was hot and direct, and not at all calculated to placate those to whom it was addressed.

"You have searched out and invented laws to suit the aim of your convenience," it uncivilly said, and besought them not to stoop to the conciliation of the base rabbling mob by the murder of this great person; it entreated them to clear their eyes of blind passion and their hearts of malice and endeavour to act like just men and in the ancient English tradition of constitutional right and law, and not like knaves bloat with malignancy, hate and fear.

Mr. Cleveland was a little dubious about these last words, having read enough English history, as well as that of other countries, to be aware that to act like knaves bloat with malignancy, hate and fear could not be accurately called altogether out of keeping with ancient English, or any other, national tradition. Still, he sacrificed accuracy to a noble sentiment, and sent the petition, signed by a hundred notable names, to Westminster, about the time that twenty thousand Londoners were signing and sending a request that Lord Strafford's issue out of his afflictions might be quite other, and the Earl of Essex was coldly remarking that stone dead hath no fellow.

All was, in fact, most unpropitious, and the Cambridge Straffordians soon perceived that they had but wasted paper and drawn upon their already suspect university the unfavourable attentions of parliament.

"The one hope's now with the Lords," Mr. Cleveland gloomily said, "and 'tis devilish thin. If they yield to the clamour and pass this bill, then good luck to that scoundrelly George Goring and his army plot, and may they seize the Tower and set the earl free, and may the King dissolve this flea-bitten mongrel assembly and kick 'em back to their kennels and reign again."

They were at supper in hall, and the high table all drank to this petition. But the master drank sadly and without hope, looking bitterly into the future, as if he saw the black clouds of doom inexorably approaching. His own quarrel with the flea-bitten mongrels, interrupted by the dissolution last May, was now, he had been informed, to be resumed, and the articles against him were a-preparing. For he, said they, had been "the encourager of Dr. Cosins in his Vice-Chancellorship to tyrannise in that Jesuitical, Popish and Canterburian religion," and his day of reckoning drew near.

But that was a small matter, in the general disintegration and darkness that he foresaw for Cambridge.

"Gentlemen," he said, and rose sadly to his feet, "I give you the King, and down with all his foes."

They rose and drank it as if in prayer, and stood in silence for a moment after.

"And may he deliver Black Tom from their hands," Mr. Cleveland added then; and, setting his empty glass on the table, turned it down, to indicate that, after this prayer, he would drink no more.

"'Twill be but a sad Port Latin day this year," some one observed. "Do you preach the *clerum*, Master?"

"Aye, I shall preach it. I shall have much to say," Dr. Beale gloomily replied. "Though, for that, they post spies on my sermons now, and carry lying reports back to my judges. . . . News have gotten abroad of this college of late which will do us no good, what with Mr. Austin's matter, and now young Conybeare flitting secretly off with the Jesuits, and away to France with Sir Kenelm Digby. That should have been prevented, gentlemen; 'twas an ill business."

He did not look towards Mr. Conybeare's tutor, but down at the table, and drummed his fingers on it in melancholy disapprobation.

Mr. Cleveland flung beneath his breath an impatient curse on the Conybeare family, who had, he was now persuaded, brought him nothing but trouble.

In sad, exasperated mood he repaired after hall to his chamber, and sat down to the pile of theses he had to correct. Weary work, he found it, instructing lads in the Latin tongue, when the fate of England seemed to hang in the scales, and he should be busy with it. He had in his head a satiric poem making game of the monster Smectymnuus, which he wanted time to write and could get none, with all the interruptions of his tutorial day.

As he sat there, with his window open to the soft May evening, hurrying through the pile of papers, there was a soft rap on his door.

"Oh, come in," he impatiently said, and in came a slim youth in cap and gown, dark and pale-faced and beautiful.

In surprise, Mr. Cleveland sprang up, and his papers fluttered to the floor.

"Kit Conybeare, by all that's strange! What do you here, sir?"

The youth stood still and looked at him, and took off the concealing cap. "It's not Kit. . . . It's I . . ."

He stared at the boyish figure in angry amaze.

"*You*, child? You masquerade in your brother's clothes, and come here to me? Don't you know it's madness, and would smirch your good name for ever were't discovered?"

The little gesture of her hand seemed to put away such good name as she might have as of small account.

"I came as a man because I could not come as a woman. Those meeting me in the college took no note of me. . . . I came because I must see you, this once. You stayed away; you never came, as you said you would . . . so I had to come to you. . . ."

"You had to? An odd compulsion!" Then, as she winced back, his anger was flooded with remorse, and he took her in his arms.

"Forgive me, child; you know I adore you, but your madness angered me. You should not have come; 'twould be ill for both of us were we discovered thus."

He went to the door and locked it, came back and stood facing her. She made a lovely and gallant boy, he thought; she was more beautiful than her brother. Desire again stirred in him.

"Y'are come to tempt me, little elf, to my stroy and your own. Alack, how easily could I yield! But look, I must not. You must steal soft away, and pray y'have not been sighted. Believe me, pretty jackanapes, I know best in this. What put it in your head to come?"

She was regarding him steadily, as if she would read his heart.

"I had to see you once more." Her low voice was thin and remote, as it had been indeed some strange, unearthly, sexless elf's. "You did not come. I had to know if you meant never to come more. I think, now, you do so mean. I sha'n't trouble you more, or risk to stroy your name."

"Sweetheart," he protested, and placed his hands on her shoulders, looking down on the small white face. "'Tis your name, not mine, I care for. We have to think, too, of your father. What would he say if he knew?"

"It would all-to break his heart," she listlessly replied. "He shall never know, from me."

Her eyes fell on a pile of manuscript lying on a table in a corner.

"I'll take my verses with me," she said.

"Ah, yes, your pretty verses. Aye, best take 'em." She did not ask if he had read them; perhaps she knew he had not.

"Now, best begone with all haste," he said. "I have a pupil waiting on me in a few minutes. Good-bye, sweet child. And be not thus rash again, for it's tempting Providence. One kiss before you go. I mayn't see you for some time, for it may be I must go up to London on a mission from the College concerning my Lord Strafford. Things look blackly for him, alas."

"Aye," she slowly agreed, and gathered up her packet of manuscript.

"Good-bye, sir. I ask your pardon for troubling you thus. 'Tis the last time."

"Nay, child, nay; we must wait on happier times. It can lead to nothing presently, but y'are always my dear."

"I am your cast miss," she startled him by replying in the same small calm voice, and slipped from his embrace like a shy child, making for the door.

"My sweet, use not those words," he murmured, as he turned the key, and, opening the door, looked down the stairs to see if any were without. "'Tis clear. Go soft and discreetly. If any should meet you, they'll swear y'are your brother's ghost that haunts his college, and will read some presage into't."

Indeed, he thought, she might well be a ghost, so white was she, and so light of foot did she go.

He turned to his seat by the window, and wiped his brow with his handkerchief.

"A crazy act. Will she do't again? I think not, for the elf bears herself proudly and is now half-angered at me. . . . My cast miss, forsooth. . . . I would not have her use such words, to both our hurts. For rat me if I don't love her still, and am physicking myself with aloes in severing us."

When young Mr. Drake, his pupil, entered, he found Mr. Cleveland somewhat impatient, absent, and distrait.

19

As Dr. Conybeare and his daughter sat at supper on the evening of the 9th of May, Francis walked in on them, dusty and hot from a day's riding. They greeted him with surprise.

"What make you here, child?" his father asked. "I had thought you in the middle of the anti-Straffordian agitations, shouting outside Whitehall."

"There's enough to do that, set aside myself," Francis grimly said. "Such a roistering and a dimification as went on all last night, and all to-day, too, I take it, outside Whitehall and St. James's (for they cry there against the Queen's mother and her Popish intrigues) would strike fear in you to hear. They say the Queen's in hysterics, and her mother too. You can imagine that, between these two screaming foreigners, His Majesty's nerves are not in the best case, and 'tis tolerable certain he'll give way and assent to the execution in the course of to-day—in fact, he has likely done so by now. He sent for the bishops and judges yesterday to advise him, and they were to wait on him to-day also. But, whatever advice he may seek, he'll yield, for he daren't other. The fury of the mob frights him. All the night they raged, and, Lord, they say the Queen's courtiers were properly starkled; confessed their sins, packed up their jewels, and made all yare for flight. The discovery of these last plots of the Queen's has exceedingly angered the people."

"Lord, there's a vain silly fool of a woman for you," the doctor commented. "But sit you down, Frank, and sup while you talk. If you rode from London merely to give us the latest news, I take it very kindly in you, for it comes through but slowly to us here. They say Jermyn and Sucklin's fled over sea, after the discovery of this newest army plot of theirs. That's another silly flighty creature, that one-time gallant of July's here, as must stick his finger into all pies. Howsoe'er, he was extreme civil and obliging to me in London t'other day when I sought Kit, so I'll not call him names."

"It's of Kit, sir, I'm come to speak," his son said. "He's back from France, and now's the time we could perhaps get hold on him. That flap-dragon Digby, it seems, fought a duel in Paris and killed his man, fled the country, and is now in London, Kit with him. They arrived in pudding-time, in the midst of the anti-Papist rioting, in time to see a pile of Popish books burned in the streets, and the mob shouting vengeance on Sir Kenelm's friend and patroness, the Queen. Within a few days, as I've heard, there'll be a committee of members wait on the fellow to make him swallow the Oath of Allegiance and Supremacy. And then they won't wait long afore they summon him before the Committee for Recusants, and he might like enough get clapped in prison. And here's Kit in his household, acting scribe and personal attendant on him, and might land himself in a pretty praemunire too, the young fool. So I thought, after taking counsel with you, to try and pluck him out of this pickle."

"Indeed, 'twould be well done. But the boy's stubborn as a mule, and worships his master, and I doubt we can induce him to leave him. Y'have not seen him?"

"Not I. He'd not let me, if I tried. As you know, sir, he and I fadge like dog and cat, and these last doings of his ha'n't bettered matters between us. If I attempt to make him go one road, he'll huff me to my face, and the more certainly run headlong along t'other."

"Y'are right there; y'are certainly very right in that. Look, Frank, I'll go up to London myself and see him, and talk over his future with Sir Kenelm, and find out if he's any more mind than he had to renounce his folly and return to his studies here. They'd take him back if he forswore Popery and craved pardon of the College. I fear 'tis near hopeless, but 'tis a chance, and, in any case, I must know what's like to befall him. Aye, I'll get up to London to-morrow. But look, Frank, are you pressed in your business? Can you take my place here for four days, till I return? For I don't wish to leave July alone; the girl's none too well in present, and mopes. Aye, chuck, you do mope, and I'll not leave you alone, to no other company than good Mr. and Mrs. Speedy."

"But I don't mind it, father. I like to be alone."

"And I like it not for thee, bud, so that's the end. What of it, Frank? Canst bide?"

"Aye, I can, if you'll carry word back to my chambers. But make such speed as you can in your business, for I can't be from London long. I had meant to ride back to-morrow. And indeed, 'tis something inconvenient to stay away presently; still, I will do so, if 'twill enable you to go with an easy mind."

Francis was a good young man, and, when he believed a

course to be his duty, he followed it. It bored him to remain from London just now, away from the stirring events that occurred there, and were likely to occur; but he was fond enough of his young sister, and supposed that his father did not decide without reason that she must not be alone; indeed, she looked sad and white enough, he thought. And there were friends he could visit in Cambridge.

So at dawn next day the doctor rode off through the green May country to London to rescue his son, and also, thought he, to see and hear the news at first hand.

20

It has often been observed, with what far greater receptivity and facility the young imbibe gossip and *on-dits* than do the elderly. A noteworthy illustration of this is the fact that, whereas Dr. Conybeare had been for several weeks going about Cambridge since his return from London in April, and had heard no word of all the words that were doubtless said concerning his daughter and Mr. John Cleveland, his son Francis, on the second day of his visit to his University, being invited to supper in hall at his old College of Christ's, heard enough to send him back to his lodging in a white heat of anger and disgust.

Next morning—it was May the 12th, and the morning of Lord Strafford's execution—Francis spoke to his young sister, and his manner was that which he employed in the courts for the interrogation of prisoners.

"Julian, I have to say to you what is bitter to me to speak and to you to hear. Do you know that men speak scandal of your name in Cambridge, coupling it with a libertine's?"

Julian, who sat idly by the window, did not look up, but gazed still out on the street. In reply to him, she moved her head slightly, but whether in protest, in denial of the knowledge he inquired after, or to signify carelessness of what scandal might be made of her name, or whose it might be coupled with, he did not know.

"Well," he shortly told her, "'tis so. And the man's John Cleveland."

Such bitterness he put into it that she looked up in surprise. What, then, had John Cleveland done to him that he should hate him?

Francis could have told her, but did not. He and John Cleveland had been undergraduates of the same year, at Christ's, both good scholars, the one plodding, the other brilliant, the one solemn and little loved, the other popular, handsome, sociable, witty, able to make any one look a fool with his quick, satiric tongue and pen. Cleveland had been of the gay, rollicking set, which that grave young man, Sir Symonds D'Ewes, had condemned as atheistical and licentious; Francis Conybeare was in a graver Puritan group, which studied more continuously, and disapproved of swearing, gambling, dissipation, and even of Sunday games. John Cleveland and he had seemed cast for rivals from the first. They had been salted together at their freshmen's orations; Francis remembered that it had cost him three and fourpence, and that he had drunk too much beer afterwards; he remembered, too, that his own discourse had been voted tolerable, and that he had been assigned both the reward of merit and the penalty of failure—a drink of caudle, and another of salted beer; but Cleveland, who had preceded him, had tickled his audience with quips and jests, and had been given the sweet drink only. Yes; from the very first John Cleveland had done better, or was reputed to have done better, what he had himself done well enough. Later, they had disputed together several times in acts in the schools; and each time Cleveland had won applause from the academic audience for unhorsing his adversary by his greater verbal ingenuity; though Francis had thought there had been more stuff in his own dialectics.

Then there had been the year that Cleveland had been chosen Prevaricator, at the Bachelors' Commencement, and had caused shouts of mirth by his flow of wit at the expense of the Puritans in the College. At his comments on their habits and their personal appearances, including his own, Francis, after all these years, grew hot and angry.

Then, in their third year, a good Latin scholar had to be selected to compose and deliver a welcome to the Chancellor and the French Ambassador, who were visiting the College. Francis had hoped for this honour, since his scholarship and his academic prowess were adequate. But it fell to Cleveland; it had been the first official oration to distinguished visitors that the future Rhetoric Reader had delivered, and every one had been delighted with it.

A little later, Cleveland had been chosen Father of the Christmas Revels, and had composed a burlesque on College life, to be acted by his sons. Again an opportunity, not missed, for mordant caricature. . . .

And so all through those seven years together; the one always a little ahead academically, a great deal ahead in athletics and in sports, out of sight in popular esteem. And since those days, John Cleveland had employed his pen in bitter mockery of the party with which Francis had thrown in his lot, and they had loathed one another like the devil. And now here was the damned fellow's name coupled in common-room gossip with his sister's, and John Cleveland had made a fool of him once more.

None of this he said to Julian, but only, in answer to her wondering gaze, " Aye, John Cleveland. Your precious tutor, forsooth. Now, tell me true, Julian. He's your lover?"

Again that denying motion of the head. In truth, he was no more her lover now.

"Not? Don't lie to me, pray, for I'll have the truth from him, if not from you. They say he was wont, while my father was up in London, to take you down the river of an evening, and they hinted that he took you to an inn at Howse for supper. That's true, a'n't it?"

Dumbly she looked on the floor, saying neither yes nor no.

"Aye, 'tis true, and you know it," he savagely went on. "He *is* your lover, and you can't deny it. God, that my sister should have come to this. D'you conceit as he wants to wed you, little ninny, and renounce his fellowship? John Cleveland the rake? Did he ever tell you such a thing?"

"No."

"Oh, so you ha'n't even that much of excuse? You were happy to be his miss, I suppose, and a nay-word to all Cambridge . . ."

"I am not . . ."

"*You are not*, say you. What are you not, pray? Not happy, not his miss, not a nay-word? I say y'are all three, and that you do but waste your breath in lying to me. What will our father say when he knows this? His daughter the quean of a College tutor that can't wed her. The truth is that he's ever cockered you and pampered you and set you up, and then was mad enough to go off and leave you to your own devices, trusting to your virtue and your honour, conceiting you so quaint you'd scarce look at a man, and not knowing you was just a frail little piece that any man could play with at his pleasure. And now y'ave dragged our good name in the dirt. D'you think 'twill advantage me to have this get about? Already I have a father tushes at all religion, and a brother a Papist fled from Cambridge, and now I've a sister a whore, God help me."

"I am not," she said again, without conviction, like a child repeating a lesson.

He looked at her coldly. It was odd how little impression his cutting words seemed to make on her, as she sat there, still and pale, her hands lying idle on her knees. She seemed remote and removed, as if she had reached some world of—was it of anguish or of joy?—that he could not touch. As if his speaking clattered over her head like a brawling brook, or like angry waves of the sea, the while she sat at the bottom of deep water in some strange drowned world. She angered him by this numb calm.

"As for your fine lover," he flung at her, "I shall wait on him this morning, and see what he's to say for himself. There shall be a reckoning at last between John Cleveland and me."

She was stabbed awake at last, and stared up at him with desperate eyes.

"No," she cried. "No. You must not go to him. Say what you will to me, but leave him be. Brother, I entreat you. He has not wronged me. For a brief while we thought we loved; then we ceased to love and went our ways. He has not betrayed me, indeed he has not."

"If he has not, then he can tell me so to my face. So I am to let him go his way, am I; take his pleasure of my sister, and walk off without paying his scot? Nay, but he shall pay it, and pay it now. Would you liefer, perhaps, that I wait on Dr. Beale, and relate him the doings of the most noted fellow of his College, the most orient, witty courtier and churchman, the prop of royalty, prelacy, and the Protestant Church of England, the mocker on Puritans and parliaments, the zealous Straffordian and Laudian, the celebrated Rhetoric Reader and wencher, Mr. John Cleveland? Which shall I wait on first, Dr. Beale or Mr. Cleveland?"

"You need be at no pains to wait on me, Mr. Conybeare," a pleasant voice behind him said, "for here I am; I hope I see you well. I think w'are not met in some years. Do you stay in Cambridge? I knew not you was here, but came to wait on Dr. Conybeare."

"He's from home, sir. Belike you knew it. Though I can well believe you looked not to find me in his stead."

Mr. Cleveland's brows went up.

"A strange greeting, Mr. Conybeare. But I seem to remember as you never had much gust for my company; though, as to that, I think I heard you say you was so good to intend waiting on me shortly."

"Yes, Mr. Cleveland, you like enough heard that. Were you come a minute earlier, you'd have heard, beside, the reason why."

"Well, since I was not come a minute earlier, possess me, if you please, sir. I trust that my presence here may have saved you putting yourself at the trouble of a visit."

"You skulking, wenching dandiprat," Francis uncivilly and bitterly remarked. "You'll answer to me here and now for my sister's honour."

"Answer to you, sir? Why so? 'Tis to your sister I should answer for that. Has she complained of me, pray?"

"No, she lies, as you doubtless will. I take no notice of either of you, for I know the truth. I have evidence. And you'll meet me, sir. You shall give me satisfaction."

"Soft and fair, Mr. Conybeare. I shan't fight you. As you very well know, duelling's not permit in the University. Nor do I intend to scandalise you sister's name by such a brawl. Nor to kill you, nor to permit you to kill me. What! Would you have us meet on the Gogmagogs at cocklight and exchange rapier-thrusts or pistol shots, like a couple of Roaring Boys who've fell out in a tavern? For shame, sir, I had thought better of your lawyerly and Puritanical precision than that."

"And I of your spirit, sir. You may soft-and-fair me as you will, but I say there lacks room in the world for you and me both, and one of us must go down. 'Tis lying, vain, coxcomical braggarts such as you, with your high proud easy airs and licentious manners and taunting tongues, as is the country's bane. But reckoning time's come between you and me, now y'have turned your fine attentions on my sister, to scandalise and tradition her; and if you'll not meet me like a gentleman, I'll thrash you like a dog. Take that for an earnest on't."

Behind the blow was the driving weight of twelve years of hate. It caught John Cleveland on the jaw, and he reeled. Before he could recover his poise or hit back, the Templar, an agile, muscular, and tennis-playing young man, had struck again, was battering him with blows.

"Stop, stop! Oh, stop!"

Julian was between them, clutching at her brother's raised arm. Violently he flung her off, flung her back; she struck her head on the sharp projecting corner of the oak table, and fell to the floor.

"Hold, man, hold," Mr. Cleveland exclaimed. "She's hurt. Good God, she's unconscious. . . ."

He was bending over her, lifting her in his arms. Francis stood by, breathing hard, the mists of passion clearing slowly from his brain.

"A leech; quick; send the people of the house for a leech. Ho, help here!"

The serving maid, already as near to the door as serving maids usually are when there is quarrelling within, did not delay to enter.

"Quick, girl, fetch a leech; she has fallen and hurt herself. Make all haste. Tell him it's a blow on the head and she lies stunned."

The girl scurried off.

Mr. Cleveland lifted the small, still form, bore it into the next room, and laid it on the bed there. It was her own bed. He sat on it beside her, and examined the red mark on the temple which was becoming a livid bruise.

"Go and fetch brandy," he said to Francis, who stood, helpless and startled, in the doorway. Francis went.

Mr. Cleveland laid a hand lightly on the childish breast, feeling for the heart, as so often before he had felt it beating beneath his hand. But he felt no movement now.

"God," he whispered. "The heart has stinted; 'tis still. Have we killed her between us? July, July, speak to me. Speak to your lover, little heart. . . . Open your eyes for God's sake. . . ."

Francis came with the brandy. They trickled a drop between her closed lips.

"No use," said Cleveland quietly, looking up into the brother's haggard face. "I think her heart's stopped."

"Impossible," Francis cried. "She's but stunned. The leech will revive her. . . ."

Cleveland pointed to the mark on the temple.

"A bad place for a blow. It bleeds not without but within, into the brain. I have known such. . . ."

Francis looked; he, too, felt for the still heart. Then he dropped on his knees by the bed and buried his face in his arms.

Cleveland sat still, his hand holding the slight form in a gentle clasp. It was a child's form, undeveloped and straight.

It was like her love, the thought came to him, running like a current in the tide of his grief; her childish unvoluptuous love, that had had a kind of difficult, brittle virginity, as if mind were ever at war with body; a monstrous perversion, he had once told her, in a woman, meant by Providence to be a man's solace in his hours of ease. Perhaps this sorry jest of death from so slight a cause, that seemed borrowed from one of gloomy John Ford's tragedies, was deeper than the cheap trick of a dramatist wishful to rid himself of an inconvenient character. Not Seneca himself would have ventured on it as fit work for the god in the machine. The Greeks had more the truth of it, and likely it was Destiny took vengeance on her for her presumption in not fitting in with any rational scheme of things. She might, if the damned Calvinists could have been right in anything, have been predestinated to this end.

Thus for a moment Mr. Cleveland the poet saw tragedy's pattern in the heavens, and the fitness of so sharp and final a conclusion to embarrassed and entangled love. Then his grief surged back. He had loved her; aye, he did love her.

"July, July," he cried in his soul to the child in his arms, "we have slain you in our quarrel. And I left you alone, and you'll speak to me no more. Forgive me and come back to me. Did I e'er think thee quiet and dull? Did I blame thee for that thy little solemn mind was on books and dreams, and wished thee a common merry wench to divert me? And now thou'lt be quiet for ever."

The memory of the passion and joy of his first desire of her swept over him; he bent his head, and hot tears welled from his eyes and dropped on to the still white face that rested on his arm.

The leech came, and pronounced that the young lady had been killed by the blow on the temple.

"She fell, I hear," he said, looking suspiciously from one to the other.

The gentlemen agreed that she had fallen.

"The wench telled me she heard sounds of quarrelling and blows within, and the young lady crying 'stop.'"

"Yes. She tried to stop us," Francis said. "I had best tell all. We had fallen out and were fighting. She came between us; not knowing what I did, I pushed her from me, and she fell and catched her head on the table."

"A very serious matter, gentlemen. A matter for the watch. I shall be obliged to inform on't."

"A serious matter . . ." Mr. Cleveland looked at him, and bitterly laughed. "You find death so, doctor? And I had thought it a jest. A serious matter, then; we grant it you, yes."

The leech decided him so strange in his manner that he was probably beside himself. He turned to the young lady's brother.

"I must ask you, sir, to accompany me to the watch and give your report of your sister's death, for the crowner."

"As you will," Francis apathetically agreed.

"Her father is from home, I understand? A message should go to him by post straightway."

"I will see to it." Francis, in his astonished misery, was still the business-like lawyer. "I will write a letter now, and despatch a post with it."

At the thought of his father's receiving that letter, his set face worked. Once more the doctor had left his darling nestle-chick behind him, and this time would be the last. Suddenly Francis's stunned composure broke, and he fell to weeping, his face in his hands, while the leech watched him uneasily, not knowing what he might next do.

Mr. Cleveland turned on him, out of eyes swollen and blackened by blows, one sad and bitter glance.

"Aye, you may weep. Weeping won't bring her back. W'have slain her between us, and though we weep our eyes out, she'll not come to life on this earth more."

21

Mr. Cleveland sat alone by the bed, clasping a cold hand in his, as if the warmth of his own life could wake that dead pulse once more, start the blood once more coursing through the deserted frame that mocked and eluded him in its marble loveliness, lying now indeed like the Lady enchanted, but enchanted by a stronger spell than any he had ever weaved.

> "If I but wave this wand
> Your nerves are all chain'd up in Alablaster,
> And you a statue; or as *Daphne* was
> Root-Bound, that fled *Apollo.*
>
> "Fool do not boast.
> Thou canst not touch the freedom of my mind
> With all thy charms, although the corporal rind
> Thou hast immanacl'd, while Heav'n sees good."

Aye; no more could he touch the freedom of her mind; that eager, grave, inquiring mind of hers, that had ever sought to rove along paths down which he would not companion her nor any woman, from which he had plucked her back with mockery and with kisses, at times with impatience, until at last she had renounced them, and followed him along the roads he chose for her. He had immanacl'd her corporal rind and possessed her lovely body, but had he touched the freedom of her mind? If he had, she had regained it now, wherever her delicate virgin spirit might be straying, gravely dreaming along the gallant walks of Paradise, untroubled by such as he; the eternal poet, virginal, sexless, free and young.

He could not have made her happy for long, nor she him; he knew that still, as he had known it before, and as she too must have known it in her soul, blind and immanacl'd with love as she had been. Poor child that lay now like a white blossom broken off by storms, the storm of his unbridled passion and her brother's unbridled rage. Between them they had beaten the frail blossom to the earth and trampled it with their feet, in the dewy morning of its life.

"Aye, we only let you have the morning, sweet bud. We slew you before noon."

Lines she had loved ran in his head; they were her apt epitaph:

> "Or like the dainty flower of May,
> Or like the morning to the day,
> Or like the sun, or like the shade,
> Or like the gourd which Jonas had—
> Even such is man, whose thread is spun,
> Drawn out, and cut, and so is done.
> The rose withers, the blossom blasteth,
> The flower fades, the morning hasteth,
> The sun sets, the shadow flies,
> The gourd consumes; and man he dies.

> "Like to the grass that's newly sprung,
> Or like a tale that's new begun,
> Or like the bird that's here to-day,
> Or like the pearlèd dew of May,
> Or like an hour, or like a span,
> Or like the singing of a swan—
> Even such is man, who lives by breath,
> Is here, now there: so life, and death.
> The grass withers; the tale is ended,
> The bird is flown, the dew's ascended,

The hour is short, the span not long,
The swan's near death; man's life is done.

" Like to the bubble in the brook,
Or, in a glass, much like a look,
Or like a shuttle in weaver's hand,
Or like a writing on the sand,
Or like a thought, or like a dream,
Or like the gliding of the stream—
Even such is man, who lives by breath,
Is here, now there: so life, and death.
The bubble's cut, the look's forgot,
The shuttle's flung, the writing's blot,
The thought is past, the dream is gone,
The water glides; man's life is done. . . ."

" 'Twas I slew thee, as well as he," Mr. Cleveland murmured. " I, that thought to take my pleasure of thee and go, like thou hadst been a light maid, as others are. 'Tis I should go before the justices and the crowner and take blame on me for thy death. . . . Not," he added wryly, " as Francis Conybeare will wish to spare me blame—but he'll be more minded to save his sister's name than to scandalise mine. I care not, and will leave him to tell his tale as he will. Thou'lt not heed, from wherever 'tis thou'rt fled to. Aye, thou'rt gotten free of all of us, thou and thy quaint proud virtue that knew failure here. Nay, but if virtue feeble were, Heaven itself would stoop to her. Heaven has stooped, and lifted thee from our mortal dust and turmoil. Belike thou has been spared much that the rest of us must suffer, in this troubled distracted land."

On his ears fell the solemn tolling of a bell. Did they mourn her passing, then? But no; he remembered; it was the hour of Lord Strafford's execution. Many thousands would be gathered on Tower Hill to stare on that great person going grandly to his death. Would their hate and execration be still, or would they howl on him to the last?

However that had been, he was at rest now, the great stormy Johnian, hated of his countrymen and abandoned of his king. Nothing remained but to toll for him the passing bell, and say a prayer for his proud, turbulent soul, that was travelling even now to its freedom. Strange, sad thought, the great murdered earl and the young murdered maiden, seeking Paradise together, defeated of men.

In that melancholy bell seemed to sound all the defeat of the sad and struggling world. Defeat, defeat, defeat, it seemed to say, as if all fine things must struggle against odds too mighty, and so perish. England itself was so struggling; was rent by faction and hate. Aye, this very city of Cambridge was so rent. For, suddenly drowning the tolling bell in clamour, other bells rang out, in a clashing carillon of triumph. The townsmen had gained access to some belfry, and were pealing their triumph over Black Tom Tyrant's death. In that clash of bells John Cleveland heard the exultation of a disloyal rebel England, that would slay not only those who sought to rule it, but all fine seemly things in Church and State, yes, the ordered beauty of Cambridge itself. Those who pealed the bells pealed them for liberty's sake; they rejoiced to be rid of a tyrant, not recking that his slayers might prove as great tyrants in their turn, nor that, whoever wins, liberty and the common, undenarious people will always know defeat.

Looking up, Mr. Cleveland's glance fell on a sheet of paper that lay on the table by the bedside. It was written over in the clear childish hand he knew so well, and seemed to be verse. He took it in his hand. It was headed, "An Epitaph on the Earl of Strafford." She must, then have written it that morning, or perhaps the day before. He was glad that she had written verses again, that he had not quite choked the stream of poetry in her, that it had welled up again at the last, in the stress of her own griefs and of the earl's tragedy.

"I would not read your verses," Mr. Cleveland murmured in remorse. "Aye, I hurt and denied you. But look, I'll read this."

He did so. Blotted and erased and ill-written as it was, he made it out.

"*An Epitaph on the Earl of Strafford.*"

"Heere lyes wyse & valiant duste,
Huddl'd up 'twixt good & just;
Strafford, who was hurried hence
'Twixt trayson & convenience.
He spent his time heere in a miste;
A *Papist*, yet a *Calvanist*;
His Prince's neerest Joy & Greefe,
He had, yet wanted, alle relife;
Y^e Prop & Ruine of ye State,
Y^e People's violent Love & Hate,
One in extreams lov'd & abhor'd.
Riddles lye heere; & in a worde
Heere lyes bloud; & let it lye
Speechless still, & never crye."

"But, child, it's good," Mr. Cleveland, in surprise, exclaimed. "Aye, 'tis beautiful. Though what that proud Protestant would say to being miscalled a Papist and a Calvanist, I know not. . . . Were thy verses, then, like this?"

He looked round the room, and saw, piled in the empty hearth, a mass of burnt papers. She had, then, burnt those prized verses of hers, at which he had not been willing to look.

"Lord, forgive me, I slew thy poetry too. But not all-thing, for thou wrot'st this one piece more at the last." And he had an odd, troubling thought that what had evoked this poem from her was the death of hope. She, like Lord Strafford, was the victim of ineluctable fate. Had she seen herself—he shrank from the thought—as hurried hence 'twixt treason and convenience, before ever Francis struck her down; as slain by him, John Cleveland? For a moment he saw himself in a strange, unwonted light. The words dropped whisperingly into his soul.

> "Riddles-lye heere; & in a worde
> Heere lyes bloud; & let it lye
> Speechless still, & never crye."

Riddles, indeed; and the puzzled child, unable, like himself and all human kind, to solve them, had willed to let them lie. She would never have appealed or cried to him again. Had this been her message to him of reassurance and renouncement? And was it now her message of forgiveness?

"And now I think thou dost give it me from where thou art; 'tis thy last gift, and I'll take it, in token thou'st forgiven me my cruelty. Yes, I'll take it and I'll print it, and men shall know thee for the poet thou wouldst fain have been."

The landlord, the landlady and the chamber-maid ever and anon stole to the door, and stared with round shocked eyes at the poor, sweet young lady on the bed; and at Mr. Cleveland who had, they knew, been the poor young lady's lover, and the most free, generous, open-handed fine gentleman in the world, and who had been assaulted so violently by Mr. Francis Conybeare, who had not, so far as they had experienced him, been generous or open-handed at all, but a prim, sour kind of a gentleman. And always Mr. Cleveland sat by the bed, his handsome head bowed, the young lady's cold hand in his.

A pretty thing to happen, in honest people's lodging-rooms; and a dreadful thing for the poor doctor to find when he should get back from London; and a pitiful sad thing that so sweet a young lady should be killed in a gentleman's brawl; and a sad grievous thing that Mr. Cleveland who had been so attentive and so doting once, even if for some weeks past he seemed to have stinted to dote, should have lost his sweetheart.

But at least, said mine host to his females, as they hearkened to the tolling and the clashing bells, at the least, Black Tom was gone to his own place, and would rob and threaten honest Englishmen no more.

"Oh, my little love," Mr. Cleveland muttered, as he folded the blotted paper and placed it in his breast pocket, "my little, beauteous, ingenious, murdered love, 'twas not thy fault thou didst fatigue me so."

And, because she could fatigue him never again, he wept.

POSTSCRIPT

" A merry mind
Looks forward, scornes what's left behind:
Let's live, my *Wickes*, then, while we may,
And here enjoy our Holiday.

" W'ave seen the past-best Times, & these
Will nere return, we see the Seas,
And Moons to wain;
But they fill up their Ebbs again:
But vanisht man,
Like to a Lilly-lost, nere can,
Nere can repullulate, or bring
His dayes to see a second Spring.

" But on we must, & thither tend,
Where *Anchus* & rich *Tullus* blend
Their sacred seed:
Thus has *Infernall Jove* decreed;
We must be made
Ere long a song, ere long a shade.
Why then, since life to us is short,
Let's make it full up, by our sport.

. . . . .

" Well then, on what Seas we are tost,
Our comfort is, we can't be lost."

ROBERT HERRICK

To his peculiar friend, *Mr. John Wickes*,
under the name of *Posthumus*.

Mr. Herrick, on Midsummer Day, 1647, seditiously, defiantly, and for the last time, for by Sunday he would be an outed minister, read the Evening Service from the Book of Common Prayer, including the Collect for the Feast of St. John the Baptist. He was supported in this parting act of rebellion by a congregation of three. One was his maid, Prudence Baldwin, whom he had desired regularly to attend church with him on week-day feasts, that there might be two, even if seldom three, gathered together, to form the quorum suggested by St. Chrysostom as a desirable condition for Divine benevolence. Prudence sat and knelt upright, making the responses in a defiant, not-to-be-brow-beaten voice. She was leaving the vicarage when her master did; she was not going to stay on to serve Mr. John Syms, the weaver to Buckfastleigh, in his usurpation of the vicar's office, even though she would have, she supposed, to sit under him and hear him pray and preach in his wild Directory way. John Syms, indeed! As if *he* could have anything to say that would do a body any good.

The other members of the congregation were Mr. George Yarde and his wife, who had come to attend their ejected vicar's last service in the parish church. The establishment of the Presbytery and the Commissions, the proscription of the Prayer Book and the substitution for it of the Directory, and the ejection of so many of the Church's lawful incumbents to make way for these low-born, ill-educated interlopers (by comparison, the squire and his wife now thought the Church of England clergymen, of whose birth and antecedents they had before thought somewhat meanly, almost gentry)—all these proceedings of the Westminster Assembly had done for the squire and for many of his brethren up and down England what the Elizabethan Settlement and the Jacobean and Caroline clericalism had signally failed to do—it had made them ardent supporters, perhaps for the first time in English history, of their parish priests. For the fallen bishops, the squire had no regrets; he had always considered them a pity, regarding them as mostly Arminian, always overpowerful and meddlesome, and too often *de faece populi* as regards extraction. Let them by all means go. But to suppress the Prayer Book, and the decent seemly ceremonies of the Church of England, and to substitute the long extempore prayings and preachings from these vulgar ignoramuses who were everywhere being pushed into the incumbencies in place of the lawful occupants, this was an outrage.

And now Mr. Herrick, his good friend and companion (though often enough they had fallen out about the limits of the authority of each, and other parochial matters) was at last to be outed as a superstitious scandalous malignant and delinquent minister, who refused the Covenant, and a Buckfastleigh weaver would pray and preach in Dean Prior Church. It was a scandal, the squire and his wife agreed.

The vicar himself had no great objection. Dean Prior in these bad times was a sad dull place. He was, in a way, relieved that his turn had come. He had begun to feel that he had been lost and forgotten, and might read the Prayer Book service for ever unmolested, amid the clash of arms and controversy that stormed over England in these bad times. Bad times indeed, now that the west was quite lost to the King. Goring's troopers had passed long since on their way, burning, plundering, raping, and now lived only in Devonshire memories as an evil nightmare. The tide had been turned;

> "The four wheels of Charles's Wain,
> Grenville, Trevannion, Godolphin, Slanning, slain,"

then Hopton's army all defeated and dissolved, the last fort surrendered, Fairfax and the New Model Army everywhere victorious and in command. Devonshire men, pressed into the King's service by their landlords, had gladly drifted into this conquering army, or laid down their arms and returned to their homes.

The Dean men had mostly been back for over a year, sullen and rebellious against those who had dragged them into this foolish fighting. They cared little for King or for Parliament, Church or Presbytery; all they wanted was to be left unmolested on their farms and fields and allowed to carry on their lives, delivered from the burdens of garrisons, quartering, and plundering.

"I had six oxen t'other day
and them the Roundheads stole away
a Mischief be their speed.
I had six horses left me whole
and them the Cavileers have stole.
Gods zores, they are both agreed.

"There goes my corne, my beanes and pease,
I doe not dare them to displease,
they doe zoe zweare and vapor.
Then to the Governor I come
And pray him to discharge the sum,
but nought can get but paper.

"Gods bones, dost think a Paper will
Keep warme my back and belly fill?
No, no, goe burne the note.
If that another yeare my veeld
no better profit doe me yeeld
I may goe cut my throate.

" And as this were not greife enow
they have a Thing called Quarter too;
Oh! that's a vengeance waster.
A pox upon't, they call it vree
'Cham sure that made us slaves to be
And every Roage our Master."

Such was the west-country farmers' view of the war. But they hated the Cavaliers worse than Fairfax's men, because of Goring and Grenville's wild, roystering troopers. The whole affair had been deplorable. Fortunately it was over, and life had settled down again, though in a somewhat tedious, melancholy manner, for no longer were there Christmas merryings, Twelfth Night mummings, maypoles, hock feasts, wassailings, or Midsummer fires, and parson seemed always in an ill humour. But now he had gotten his quittance, and John Syms to Buckfastleigh was to come and be parson, which seemed queer, but haply he'd do well enough.

As the vicar and the squire and his lady came out of the church together, on this fine midsummer evening, the sweet smell of hay filled the air. They were carting the hay from the fields above the church, and now once again they were carting it across the churchyard, since the Metropolitan visitors would trouble them no more.

" That will be for Mr. Syms to deal with," the vicar said; to which Mrs. Yarde returned:

" Marry come up! If John Syms thinks to meddle in village matters, he'll find he hath to reckon with the squire. John Syms, forsooth! 'Twill be a sorry business enough to have him whining and prating his prayers and preachments in church, and let him not lift his voice without it."

" My dear," said the squire gravely, " since this weaver has been put upon us, we should endeavour to sustain him with patience, and not hinder his ministry in the parish more than need be. 'Tis a sorry business, but we must make the best on't, as of all else in these bad times."

> " O times most bad,
> Without the scope
> Of hope
> Of better to be had!"

Mr. Herrick declaimed,

> " Where shall I go,
> Or whither run
> To shun
> This public overthrow?

My answer is, I go first to my dear John Weekes at Sherwell, who still remains unmolested in his parish, leading his good hard diligent life, though the devil alone knows why he's not dispossessed long since. But I shan't burden him long, for London calls me. I shall live in poverty there, since not even the outed parson's fifth will come my way, poor bachelor as I am; but I have friends, and at least I shall live free, and far from these rude barbarous churls that think on naught but filling their own bellies and care naught for king, country, or church."

" You must not blame the people over much," the squire said. " They have not the means to look at the larger issues of policy in Church and State, nor beyond their own fields. They have suffered much in these troubles, and still do so, and they blame you and me and Sir Ralph Furze, and our like for leading them into the business. Though, did they but know it, we have lost more heavily than they, and shall do so in the future."

He sighed. He, who had put himself with a sad heart and a divided conscience at the head of his tenant bands, and led them to fight for a king whom he distrusted but would not serve against, lived now in fear of the sequestration of his estate. His grandson, Giles, had fallen at Exeter, and (more unexpected tragedy) his granddaughter Meg had donned her brother's clothes and arms, and ridden out secretly to join the troops that fought Fairfax round Ashburton, and had been killed in the first skirmish.

Both those merry children slain, in a cause that seemed itself slain too; the country ravished and torn, soaked in the blood of peasant and yeoman, squire and townsman, loyalist and rebel. Only the midsummer countryside smiled on, smelling sweetly of new-cut hay.

The vicar walked with his friends up the lane. At the turning to Dean Court they met Mrs. Lettice Northly, grown thin and peevish, two children dragging at her hands. Her husband lay sick at home, shattered in health by his campaigns, and she was grown weary of this sad Denshire world, where one saw no life, and would, perhaps, never see London again.

"We shall see you to supper this evening then, parson," Mrs. Yarde said, as they parted.

"Aye; for the last time," Mr. Herrick returned. "After this you'll be entertaining Mr. Syms."

Mrs. Lettice gave a little scream of disgust.

"Don't mention that dirty fellow's name, parson! I swear I shall never speak to him once while he's here."

"Peace, child," her grandfather reproved her. "We shall look for you, then, Mr. Herrick, in a short while."

"Thank you, squire. I have some business to do in the village, and will be with you suddenly."

They parted. The vicar called on his churchwarden, and then strolled along the road to the bridge. There he stopped, and stood leaning against the old rough stone wall, looking at the brawling burn below. How it dashed and tore at its rocky bed, in its restless running! Not a peaceful, civil kind of a stream; nor in these days, was Dean a peaceful, civil kind of a place. The men, half of whom had ended their fighting in Fairfax's army, angered him by their stubborn wrong opinions. Ashburton and all the neighbouring towns, were still garrisoned by Roundhead troops; over the country brooded the harsh alien bitterness of strife hardly ceased; a strife which had left the vicar, a non-combatant, more bitter than the fighters.

He was glad to be going from Dean Prior, grown so empty and so sad. His kind, good sister-in-law had died last year, and left him lonely in the parsonage but for faithful Prue. Tracy too was dead. And his dear little pupil, Julian, dead six years back, killed in a brawl, and her father gone near distracted, and only returned once to Dean for a few weeks, to dismantle the little house at Deancombe and depart for ever, to write his bitter, wicked, wild, heretic books in London; and then, when none would print them there, and England went mad over this war, he had fled to the Hague, and lived there among foreign doctors of learning, writing seditious, atheistical pamphlets, and melancholy letters to his friend the parson at Dean Prior saying that he had no hopes now for liberty of conscience or of thought in this world, and had given it up as a bad business. As to his son Kit, he was living somewhere in Paris, hanging on to the beggared English court.

London was the place for a tired, ejected parson to end his days; even though it was a new, grim London, in the hands of the Presbytery and the parliament men, and the best men (including that patron of poets, Mr. Endymion Porter) either ruined or fled overseas, or both. But, at least, he would there be able at last to print his poems, his *Hesperides*, as he had called the collection, dedicating these children of the west country to Prince Charles. And those other less earthly and profane poems, too, his Noble Numbers, which were more apt from a clergyman's pen.

Would they be well received, he wondered? Six years back, at Cambridge, he had felt disappointed and discouraged; the young poets there had made him feel outmoded, unimportant, out of date. He had written, on his return from Cambridge, some cautious lines to his Muse:

> "Whither, *Mad Maiden*, wilt thou roame?
> Farre safer 'twere to stay at home: . . .
> There, there (perhaps), such Lines as These
> May take the simple *Villages*.
> But for the Court, the Country wit
> Is despicable unto it.
> Stay then at home, & doe not goe
> Or flie abroad to seeke for woe.
> Contempts in Courts & Cities dwell;
> No *Critick* haunts the Poore mans Cell . . .
> That man's unwise will search for Ill,
> And may prevent it, sitting still."

But he had recovered a little from that discouragement, and felt that his *Hesperides* would give him at last the fame, the promise of immortality, that was his due. Other men were publishing their poetry. He had sent the other day for the book just out containing John Cleveland's verses: a collection ingenious and witty enough, and the satires on the rebels good spiteful stinging stuff but most of the other verses too elaborate, quaint, and Clevelandised to please his own more musical, terse and direct taste. He did not really regard John Cleveland, the most popular poet of the day, and the busiest in the King's cause, as a poet at all. The best thing in this volume was an epitaph on Strafford; that seemed to Mr. Herrick to have a sad brief poignancy and beauty that the others lacked. He might, thought he, almost have written it himself.

Where was he now, that lover and betrayer of little Julian?

He had left Cambridge for Oxford when Cambridge was garrisoned and fortified, battered, plundered and desecrated, by Cromwell's soldiers and Colonel Dowsing's wild, hacking iconoclasts. In the more fortunate, though inferior, University he had lived, as satirist-in-chief to the King's party; then had helped to govern and hold Newark till its surrender to the Scots threw him, a ruined but still vocal man, into a world grown hard for destitute Cavaliers. "For my part," he had written to the army that summoned him to surrender Newark (and let the bold words count to his credit, thought Mr. Herrick), "I would rather embrace a wreck, floating upon a single plank, than embark in your action with the fullest sails to dance upon the wings of fortune." And now he was, presumably, embracing that wreck, floating upon that plank, drifting about London, hoping that better might come; visiting sometimes his beloved Cambridge, to be further embittered and enraged by the sight of those ravished and plundered Colleges, smashed and desecrated chapels and churches, broken bridges and cut groves, usurped offices and emptied lecture halls, to which "the Kipperdollings of the age" had "reduced a glorious and renowned University; and did more in less than three years than the apostate Julian could effect in all his reign, viz., broke the heart-strings of learning and learned men." Thus John Barwick of St. John's complained, in his *Querela Cantabrigiensis*, lately printed at Oxford; and went on to picture that consoling being, Posterity, inquiring, "Who thrust out one of the eyes of this kingdom? Who made Eloquence dumb, Philosophy sottish, widowed the Arts, and drove the Muses from their ancient habitation? Who plucked the Reverend and Orthodox Professors out of their chairs, and silenced them in prison or their graves? Who turned Religion into Rebellion, and changed the Apostolical Chair into a Desk for Blasphemy, and tore the garland from off the head of Learning, to place it on the dull brows of Disloyal

Ignorance? If they shall ask, who made those ancient and beautiful Chapels, the sweet remembrancers and Monuments of our forefathers' Charity, and kind fomenters of their children's devotion, to become ruinous heaps of dust and stones? Or who unhived those numerous swarms of labouring Bees, which used to drop honey-dews over all this Kingdom, to place in their rooms swarms of senseless Drones? 'Tis quickly answered. . . ."

But not so quickly after all, for it had taken Mr. Barwick several hundred words of romantically descriptive invective, which Mr. Herrick endorsed with full agreement, as he thought bitterly of his mutilated Alma Mater in the hands of Vandals, her learned loyal sons exiled and deprived, their places taken by unscholarly usurpers. For so Mr. Herrick, and so the authors of the *Querela*, saw it without discrimination, forgetting those calm, if melancholy, dons who remained, so occupied in scholarship that they could swallow the Covenant down without noticeable indigestion; forgetting how Dr. Whichcote still gave his afternoon lectures in Trinity Church, and Henry More still paced the Fellows' Gardens at Christ's and disputed with Ralph Cudworth concerning the plastic medium and the Intellectual System of the Universe, and Dr. Duport, the little Greek professor, lectured, oblivious of turmoil and chaos, on Theophrastus and Demosthenes, to whomsoever, in these days, would attend.

Mr. Herrick saw Cambridge as gone utterly into chaos, darkness and ignominy, like the Church, like the country, like the times. Yet he would still be a poet, still wear, whether mortals conceded it him or not, his little parsley crown. Still the pastoral country smiled, and flowers blew; still, though maypoles were down and midsummer bonfires extinguished, the may flowered white on the bush, and girls and boys would go a-maying, and the June country smell of hay, and the elves dance beneath the moon.

A pox on all politics. And a pox on all those new, modish versifiers, John Cleveland and the rest.

"By God," observed Mr. Herrick, and struck the bridge wall with his open hand, "I'll write 'em all down yet.

> "And once more yet (ere I am laid out dead)
> Knock at a star with my exalted head."

A little cool breath of wind stirred the scented warmth of the evening; he shivered, and pulled his coat more closely across his broad chest. A breath, it seemed, of doubt, of question, hinting at the mortality that waits on all desire.

But Mr. Herrick remembered that he was, after all, a clergyman, though now an outed one, and it was rather of immortality he should be thinking than of pleasure, fame and parsley crowns on earth.

Slowly he walked from Dean bridge across the meadows to the Court; and he seemed to have already put on immortality, for he might have been some sturdy sylvan god in that serene pastoral landskip, passing on his way to eat and drink with his friends.

THE END